SIMPLY DEAD

Pat Arneson

BG SKY PUBLISHING

ISBN 979-8-9922562-0-8

The author wishes to thank:

Greg Kersten—President, OK Corral Series, Founder of Equine Assisted Psychotherapy (EAP), Equine Services, Inc., EAGALA; Guy Kaufman—Founder, Executive Director Changing Gaits, Inc; Cathy Cleary, MD; Joey Zezulka—Mechanic, endless source of useful information; Sean Miner—Author, journalist, editor; Kelsey Miner—Beta reader; Katie Zezulka—Facilitator; and Karen Phillips of PhillipsCovers.com—cover artist.

Additional thanks to those too numerous to mention, who provided ideas, technical information and instruction, and encouragement.

Chapter One

I never saw it coming. The bear filled my headlights. My little hatchback slammed into it and launched.

Two lanes in the blackness, thick pine woods on both sides. No one else for miles, then suddenly, people out of their car on the shoulder. My eyes were on them. I landed on the blacktop, still moving. I pulled to the side and sat, frozen, heart pounding.

"Listen." She got a *nice* job. She wanted *me* to get a nice job. I could still hear her, speaking in italics. Persuasive, earnestly convincing. She settled back in the diner booth and ticked things off on her fingers. "No one has hit me, kicked me, bitten me, peed on me, pulled my hair out or tackled me," she paused for emphasis, "in *months*. I swear to God. No one has tried to shank me with *anything*. I haven't even *watched* anyone getting shanked. I feel..." she waved her hands in front of her, as if searching for words, *"relaxed."*

I bit my lip, studied her. I'd never seen her so relaxed. Was she on something? I cocked my head a little. "Is all of this—" I waved my hand in a circle that encompassed her— "a regular prescription or more of an off-label thing?"

"I mean it, Abby." She poked her finger at me. "You need to get a piece of this. A couple months in, you won't know what hit you."

I swung out of the car and walked around to check my front bumper. In my headlights, it looked fine. How could it be fine? I peered underneath. I couldn't see anything in the dark. I heard a loud thump—an SUV slowed and pulled to the side. I shielded my eyes from the headlights behind me, blinding in the surrounding darkness. A frantic woman approached. "It ran right in front of us! Our truck is just ruined, I don't know what to do. Does Deergrass even have a police department?"

"I don't know." I hugged myself against the chill in the air. "You could call 911." I couldn't remember if this was a state or county road, or how far from the town we were. "I'm sure someone will come."

A heavy thud and then another. More vehicles slammed into the bear and slowly pulled ahead. We were getting quite a line of taillights along the shoulder. I returned to my own car, did a walkaround.

A man appeared from the SUV ahead. "What was that? It ripped off my entire back bumper!"

"A bear." I gestured vaguely toward the blackness behind us, the glaring headlights. He stared at me, mouth open, then wordlessly moved away. I got back in, turned the key. It started just fine. I decided to leave them to it and drove into town.

I found a gas station with a dry parking space under a light post and killed the engine. I thought again about the former co-worker who talked me into this in the first place. She was probably at her own "nice new job" right now, in her own "nice, calm setting."

I started the car and backed out. The pavement was clear—no leaking fluids. I parked again and took a look outside. Something was broken under the front bumper, but it probably wouldn't fall off. I went into the gas station, got a bottle of water, and grabbed a bouquet of flowers by the cash register.

Back in the car, I restarted the GPS. I arrived ten minutes and a couple miles of gravel road later. I'd had some weird gigs, but this might just top them all—a horse ranch out in the Minnesota woods. I turned into the long, dirt driveway and stopped, rolling down my window to get a better view under the yard lights. An old house. A metal silhouette of two horses and a cowboy. A wooden wagon with 'Trail Rides' painted on the side. I could see the edges of several different pastures—some with wooden fencing, others with wire, probably electric.

A few horses peered curiously over a fence at me. I looked back but had little else to add to the interaction, so I rolled my window up and drove to the small, gravel parking lot just ahead. The barn had a regular door and a huge sliding door, standing open under a line of mounted outdoor lights. Wooden stairs led up to a narrow platform and another standard-sized door. The key would be under the mat, my new employer assured me.

I parked close to the barn and grabbed one box for my first trip up the stairs. Locating the key, I pushed the door open with one hip. The apartment was simple but clean, built along one side of the barn. A compact bedroom, an open living area. A sofa and chair in a worn plaid. A white Formica table with unmatched wooden chairs. A window with brown curtains pulled closed. A nice little kitchenette that smelled like lemon cleaning fluid. A bathroom with a tiny shower, brightly colored towels, and a new bar of soap.

I opened the box and pulled out my coffee maker. I filled my cut glass vase with water and centered the gas station flowers on the table. A few framed photographs fit nicely on a shelf. I smiled with satisfaction. Home.

"Hello!" A man stood in the doorway, holding one of my boxes. "Max Turner, ranch manager. I live in the house there. I was just doing the rounds and saw you pull in." He gestured with the box. "Welcome! We're sure glad you're here."

Max looked to be about my age—fortyish, give or take—with a wiry build. Dirty blond hair curled over his ears and the back of his collar. His neatly trimmed beard almost covered scarring along the side of his face and down his neck. He wiped worn cowboy boots on the mat. His jeans and untucked flannel shirt were clean, smelling vaguely of cigarette smoke. The edge of a tattoo peeked out from one rolled-up sleeve. His dark eyes were alert, intelligent, curious, sizing me up.

I'm not exactly imposing—five and a half feet tall, weighing in at a solid buck and a quarter. My rusty hair and green eyes are fine, but it can be hard to be taken seriously with freckles. I took the box, set it on the floor, held out a hand. "Abby Maguire. Thank you for bringing my box up!"

Max grinned, his smile relaxed and natural. "No problem. I'll help you carry the rest of them up, too. Looks like it shouldn't take too long. You travel light." He turned and I noticed a hip holster under his shirt. Why was he walking around in the dark with a gun?

Ten minutes later my boxes were all stacked on the floor. Max smiled at the coffee maker. "You're gonna fit right in." He leaned against the kitchen sink. "So, you work for a temp agency. You travel a lot for that?"

"I do." I waved him toward a kitchen chair, sat in another. "Different states. A few months here, half a year there."

Max tilted his head, raised one eyebrow. I was immediately flooded with jealousy. I always wished I could raise one eyebrow. There were so many situations where it was the perfect reaction or silent comeback—

"I'm not real familiar with that," he said. "You like it?"

"I do. Keeps things interesting. I like variety." I did not add that with temp work, the irritating aspects—and people—that you get with any job were less annoying. You knew they were time limited. "Sometimes I end up doing something just for one job, so it's constant learning. I have no experience with equine-assisted therapy, for instance. I just got certified for this position. And I know nothing about horses. I do love this apartment!"

Max stretched out his legs, rolled his shoulders. "You might get kinda bored out here. It's pretty quiet."

I shook my head. "One of my requirements is access to a quiet place to live. The temp life skews fairly young, and I'm really past the loud-music-all-night stage. I like my own space. Month-to-month apartments can be hard to find, so this is wonderful."

We sat quietly for a moment. "I used to be in the Marines," Max said. "Had some trouble after I got out. Equine therapy literally saved my life, so I always like to hear someone's getting involved with it. I hope you'll find it worthwhile." He stood. "Well, I'll let you get situated. You'll probably hear me in the morning, bringing in the breakfast crew. Some of the horses get supplemental feed or meds, so I get them in early. Feel free to make yourself at home."

I left my windows open and woke to sunlight, shouting and hoofbeats. I looked down to see horses running out of the woods and into a corral near the barn. I moved to the step outside my door. Max walked along the fence line, waving a long, black stick. He waited until all the horses were in the corral, then came in and closed the gate. He looked up, saw me leaning on the railing, and waved. I smiled and waved back.

The morning air was cool. I stepped back inside, started a cup of coffee brewing, then dug in a box for running clothes. A quick hit of caffeine and I was down the stairs.

"Good morning!" Max was leading a horse out of the corral. "You a runner?"

"More of a trotter. I thought I'd check out this dirt road past the ranch. Does it go far?"

"It's a whole network of dirt roads," he said. "Tiny little towns, farms. As far as you want to go. Mostly flat and quiet. No worries about vehicles sneaking up on you. You'll hear them coming."

"Perfect." I turned to leave. "If you're ready for a break when I get back, come on up for a cup of coffee."

"I definitely will." He led the horse into the barn.

I jogged down the driveway and surveyed the area by daylight. Both sides of the road were thick with birch, poplars, oaks. White and dark trunks intermixed with pine trees. A slight breeze wafted through. Leaves quivered and danced in the bright sun. Small ponds appeared here and there. I could hear frogs singing as I ran by. Fences outlined grassy fields—the neighbor had cows. I smiled in delight. Cows!

Max was right about hearing vehicles. The crunching of my shoes on the road seemed loud. The occasional pickup slowed as it passed. I waved a thank-you for not spraying me with gravel. Each driver raised two fingers from the steering wheel.

I ran past woods and fields, feeling my muscles gradually loosen. The smell of cows and horses mixed with dank marshes and musty soil. Dust from the road clung to my arms and legs. I went as far as the first small town, only a few blocks long, and turned back. I didn't want to get lost on my first run.

Max was adjusting a gate when I came in. He glanced up. "You were gone a while. How far did you go?"

"I have no idea, but it felt really good to work the kinks out." I bent down and examined the front of my car. A cracked piece of plastic, but still nothing major. I laid down in the grass and tried to see underneath.

Max stood and walked over. "Everything ok?"

I looked up at him. "I ran over a bear last night. I'm trying to see if there's damage."

He stared at me. "A bear?"

I waved a hand vaguely. "It was really dark."

He knelt and peered under my car. "Seriously?"

"I didn't kill it. I hit it second." I sat up in the grass. "Then a bunch of people hit it after me."

He looked under the car again. "Looks like you came out of it pretty good."

"I guess I did. I'd better go get cleaned up. I'm meeting with Walt this morning. If you still want that coffee, give me ten minutes and come on up."

"You're on," he said, and went back to the gate.

Max did not appear for coffee. After about twenty minutes I stuck my head out the door to see if he was in the middle of something. Smoke rose from behind a shed. It smelled mechanical. I went to investigate. Max sprayed a fire extinguisher over a small tractor while two men stood, watching. I walked up to the bystanders. "What happened?"

They glanced at each other. "Hell if I know," one of them said. The other man just looked away.

Max thunked the fire extinguisher down. He kicked the ground, sending up a puff of dirt. Glancing over, he saw me standing with the men and scowled. I took a step back. He pulled out his phone and turned away.

Chapter Two

I presented myself in the barn and looked around. A wide area with a dirt floor was surrounded by blue painted fencing. Sunlight poured in through the huge, open sliding doors. The sides and back of the barn were darker, shaded. Sturdy wooden fenceposts had ropes tied around them. Doorways along one side—under my apartment—were labeled Water Closet, Sheriff, Meetin' Room. Swallows flitted through the sunlight. They perched on high wooden rafters spotted with bird droppings, swooped through shafts of light and back into shadow. A few nests were squeezed into the junctions of rafter beams.

I walked out into the sunlit dirt and felt the heat immediately on my back and legs. A huge stack of hay bales filled the rear of the barn. A man in dirty, faded blue jeans, a dirty white t-shirt and a cowboy hat was standing on a bale halfway up to the roof. I couldn't tell what he was doing up there. He saw me, climbed down, and brushed his faded work gloves on his jeans. He looked about as solid as a paving stone.

He took off his hat, revealing short, graying black hair. He wiped his forehead on a sleeve and replaced the hat. His skin was a warm tan, his eyes nearly black and sharply focused. He took off a glove to shake my hand. "Good morning! Walt Bravo, founder and director here. How's the room for you?"

"I love it. Abby Maguire. I hope you believed me that I don't know much about horses. I've had a little training, but I'm really starting from scratch."

Walt grinned. "Did you really run over a bear?"

That was fast. "Unfortunately."

He shook his head, moved on. "You got equine certified, right?"

"I did, but only just. I haven't used it yet."

He waved that away. "You'll catch on quick. Like I told you on the phone, we've got a great deal of new programming, but our clinical person fell through. So, we need you for the actual psychotherapy until we get a new person on board. You're welcome to join in on other sessions. They're all therapeutic. We're glad to have you."

He made a wide, sweeping motion around the barn. "Now, this doubles as our indoor arena. We've got the outdoor arena too—I'll show you around as we go. See, now, I'm not real worried about you not having equine experience, because we work as a team. One clinical person—you—will focus on the clients. Then you've got the equine specialist—me, or Max, you met him, or another gal, Ida. You'll meet Ida in a couple days, she's out of town right now." He pointed to himself. "We focus more on observing the horses, watching their behavior. So that gives us information to work with."

He walked toward the back of the barn, so I followed him. He opened a gate and latched it tightly after me. "Gates are important. You open a gate, you close it."

Outside, several horses gathered around hay bales in metal rings. Others stood idly in the sunlight. A few drank from water troughs. There was absolutely nothing between the horses and me. I bit my lip and stepped back closer to Walt.

"Ok," he said, pointing with his gloves. "We'll get started. You go ahead and go meet the horses, figure out which one you're going to work with. I'll be back in a little bit."

My mouth opened, but nothing came out. I shot a panicky glance at Walt's back as he disappeared through the doorway. This had to be a joke.

I was alone. The horses seemed unconcerned. Several glanced at me, but went back to eating hay. How do you meet horses? I turned back to the barn hoping to see Walt stick his head out, laughing at how he'd gotten me good. I waited. He wasn't coming back.

Oh, hell.

I took a breath, blew it out. I tentatively approached the closest horse, an enormous brown one, and patted it on the side. It stopped eating and looked at me.

This is it. This is how it's going to end. Trampled by horses.

The horse went back to eating. Ok. I scratched the next, also brown, on the neck. "Hi," I said. It ignored me. Alrighty then. I began moving from horse to horse, studying them. Most of them were various shades of brown. They were all huge. Their teeth were huge. Their hooves were enormous. "Hi, there! You're a sweetheart, aren't you?" I hoped it was. "How do I know which one of you I'm supposed to work with?"

One of them picked up its head and focused on me. "Oh, is it you?" It put its head back down, turned away. Fine. I wandered some more, scratching and patting. A horse swished its tail. I jumped nervously. I turned toward the hay rail.

"Nope!" Walt was standing by the barn. "Don't go back to the ones you already looked at until you meet them all!"

I hadn't been aware of him watching me. Worse, I thought I did look at them all. I gazed around, not wanting to admit it. Which ones didn't I meet? Some of the brown ones? I bit my lip, studied the ones by the water trough, sighed. "Which ones did I not look at?"

He tipped his head toward a small crowd standing in the sunlight. I dutifully walked over, patted one, scratched another. One of them watched me with big, soft, brown eyes while chewing. Unsure, feeling stupid, I turned to Walt and pointed at the horse. "Is it that one?"

He grinned. He was thinking something, but I had no idea what. "Ok, hold on." He disappeared into the barn, reappearing moments later with a halter and a rope. He eased the halter around the horse's head, buckled it on, and clipped the rope under the horse's chin. "We never move the horses around without a lead rope. You might think they're fine, but something could spook them, and someone could get hurt. It's safety first."

Sounded good to me, until he handed me the rope. "Ok, you hold your right hand here, just under the clip, and your left hand is going to hold this coil of rope, like so. Then you say, 'Walk.'"

I took the rope, which required standing very close to those gigantic hooves. Walt walked away. "Ok," he called back. "Keep an eye on where her feet are, and where your feet are, and bring her in here." He disappeared into the barn.

I made a mental note that this was a female horse. I hadn't been sure. It blinked at me slowly. "Walk," I said. The horse didn't move. I glanced toward the barn. Walt was still gone. "Walk." The horse's ears swiveled around. One of them pointed at me. "Walk, please?" The horse looked away.

Walt stuck his head around the corner. "Tell her to walk and then start walking." With that, we managed to get into the barn and up to the post Walt indicated. "You're going to work with Rosie," Walt said. "You'll get her every time and build a relationship with her. Outstanding horse."

He took me into a room labeled "tack," an L-shaped area lined with saddles, bridles, halters, shelves of bins. A locked tool area was enclosed by metal grating. There was an open shelf with general tools. For a barn, it was immaculate. Everything was labeled. Walt told me to find the container marked "Rosie," and get her brush.

We went back out to where Rosie was standing, clipped to the post, looking sleepy. "Alright," Walt said. "Now I'm going to have you brush her out." He demonstrated how hard to press. He brushed her legs, which involved bending over close to them. Rosie did not kick him in the head. I swallowed hard. He leaned farther. "Then you can reach under here and do her belly." I started seriously doubting this career move.

"This is where the girth strap goes, when we saddle her. You really want to make sure there's no dirt here, or it'll rub her raw, under that strap." He stood up, glanced at me, and laughed. "Now don't worry. You'll get used to this in no time. Let me show you how to walk behind a horse."

Walt demonstrated two ways—far enough back to be out of leg reach, or else pressing up against the horse's rear end. I felt myself pull slightly back. "Now, if you stay in close," he said, "you want to let her know where you are. Horses can't see straight behind them. Touch her hip, then slide your back against her like so, all the way around, so she feels where you are."

Like hell.

I walked around ten feet behind her. "Okay."

Walt laughed again and handed me the brush. "Go ahead and brush her out, and talk with her. I'll be back in a few minutes." And he left.

I walked back around, ten feet behind those legs, and started brushing. "Listen. Let's make a deal. You don't kill me, and I'll do the best I can. Sound good?" Rosie stretched her neck against the brush.

"Oh, does that feel good?" I brushed that spot some more. She sighed, smacked her lips. I started to relax. There might be something to this, after all. I brushed, Rosie sighed. I felt the tension easing out of my shoulders. "I could get to like this, Rosie," I told her. Then I ran out of back and side.

I looked at her legs and belly. I had to either bend down—and maybe get kicked in the head—or skip all that and go, ten feet behind her, to the other side. I took a deep breath and leaned in. "Remember, don't kill me." I brushed all the way down to those killer hooves. I stood up, turned, and jumped—Walt was standing there watching me.

"Ok, see, I'm learning about you," he said. "I see how you do when you're afraid of something. Instead of avoiding it, you put your head down and wade right in. Now, tell me something that's a challenge in your life."

I immediately thought about the accumulated trauma of doing trauma work. I didn't want to go into it. "Well, I've got quite a learning curve here. I'm not used to being the one who doesn't know what I'm doing."

Walt nodded. "Now, something else niggled at the back of your mind. You paused, then shifted gears. It was real subtle, like a hiccup, but the horse kind of looked at you at the same time, shifted her hindquarters just a bit. There was something there. Now, we wouldn't necessarily push too hard with a client, maybe just make a note of it for later, depending on the situation. But I'm going to push you a little."

I sighed heavily and rested a hand on Rosie's neck. "I started to think about the aftermath of the difficult jobs I've had."

Walt dipped his head in acknowledgement. "That's more like it. Don't just keep it surface level. If it's not real, it's not worth much." Walt handed me the rope. "Why don't you clip that back on her. You can do a more thorough job brushing her later. I'd like to show you something else."

We walked out to another area, where Walt had me take the halter off and let Rosie go. Several horses moved around us in alarming bursts of speed, then slowed again. Walt did not seem concerned.

"Now, observation," Walt said. "Observation gives us information. We can use information to gain knowledge. I want you to watch the horses for a while here. Then tell me which horse reminds you of yourself at a younger age, and which one is more like you now. I'll give you a few minutes, then we'll talk about it."

And he just left me in this pasture with a bunch of horses running around. To be fair, a lot of them were standing around, like I was. But Holy Moses, some of them were big. A couple of them got curious about me. Came right up, sniffing, eyeballing me. I wondered if the friend who was storing my things in his basement would sell it all when I got trampled.

I climbed up to sit on the fence so I could observe better. And swung one leg over to the other side. Purely for balance. "Okay, give me something I can work with. Remind me of myself. I've never sniffed anybody." Although broadly speaking, that wasn't necessarily true. Did that include being nosy? I decided not to dwell on that. I realized with dismay that I was no longer sure which one was Rosie. She disappeared into a mass of brown horses. I watched the lot of them standing, running, stopping as suddenly as they burst into motion. Milling around in small groups. Hovering alone on the periphery.

One of them made me smile, traipsing around. It ducked right under the rope fence that surrounded the outdoor arena, going in and out at will. It stuck its head in a barn window to see what was going on in there. It investigated various groups of horses, sometimes being chased away. I was grinning at that horse when Walt came back.

His face crinkled into a smile at the sight of me. "What did you come up with?" He didn't say anything about me being halfway over the fence.

I pointed at the traipsing horse. "That one is like me as a kid." I described the antics I was watching. "I was always curious, always interested in everything."

Walt nodded. "And the older you?"

I scrunched up my nose, thinking, looking around the pasture. "I think that one, over there." I pointed at a lone horse standing on the edge, watching quietly. "That's kind of depressing, though, when you think about it."

"What do you see about this horse that's depressing?"

I sighed. "Well, it isn't exploring with energy and wonder. It looks wary."

Walt put a hand on my shoulder. "This is exactly the point of this exercise. Look at all that information we have now, to work with. You made a point to yourself that I guarantee you'll think about later. How long do you suppose that would've taken us, sitting in an office, to uncover that same belief about your life?"

I nodded. Made sense.

"This is very important," Walt said. "The horse is not just a prop to use in experiential therapy. You let them act like horses, they're an active participant in every session. They will give you feedback, if you're able to perceive it. You'll learn about natural horse behavior and that'll help you observe more. The client decides how it connects to their life. There's no right or wrong—it's all information. You'll be amazed, I guarantee it. You'll see things happen that you just couldn't make up."

I climbed down from the fence. Walt looked out at the horses. "Whatever we have people do, remember, it's not about completing the task. It's observing the whole situation. Gaining understanding. We don't interpret—we point out what we see and the client tells us what it reflects in their life. That's where the rubber meets the road." He signaled an end to our session and walked away.

I leaned on the fence and watched the horses. The wary, watching horse ate some grass. It looked comfortable enough. I stood in the warmth of the sun. I was comfortable, too.

Chapter Three

I woke in the middle of a panic attack. I sat up, heart pounding. I swung my legs over the edge of the bed, looked at the clock. Two AM. I closed my eyes, but opened them immediately. Closing my eyes made it worse—panic rose again. I got up and walked out to the main room, turned on a lamp. I hugged myself, paced the apartment, focused on breathing. Deep. Slow.

I heard footsteps outside my door, and a quiet knock. At two AM? I looked out the window. Max. He met my eyes, and I opened the door.

"I'm sorry, knocking this late. I just wanted to make sure you were ok."

I sighed heavily. "Did I yell?"

Max smiled, tipped his head. "Don't be embarrassed. I was up anyway, walking around. I promise, of all people, I am the last to judge someone for having nightmares." He waved a hand dismissively. "I won't hang around. Really, I just wanted to check on you."

"Do you want a cup of tea?" I was curious. Why was he walking around at this hour? And company might be nice—a friendly face, even for a short time.

He smiled again, shrugged. "If you're going to be up anyway, sure."

I stood back to let him in. "Why are you the last to judge? Are you familiar?"

Max stepped out of his boots, walked to the kitchen. "Yeah, well, I told you I had some trouble after the service. I've had my share of sleepless nights. Waking my girlfriend up, yelling. Sometimes it helps not to be alone on a bad night."

I started heating water, waved him toward a chair. "Do you still struggle with PTSD, or have you resolved it?"

He hesitated. "Well, I'd be lying if I said I was done with it. There's better times and worse times." We sat and nodded at each other.

"How come you're out walking around at two AM?" I didn't mention that he was wearing his holster.

He seemed to answer carefully. "I don't always sleep very well. Sometimes I decide to do the rounds, check on everything."

I left it alone. "It was nice of you to come up." I got two mugs out. "Do you like lemon? No caffeine."

He nodded. "I don't want to pry or make you think about something you don't want to. Just say, if you don't want to talk about it. Your resume talked about working with high-conflict situations, aggressive behaviors?"

"Yes." I set a mug in front of him. "It takes a toll after a while. A lot of assaults, a lot of physical restraints. A lot of dangerous situations." I sat across from him, rubbed the table with my fingertip. "You think you're fine while you're in it. You take care of each other, develop a dark humor about it all, a camaraderie. Then one day you realize you're not fine."

"I get that." He tried his tea. "Thank you for this." We sat quietly together in the semi-darkness.

"I was thinking this might be a nice change," I said. "Take a more peaceful job, get a break. Then decide where to go from here."

"We were kind of wondering what made you want to come here." Max set his mug on the table. "I mean, we were excited about it. You were way more qualified than our usual applicants. Looked like maybe a step down for you."

"Depends on what you think of as down, I guess. Maybe a step in a different direction."

We were quiet again for a long moment, then Max stood and pushed his chair in. He set his mug in the sink. "I should go. We both could probably use some sleep."

I nodded. "Good luck." I watched as he walked back to the house. I wondered how often he did night rounds, how often he didn't sleep. I crawled back in bed and eventually drifted off.

I was scheduled to meet with Max and found him in the outdoor arena with Rosie. He climbed up on the fence, cupped his hands around his mouth, and yelled, "Quincy! Quinceee!" A big grey horse came trotting out of the woods. Max put a halter on him and led him into the arena with Rosie.

Max gave no impression that anything unusual had just happened. "Now, you most likely covered this in your certification class." He studied me. "Actually, it will be good to see how you feel about all this. We've had a couple more experienced therapists kind of struggle to transition away from the office. It goes a little different in the arena."

He seemed to be waiting for a response.

"I tend to use a very multi-systemic approach anyway," I said.

Max frowned slightly. "What's that, when it takes its boots off at night?"

I grinned at that. "I pull from a lot of disciplines, depending on the client and where they're at. Some clinicians specialize, and some clients do well with that." I shrugged. "I tend to work with people who respond better to a mutt approach instead of a pure-bred approach. So, I learn as much as I can, with a few guiding principles. I'm happy to learn. Teach me."

Max nodded. "Someday I'd like to hear what those guiding principles are. This might be real good, because we get a lot of people, traditional therapy didn't work for them." He paused. "Never heard of mutt therapy." Max turned back to the horses. "Now, being a prey animal, the horse is sensitive. They look, but they also feel. They sense our heartbeat from several feet away. They know when it picks up, and if our breathing is relaxed or tense."

"So, Rosie knew I was terrified of her."

Max nodded. "She absolutely did. She can tell better than we can, day to day, how much more comfortable you get. Now, if you act all cool and put together, we might be fooled. But if you're all jacked up inside, the horse doesn't like that discrepancy. How you look doesn't match how you feel to them, they'll be less comfortable, don't know what you're gonna do." He tapped his fingertips on his chest, like a fast heartbeat. "If something triggers you and your pulse quickens, the horse feels that. Then we'll see it in the horse's mannerisms. They'll give some kind of a little tell."

I glanced at Rosie. "And she doesn't have to speak English, because you speak horse."

He grinned. "We do our best. Now, with you, I've noticed that you're in your head a lot. What are you thinking now?"

I sighed. I'm in my head a lot? I decided to be honest. "I was thinking that I was twelve years old the first time someone told me I was a prey animal. Some guy came to the gym and taught the girls about situational awareness and basic self-defense moves. He told us we were deer and men were wolves and we needed to understand that."

Max stared at me. "Well. That's depressing."

I made a rolling let's-move-on gesture with my hand. "Anyway. Sorry. You watch the horses to see how they react."

He nodded. "That's right. You'll develop a good connection with us as we go. We watch each other, cue each other if we see something."

Quincy and Rosie quietly chewed grass, heads stuck under the ropes outlining the arena. "They seem like they're ignoring us," I said.

"While being completely aware of us on another level."

A loud bang made me jump. Both horses ran to the far side of the arena, turning to look back. "You see that?" Max said. "They perceive a threat, they come together, circle away together—then from safety they figure out what's going on. If it's a mountain lion, they don't want to stop to identify it first." He looked at the horses. "We talk about this a lot as a metaphor. Sometimes in life we need to take a step back—that isn't weakness, it's wisdom. We reassess, see what resources we need, then when we're ready we can circle back and re-engage with the situation more effectively."

Max pointed for emphasis. "We want people to do that as a herd, see how they're still together there? Not like a pack, turning on each other under stress, like wolves or something. Now they can see it was just somebody slamming the door against the barn." He watched for a moment. "Although I don't know why they're doing that."

There was a series of smaller banging noises as someone wrestled with the door. Max shook his head. The horses moved to the fence to watch. "See, now they're curious," Max said. "They also noticed that I'm not worried. They aren't gonna trust you yet, to go off your reaction, but they know I won't let anything happen to them."

A younger man in worn, dirty jeans and a faded Metallica t-shirt walked toward us.

"Have you met Mason?" Max asked. "He's a general ranch hand, does a lot of work around here."

Mason focused on Max. "The door's broke again. And there's something wrong with the skid loader. It won't start. It's not even turning over."

Max blew out angrily. He took off his ball cap, ran a hand through his hair, looked at me. "Are you ok putting the horses back out? I gotta go deal with this."

I nodded and Max left, smacking his cap against his leg. I got Rosie out just fine. I took Quincy out, unclipped the rope, and he ran away before I could take off his halter. If I got within a few feet of him, he walked away. Just fast enough. I tried coming from a different direction. I tried putting on a burst of speed at the last second. I told him to keep the halter. I walked back to the barn and put away Rosie's halter and the lead rope. As I left the barn, Max came storming in, not looking in my direction. He strode into the office and closed the door.

Mason stood outside with another man. I walked up to them. "Everything okay?"

Mason shook his head. "One more thing going wrong. Max is pretty mad."

The other man looked away, avoiding eye contact. Huh. One more thing. How many things? Going wrong, breaking, burning. I thought of Max walking around strapped in the dead of night.

"I couldn't get Quincy's halter off," I told Mason. "He's out there still wearing it."

Mason looked in that direction. "Yeah, okay. No problem. I'll get it." He walked through the various fenced-in areas and out to the woods. I watched him walk up to Quincy, take off the halter, and come in with it.

"I feel pretty stupid," I said, as Mason returned.

"Naw, he's just playin' ya. He always does that. Maybe next time leave the lead rope clipped on until you take the halter off."

It was still dark. I felt groggy—I was sound asleep. Something woke me. A car door closed. I looked at the clock. 3:30. I swung my legs out of bed and padded to the door. I could dimly see a car in the middle of the parking lot, lights off, turned to face the road. The cherry of a lit cigarette hovered over the driver's seat. I picked up my four-cell Maglite, slipped on my boots. A noise came from the barn. Someone was down there. Probably breaking something!

Suddenly angry, I switched on my flashlight and ran down the stairs. "Hey!" I yelled into the barn. "What's going on?" I shone my light around the arena. I didn't see anyone. Well, I knew where the driver was! I stormed back out to the parking lot and focused my light on the back of the car. No license plate. The car took off, spraying gravel.

"That's right!" I yelled. "Just leave your partner! Coward!" I turned and went back into the barn. "I know you're in here! Your partner took off on you! You might as well come out!"

The back door banged. I ran through the barn and saw someone slip through the gate. I heard zapping and cursing as they went over the electric fence and into the woods. I went far enough to latch the gate behind them.

"Stop right there!"

I froze. "Max, it's me. They're gone."

Max appeared out of the darkness. "What happened?"

I told him. He looked at me like I was an idiot. "You have my phone number. Could you not call me instead of charging down here on your own? Seriously?"

I blew out air. "I know." I shone my light around the arena.

"Hell, turn the lights on," Max grumbled. He stalked over to the entrance and flipped switches. "I'm turning this place inside out."

We walked every square foot of the barn and found nothing. "You scared them off," Max said. "That's good, anyway." He caught himself and glared at me. "Don't ever do this again. What were you gonna do if you cornered the guy? What was your plan? Being a pain in the ass when you get irritated isn't a plan!"

I narrowed my eyes at him. "That was a little harsh."

Max turned away. "Well, it's too early to feed the horses. We might as well go back to bed." He looked back at me, pointing a finger. "If they come back, you call me."

I nodded. "Promise." I went back upstairs and locked the door behind me.

Max was still irritable in the morning. He was standing by the office talking to Walt when I came down. They both looked at me and shook their heads. I turned to leave, but Walt waved me over. "I'm not going to bother scolding you, Abby. We're making a police report. I need you here." He opened the office door and tipped his head toward a chair. I obediently sat and told Walt everything. He rubbed his face and stared at the ceiling. "Alright. I said I wouldn't scold you." He closed his eyes.

Max came in with two police officers, and I went over it again. The younger cop wrote everything down. The older cop looked at me like I was an idiot. "Property damage isn't worth getting hurt or killed over. You think about what you were gonna do if you caught them?"

"No," I said. "Apparently I'm a pain in the ass when I'm irritated."

Walt flicked his eyes to Max and back to me.

"I don't doubt it," said the cop, and rose to leave.

Chapter Four

I showed up for my first staff meeting with coffee in hand—I already knew this was acceptable behavior. A sturdily built woman with short, salt and pepper hair and weathered skin was pouring coffee for herself and Max. She looked up and smiled broadly. "You must be Abby! Or should I call you Maguire? Max called you Maguire."

I laughed. "Either one."

"I'm Ida," she said. "Ida Gill. I'm sorry I wasn't here earlier. I was on a road trip with some girlfriends. We call ourselves the Old Bats Club." Ida was wearing a t-shirt that said OBC World Tour. She returned the carafe to the coffee maker and sat down. "We went up to Canada this year—first time we've ever gone international." Ida peered at me over her coffee cup. "Did you really hit a bear?"

I couldn't help grinning at this woman. "I did. I had no idea it would make me famous. Maybe I should get a t-shirt."

Ida nodded. "You should. I can make you one."

Walt came in and Ida stood to hug him. "Welcome back," he said.

The meeting was relaxed and friendly. Walt, Ida, and Max laughed easily, teased each other fondly. The paperwork systems were efficient and up to date, a very good sign. As we finished, a man walked in from the parking lot. I blinked. Holy Hannah. He looked better in a pair of jeans than any man I'd ever seen. Cornflower blue eyes, carefully mussed blond hair, and fancy cowboy boots that had probably never been in a barn.

"Good morning," he said. He focused on me.

"This is Abby Maguire," Walt said. "She's our new therapist for the next couple months. Abby, this is Luke Morgan, a probation officer with the county. He meets with some of his caseload here, and they volunteer with us. It might be a probation requirement, or just a good, positive environment for them. Who you after, Luke?"

"Nice to meet you," I said.

Luke held out a hand to me. It was strong, but smooth. He met my eyes, then turned to Walt. "Looking for a few folks today. Starting with Janice."

Walt directed him, then looked at me. "We don't have anyone with any violent offenses, and no sex offenders. We make sure we screen them. We get some juvenile volunteers, and of course our clients. We want to be protective of them."

I nodded.

"Now, this is generally an all-hands-on-deck kind of place," Walt said. "But that doesn't necessarily apply to your position. We all tend to clean up poop when we see it, move horses around, or what have you. But you aren't expected to do any of the physical work. That'll be entirely up to you. We've had some therapists who just draw a firm line there, and that's fine."

"I'm happy to pitch in," I told him. "I'd like to learn it all."

"I like you already," Ida said. "You're going to want some muck boots and some gloves, if you don't have any."

"I need some groceries, too," I said. "Maybe you can point me in the right direction."

"I'll do you one better." Ida nodded. "I need to do some shopping anyway. Why don't we just go together?"

I offered to drive, but Ida saw my hatchback and stopped abruptly. "Honey, I'm not squeezing into that little thing. We'll take my truck, and let's drive into Deergrass. It's a few miles farther, but Jack Pine just has a convenience store. Post office, bar-and-grill, that's about it."

I wandered up and down the aisles grabbing produce, eggs, yogurt. Ida surveyed my cart. I added peanut butter sandwich materials and an extra-large bag of coffee beans. I paused, then took a second bag of coffee beans.

"Hunh," Ida said.

I glanced at her cart. Milk, ground beef, some canned soups and a box of individually wrapped cookie sandwiches filled with marshmallow cream. "A little treat for Max," she said. "He just loves these things."

I grabbed a stack of frozen spinach cartons and Ida grabbed ice cream. In the parking lot, she handed me her keys.

"Here, you want to drive? See if you like a pickup truck. We're going to make a country girl out of you."

I climbed up into the cab. Automatic transmission. "Thank God."

"What was that?"

"I'm starved," I said. "Where's a good place to grab something?"

"Oh, we've got the best burgers," Ida said. "But I don't know if you eat fast food. You're kind of into healthy eating, I noticed."

"I am." I stopped for a red light. "But I'm not religious about it. I eat to have the energy I want. But I do like burgers." I glanced at her. "And tacos. I love tacos."

Ida pointed. "Turn up there, after that mailbox. I am religious about it, but not how you're thinking. I figure I mostly ought to eat things as close as possible to how the good Lord made them, seeing as how He made us too, so He knows what He's doing. But you gotta try Burgers 'n Bait."

I almost hit a parked car. "Bait? Tell me they don't."

Ida laughed. "Well, you can't get leeches and nightcrawlers through the drive through. It's a whole separate entrance. I think it's a health department thing."

A few blocks later I pulled into the Burgers 'n Bait parking lot and joined the line for the drive through. Ida chuckled. "The last time I was here, oh Lord, was I in a mood. I was working hard on eating healthy, but that day I just wasn't feeling it. 'Yes! I know my body's a temple! But I just want some FRIES! Is it THAT big of a deal? Is it REALLY?' The whole time I was waiting in line, thank God no one else could hear me, I was yelling at Him. I just ordered a burger, nothing else. 'Well, I hope you're happy!'"

I pulled ahead as the line moved, and looked at her.

"Well, do you know, when I got my order they accidentally gave me a large fry! They didn't charge me for it, but there it was at the top of my bag!"

I grinned. "Did you eat them?"

"Damn straight!" She laughed. "God gave me those fries! Probably His way of telling me to lighten up a little. It would've been rude not to eat them. They were the best fries I ever had, too. Fresh and hot and crispy and salty..." She sighed, thinking about it. "Of course, I thanked Him."

We pulled up to the intercom. "I want a cheeseburger, no onions," Ida said.

I leaned out the window towards the speaker. "Two cheeseburgers with no onions and a large fry."

"And two Diet Cokes!" Ida shouted over me.

I handed the food and drinks to Ida. "Do you mind if we go to my house to eat?" she asked. "I can put my ice cream in the freezer."

We pulled into her driveway a few minutes later. Her house was small, with light blue siding, a freshly mowed lawn and neatly kept flowerbeds. As Ida unlocked the back door I heard squawking from a chicken coop in the yard. We stepped into the kitchen.

"Go ahead and start eating. I'll just quick put these things away." Ida set two plates on the table. She stuck my spinach and her ice cream in the freezer as I divided the fries between us.

We stacked our plates in the dishwasher. Ida took an empty egg carton from the top of the fridge and filled it with eggs from a wire basket. "I want to bring these back for Walt. Well, really for little Clara, his granddaughter. She and his daughter live with him. There's a few others at the ranch who keep chickens too, if you want fresh eggs. Now, they have a natural antibacterial coating, so you don't have to refrigerate them. Once that gets washed off, of course, then they need to keep cold. We'd better get going if we're going to stop at the farm and fleet."

Ida drove into the ranch parking lot as another car pulled out. "Max's girlfriend. Hunh."

I didn't ask. Ida grabbed my new rubber boots from the back seat. We both loaded our arms with bags and carried them up the stairs.

Walt decided to have a team-building ride. I needed help getting Rosie ready. The whole saddling thing was complicated. Plus, it involved reaching under the horse. Walt offered to let me put the bridle on—put my hand up to Rosie's face, stick a thumb in the back of her mouth. "There are no teeth there," he said. "You just give a little bit of pressure to encourage her to open up."

I stepped back, fingers curled protectively into my palms. He laughed and put the bridle on.

Walt's horse was a big brown one named Maverick—apparently one of the most experienced therapy horses. Max was tacking up Quincy. As Max paused to talk to me, Quincy leaned over the rail, picked up a lead rope in his teeth and hurled it at Max. Max threw his head back and laughed. Quincy glared at him.

My mouth hung open. "I had no idea a horse would do that!"

"Quincy has a mind of his own! He will definitely share his opinions." Max picked up the rope.

Ida walked in leading a beautiful black and white horse. "This is my girl. Her name's Rebel."

Walt leaned over. "The horse mimics the person!"

"Damn straight," Ida said.

Walt said the horses knew the trails and knew when they were working. I was in the back— "Rosie does tend to kick other horses if they get too close, so we'll put her on tail today." Rosie followed Quincy with no input from me.

The trail wound through the woods. When conversation ebbed, I could hear the wind rustling the leaves. I felt my shoulders and back relaxing. My breathing slowed, deepened. We rode into the open prairie over a land bridge that crossed a culvert. Geese floated in a pond, swimming away as we passed. We rode out to the far end of the property. The neighbor's cows grazed across the fence.

Walt twisted around in the saddle. "Now, be alert here. There's a couple turkeys in the brush. They might startle the horses, so just be ready. If the horse spooks it'll jump sideways on you, but don't panic and the horse won't panic."

I gazed at the wild turkeys in wonder. The horses didn't seem concerned. We wound back through the woods and into the barn. Rosie automatically walked up to her own post. I dismounted like Walt showed me, landing on my feet without embarrassment. I couldn't stop smiling as Max helped me untack Rosie and put everything away. What a wonderful job this was going to be.

I decided to spend a little time in the office, reviewing the paperwork systems. When I stepped out, Max and Walt were huddled together near the feed room. Leaning in, speaking intensely, both making short, emphatic gestures. Walt put his hands on his hips, looked away, scowled. Max kicked the wall.

Ida came into the barn and saw me watching them. "They're just frustrated about the Kubota being out of action." She waved a hand toward the door. "Let's go open the gate so the horses can all go out for the night."

I gave the men another glance as we walked away. I was being distracted. Whatever was going on, no one wanted me involved.

Chapter Five

I got more familiar with the ranch as the days went on—model of therapy, chores. Whenever we finished a session together, Walt sat down with me to review. We noticed very different things in the same situation. Comparing notes was fascinating as we blended our perspectives into a whole. I hoped this was standard procedure and not just training. It was fun.

That said, this was hard work. The saddles were heavy, carrying them from the tack room. Hoisting them onto the horses, especially the tall horses. Heaving them back up on their posts. And mucking. Pushing a full wheelbarrow, dumping it on the six-foot-high, twenty-by-thirty-foot pile of manure they called Poop Mountain. My shoulders and back ached. My arms ached.

It had dirt mixed in, Poop Mountain, and lush grass growing on it. Sometimes horses wandered up to munch that grass. I was startled the first time I saw a horse on top of the mountain, but no one was concerned. Eventually, I stopped noticing the mountain, too. It was part of the landscape.

I finished my morning clients and went outside for a break. The mechanic was bent over one of the ranch vehicles. He was introduced as Jared, but we hadn't gotten past hello. I wondered what his take was on things breaking down, starting on fire.

Jared's clothes hung loosely on his frame. Extra holes were punched through the leather of his belt, probably with a screwdriver. His face looked like he'd been picking at it. He became aware of me standing there, and looked up.

"Jared, you pretty much know everyone around here, don't you?"

He nodded. "I guess so. I've been around about the longest."

"I see you fixing things all the time," I said. "Are you the only person with mechanical know-how? I mean, I wouldn't begin to know how to do anything with a skid loader."

He wiped a hand across his forehead. "Hard to say, isn't it? People have histories. You don't know what people know, if you've never asked."

"Huh." I peered at the engine he was working on. "Excellent point. I haven't seen anyone else fixing any vehicles, though. I guess it's job security in a place like this."

He stared at me for a long moment, then went back to his work.

A car pulled into the parking lot and a woman waved to me from the passenger seat. I knew I'd met her. Janice. She kept chickens. I walked up to meet her as she got out.

Janice held up a plastic bag. "I brought those eggs you wanted! Fresh this morning."

"Wonderful! Come upstairs and I'll get you some money."

She waved as her ride drove away, and followed me up the stairs. "I don't clean them. They don't have to go in the fridge."

I nodded, digging in my purse. "Ida explained that to me. I can't wait to try them."

"You just let me know when you want more." Janice leaned back against the counter, looking around. The smell of cigarette smoke emanating from her clothing was strong in my small kitchen.

I handed her some cash. "Janice, do you know anything about machines or engines?"

She snorted. "Me? No. I do wanna get my driver's license back, when I'm off probation. Why would you think I knew about engines?"

I shook my head. "I just don't want to assume that only guys might be mechanical. There are women who are good at it."

"Yeah, not me," she said. "I just take care of the horses."

"Do you have much probation left? Bet you're counting down the days."

"I still got five years." She rolled her eyes. "I'm trying to get off early, though. I might get it reduced. Plus, I have community service hours I gotta do from before. I got almost 200 hours, but I'm working on it now."

"You're here a lot, that's got to help. Have you been coming out here long?"

"It better help!" She cackled. "I ain't doing it for my health!" Janice nodded at me inclusively while she laughed. We were sharing a joke. "I just got sentenced in January. My P.O. said it would look good if I volunteered here. My grandpa had horses when I was little, so I been around them before. Course, I didn't muck out the stalls then, but that ain't no big deal. I'm happy to shovel crap if it gets me off paper quicker."

I nodded. "No kidding."

Janice cackled again. "Jail ain't that good, and poop ain't that bad."

I grinned. "Seems like this is a big place for Jared to be the only one who can fix things. I was just wondering if anyone else helps him out at all."

"I don't know," she said. "Never really paid attention. Why?"

"Just getting to know people. There's a lot of work to go around, isn't there?"

"There sure is. I better get to it." Janice pushed the door open. "Let me know if you want any more eggs." She waved and left. The smell of cigarette smoke lingered after her. I opened the window.

I looked in the egg carton and recoiled. The eggs were covered with thick gobs of chicken poop that held straw and dirt on the shells like paste. I set them down, covering my mouth with my hand. My breakfast rose to my throat. Ida's looked nothing like this. I closed the carton and went back downstairs.

A group of people was gathered around the farthest picnic tables, where smoking was allowed. The non-smokers also perched on benches or edges of tables. I wandered over, hoping to join in.

Max was saying something about his girlfriend, who lived in a nearby town. A couple of people nodded, laughing.

Luke the Hot P.O. was there. Must be checking on his caseload. He leaned back against a table, fingers stuck into the front pockets of his jeans. He pushed a wad of chewing gum into his cheek with his tongue. "So, Abby, any special someone out there you left behind, to come to Minnesota?"

I shrugged. "Short-term temping doesn't really lend itself to long-term relationships."

"Makes sense," Ida said. She wasn't smoking, but pulled a Diet Coke out of a small cooler and offered another to me.

"Hey, did you really run over a bear?" someone asked.

I laughed. "Oh my gosh. Yes, I did. But someone else did first."

Luke tilted his head. "Got anyone semi-special? Not to be nosy or anything."

"Not really." I cracked open my can.

"Me either." A woman with young hair and clothes, but a worn face, took a drag. She blew out smoke. "Easier that way."

"Oh, I always gotta have someone," said a man, who looked about seventy. "Don't like sleeping alone!"

"You're a grown-ass man," someone told him. "Buy a night light." General laughter. I guessed there was a story there.

Luke brought it back to me again. "Hard to believe you haven't been snatched up. Unless you just don't want to be?"

"Aw, let her be, Luke," the older man said. "She's a grown-ass woman, she can date how she wants. Maybe she does prefer sleeping alone!"

"It is easier that way," I said.

"Damn straight!" Ida toasted me with her soda. Several people grinned and raised their cans to her. Ida seemed to bring laughter wherever she went.

Another woman leaned in. "So, you really go live all different places around the country? Did you just decide you're not going to date until you live in one place?"

I studied her briefly, looked around the group, took a cold swallow. "I do move around a lot for jobs." How far did I want to go with this? They all watched me, waited. "No, I haven't sworn off dating. Thing is, I'm just not into casual sex, just as an expected part of going on a date. A lot of guys, I tell them that, they suddenly remember they have to wash their socks every night for the next month. Or some guys, they think that's fantastic, they love that! But if it gets to a couple dates, they're shocked that it would apply to them."

"Good for you." An older woman punctuated with her cigarette. "You don't want to put out, don't."

Luke laughed. It made him even more attractive. I noticed the golden curl hanging over his forehead, the sparkle lighting up his eyes. "I bought you a burger!" he exclaimed. "I even sprang for a Coke! Now you really owe me sex!"

"That's not far from the truth," I told him.

He stood up, stretched. His soft-looking Henley rose to show an inch or so of belly. I couldn't tell if he did it on purpose. "Or how 'bout if it was tacos? He buys you tacos, you definitely owe him sex for that."

Everyone laughed. "Well, tacos," one of the women said.

"Maybe she's holding out for a steak!" The older man looked around at his audience as he laughed.

I shook my head. "Tacos are fabulous. Steak is alright. But sex is never transactional. Where are the best tacos around here?"

This started a lively debate, and my personal life—or lack thereof—was thankfully left behind. When the group broke up, I went to find Rosie.

I was brushing Rosie in the barn, working on the scary parts. "I appreciate you being calm," I told her. "And not kicking me in the head." Rosie yawned. I walked ten feet behind her and brushed the other side. I noticed her ears swiveling. She pivoted on her lead rope, moving her hindquarters away. "Did I do something wrong?" I asked her. I heard movement and turned. Luke was standing behind me.

"So, Abby, you want to grab some dinner later? I'd be happy to buy you tacos, or whatever. We can go into Deergrass. You can get anything you want there—tacos, burgers, or pizza. No strings attached. Kind of a welcome to the neighborhood kind of deal."

I couldn't help returning his grin. "Sounds good."

"Great! Tonight, around seven?" He nodded and angled off toward the parking lot. I watched the embroidery on his back pockets swing out of the barn. Was this really just "welcome to the neighborhood?" Did I want it to be? Either way, I should probably wear clean boots.

Luke was a little early, smiling on my doorstep.

"Come on in for a minute," I said. "I'm just about ready."

He must have gone home and showered. His hair was freshly tousled. I wondered how long it took him. Longer than I spent on my hair, for sure. He stepped in close. "How do you like living in the upstairs of a barn?"

"Actually, I love it." I closed the door behind him.

Luke walked down the hall, taking in everything as he moved through the apartment. I was glad I'd whipped through the little kitchenette, shoving dishes in the cupboard, wiping drips of coffee from the countertop.

"You don't mind being out here in the middle of nowhere, all by yourself?"

"I don't. I get a lot of people-time at work."

He wore clean Wranglers as well as clean boots. Immediately the advertising jingle popped into my mind. "Wrangler butts drive me nuts." Stop it. Do not look at his butt. He pushed up the sleeves of another Henley, snug around his forearms. I wanted to touch it, see if it was as soft as it looked.

"Let me grab my coat." I escaped into the bedroom to grab a denim jacket from the closet. Get yourself together. This is ridiculous. I took a few breaths and stepped back out to the main room. He was leaning on the sink, looking around. I saw him take in the coffee maker sitting alone on the countertop, the few framed photographs, the kitchen table where my laptop and some worn paperbacks took up residence. He could probably tell I ate standing over the sink, right where he was resting that butt.

"You must travel pretty light," he said. "Is it hard living like that, being ready to up-stakes all the time?"

"Everything I need, I can pretty much fit in my hatchback." I scooped my purse over one arm, walked to the door.

Luke scanned his eyes over me, smiled. "You look real nice." He put his hand on the small of my back as he eased past, and my entire body tingled. I had to get this under control. He looked back at me with a mischievous grin. He knew exactly what he was doing to me. I sighed and locked my door.

"It really wasn't awkward, once we got there," I said to my picture of Papa later. "Luke is one of those guys who can talk easily and comfortably all night." I straightened the frame on the shelf. "Mostly about himself." There was already dust. It must be a hazard of living over a barn. I grabbed a dishcloth and wiped the picture and the shelf around it. "No, you're right," I told Papa. "This isn't going anywhere. But it was sociable. And entertaining, in a way." I put the frame back on the shelf and carried my clean boots to the closet.

The night was clear. I could see shadowy groups of horses in the woods. They vacated the corral when the gates were opened, and spread out to the trees and pastures. The air through the window was still warm. I pulled on my barn boots and went exploring.

I could see the trails in the moonlight. The white trunks of birch and poplar almost glowed against the blackness of pine and oak. I walked along the path, hearing a rustle of movement in the brush. It was one of the brown horses. "Hi there," I said. We stopped to look at each other. I took a step closer. The horse closed the distance between us. I scratched its neck. "I'm not sure who you are, but you're a sweetheart, aren't you?" The horse leaned in.

After several minutes I moved along the path again, the horse following along. We walked together out to the farthest pasture. The air seemed to vibrate with the high-pitched buzzing and creaking of frogs. Horses watched as we passed. Some of them ignored us. Others approached, seeming curious. I stood in the middle of the field, looking up at the stars. They were brilliant, so far from the city. Varied in brightness, they flooded the sky. I could hear the hooves of horses stepping around me on firm ground. Breathing, deep and rumbly. A quiet ripping and chewing as they cropped the grass. A slight breeze touched my arms and legs. Staring at the sky, I was startled when something brushed my neck from behind. The horse that walked out with me nuzzled my shoulder.

I finally went back to the barn. The horse moved with me. Several others followed behind. As we ambled along together, joyful laughter bubbled up inside me. I was in a herd! I shook my head in wonder. Most of the horses peeled off in ones or twos, heading in different directions, but the first horse saw me to the fence. "Goodnight, buddy," I said, giving it a final scratch. I stopped halfway up the stairs to look out over the night. I heard a horse nicker in the distance, and smiled.

Chapter Six

There was shouting in the barn—men's voices, rageful, violent. I looked up from my paperwork. My stomach tightened. It sounded like trouble. I stepped out of the office. Mason the ranch hand and another man stood in the middle of the arena, each with a horse on a lead rope. Red faced, screaming. I couldn't understand them. They didn't seem to notice the horses pulling away.

"What the hell is going on in here?!" Max came striding in.

The men stopped shouting. The one I didn't know dropped something on the ground and stepped on it.

"Get out! Out!" Max grabbed both lead ropes and jerked his head toward the parking lot. "You got a problem, you take it the hell away from these horses!"

The two men looked at Max's face and didn't say a word. I wouldn't have either. His eyes blazed. He seemed to radiate restrained fury. The men both hesitated, then walked away. Max raised the lead ropes toward me. I walked over and took a rope in each hand and led the horses over to their posts.

Max toed at the sandy ground where the man dropped something. His eyes bulged. "Are you out of your damn mind?" He bent over and picked up what looked like a cigarette butt, and stormed out to the parking lot. The men resumed their argument, but with less energy. Max shouted, stabbing a finger towards their chests in turn. They climbed into their trucks and drove out, one leaving a spray of gravel in his wake.

"All right," I said to the horses. "Well." I had no idea what to do. I was halfway done brushing the first one when Walt appeared.

"What just happened in here?" he asked.

I described what I'd seen. "It sounded violent, but it was all verbal." I leaned with both forearms against the horse's back, looked at Walt. "Max was just verbal too, but the guys seemed like they were scared of him."

Walt shook his head in disgust. "They should be." He seemed to catch himself. "I mean to say, he's right. We can't have that." He walked over to the other horse and put his arms around its head. The horse nuzzled its face into Walt's shoulder. He scratched its neck quietly. "Flame in the barn, think what could've happened."

We finished our post-session dialogue and documentation. Walt hooked a chair with the toe of his boot, pulled it toward him, then put his feet on the chair. "You're a good fit here, Abby. I'll confess I wasn't expecting someone with your level of experience, didn't think I could afford you." He studied me, tilted his head, paused as though there had been a question there. "I suspect you took a pay cut to come here. I've been nothing but impressed with your work, your professionalism. I do wonder what you came here looking for? I understand you like novelty, but I feel there's something more."

I searched Walt's eyes for some indication that Max discussed our nighttime talk, but saw none. "I kind of got talked into it by a friend. I mean, not this job, specifically." I did air quotes. "A 'nice' job. But she made a good point. My work has been too high in trauma for too long."

He waited.

I smiled, shook my head, told him about the dinner with the sometime co-worker who got a nice, quiet job and stopped getting shanked. It seemed like a long time ago, now. I realized I was frowning at Walt. "I didn't really believe her," I finished lamely. "About feeling relaxed."

Walt stared at me.

I cleared my throat. "Anyway. So, I'm considering something of a change in direction. Basically."

He nodded. "Alright. Thank you." He rearranged his papers in a neat stack, closed his binder, stuck his pen in the chipped mug on his desk. He looked at his feet for a moment, then sighed and pushed the chair away. His boots thumped down to the floor, one after the other. He stood and stretched.

I took the cue and stood.

Walt picked up his coffee mug. It said, "Horses make me happy. You, not so much." He pointed it at the countertop. "You want some coffee?"

I glanced at the coffee pot. It was about a third full of murky liquid, a layer of sludge on the bottom. I took a breath. "Hey, I know. Do you want to come upstairs for some really good coffee? Not that this isn't, but I just ground the beans this morning. Really fresh."

Walt eyed the sludgy coffee. He set down his mug. "Let's go."

Walt pulled off his boots at the door, came through the living area. "This is nice. You haven't added a whole lot, but it feels more personal." He took in my vase of cut flowers, my framed photos. "Who is this?"

I waved him toward a chair and started some coffee. "That's Papa. He raised me."

Walt studied the pictures. "He did a fine job. A real fine job."

I was surprisingly pleased with Walt for saying that.

"Tell me something about him," he said.

I sat down across from Walt. "Technically he was my Uncle Seth. I called him that for the first four years or so—until I found out what my name meant." I smiled at Papa on the counter, then at Walt.

Walt leaned his weight back in the chair. "I hope you're going to tell me that story."

I eyed Walt. It wasn't really a story I told, but I'd opened the door myself—to my own surprise. Something about Walt invited confidence. I took a breath. "I was four when my mother died. She'd been sick. My father just disappeared. I overheard people talking, not knowing what to do with me. Then my Uncle Seth showed up, and he just put me in the car and took me home like it was the natural thing to do." I smiled again, thinking about him while the coffee hissed and gurgled into the pot. "He always acted like, of course we should be together. Like I belonged to him. He died just a year ago."

Walt nodded, waited for me to go on.

I told him about the day in grade school when we learned about the meanings of our names. We were supposed to write a little story or do some kind of art project about it. I went home that day and sat at the kitchen table with my knees drawn up against my chest, hugging my legs, until my uncle came in and found me.

"What's wrong, Abs?" Uncle Seth sat next to me.

"I have to change my name." I stared at the floor.

"The whole thing, or just part of it?"

"No, I want to keep my last name. I like having the same name as you."

He nodded, paused a beat. "So, is there a name you're looking at, or you just don't want Abby anymore?" He sat quietly until I answered.

"Abigail means *her father is overjoyed*." I turned back to the floor. Tears welled up in my eyes. I tried to blink them away. "I have to get rid of the Abby part. Maybe I'll just keep Gail." My voice trembled.

He didn't respond for some time. "No," he finally told me. "If you want to be Gertrude, or Millicent, or Goldilocks"—

I smiled a little, despite myself.

"I could go with that," he continued. "People should have a say in what they want to be called. And Gail's a fine name, especially if it means joy. But I can't call you something that, to you, means unloved or unwanted. That would be a lie."

I stared at the floor some more.

"Abby, I'm sorry," he said. "I'm sorry about your dad. I truly am. I can't tell you what is or isn't going through his mind. I know he tried to be a good father, before your mother died." He paused. "I hope you know that I'm overjoyed about you."

I looked up.

He cocked his head. "Another idea could be, I could change my name."

I frowned. "How would that help?"

"Well," he said, "what if you and I just decided to adopt each other? I wouldn't be Daddy, but what if I was Papa?"

I was astonished. "Can we really do that?"

He raised his chin defiantly, crossed his arms over his chest. "We can do whatever we want. Who's going to stop us?"

I laughed with pure delight. Who could stop us? I felt like an outlaw, or a pirate—a daughter chosen against the rules. I clapped my hands. "Can I really call you Papa?"

"If I can call you Abby." He stood and put his hand on my head. "Let's get some dinner, shall we?" So, we did. I couldn't remember what we ate, but I remembered Papa smiling at me over the red painted tabletop, the late sun angling in through the curtains. I remembered the wrinkles on his face, the graying stubble on his chin. I remembered feeling happy. Safe.

Walt sat quietly for a moment. "Thank you for telling me that," he said. "It helps me know you."

I got up and poured the coffee. "I think I heard your daughter lives with you?"

He nodded, took a sip. "Oh my. This really is good coffee."

I smiled. I didn't say anything about the sludge downstairs.

"My wife passed about ten years ago. I don't know if I can say I really got over it. I just go on. When my daughter's marriage broke up and she wanted to go back to school, she and my granddaughter moved in with me. And I love it." He smiled, drank some more coffee. "I wish they'd live with me forever. I really dread the day that Marcia—that's my daughter—decides she's ready to go on her own. They really light the place up." He paused. "Marcia looks just like her mother. It's like I get to keep a little part of her. And little Clara, well, you'll meet her. I like to have her out and put her on a horse." Walt beamed, thinking about his family. He thought for a few minutes while he drained his cup. I got up and refilled it. He nodded thanks, and went on. "You know, my wife never got to meet Clara. She would've loved that little girl. She never got to be a grandma. I guess I try to hold on to Marcia and Clara a little tighter because of that. I know it irritates Marcia, though. Eventually she'll want her space." Walt seemed a little embarrassed, like he hadn't planned on sharing that. He shifted his weight in his chair.

I smiled. "It will be fun to see Clara on a horse. Who does she ride?"

"I put her on Teddy. She loves how affectionate he is. Thinks Teddy's her best friend." He finished his cup and set it down. "Thank you for this. I could make this a habit."

"You're welcome up here any time, Walt. I always have some ready to brew." I put our cups in the sink. "Really. I love sharing coffee. Come up any time."

The wind kicked up and was howling around the barn. The partially open sliding doors blew in and out, slamming against the walls, straining as though they would break. "We've got to shut these doors," Ida said.

I ran over and tried to push one closed. I could barely move it. I shoved harder, leaned in, put my weight against it. It slowly inched along the track at the top. Ida took hold of the other door and pushed it shut. Without a track on the bottom, Ida's door still blew in the wind. "We'd better block it with something," she said. "This wind is something terrible!" She put a chair in front of the door, but the next gust pushed it over.

I finally got mine closed. "Maybe put something heavy on the chair?"

"Let's try buckets of water," she said. We started filling buckets. I picked one up with both hands and staggered over to the chair, trying not to slosh too much as I bent under the weight. I heaved the bucket up on the chair and shook my arms out. Ida came striding across the barn, a bucket in each hand, and set them on the ground in front of my door. I stared at her. She seemed not to notice. She was looking at the doors, not at me. The wind still pulled the doors outward, with loud groaning and creaking, then slammed them into the water buckets. "We've got to get something on the outside." Ida left the barn. Moments later, I heard a motor start, and Ida returned. "Mason's going to park the skid loader in front of the doors."

That seemed to work. With only inches of room, the doors rattled and banged less violently. "We'll just bring the horses in the other door," Ida said. "They may not like it much. They like what they're used to."

We brought in Rosie and Teddy, who turned out to be the brown horse that loved scratches. They were both extremely cooperative coming in out of the wind. A few more horses tried to follow us. "Sorry, guys." I shut the gate on them. "Go stand in the lean-to." They stuck their faces over the rail.

"Hello! Boy! It's windy out there!" Luke Morgan appeared, shivering dramatically. "Seen Rodney around?"

"He knows he's meeting with you," Ida said. "He mentioned it earlier. I'll go see if he's still out in back."

When Ida left, Luke sidled up to me. He slipped an arm around my shoulders and gave me a quick kiss on the cheek. "Hey. Nice to see you. Been wondering if you want to have dinner again."

My heart beat faster as he leaned close to me. The warmth from his body made me tingle. He smiled at my shiver, ran a hand up my arm. His face was a little rough as it brushed my cheek. He spoke quietly into my ear. "Been a long time, hasn't it?" His finger traced down my throat. "Ground gets too dry, a tiny little spark'll set things off." He kissed my ear. I couldn't breathe.

"Here he is." Ida walked back into the barn with a younger man a step behind. I hadn't been sure who Rodney was, but I would remember now. Scowling Rodney. I'd noticed him more than once. Debated with myself whether his demeanor was due to a depressive disorder manifesting as anger and irritability, or just a generally obnoxious personality.

Luke took a step back at the first sound of Ida's voice and assumed a casual stance. I blinked. Luke gave me a quick smile and said quietly, "Dinner tonight? Seven?"

"Ok!" I smiled back.

He and Rodney left for the conference room as our client walked in.

A few hours later, I ran into Luke in the parking lot. He hurried by, frowning. "Sorry," he said. "Gotta cancel for tonight. Something's come up."

"No worries. Another time." I watched him drive away.

Rodney, still scowling, came out of the barn with another man. They glanced from me to Luke's departing truck, and back to me. I smiled. "What's Luke like as a P.O.? Is he ok? Strict? What do you think?"

"Don't even talk to me," Rodney said. "I don't need no trouble." He turned abruptly and walked away. The other man stood, eyes wide.

I tried to look friendly. "Goodness." I shook my head a little.

"I don't mean no disrespect," he said. "Don't ask me about Morgan. I don't need to get violated. I don't want no trouble either. I gotta keep my head down." He shot me a panicky glance and hurried away.

I leaned against the fence and pondered that, as they fled.

Chapter Seven

Max and I were having a bit of back-and-forth before the staff meeting. Ida and Walt came in, studied us to see if we were arguing, saw that we were not, and settled in comfortably.

"Let him bark on his way out the door, to save face if he needs to," I said. "It doesn't matter. He got the message."

Max was unmoved. "I'm not going to let him talk to you like that."

"That's good, but you don't need to do it in front of me. It'll be easier for him to stomach if you pull him aside later. Maybe he'll hear you better, if he doesn't feel humiliated."

Max wrinkled his brow at me. "Is that one of your rules?"

Ida and Walt both gave Max questioning looks.

"She has rules of engagement," Max said. "Uses a mutt approach to therapy, picks up different things to use with people, has a few hard and fast rules. I don't know what they are yet."

Ida paused in passing out agendas. "It sounded like you said 'mutt'."

Walt took one, but set it aside. "I would like to hear those rules."

I rubbed my temple with my fingertips. "Rule one, everyone gets to keep their dignity. Always. We never use or tolerate shame.

People get to save face when they need to. We find a way to work around it. We never make people small. There's always another way."

"He's not too worried about your dignity," Max said.

"It's not his rule."

Max raised an eyebrow at me.

"I think most people mean well," I said, "but it's easy to be sarcastic or dismissive. Laughing at people, not being sensitive to their embarrassment. Getting impatient can make people feel stupid. We lose track of how hard it is to come in and be vulnerable. Respect matters."

Max tilted his head in acknowledgement. "How many rules you got?"

"Two."

The corners of his eyes crinkled in a smile. "Ok, you gonna make me ask? What's rule two?"

"No one is disposable. Everyone matters."

"That sounds pretty basic too," Max said. "I think most people would follow those rules."

"Well, again, it sounds basic until you put it into practice. I tend to focus on the hardest people to work with." I slid my agenda closer to me, pulled a pen from the mug in the center of the table. "See, if everyone matters, we don't just go after the low-hanging fruit. The people we really enjoy, everyone enjoys. They're better at the whole interpersonal thing, they're fun. The people that you brace yourself when you know they're coming, everyone does, everywhere they go. No one's face ever lights up when they walk into the room. Imagine no one ever being happy to see you."

"We're always friendly with people," Max said. "We would never scowl at someone when they get out of the car."

"But some people, our faces light up. People can tell the difference, even if they're young, or old, or have a ton of disabilities. People pick up on way more than we think." I paused. I felt my face getting warm. "I'm ranting."

"You're passionate—I like that." Ida smiled at me.

"All right, so how do you operationalize that?" Max settled his weight back in his chair.

"Find something to like. Some connection. Have fun with them, enjoy them, notice them. If people get themselves or their kids out here, they're trying. So we show up for them, for the time they're here. We get tired, doing session after session, but we show up for everybody. Not one single person is disposable."

"I like your rules," Walt said. "We'll take a look at this. Never hurts to reevaluate ourselves."

"Did you really say 'mutt'?" Ida asked.

Max pointed at me with his head, did an exaggerated shrug. I stuck my tongue out at him. He laughed. Walt knocked his empty coffee cup on the table like a gavel. We all picked up our agendas, the meeting called to order.

I began to think of it as scooping therapy. I felt a real sense of accomplishment after cleaning an entire corral. I put on my gloves when I felt frustrated or edgy, grabbed a wheelbarrow and a rake, and picked an area to clear of manure. The things you don't see coming in this world. I moved the wheelbarrow from clump to clump. The people with years of experience were good at placing the wheelbarrow in a central location and heaving poop into it. It seemed to be an acquired skill.

I piled the wheelbarrow high, trying to avoid an extra trip to the manure pile. Pushing the wheelbarrow through each gate, while keeping anyone from escaping, could be tricky. Plus, a full wheelbarrow was heavy. I carefully balanced the last scoop of manure on top of my load and tossed my rake over the fence. I was halfway back to the wheelbarrow when one of the ponies approached. "Hi, there. Aren't you pretty?"

The pony looked at me. It walked up to the wheelbarrow and leaned against it. "No!" I shouted. "No! Don't—" The wheelbarrow tipped over sideways. The pony shot a look directly at me and walked away. "I can't believe you did that!" I shouted. I looked at the wheelbarrow on its side, poop spilling out in a huge pile on the ground. I waved my hands at the pony in disbelief. "What—I can't believe you did that!" It was clearly deliberate. I had no idea horses did things like that! "You're not pretty," I said. The pony ignored me.

I righted the wheelbarrow, which was difficult with the weight of the manure still in it. I retrieved my rake from the other side of the fence, and came back to the pile. The pony was eyeing the wheelbarrow. "No!" I waved the rake. "Don't even think about it!" I looked at the pile. It was huge, but it was all in one place. It would go more quickly this time. I filled my rake with manure, pivoted to sling it into the wheelbarrow, and slipped, falling on top of the pile. I scrambled to my feet. Nothing about this was pretty. I glared at the pony. It sauntered away. I finished loading the wheelbarrow for the second time and wheeled it to the manure pile to dump. One horse tried to sneak out the gate when I opened it to push the wheelbarrow through, but I was in no mood to be intimidated. I ordered it to back up. Unlike the pony, it listened. I put the wheelbarrow and rake away. Thankfully, I had time for a shower.

"Abby!" One of the volunteers called to me. "Hey, I'm sorry, but we had to turn off the water to the whole barn. You won't have any for a couple hours."

I looked down at myself and cringed. I had a session! I could use Max's shower. No, Max was off buying feed. I leaned against the wall, closed my eyes. Footsteps approached and stopped. "Oh, Lord, help." I opened my eyes. Ida was staring at me.

"It was that pony," I said.

She nodded. "I know just the one you mean."

"Ida, I have a client in a few hours. Look at me! Smell me!"

"I'd rather not. Let's grab a couple of towels and put them on my seat. I'll take you to my place, you can shower there."

I ran upstairs for clean clothes and towels. "We can take my car!"

"No," she said. "I'm not crawling in there. Just don't touch anything."

We walked through the back door, into the kitchen. I wondered if Ida ever used her front door. As I stepped out of my boots, an owl hooted in the next room. I froze, then turned in that direction.

"That's my bird clock. There's a different bird every hour," Ida said.

I glanced at my watch. It was ten minutes after two.

"Well, supposed to be on the hour," she said. "It does what it wants, when it wants. Kind of like my Johnny used to do, God bless him. It does keep things interesting." Another bird chirped loudly. Ida laughed. "Sometimes it doesn't make a sound for half the day."

I had to see the bird clock. It hung in the living room with several pictures of Ida and an always grinning man, over decades of life. Ida tapped the top of one frame. "Johnny passed on, oh, seven years ago now. He was a prize." She smiled and nodded. "He was a prize."

I smiled back at her. "The two of you together must have been fantastic."

Ida beamed. "Oh, we had fun." She led me into the bathroom. "You can put those towels on the floor and put your dirty clothes on top of them. Grab a clean towel off the rack. And use whatever you need." Her shower curtain was just a clear liner. She patted it. "Don't mind my not having a real curtain. My Johnny, God bless him, he liked it this way. He used to call it a show-er curtain. He'd come in for his show." She laughed. "Do you know, no matter where I was at with my weight, up and down, even when my hind end was roughly the size of a Buick, he stood there goggling at me like I was some centerfold." She shook her head, laughed again. "God love him. I don't have the heart to change it."

I scrubbed myself and washed my hair twice. I heard the bird clock as I toweled dry. It sounded like a mourning dove. I wondered briefly if Ida talked to Johnny when she was alone, or if she just smiled, thinking about him. I bundled up my dirty clothes.

Ida sat at her table. "Abby, I'm worried about Max and Walt. They're under too much stress."

I set my bundle on the floor. "So, what's going on, Ida? Nobody wants to talk about it. Something's on fire, something's broken, people don't want me to see it. Clearly the three of you are close, but everyone's putting on a happy face and pretending. What's really happening?"

She sighed, shook her head. "We do love each other. And we're trying to carry on as best we can, but we don't know what's going on. We don't know why things keep breaking, or God help us, burning. Someone must be doing it on purpose, but we don't know who. We don't know why. Max and Walt are both exhausted, drawn. Walt is getting depressed. We need to do something. I want you to help me."

"Have you gone to the police?"

She waved that away. "We've filed reports. What can they do? There's no proof it's not just a terrible string of bad luck. Help me, Abby. You've got a good brain and fresh eyes. You might see something we don't."

"I'm not sure what I can do," I said. "I'm just getting to know people. But I'll try. I'll keep my eyes open."

Ida nodded, satisfied. "You always have your eyes open. You're always watching, always noticing. Nobody's been fooling you one bit. I figured it was time to talk to you."

I brought in the wrong horse again. I knew I wasn't after one of the brown horses, I got that much right. I brought in the wrong paint. I should have known something was off when I was leading her along, saying in a sing-songy voice, "Come on, Molly. Good girl, Molly," and she bit me on the arm. All she got was my jacket, just telling me she wasn't Molly, dammit. I had her all tacked up with Molly's saddle when a volunteer came in and laughed at me for bringing in Lego.

"I'm David," he said. "I don't know if you remember meeting me."

I'd seen him around quite frequently—an older man, retired, always talking—but I did not remember being introduced. I smiled sheepishly. "I guess I didn't remember meeting Lego, either." I took everything back off while Lego glared at me from Molly's post.

David smiled. "Don't worry, you'll get it." He walked with me to take Lego back out. "Now, observe. We call Molly the Llama Killer. When you look at Molly, it looks just like there's a dead llama slung over her back. See, there's even an eye, see that dark spot there, on the white llama?"

He was right. It did look like a llama slung over her back, as disturbing as that might be. David continued with his lesson. "Lego is also a paint, but she looks like a flock of birds flew over her, see the white drops?"

I smiled, nodded thanks, and put Molly's halter on. She didn't even bite me on the way in. David walked in with me. "You'll be familiar with the horses, in time. But don't be afraid to ask."

"I appreciate that," I said. "Especially with all the brown ones. You must spend a lot of time here?"

"My wife doesn't like me underfoot," he said. "I always tell people that, and it's the truth!" He laughed jovially.

I was struck by the feeling that he was performing. Was he a retired teacher, or a politician? Someone used to each day being a presentation. I was trying to decide which was more likely, when I realized he was still talking.

"Young people just getting started, or some starting over. A real opportunity to have an influence. Steer them, as it were. Of course, they're learning about the ranch, as you are. But people can be directed in other ways, as well."

I reached Molly's post again, so I thanked David for his help and started brushing. I was running behind now, so I wanted to focus. David wandered away and started talking to Rodney, who looked peevish about something.

"Okay, Molly," I said. "Bear with me. I'll try to get this right."

We had two late afternoon clients. I was tired and hungry by the time Walt drove away. I pulled out a frying pan, found vegetables to cut up for an omelet, and opened the egg carton still sitting on the countertop. I stood for a few long moments, looking at globs of solidified chicken poop, shells stained with liquid blotches. I closed the egg carton, put the vegetables back in the refrigerator, and grabbed my car keys. Burgers 'n Bait sounded perfect.

The inside of my car was disgusting. How did the cupholders get horsehair all over them? I tried to wipe it off, but it stuck to the console with static electricity. I turned out of the driveway and saw beer cans in the ditch. I pulled over and swung out of the car. I popped the hatch, picked up the beer cans, and was putting them in a trash bag when a car approached and slowed to a stop. The passenger window rolled down. Janice, the egg lady, stuck her head out. "Everything okay?"

I raised a beer can toward her and smiled. "No problems! Thank you! I appreciate you checking."

She studied me, squinting, then shook her head and said something to the driver. The window hummed back up and they drove away, tires crunching over the gravel. I frowned at the retreating car. What was I going to say when she asked if I needed more eggs? I twisted the top of the trash bag so it would stay shut. Maybe I needed tacos.

I woke in the night, noted the darkness out the window, and sighed. At least I wasn't having a panic attack. I stared at the ceiling, then rolled out of bed and went out to the kitchen. I turned on a lamp by a window, in case Max was up, wandering around in the dark. My tea was still steeping when he knocked on the door. His eyes looked red, his shoulders tense. I waved him in and heated more water. "Rough night."

He nodded.

"Max," I said, handing him a mug, "you told me that equine therapy saved your life. Have you ever done therapy for PTSD?"

"I don't need therapy," Max said.

If I could raise one eyebrow, I would have.

"I'm not sitting in any office getting my head shrunk." He blinked slowly. "I know we have clients with trauma, I know it helps. But for PTSD, I don't know what that would be."

"I do. I can help you with that," I said. "With horses or not. We can chip away at it in the middle of the night. You don't have to sit in an office, if you feel like you're being commanded to relive things."

He eyed me through the steam rising from his cup.

"I mean, I wouldn't be your therapist. But I can tell you how it works. We can support each other—we don't need to be proud, here." I put my feet up on a chair and settled back. "Do you understand basically what's going on in your brain, with nightmares, flashbacks?" I sampled my tea. It was pretty good.

Max shook his head. "Not really."

I set down my mug. "Five second version. Your brain has two places it keeps memories. Short term storage, call it Point A, is also where the emotions are. Long term storage, Point B, is in the thinking area. Memories are supposed to get moved to long term storage, but if an experience is too powerfully emotional, your brain can't get it in there. So, it gets put back in point A, the temporary holding place, with the feelings." I tapped the table for emphasis. "But it can't stay there. It's supposed to be at point B. So your brain keeps bringing it up, bringing it up, trying again and again to file it with the thoughts. If the feelings are too overwhelming, it can't. All those nightmares, all those intrusive thoughts, that's your brain trying again to refile that memory."

Max took another drink. "It's trying real hard. My brain's not a quitter, apparently."

"Nothing about you is a quitter. Now, something about putting things into words helps with the refiling. But that doesn't mean you have to sit down on someone else's timeline and force yourself to describe things. If it's too overwhelming, it's counterproductive. Make sense?" I pointed my mug at him. "It's got to be you opening that door, deciding how much to let out, and closing the door when you want to. Thirty seconds or thirty minutes, doesn't matter. You are in control."

He studied his tea as if something was floating in it. "And the horse?"

I tilted my head in a shrug. "You know better than I do. The horse gives you another focal point, gets you out from under the microscope. If you've deadened your awareness of how you feel because you just suck it up and move on, Quincy can show you what he senses coming off you. We let Quincy show you the parts of yourself you turned off—shut down so you could function, survive."

I heard his breathing change. The bit about deadening his feelings had struck a nerve. "The thing is—" I heard my voice gentle and hardened it a bit. Matter of fact. Mustn't sound like pity. "You need to bring back awareness of what you're feeling, to heal and make the trauma cycle stop. Using things in the arena to represent what's going on makes it easier. It works. There's research. Really."

Max rubbed his temples. He didn't say anything for several minutes. I let the silence stretch out and fill the room. "Maguire," he finally said, "out of all the therapists we've had, you're the only one I would even think of touching this with."

I felt my eyes tear up. I blinked it away. We were both exhausted, sleep deprived, but his words touched me. "Just let me know, Max. Any time."

Max nodded, finished his tea, and stood. He seemed at a loss for words. He nodded again, turned, and walked away. I stood at the door and watched him walk back to his house, then turned off the light.

Chapter Eight

I was sitting at the table trying to figure out what still stunk, when Ida hollered in from the door. I yelled back to let herself in.

She came from the barn. The smell wafted into the room with her like a poison gas cloud. "Just thought I'd pop in and say hello before I start getting ready for my session, see if you were busy."

It wasn't just my boots. It permeated my clothing, my hair—but I'd showered, changed, scoured my fingernails. Every time I raised my sandwich to my mouth, I smelled manure. I sniffed up and down my arms. It was my watchband. "I'm not. I can help," I said. "Just trying to figure out what still stinks, and I got it."

Ida frowned and turned her face back and forth, sniffing. "I guess you did get it, I don't smell anything."

I tossed the sandwich and followed her out.

Ida organized the post-session paperwork while I made us both a good cup of coffee and brought it down. She nodded her thanks and kept writing. Then she smiled. "Say, Abby, let's go to my place for dinner tonight. We'll make something fun."

"I want to make a Minnesota hotdish."

Ida laughed. "That's good. And hotdish is right. Casserole is for a fancy occasion, a dinner. Family and friends get hotdish."

"I definitely want hotdish, then."

It really was fun. We stopped at the grocery store for canned soup and wild rice, and settled into her kitchen. Her bird clock sounded off unexpectedly, at odd intervals, then fell silent for hours. We laughed while we cooked. We talked into the night. I found myself watching Ida affectionately. She was looser than I'd seen her. Relaxed, at ease. Realizing how relaxed I was distracted me. I looked at my watch. "Oh, Ida. It's after midnight. I hope you don't have to get up early."

She shook her head. "Let's get you home, though. Don't forget the hotdish and the rhubarb bars we packaged up for you. You might be too tired to cook tomorrow."

"What is it? Hey, hey, hey. What is it, girl? What's wrong?"

I took my coffee to the doorway to look out. Max was trying to lead a horse into the barn, but it came to a full stop. I leaned out over the railing. "What's going on?"

"Hell if I know! She's too distracted to focus on breakfast, for the first time in her life."

I trotted down the stairs, set my coffee on a step. "Can I help?"

"I don't know," Max said. "She must smell something. Look at her nose." The horse's nostrils were flaring. She turned her raised head back and forth, surveying the area by scent. I hoped it wasn't some kind of sabotage. What if there was a fire smoldering in the barn and we couldn't smell it?

"Did you hear anything out here last night?" Max asked. "I don't know, maybe a coyote was prowling around. We do have them out in the woods. The horses don't always like to cross their scent path, if they've walked across the trail."

"I didn't hear anything." I looked at him suspiciously. "Do coyotes seriously come this close to the barn?"

He sighed. "No. We've never known them to. I'm just grasping, here." He looked at the horse. "You ready to come in? Breakfast!" He gave a little tug. The horse gave him a sidelong glance of disapproval.

I looked at the ground between the gate and the barn. The dirt was dry, showing no tracks other than deeply embedded hoofmarks, hardened in the sun, worn from being walked over for days. I looked in the barn. "There wouldn't be a coyote in there, would there?" I wasn't sure I wanted to go find out, but the thought of walking out of my apartment some night and tripping over a predator was compelling.

"No," Max said. "I can't even imagine that. I need to get these horses fed and medicated so I can move on here." He turned back to the horse. "Come on. Walk." He started into the barn and the horse came with him, ears pricked up, eyes alert, nostrils wide.

I walked into the barn and looked around tentatively. It smelled like the normal pungent mixture of dirt, manure, and hay. Max already got the buckets measured out and hung on the rails without concern though, so it wouldn't be obvious. I grabbed a lead rope and halter and went out to get another horse. Within minutes all the horses were tied and eating. "Every horse I brought in did the same thing," I said. "Sniffed around and looked offended. What in the world kind of smell offends a horse?" I patted the closest one. "No offense."

Max leaned on a railing, looked around the barn, and shook his head.

"If there was a coyote in here," I said, "there might be tracks in the back, where the sand is looser, or some scat or something. I'm going to go look around a little."

"Have at it," Max said. "I'm going to muck out the pasture while the breakfast crew is out of the way."

I hesitated, imagining a wild dog of some sort bedded down in the tack area, startled at my presence, snarling to life...or a cougar? What if it was a wildcat? There were black bears in the woods, though seldom on the ranch itself. How did I know what would make a horse uneasy in the barn? Maybe it was a snake. A big one. Whatever it was, it didn't mind us in the middle of the barn, or apparently the feed room, but did I really want to go poking around in the corners? Maybe I should wait for one of the guys who were always talking about the different guns they owned. Maybe I should call them and ask them to bring their guns.

Imagining Walt's reaction to that, I shook it off and picked up a rake. I could keep something away long enough to back off. I edged my way into the tack area, peered around the corner, scanned the ground, tried to see farther in. Nothing. The sand even looked freshly raked, with only a few trails of boot prints across it. There was a plastic food wrapper on the ground, unusual in Walt's tidy barn. I picked it up and shoved it in my pocket. I followed the boot marks, holding the rake in front of me at waist level. Something did smell off. I couldn't identify it, but the mustiness was somehow different. Was it an animal smell? I took a few deeper sniffs of the air, my nose wrinkling, but I couldn't quite place it. I glanced behind me, halfway hoping that Max became curious and followed me in, but I was alone.

I sidled toward the wall, giving whatever-it-was room to escape past me if startled into flight. I reached over and flicked on the light switch, ready with the rake if anything sprang from the depths of the room. Nothing moved. I banged the rake on the wood paneling. "Hey! Anything in here?" I waited. Nothing was scrabbling under the saddle mounts or behind the shelves of grooming tools. I took a breath, blew it out, and edged along the wall. I stopped, jumped back—a shape caught my eye. There was something on the ground where the room dog-legged. Something sticking out around the corner. I looked again. It was a boot. I took another step forward. It was a pair of boots, and jeans. A man was lying on the ground.

I rushed forward. "Are you alright?" It was Mason, face down, motionless. My first thought was that he was drunk, passed out. Then my brain processed the smell, as my eyes registered the blood pooled around Mason's head. I froze for a long moment, swallowed hard as my stomach clenched and a wave of nausea swept over me. I propped the rake against the wall and knelt over Mason, feeling for a pulse, knowing I wouldn't find one. His skin felt cold. A shovel lay next to him, the long shaft going over his arm as if tossed there. A shovel I'd used many times. I stood, backed away. Feeling my way along the wall, I wobbled my way out of the barn.

The bright sunlight seemed disorienting. I looked around, located Max in the corral scooping manure into a wheelbarrow. Had it only been a few minutes? I tried to call out to him but couldn't speak. I climbed over the fence and walked towards him. He looked up, opened his mouth to say something, but stopped abruptly at the sight of my face. He put down his rake. "Are you ok? What is it?"

I took a deep breath, steadied myself, and pointed at the barn. "We need to call Walt. And the cops. You'd better come."

Chapter Nine

There were cops from Deergrass, which was apparently the local station. Jack Pine was too small to have their own. There were county deputies. There was a plainclothes detective from somewhere. I went over everything again and again. I was out late with Ida. I hadn't seen anything, or anyone. I slept through the night. I didn't tell them that was rare. I didn't mention Max's midnight walks. I was still getting to know people. I really didn't know who'd want to hurt Mason. I was finally dismissed, so the police could talk to Walt and Max.

Ida sat at one of the picnic tables, blankly looking at the parking lot full of emergency vehicles. I walked over and sat by her. Ida turned to me, opened her mouth, but closed it again and looked away. We sat quietly for several minutes. "Abby," she said. "What can this possibly be about?"

I shook my head. "I have no idea. This is way beyond sabotage. I don't know what to say."

She rubbed her forehead. "I've known Mason for years. Most of us have known each other for years. It has to be an intruder, don't you think?"

"I don't know why there would be an intruder in the tack room. Are used saddles worth stealing?"

"They're not worth killing someone over." Ida sat and watched the uniforms walking around. "What can we do, Abby? We have to help Walt. There must be something we can do."

I thought. "What matters to Walt is helping people. We can keep doing that, as soon as we can open again. Not let this destroy the place."

Ida nodded. "You're right. That will help him. And we've got to keep our eyes open. Like we were before. No one's going to be comfortable until we know what's going on."

"People like coffee," I said. "Someone knows something around here, and coming up for coffee might get them to relax a little, maybe give something away."

"I'll make cookies." Ida looked a little less miserable, if only for a moment. "People love my cookies. When I put them in the break room, everyone wants to sit and eat them, and talk. I'll bring you as many cookies as you need, to serve with your coffee. You just let me know." We nodded at each other. We had a plan. We could move forward. Not feeling paralyzed would help.

Not knowing what else to do, Walt closed for a week. We said there'd been an incident, and someone was hurt. The local gossip probably reached everyone before we did—there were fewer questions than I expected. Meanwhile, the horses still needed to be cared for, fed, kept in a riding routine. Ida and I brought horses in, but Ida went to the tack room. Even after the police cleared us to go in, I didn't much want to.

Walt walked into the barn with a man I hadn't seen before. Clean cut. Dark hair, barely long enough to show that it was wavy. Something of an ex-military air. He wore faded jeans and a plaid button-up, sleeves rolled to his elbows. Built like he was used to physical work. His boots were scuffed, but clean—no dried, caked mud and manure on them. Walt gestured for me to come over. "Abby, this is Ben Murphy. He's going to be joining us as a ranch hand." He did not point out that Ben was taking Mason's place, after only a few days.

I held out a hand and introduced myself. Ben nodded a greeting. His eyes scanned the arena, taking in not only me, but the entire situation. He was almost attractive in a rough sort of way. The slight wrinkles on his face were laugh lines, though he was serious now. His nose might have been broken at some point. His hand, shaking mine, was firm and calloused. Something felt off. I looked at Walt. He just looked tired. I studied Ben. It was his eyes—the intelligence there was bright, quick, assessing. Brown eyes, smoothly cataloguing his surroundings. Outwardly he might look like a laborer, but he was up to something.

A fed. Would the feds come in for a murder? Would local law enforcement put an undercover detective on a ranch? Had Ida told me everything? What did I still not know about? What would bring a fed? Ben was staring at me. I realized I was squinting at him. I felt my face getting hot. I looked away, then glanced back. Those scrutinizing eyes registered my suspicion. Now he studied me.

"Nice to meet you," I said. "I'm sure we'll see a lot of each other." I nodded and walked back to the horse I'd brought in. When I looked back, Walt was gesturing at something across the arena and talking, but Ben was still looking at me.

Ida came out with our grooming tools. Her eyes cut from me to Ben, and back. "What's going on?"

"A fed. That's just my guess. A new ranch hand, officially."

Ida watched him, while trying to pretend she wasn't. "Why are the two of you eyeballing each other?"

"I stared at him too long. He knows I suspect him." I took my horse's brush. "Is there anything you haven't told me, Ida? Anything else going on, that would elevate this to fed level?"

"No." Ida put down her tools and brushed her hands on her pants. "I'm going to introduce myself, though. There's not going to be a fed here, without my finger on his pulse." She gave Ben the Probable Fed her most charming smile and shook his hand. He smiled politely but barely looked at her after that first scan. Good. He would underestimate one of us, anyway. Old ladies were great to have on your team. They were always underestimated. I made a mental note to tell Ida that. The Old Bats Club could add it to their organizational mission statement.

Walt and Ben walked on, and Ida returned to her horse. "We need to stay sharp, Abby. We're in uncharted territory here. We've never had a fed before." I nodded, and we quietly tacked up our horses.

I found Max in the round pen with a horse on one end of a very long rope. Max held the other end of the rope and a slender whip. The horse ran in circles around Max. Waving and pointing the whip like a wand, Max turned the horse around. It loped along in a lovely arc, smooth and elegant. A ballroom dance. I leaned on the fence to watch. Max saw me and grinned. "He's doing great, isn't he? Want to try?"

I climbed over the fence. "I'm not sure if I do or not. Have you ever been trampled doing this?"

He laughed. "Never." He handed me the rope. "This is a lunge line. Getting the horse moving at the end of it is called lunging. Now, you use this whip—of course we never whip them. It's a pointer, or you can wave it to get them going in the direction you want. Here, give it a shot."

I studied the horse. It gave me a side-eye. I waved the whip. The horse glanced at me. I gave a little tug on the line and waved the whip again.

Max made loud kissy noises, and the horse started walking. It came closer to me, in a smaller circle, causing slack in the line. I moved back to tighten it again. I waved the whip. The horse broke into a slow trot. After several steps, it cut in again. I stepped back to tighten the line. The horse stopped, turned, and walked straight towards me. I moved back, and circled away from the horse. How did Max keep the line tight? I waved the whip. The horse walked in the other direction. I trotted over to be in a better position. The horse cut in again, making a smaller arc. I circled around it, to compensate and tighten that line. I glanced at Max.

Max smiled. "Do you see what's going on here?"

I waved the whip and took several steps sideways. "Nothing very graceful."

"Who's doing all the work?"

I stopped and let the whip fall to my side. "That would be me."

Max grinned. "Who's being lunged?"

I turned to look at the horse. It yawned. "Oh, for crying out loud. The horse has me going in circles." I gave the line back to Max. "How do you keep the horse from lunging you?"

"I'm real glad this happened," Max said. "It kind of relates to a philosophy we have here. Sometimes it's not what you do, it's what you don't do."

I handed him the whip. "Explain."

"We want to help," he said. "It's natural. We try something, it doesn't work, we try something else, it doesn't help, we wrack our brains trying to find something to do, the client keeps telling us nothing works. Maybe they don't take part, maybe they act compliant but never really engage."

"I know exactly what you mean," I said.

"We figure you can lead a horse to water, but you can't make it drink. Which you can see literally, every day of the week here, if you ever wanna point it out to a client. We do our best to match client to horse, client to activity, but we also do our best to not be the only ones working hard. The client lunges us, it helps nobody. See, this horse is real comfortable, and you're not. You're trying real hard—you're trying harder than the horse is, right now. With this horse, it's because he knows you have no idea what you're doing, so he's playing you." Max twitched the whip in the air and the horse came to attention. "With clients, I'm not saying they're all playing you. Some of them are." He made a tsk-tsk noise, and the horse became the very picture of grace, gliding along at the end of the line. "Some of them, it's probably a defense they came up with, because therapy is such hard work, they're avoiding pain. Lot of things in life, the idea of it is better than the reality. You know, like eating salad." He cut a glance at me, smirking.

I ignored him.

"Or maybe they're not looking for the same thing the therapists are looking for." He pointed with the whip and the horse moved in that direction.

"I'm glad to hear you say that," I said. "I think it's critical to know what people actually want, and why."

Max nodded. "And the ones do that come in wanting to lunge us, we just don't respond like they're used to, and if they keep coming, maybe for once in their life they get a different result."

I finished cleaning up after a session. Ben was sweeping stable pads. He rested his broom against his shoulder. "Got time for a cup of coffee? I'm ready for a break, here."

"I do," I told him. "But let's go upstairs and I'll make some fresh. You don't want to mess with this coffee down here."

He put the broom away and followed me up. I waved him toward the table, while I measured water and grounds.

Ben pulled out a chair and sat down. "So, I've been wondering. I don't really want to be awkward, asking people. This guy that I'm replacing. Do you think there's anything I should worry about myself, here? Or do you think he was mixed up in something?"

Wow, he got right to it. "I haven't been here that long myself," I said. "I really didn't know Mason that well. It seems like most of these folks have known each other forever, though, so whatever happened, I'd guess people will see you as entirely separate." I eyed him over the table. He was scanning the apartment, taking in every detail with one broad sweep. He seemed to be pretty good at that.

We established how my position worked and what I liked about temp jobs. He lived in a town nearby, he said. Knew people with horses, growing up. I poured Ben some coffee.

"This is excellent," he said. He took another drink.

"So," I asked. "Are you a fed?"

Ben jerked and spilled his coffee, sloshing it onto his shirt. He coughed, choking mid-swallow.

I sat back and took a drink of my own coffee. It really was excellent.

Ben put his mug down. He took a napkin and dabbed at his shirt, but the wet spot was too big.

"Too soon?" I asked him. "I figured we'd covered the niceties."

He shook his head slightly. "Why on earth would you ask me that? I wasn't sure if you were joking." He looked down at his shirt and frowned. "This is going to be mud within five minutes of walking into the barn." He dabbed at it again. "I'm meeting Walt later. Crap, I'm sorry, I spilled some on your table."

"That's fine," I told him. "You know, I bet I have a clean shirt that might fit you."

He looked at me, looked down at himself, spread his hands in a you've-got-to-be-kidding gesture.

"No, really. I have some large men's shirts I sometimes pull on after running. Let me see what I can find for you." I went in the bedroom and dug through my drawer, pulling out a nice, roomy t-shirt. When I got back out, Ben was standing by the window. He glanced at the shirt in my hand.

"This should work," I said, handing it to him. He held it up. The picture on the front was a mug shot of Bigfoot. It said he was wanted for Failure to Appear. Ben stared at me. I shrugged. "I thought, being in law enforcement, you might appreciate a little FTA humor."

He blinked. "Why are you calling me law enforcement?"

"Oh, please." I took his cup and refilled it. I set it back down on the table. Ben changed his shirt, looked down at it and frowned, shaking his head. I wiped the table with a dishcloth. Ben eyed me dubiously, picked up his coffee and carefully took a sip.

"What are you meeting with Walt about?" I asked. "Maintenance? Horse care?"

He narrowed his eyes at me. "Yes. Moving the horses between pastures, things like that."

I raised my cup to him in a toast. "That's important," I said solemnly. "It's the details that keep the place running smoothly."

Ben drank his coffee and set down the mug. "Thanks for this. I'd better head back down." He turned to look at me from the doorway. "I'll wash the shirt and get it back to you."

"Please don't dry it. I always hang my clothes, so they don't shrink."

He nodded and left. I looked at Papa. "He didn't even pretend to answer me, did he?" I rinsed out the coffee pot and went back down.

Janice was in the barn, brushing a horse. I ambled up to her. "Hey. How's it going today?"

She stopped brushing. "Ok. Why?"

"Just thought I'd say hi. See how your day's been."

"Oh. Fine. Thanks." She walked around to the other side of the horse so she couldn't see me anymore and immersed herself in brushing. Alrighty then.

I wandered back outside. One of the volunteers was standing by the fence. I leaned on a nearby picnic table. "Hi! Nice day, huh?"

He glanced at me, and his face turned grim. He gave an almost imperceptible nod. "Yeah." He climbed through the fence and became very interested in the water trough.

Fine. I went back upstairs and poured more water into the coffee maker. "I can understand people being a little uneasy," I told Papa. "I did find Mason. They can't possibly think I did it, can they? Mason was at least three times as strong as me." I looked at Papa and thought for a moment. "Probably just people being on edge." I heard knocking and moved so I could see down the hall. I waved Ida in. "You're just in time. I haven't started brewing yet. Want some?"

"Absolutely. And we need to talk."

"At least someone wants to talk to me. I feel like I've been blacklisted."

Ida processed that, but didn't comment. "We need to compare notes, Abby. Have you picked up on anything at all?"

I shook my head. "I've only had a couple people up for coffee, and one of them was Ben. People are avoiding me."

She frowned. "I haven't heard anything yet, either. Not a lot of people talking, which is strange in itself. The rumor mill has got to be positively electrified, but I guess all the buzz is happening somewhere else."

"Ida, people can't think I killed Mason, can they?"

Ida laughed. "You? Oh, Lord. No." She waved a hand dismissively.

I almost felt insulted.

"Be serious, Abby. Someone must have heard something. Maybe that Mason was going to meet someone. Why in the barn? Why so late?"

Nothing would be gained by defending my potential as a villain. I let it go, taking two mugs down from the cupboard. "Isn't it most likely it's someone from the ranch? We need to think about people we know whether we want to or not."

Ida pulled out a chair. "Maybe it was Luke Morgan. He's here a lot. Just because he's a probation officer doesn't mean he'd never break the law."

I hoped she didn't notice my little shudder. "I doubt it."

"Why? What was that?"

I went quiet.

"Are you getting all up-close and personal with him?" Ida looked appalled. "What were you thinking?"

"Mostly about his butt in those Wranglers," I admitted. "But I got to fondle that soft-looking Henley he wears, so that was nice."

Ida snorted. "I'm not kidding. You watch that one—he always looks like he just walked out of a western store. You ask me, he's trying too hard to look like something he's not."

"Oh, Ida. Let's be fair. The guy works in an office. His jeans and boots are going to be clean. He probably just reminds you of someone you didn't like."

"Well, maybe he does, but that doesn't mean I'm wrong, either. I'm probably picking up on something. You gotta listen to your gut, you know. He's fine as a P.O. You just leave him there."

"Listen." I was ready to change the subject. "Do you have any idea what kind of trouble Max had when he got out of the service? He was vague when he mentioned it."

Ida's face hardened, her mouth a tight line. "No. It's not Max."

I opened my hands, palms out in surrender. "I'm just asking. That day he threw those guys out of the barn, he looked scary as hell. They both looked like they were afraid of him. Walt said they should be. Max was a combat-trained Marine. I'm just saying we should consider everything here."

Ida crossed her arms over her chest and glared, her voice growing louder. "It's not Max. I've known him a long time, Abby. He's a good man. He helps a lot of people, changes a lot of lives. We've been through a great deal together. I'm telling you it couldn't be him."

"Anyone can do something bad in a single moment, depending on the provocation. I'm just wondering if you know what his trouble was. Drugs? Alcohol? I know he doesn't drink now. Does he have a record?"

"It doesn't matter what he came through in the past!" Ida smacked the table. "He came through it. He did not do this. It's a lot more likely it was your boyfriend!"

"I don't have a damn boyfriend!" I blew out air, looked at the wall, composed myself. I raised my hands again, signifying a truce. "Honestly, I don't really think it was Max." I sensed Ida starting to relax across the table. "If Max was going to club somebody over the head," I said, "he'd do it somewhere a lot farther away from the horses."

Ida's coffee cup returned to the table with a thunk. She leveled a steely gaze in my direction, then sighed, looked away. "Max told me you're helping him work through some things. If you think he's a killer, why would you do that?"

I examined my cup. "Well, that's for Max to talk about, not me. And I've worked with killers, but that's not my mandate here. Although none of this entire conversation is my mandate, so there you go. This whole situation is ridiculous. What are we doing?"

Ida didn't answer.

"Okay," I said, "since you're already mad at me..."

Ida narrowed her eyes. "What?"

"What about Walt? Does he have a dark side? What's his history?"

Ida raised her eyebrows. "Why on earth would Walt risk everything he has built here, to kill somebody in his own tack room? That doesn't wash."

What was the deal with Ida and Max?

She shook her head. "I've known Walt forever, Abby. This is something new."

We sat with the silence heavy between us for several long minutes. The sound of gates opening and closing drifted in the window. A motor started somewhere. The Kubota. I was glad to hear it running. And not on fire. "Ok," I offered, "What do you think of Ben?"

"Well, I don't know anything about him," she said. "But he wasn't even here. He's Mason's replacement, remember?"

"Did you ever ask Walt or Max about him? You might get a straight answer."

Ida huffed. "I got nothing. They got evasive. What do you know about him?"

I paused. What did I know? "Well, he doesn't like spilling on himself. It makes him cross."

"He spills on himself?"

"We were making conversation, so I asked him if he was a fed. He spilled his coffee and got cranky about it. He never did answer me."

"Hunh. Guilty as charged, I'd say."

I ran my finger around the rim of my cup and studied Ida. I thought about how physically strong she was, how she strolled along with full water buckets in both hands. How her moods flared up and subsided with little warning, especially if she thought Max needed defending. How well did I really know Ida?

She squinted at me. "Have you really worked with killers?"

"Some. And people who care about them—a whole lot of trauma there, I promise you. But really, Ida, you might have, too, and just didn't know it. That's kind of our point here, isn't it? Not knowing who's killed someone." I rubbed my forehead, suddenly tired. "We just circled back to the beginning."

Ida drained her coffee cup and set it down. "Have we resolved anything at all?"

"Only that I need to lock my door at night," I said.

"Damn straight. Make sure you do."

Chapter Ten

I circled the arena close to the fence, but Rosie kept cutting the circle smaller. I steered her back to the perimeter. I reversed direction and tried it again. Walt brought in another horse. "Now hop down, and let's give Lucy a try." He explained that she was young, less experienced. "Smart horse. Really good horse."

Lucy took a few steps and my pulse immediately shot up. "She's going to run! Whoa! Walk! Slow!"

Walt grinned and put a lead rope on Lucy's halter. "Let me walk you a little bit first, while you get the feel of this." Lucy followed Walt, every step brimming with energy, as though she might take off wildly at any second.

"Don't let her run!" Would she trample Walt? Could I stop her if she did?

Walt turned and smiled at me. "Now, remember, you're in control."

Like hell I was. Ok. Deep breath.

"Scoop your seat down into the saddle," Walt said. "Sit your weight back. That's telling her to take it slow. Legs relaxed. You squeeze your legs, you're pressing the accelerator. If you do want to slow with the reins, just tap the brakes at first. Just a few gentle pulls—ask nicely. If the horse doesn't respond, you can be a little firmer, but don't forget that's a piece of metal in her mouth."

Walt unhooked the lead rope. "Ok, now you just walk her. Relax, breathe." He stood back to watch. "You need to let go, Abby. Stop trying to be perfect. You don't want to be all high-strung with Lucy."

"Ok, Lucy," I said. "I'm relaxed. Don't buck me off."

When I'd made it around a few times, Walt changed his posture, and Lucy immediately slowed and walked over to him.

"Wow, she's focused on you," I said.

Walt nodded. "Like I said, this is a smart horse. Now you go back to Rosie, and feel the difference in the energy she puts out."

Rosie and I did a couple of laps. "How does she feel?" Walt asked.

I stopped. "Ok, I know Rosie can have an attitude—"

Walt grinned. "The horse mimics the person."

I ignored that. "But her calmness is amazing after Lucy. I had no idea."

He nodded. "That's good for today."

"Walt, what is that mimicking thing? No one says it seriously, but you all say it."

Walt smiled. "Many folks will say that the horse mimics or mirrors the person. We see the horse being itself, bringing itself into the situation, but it does respond based on what it senses. That's probably what a lot of people mean anyway." He grinned. "We do use it to tease each other. And a horse may behave more stubbornly if it senses resistance in a person. Or the person having an attitude."

I nodded. "Uh huh. That's good for today."

I got a late start the next morning, taking a jog and a hot shower at a leisurely pace. I didn't have any sessions until afternoon, but I wandered down to the barn.

Ida had a couple of horses tied to their posts. She gave me a friendly wave. I picked up a brush and started in. I was putting the saddle on when we heard the crunch of tires on gravel, and car doors.

A couple of uniformed police walked toward the office. A cop in a suit came in a step behind them. The detective, I remembered him. He saw Ben leading a horse in from the pasture, and slowed for just a beat. Ben looked away quickly. The cop recalculated and kept walking.

Ida looked at me. "Hunh. You see that?"

I narrowed my eyes in Ben's direction. "Ranch hand, my ass."

Ben tied his horse to the post as if nothing had happened. Ida continued brushing, but I was feeling testy. I stared at Ben just long enough for him to see me. His eyes registered that I was watching. Only then did I turn and bridle my horse. When I glanced back, Ben was brushing his horse, but looking at me.

Irritating him was probably counterproductive. I purposely ignored him until he was finished tacking up his horse—Lucy, the high energy one. How experienced a rider was he? Part of me hoped this would be interesting. I caught his gaze. "Hey, want me to open the gate for you?"

He nodded. "I'd appreciate it. Thank you." He put his foot in the stirrup and swung up as easily as most people sit on the couch.

Huh. He rode in a few small circles, he and Lucy getting a feel for each other. I felt a little guilty for being disappointed.

I pulled out my phone. "You look great on her, Ben." I took a few pictures. "I'll send them to you later, if you want."

He nodded again. I went to open the gate so he could ride out.

Walt came out of the office, looking strained to the point of breaking. I froze. What now?

He waved us over, took off his hat, ran a hand through his hair. "Ida. Abby. I'm so sorry. So sorry. I—they need to take everyone's fingerprints. For elimination purposes. The shovel was so full of prints, of course—" his voice was choked. He couldn't finish.

Ida put an arm across Walt's shoulders. "You never mind, Walt. We'll be fine. I've never had my fingerprints taken before. It might be interesting."

I nodded. "I had to get fingerprinted for my licensure. We're fine, Walt."

He blinked hard and took a deep breath. "I can't bear this. We've come so far, through so much, for our staff to be fingerprinted by the police, to have a death... How can I tell people they must be fingerprinted by the police?"

Ida squeezed his shoulders and gave him a tiny shake. "Walt, you know as well as I do, half the volunteers are already in the system. The ones that aren't, well, they'll either think it's a kick, that will give them a story worth free beers for a week, or else they'll want to do their part to help. No one's going to be traumatized by having their fingerprints taken."

Walt swallowed and nodded to her. "Thank you, Ida. I hope you're right."

She patted his back. "You know I am. Walt, you go on up to the house and sit in Max's kitchen for a few minutes." She turned to me. "Come on, Abby, let's go first. Then we can tell everyone else how it was. Encourage them."

We watched Walt's back as he moved toward the house. "I hope they find some prints that don't belong to anyone here," I said.

Ida looked startled. "Of course they will! Oh, do you mean the person might have worn gloves?" That wasn't what I meant, and she knew it.

Cleaning up after the last session of the day, I found myself alone in the barn with Ben. He came over to put away his rake next to mine.

"Been a long day," he said. "What do you think about grabbing some dinner? The taco place in town is pretty good."

I studied him. Tacos did sound good, whatever his intentions. "Let's do it. I should change into clean clothes."

He looked down at himself and spread his hands in a gesture of futility. "I've got nothing to change into. Let's just stink together."

I laughed. "Let me dump this wheelbarrow, I'll be right with you." I wheeled it out to Poop Mountain and dumped it at the edge. Ben was by the parking lot, scraping his boots on the grass.

"Do you want to drive separately," I asked, "so you don't have to come back out here?"

He waved that away. "It's not that far. Let's go together in case we decide we're too ashamed to go in, and eat in the truck."

I climbed up into his pickup, an older single-cab with a long bed. "You seem like you're settling in really well," I said, as he drove. "I always see you talking with people."

Ben looked straight ahead. I suspected he could see me just fine in his periphery. "I hope to fit in as well as you. Not that you don't work hard, but you're always chatting someone up."

I smiled warmly. "Occupational hazard for me. Talking is my life."

He grinned and watched the road.

"I've been trying to meet everyone," I said casually. "Get to know who does what, what people's strengths are. Did you ever figure out what people expect from you, compared to Mason?"

Ben said nothing for a few beats. "I'm getting to know the horses," he finally said. "Routines. How things work."

Moments later, he pulled into the Taco Tio parking lot and turned to look at me. "Ok. You call it. Do we go in, or drive through and eat in the truck?"

I looked at my clothing, then his. "We're gross. Drive through."

He nodded. "We don't want to create an exposure incident." He maneuvered up to the speaker and ordered enough tacos for four people, with extra napkins.

"I'm sorry—I didn't even think about getting tacos all over your truck." I took a bite and my taco shell cracked, spilling meat and fillings onto the wrapper spread over my lap.

He laughed. "I'll hose it out tomorrow when I fill the water troughs." He bit into his taco and shredded cheese fell out.

I leaned back against the door, extending manure-caked boots across the floor of the cab, waggling my toes at him. Hot sauce dribbled onto my shirt. "I meant to ask, is this a date?"

Ben laughed with a mouthful of taco. He put a hand over his mouth and choked a little, coughed and cleared his throat. "How could I possibly say no to that?" He crumbled up his empty wrapper, dropped it on the floor and reached for the bag. His hand brushed against my arm. Every muscle in my core contracted. A tingle swept over me. My toes curled.

Luke got one thing right. It had been a long time. I crumpled up my own wrapper and reached for my drink. "Hey!" I set my drink down again. "I was going to send you that picture of you riding Lucy. Do you like her?" I dug in my purse for my phone. "I've only been on her once, and I couldn't believe how different it felt. I thought she was going to take off running. Way higher energy than I'm used to!"

Ben nodded. "I like her a lot. She's smart. Super intelligent horse. I love that feeling of restrained power, just ready to go."

I peered into my purse. "I know I dropped my phone in here." I rummaged in the corners. I felt the outline of something in the back zipper pocket. Rectangular, but too small to be my cell phone. Puzzled, I unzipped the pocket. My hand closed on something smooth, with rounded edges. "What in the world is this?" I pulled out a little black plastic rectangle. I frowned, staring at it.

A tiny flinch of alarm—Ben recovered, but not in time.

I narrowed my eyes at him. "What—" Then I understood. "Is this a recording device? Are you surveilling me?"

His mouth opened, then closed again.

"I knew you were a fed, but I didn't know this was a fake date." I threw the device at him. "This is not admissible in court."

Ben bent over and picked it up. "I'm not a fed. And this is not a fake date, Abby."

"Ben! You can't spy on me, I'm a therapist! You cannot listen in on confidential sessions! You cannot do that!"

He leaned back and gave me a level gaze. "You never take your purse into sessions. You never take it to the barn at all."

I stared at him. "How many people are listening in on this?"

He held his hands out in front of him, as though warding me off. "Just me—no one else."

"And you're going to tell me you're a stable hand."

He didn't say anything.

I opened my door and climbed down from the cab, slammed the door behind me, and stormed across the parking lot.

Ben slid down from his side and followed me. "Abby. I know you're angry, but let me take you home. It's too far."

I kept walking.

He caught up and reached for my shoulder. "It's going to get dark, Abby. It's not safe."

I shook off his hand and dug in my purse again, finally locating my cell phone. Turning my back on Ben, I dialed Ida.

She answered cheerily. "Hey, Sunshine."

"Are you busy?"

"I'm not," she said. "What's up?"

I sighed. "I'm at the taco place. Honestly, I feel like I'm in high school, but I need a ride because I walked out on a date."

"Hunh. I'll be right there."

Ben returned to his truck and sat, watching me, until Ida arrived. When I climbed up into her cab, he drove away.

Ida looked me over. "You went on a date like that?"

"Ben the Fed offered tacos when we got done cleaning the barn. I actually liked him for a minute. Ida, he put some kind of a voice recorder in my purse! He was spying on me!"

"No! Let me see it!"

"I threw it at him. I shouldn't have let him get it back that easy."

She shook her head. "Lord, help. I never heard of such a thing."

"I was hoping to find out who he's been talking to, whether he's heard anything, but he's cagey."

Ida drove out of the parking lot. "I suppose feds are trained to be cagey."

I turned in my seat, leaned on the door. "I've been trying to figure out who at the ranch has mechanical knowledge, but I'm coming up empty."

"Other than Jared and Max, not many people fix things," she said. "And Max doesn't do engines. Jared's the mechanic."

"I think you have to understand about mechanics to effectively sabotage things," I said. "Don't you? That's where I'm drawing a blank. If we could come up with a why, that would help. We could follow why, to who."

"Don't think we haven't tried," Ida said. "Since day one, and we haven't made the least bit of sense out of it."

Max was walking towards his house when Ida dropped me off. He stopped, raised one eyebrow, then turned away as if catching himself looking nosy. I pretended I didn't see him. He'd probably seen me leave with Ben. I didn't want to talk about it.

Chapter Eleven

I tried to stay as far away from Ben as possible. Shouldn't be hard—I mind my business, he figures out the horses and barn routines, the liar.

I was carrying materials to the outdoor arena when I heard a truck door close.

"Hey! Morning!"

I looked up. Luke walked toward me, grinning. I was in just the mood for this.

He leaned on the fence, smiling. I set down my cones and poles, and walked over.

"Luke. I'm glad I ran into you. I've been wanting to talk."

He made a comic frown. "Uh oh. Sounds serious."

I had to smile. He was cute, give him that. Too cute by half.

"Luke, I need to not be dating. We need to not be dating. You really are a great guy, and you're fun, but I need for us to just be colleagues."

Luke reached over and ran his fingertips down my arm. "I know you like me."

I sighed—his touch made me tingle. "That's hormones."

He laughed. "You like playing with fire, but can't decide if you should or not."

"I shouldn't." I took a step back.

Luke straightened. "We can totally be colleagues. You let me know if you change your mind. I'm available." He shot me a charming grin.

I watched his back pockets swing away—Levi's this time—and turned back to my obstacles. Ida was bringing horses in. Our client would arrive soon. I needed to focus.

After the session, Ida went to start the paperwork. I went to the barn to get a muck rake. Ben the Liar was standing by the rakes. Of course he was. I grabbed a wheelbarrow without looking at him.

He helpfully handed me a rake. "Can we talk?"

I took the rake and set in in the wheelbarrow. "About what?" I pointed at the horse in the arena. "That's Lego."

He glanced at Lego, then blew out a breath. "Yeah, I got that. Thanks."

I pivoted the wheelbarrow and turned to leave.

"Abby."

I stopped.

"We want the same thing."

I raised my eyebrows.

"It wasn't a fake date." Ben took off his work gloves and restlessly slapped his leg with them. "Can we try it again? Can you let me start over?"

"Dating is a bad idea for me." I pushed off with the wheelbarrow and walked away.

I rode slowly and awkwardly around barrels. Rosie was cooperative, but it was clear which of us was the brains of the operation. She was schooling me.

"Now," said Walt, "tell me something you struggle with."

The sun was hot. Beads of sweat ran onto my forehead and down my back. I was afraid to let go of the reins with one hand to wipe my face.

Walt stood with his thumbs tucked in his pockets and waited.

"I'm not used to feeling incompetent," I said. "I'm not very good at it."

He nodded. "Now, first of all, you're going to want to hold the reins in one hand. I'll show you again. This finger between the reins, like so. Now, as you ride around that barrel, think about letting go of that difficult thing. Just letting it go. As fast or slow as you want—your speed."

I nodded, lifted my reins in one hand, tried to surreptitiously grip the front of the saddle with the other hand, and gave Rosie a tiny tap with my heels. She slowly walked toward the barrel. She kept walking right past it.

"No!" I hissed, as if Walt couldn't see me. "Turn!" I pressed with my leg. I tugged the reins. I leaned. "Walk! This way!" She stopped cold. "Walk!" She ignored me. I glanced back at Walt. He was grinning.

Walt walked over. "Looks to me like you're stuck on feeling incompetent."

I sighed, staring at the back of Rosie's head.

"Couple of things," Walt said. "First of all, were you thinking about letting go of your need to feel competent, or were you in fact still trying to appear like you had everything under control?"

How did he know everything? I tried to smile. Sweat dripped in my eyes.

Walt grinned again. "Okay. Now I want you to remember this. Pay attention to where you're looking— look where you want to go. The horse can tell by your body. If you look down or stare at the horse, many times the horse will just stand." He waved a finger for emphasis. "When you get stuck, think about where you're looking."

I looked at the barrel. Rosie started walking in that direction.

Walt laughed. "Remember, it's not about nailing the exercise. It's about what we bring with us into the arena, how we reenact our lives, how the horse responds. Today, it's about you getting paralyzed by perfectionism." He walked away, then called over his shoulder, "Ride back into the barn. We'll call this good for now."

The day was hot, but the temperature dropped with the sun. I liked watching the sun set in the country, rich orange and gold flooding a wide-open horizon. My apartment was quite comfortable in the cool of night.

Max sat hunched on the couch, cupping his midnight tea in his hands, soaking in the warmth of the mug.

I leaned back, feet propped on the coffee table. "Max, you're so tired, you're shivering."

His eyes flicked to me, then back to his tea. The darkness was quiet around us.

He drew a deep breath in through his nose, huffed it out. "I've been thinking about what you said, about numbing. Not feeling."

He heard me. Good. And didn't blow me off.

"Seems like the only thing I really, a hundred percent feel is anger. I try to hold it in, but it's getting harder. There's so much going on. Too much going wrong."

"A little girl told me once," I said, "holding in your anger is like holding in your pee. It gives you a stomachache, it can make you sick, and it comes out all over the place when you don't expect it."

He blinked. "I never know what the hell to say to you."

I sat up. "Max, do you trust me?"

He eyed me warily.

"Can we talk about the F-word?"

Max's eyes widened. "Am I swearing too much? I'm sorry."

I smiled. "No, I mean the really bad F-word."

He braced himself.

"Max, I know you see anger as the problem, but anger just protects you from things that are far more painful."

Max pulled himself back into the sofa cushions.

"I mean fear. The thief. The very worst F-word." I cocked my head and studied him. "Fear is paralyzing. Fear of flashbacks, of thoughts that come out of nowhere. Of getting triggered." I shrugged, admitting my own part in this. "Fear of someone hearing you yell at night."

Max smiled at that. "I'm glad I did. Look at us now."

I felt a flood of affection, seeing him tense, expectant, on the worn sofa. Looking at his red-rimmed eyes and tousled hair, his tired, wrinkled clothing. Look at us.

"Fear of looking broken," I went on. "Of the damnable sadness and pity on people's faces. Fear of what we've become, in front of people. Fear stops so many people from ever being free. Fear is the thief. But we can rob the thief."

Max became intensely focused on a loose thread on his sock.

"We can take it back, Max. Our life, our time. Our strength. Even joy. Our ability to make plans without dreading what could happen. We can refuse to back down."

He swallowed. "How?" His voice croaked.

"Well, part of it is what I told you before—putting it to words, in a way that doesn't re-traumatize you." I sampled my tea. "Pull something out of the darkness, hold it up, name it, it loses so much power. It's also training yourself to focus on the present."

Max raised one eyebrow.

"I know, I know," I said. "Sounds like a bunch of hoo-ha. Listen. Worrying invites more fear than anything else people do. Focusing on the moment at hand short-circuits fear. Robs it of its power."

Max said nothing.

I shrugged. "It's true, Max. Try it. It's not just fruity-loopy. It's a strategy of war. Sitting here right now, smell the lemon cleaning fluid I used earlier. Notice what a mess my hair is, feel the sagging cushions behind your back. That totally distracted you, didn't it? By grounding you, it shakes the hand of fear from its grip on your throat."

"It did distract me. For a minute."

"The minute we're in is all we ever have, to work with. That's where everything really happens." I paused. He was listening, if only to humor me. "If you refuse to look at what fear is trying to show you, and defiantly look at something else—something right here, right now—it loosens the grip. Distract yourself on purpose—it's five seconds of not feeling that boot on your neck, repeated, and multiplied outward. You get better at it. You get better and better at bringing down the biology."

Max squinted at me. "Biology?"

"Breathing," I said. "Pulse. You start with breathing. And mental focus. That brings the heart rate down. It's a process, but everything you've ever learned in your life has been a process. Walking. Tacking up a horse. Shooting. Wiping your butt, for that matter, but you had to learn, or spend your life stinking in your own mess."

"Honestly, Maguire." Max blew out a breath. "Strategy of war? Learning to wipe my ass? You're a piece of work, you know that?"

I sipped my tea. "It's been said."

He shook his head. "I'm not trying to be rude, but...deep breathing? Really?"

"Max, have you ever controlled your breathing to improve the accuracy of shooting?"

He narrowed his eyes at me.

I nodded, claiming the win. "So why is it any stupider to control your breathing to deliberately impact your own physiological responses?"

He looked away. Silence grew. I let it sit between us.

Max shifted in his seat. "You're the craziest excuse for a therapist I ever met in my life. I never know quite what the hell to do with you." He leaned his head back and closed his eyes.

I waited.

He picked his head up and focused on me again. "I guess I never did meet a normal therapist I much wanted to talk to. Nothing against normal therapists. They've all been really nice people. Every one we've had. Just not someone I wanted to take off the Kevlar for. But Maguire—" His tone changed.

Now I looked at him warily.

"What about you, Maguire? Are you going to talk about what you're afraid of?"

I picked up a pillow and threw it at his head. "That's entirely different."

He snorted and threw it back.

Chapter Twelve

Ida came up for coffee with two volunteers, sisters earning high school credit through work experience. I'd forgotten about the drying racks all over the room, draped with laundry.

"I'm sorry!" I called back as they filed in the door. "Just step around all this."

"Don't you use a dryer?" one of the sisters asked.

"Only for socks, underwear, towels, things like that. I kind of ran down in a hurry this morning. I forgot about all this." I flipped over one of the bras. "I'm glad I didn't bring a guy up here."

Both girls laughed. The younger one covered her mouth in horror.

"You start the coffee," Ida told me. "I'll show these girls how old-school laundry works." She felt the clothes for dryness, moved from rod to rod, flipped and rearranged shirts and shorts. "You want to think about air flow. The taller things are a little trickier since they have to be on top." She pulled out a pair of jeans and felt the seams for dampness. Something crinkled. She shot me a look. "Abby, you didn't empty your pockets. If this is cash money, I'm keeping it as a tip."

"If it's cash money, those aren't my jeans," I said. "I haven't got any."

Ida laughed as she held up a plastic snack wrapper. "You are caught! Max's bad habits are rubbing off on you!"

I froze over the coffee pot. I'd forgotten about the wrapper from the tack room.

Ida registered my reaction. She shoved the wrapper into her own pocket and draped the jeans back over the rack. "All right, girls, pull up a chair. I'll grab the cups."

I took a deep breath, finished making the coffee, chatted casually with the girls. I couldn't wait for them to leave. Two cups each and a plate of cookies later, they giggled their way back to the horses.

Ida closed the door behind them and turned on me. "All right, give."

"Ida!" I wrapped my arms around my chest, started to pace.

"Abby, what is it?"

"I forgot about it. I picked it up from the floor in the tack room. I thought it was weird, garbage in the barn. Walt would lose his nut. So I just stuck it in my pocket, but then—"

Ida waved a hand in a circular "get on with it" motion.

I swallowed. "Ida, it was just a few feet from Mason's body. After I found him, I forgot all about it. And now I washed it. What if it had fingerprints on it or something? What if the killer dropped it there?"

She sat down heavily. Neither of us spoke.

Ida looked at me sternly. "Abby, it's a wrapper from Max's cookies. If the killer left it there, he was trying to point the blame at Max. You know damn well Max didn't kill Mason and drop a wrapper from his favorite snack, in a barn he has never, ever littered in before. You know that, Abby."

I shook my head. "That would never happen. It doesn't follow. The question is, what do I do now? I don't want to tell the cops I found this and ran it through the laundry, but thought I should implicate Max anyway, so here you go."

"Well, you can't give it to the cops, because it's in my pocket now. And if you tell them I have it, you're implicating me for concealing evidence."

I sat, put my head on the table. Neither of us spoke.

Finally, I straightened up. "This never happened. It's just garbage. It's not connected to anything. We'll throw it away."

She nodded, stood, and cleared dishes from the table.

I turned to face her. "Ida, why isn't Jared part of the in-crowd? He's been around forever. You have smoke break gatherings, shoot the breeze with everyone. I see you talking to all kinds of volunteers. If Jared isn't included, why is that?"

She stopped halfway to the sink. "I don't know, Abby. It's not like we haven't tried. He's prickly. I don't know if that's just his nature, or from something from his Army experience, or from prison—"

"Jared was in prison?"

"Yes, I think drugs. Not violent. Years ago, now." Ida rinsed the dishes. "We should get going. Coffee break's over."

The next few days were continuously wet, transforming the arena, the trails, the corrals. Manure-mud squelched around my boots. I let the horses lead the way as I brought them in. They knew where they didn't want to walk, knew the deepest puddles of rain and dissolved poop, the thickest mud. Then I realized they didn't care where I walked, next to them. The mud was halfway up my boots, ripeness assaulting my nose. I lifted my knees higher, pulling upward with more and more effort as my boots sank deeper. One got stuck. The lead rope taut, Lego kept walking. My foot started to come out of my boot.

"Stop! Wait!" I tightened my grip on the rope and tugged upward with my foot. Lego looked annoyed, turning to see what my problem was. "Hold on!" I got free and moved over to find a more solid path, letting her walk ahead of me when we didn't both fit between the bad spots. In the barn, away from the breeze, I smelled myself full-on. The stench wafted up from my clothing in the humidity. I was covered with mud, with melted manure and acidic urine mixed in. My eyes watered. My morning coffee was in my throat.

"Kinda pungent, huh?"

I looked up. It was Ben. His rubber boots were also caked with muck, but his jeans were less muddy. I shook my head. "This is probably the most disgusting I've ever been in my life."

"Do you think we're gross enough to go for tacos again?" He looked at me hopefully. "Eat in the truck? With the windows cracked open? It was fun last time, until I ruined it."

I didn't answer.

"Or we could just warm up and have some coffee?" He raised his eyebrows, smiled.

I looked around the barn. The horses were tucked into their feed buckets. It would be a while before they wanted to go out again. "Let's make some coffee."

Ben beamed. I belatedly realized I would not be able to strip at the door and leave my manure clothes in the entryway. We left our jackets and boots by the door. Ben sat in the same chair as before.

I leaned back on the counter and studied him as the coffee gurgled and spat behind me.

He sat quietly, watching me. We waited. I was determined to make him crack first. What direction would he go with this? I could be very good at waiting.

Ben smiled.

I smiled back.

He studied his surroundings. Glanced at me. His brow furrowed a little. He took a breath, exhaled, gave up. "I owe you dinner. Listen, I'm not a bad cook. You've got a serviceable kitchen here. What do you say I bring in the fixings for a simple meal some night?" He held up his hands. "I'm not trying to be forward or make any assumptions. It just might be more relaxed, casual."

I cocked my head, considered him. It would be much easier to grill him for information in a private setting than in a restaurant. "That's not a bad idea. If we even sat in your truck on a day like this, we'd asphyxiate ourselves. There's a point where gross is too gross."

Ben positively glowed. "Just tell me when. I'll hit the grocery store and pick up what we need. Is there any kind of food you don't like?"

"I always eat whatever people give me, in different places." I poured some coffee and handed it to him. "It's better to be flexible about food. Makes life easier."

He nodded thanks, and took a drink. "You make great coffee. I see why people like it."

"People talk about it?"

Ben looked surprised. "Oh, yes. Everyone talks about your coffee. And Ida's cookies, when she brings them."

This could be useful. "Huh. Well, I do actually have some of Ida's cookies, if you'd like one."

His face lit up again, so I put one on a plate and set it in front of him. He smiled and ate half of it in one bite. I sighed inwardly, and added several more.

Ben settled his weight back in the chair. His smile widened as he stuffed the second half of the cookie in his mouth.

I made a mental note to ask Ida for more cookies, and sat down with my own cup of coffee. "So, how do you like working at the ranch?"

He nodded, mouth full. He swallowed, drank some coffee. "I like it a lot. Days like this aren't the best, but it's still better than sitting in an office. How about you? You like doing therapy here, as you're getting more time in?"

"It's a nice job. It doesn't hurt that people liked the therapists that came before me. Makes people more inclined to be welcoming." I stopped short of asking if he was having a similar experience. No need to be crass about it.

He got the point anyway. He said nothing as he ate two more cookies, but it wasn't the blank silence I got from people who might be a little slower at processing. I could practically hear his brain humming, information spinning in his head. He needed to start spitting out some of that data stream.

I decided to lob him a nice, fat one right over the plate. "You know, Ben, it's the craziest thing."

Ben took another cookie, but held it in his hand and waited for me to go on.

"This just occurred to me, just recently. When I first got here, really from day one, there were a lot of things going wrong. Weird. Like sabotage. Machinery breaking, fires. But after Mason was killed, it just stopped. I mean, no one is suggesting that Mason was responsible. Sounds like he was a hard worker, you know? Not really mechanically inclined, maybe not a real independent thinker, but happy to do his job. Took me awhile to realize it all just stopped. At least so far. Paused, anyway."

And all the air got sucked out of the room, just like that.

It wasn't even a swing and a miss. Everything stopped. Ben held his cookie in mid-air, his thoughts turned inward. Then he blinked, drained his coffee cup, and stood to leave. He grabbed a few more cookies to take with him.

"Thanks for this," he said, as if he were not bolting from the room. "Let's figure out a time for that dinner." And he was gone.

The rain eventually stopped. The sun and the wind took a few days to dry things up, but the squelching mud disappeared, first from the open areas, then from the woods and the lean-tos. Things returned to normal, but Walt was clearly not himself. Ida said he was getting depressed. I didn't know him before, but I could see it. He was like a wrung-out rag draped over the rail, barely holding his shape through the day. I came into the office one afternoon and found him sitting at his desk, staring blankly into the air. He didn't seem to notice me.

"Walt."

He slowly turned his head to look at me.

"You need to move from this desk. I bet you need some good coffee. Why don't you take a break and come upstairs?"

Walt pondered that. He slowly rose to his feet. He followed me up the stairs, pulled off his boots at the door, and sat at the table while I got some coffee brewing.

I sat across from him, and studied his worn face. "Talk to me."

He regarded me numbly, as if the decision was beyond his ability to calculate.

"I'm neutral territory. Whatever this is, it was well in play by the time I got here. I have no part in any factions, no alliances. You need to unload some of the weight you're carrying."

Walt sighed heavily as the coffee gurgled behind me. He lowered his defenses, and underneath he just looked sad. "It is a weight, Abby. A terrible weight. I don't know what the right thing is, to do. Are people at risk if I stay open? I cannot have someone else hurt. Yet, a lot of people will suffer if I close." He rubbed his face, stretched his legs under the table. "I don't even know how to think about this. We're a therapy ranch. Things like this don't happen. As to why, I can't even get there. I'm stuck on fathoming that this is really going on, in my place." He disappeared down some trail of thought and barely noticed when I set a cup of coffee in front of him. Then he picked it up, took a sip, and closed his eyes. I almost smiled. No one loved my coffee like Walt did.

He took a deep drink, then shook his head. "Little Clara wants to come out, but I don't feel I can allow it. How can I? She wants to see Teddy. Worries about him being lonesome. Thinks he's a heartbroken horse, since she hasn't been to see him. She drew a picture for him, a little girl on a horse, with a big heart on it." Walt rubbed his fingertips on the table. "She wants to know why I'm so sad. I just tell her I'm tired, try to smile. Ida's right, though. It's more than that. This thing is wearing on me." Walt drank his coffee quietly. The tension seemed to be easing from his back and shoulders, if only a little. Then he focused his gaze on me. "Abby, what do you think I should do? Do you have an opinion?"

I hesitated, turned my cup in my hands. "I'm not the best person to ask. I'm strongly biased. It's so disruptive for people to have sessions cancelled, once they form a connection with a therapist. I'd be the one showing up for sessions on the deck of a sinking ship, in case someone needed to talk about the waves coming over the bow."

Walt chuckled in spite of himself. "I believe you would. You're a brilliant woman, without a lick of sense sometimes."

I was so glad to see Walt smile, I couldn't be mad at him. "Whatever's been going on, the sabotage, no one has been hurt until Mason, late at night, with no one else around. It's been more like harassment. Driving you and Max to distraction."

Walt nodded. "That's a fair point."

I thought about the idea I'd shared with Ben the Fed, that the damage seemed to stop with Mason's death. Walt would probably accuse me of meddling. I looked up and realized he was staring at me, waiting for me to talk.

I blinked. "You know, Ida left me a bunch of cookies. Would you like one? They're really very good."

"No, thank you. I'd rather know what you were just thinking about."

I blew out a breath. "I just realized yesterday, while I was talking with Ben—" I glanced at Walt. "Since Mason's death, there doesn't appear to have been any more sabotage. Like maybe whatever was going on..." I didn't finish my thought.

Walt sat up straight in his chair. "Abby, noticing is one thing, but I do not want you getting involved in this. Don't think that I don't see you and Ida, walking around looking at people, talking to people. Ida is a dear friend, a precious friend, but she is loyal to a fault, and I'm well aware of that fact. Ida would blunder into the path of a grizzly bear, trying to protect Max and myself, and I will not have you encouraging or following her."

I cocked my head at him. "Have you told Ida that?"

Walt scowled at his coffee. "Like talking to a damn bull moose. Smiles and pats me on the arm, and does whatever she damn well pleases."

I laughed before I could stop myself, then put a hand over my mouth. "I'm sorry. Ida's something else."

"Woman's a force of nature," Walt grumbled.

I couldn't help but smile. "Did you know her husband?"

"Oh, yes. We were all friends, from way back. The two couples. Johnny was a force of nature himself, in a different way." Walt had a faraway look in his eyes. "He was like a big ol' rock in the sunshine, holding onto that afternoon heat no matter how the wind of Ida blew this way and that." He shook his head. "He and Ida were really something. Then, too, Ida and Clara—" Walt met my eyes. "Clara was my wife. You see, little Clara was named for her. Ida and Clara would get together, Johnny and I just sat and watched the weather phenomenon."

Walt leveled a gaze at me. "I won't lose Ida, too, Abby. I'd appreciate your help in that. She won't listen to me, but maybe you can be a mitigating influence, somehow. Just don't encourage her to be reckless, trying to do the job of the police, messing around in things, however good her intentions may be."

I almost felt guilty. Could I stop Ida if I wanted to? If I backed out now, would she listen? Probably not. "I don't know if I qualify as a force of nature, Walt. Or anything that could move the wind."

He finished his cup and stood. "Thank you for this. I do feel a little better, just being able to speak my thoughts out loud."

"Come up here again, Walt. You can't carry this by yourself. And you know the coffee down there is terrible, even if no one admits it."

Walt ducked his head in acknowledgement and left.

Chapter Thirteen

I found myself avoiding Ben. What do you do when you're attracted to a spy? It was too awkward trying to pretend he wasn't one. I wandered down to the barn one morning, and Ben was raking the sand. I made a hand-in-the-air gesture like I just remembered something, and walked back out. Ida pulled into the parking lot. I stood and waited for her.

"Good morning, Sunshine." She brought a large container from the seat beside her. "I whipped up some cookies last night, when you said you were going through them too fast."

"Wonderful! Come on up. I just put half a pot of coffee in the thermos to stay hot." I took the container so she could grab her purse.

Ida followed me up the stairs, poured herself some coffee. "What's going on with you and Ben?"

I squinted at her. "What are you talking about?"

"Well, I notice you don't look at him. You just walked into the barn and walked back out. Was he in there?"

I scowled instead of responding.

"You're avoiding him. What's that about? Is it just because we think he's a fed?"

"He put surveillance equipment in my purse! Clearly, he doesn't know how to behave. And...he has too many of my weaknesses."

"He doesn't wear look-at-my-ass jeans. I thought that was your weakness."

I smiled. "I mean I could really like him. I'm not sure I want to go there. My life is complicated enough. And he's probably a fed. And not admitting it, more to the point."

She looked at me over her cup. "What boxes does he check?"

I sipped my coffee. "Well...he does have a nice butt, with or without embroidery. I couldn't help but notice."

Ida shook her head.

"Sexy laugh lines. The humor in his eyes," I said. "Intelligence is nice—and necessary—but intelligent humor is hot." I took another drink. "I'd rather poke myself in the eye than have him catch me looking."

She shifted her weight back in the chair. "He's got a few years on Luke. Of course, that's not a bad thing. Nothing wrong with a juicy, ripe tomato. Had a little more time in the sun before you pick it. Who knows, maybe Luke will be alright someday himself. I know some people like green tomatoes, but I never did see the attraction." She smiled. "Nope, give me that nice, full, mature one." She nodded. "Juicy."

My cup clunked on the table. "Ida!"

She laughed, drained her cup. "You know exactly what I mean. If you didn't, you'd be able to look at him."

I grabbed the thermos to pour her another cup. "I had him up to try to interrogate him, but he got up and ran when I pointed out that there hasn't been any sabotage since Mason was killed."

Ida didn't say anything for a moment. She exhaled loudly. "There hasn't been, has there?"

I met her eyes. "That doesn't necessarily mean Mason was doing it. He could have been, and someone caught him—"

"Max did not do this."

"Yeah, I got that," I said. "I don't think Walt did either. Help me walk through this."

"Could be it's on hold while there are cops around." Ida pursed her lips, thinking. "Too much attention."

"Maybe he walked in on the person, caught them," I offered. "They killed him to get away, but now they're scared to do it again."

She nodded. "Takes it to a whole new level. Not so funny anymore."

"I pointed out to Walt that the damage stopped, at least temporarily."

Ida raised her eyebrows. "What did he say?"

"He told me to stay out of it and keep you out of it."

Ida snorted. "Comes to therapy, he's my boss. Other than that, I don't recall having a boss, other than the good Lord Himself."

I nodded. "I'm not even sure how to proceed."

Ida drank her coffee. "Something will break open. We'll just try to be ready when it does."

Jared was picking up tools from the ground and packing them away.

"You look like you're at a good stopping point," I told him. "Want a cup of coffee?"

Jared eyed me suspiciously, then shrugged. "Ok, sure." He followed me up the stairs and pulled his boots off at the door, looking around. He hitched up his sagging jeans. "I've never even been up here. They've had top-secret meetings up here, but Walt thinks I'm too stupid to be one of the cool kids."

I set down two mugs. "Jared, I'm surprised to hear you say that. I've never had even the smallest idea that Walt might look down on you. If anything, he relies on you. You keep the place running."

Jared scowled and scratched his cheek. He sat and tried his coffee. "It's always him and Max, isn't it? Walt and Max, off having secret conversations, or Walt and Ida, or now you, always off having important talks away from the rest of us. Yeah, yeah, I know, confidential therapy, but Max didn't come here any kind of counselor. He was in the Marines the same as I was in the Army, except guys like me saved the asses of guys like him."

He took a drink. "I was EOD, and what was he? He's so damn smart, he can't even fix the skid loader. Then even after I fix it, Walt's still off with Max. He's never once had a private conversation with me. Max can walk up and join anything, but all the rest of us need permission to approach. Well, who's the smart guy now, huh?"

I sat back in my chair and took a swallow of coffee to gain a moment to think. I wasn't sure if I should take the direct approach. "What does that mean, 'who's the smart guy, now?'"

Jared shook his head. "Doesn't matter. So, you have pretty much everyone up here?"

I shrugged. "It's not like I plan it out. I like coffee, and I like sharing coffee."

He gave me a speculative look. "I hear you share more than that with Morgan." He sat and waited for me to respond.

"Let's back up," I said. "I'm more interested in getting to know you a little. Did you grow up around here?"

"Nah. Over by Deergrass."

"Did you go into the Army right from high school?"

He finished his coffee and set the cup down. "I like you. You should go get a different job somewhere. Things are kind of going to hell around here."

I tilted my head, studied him. "But less than they were, do you think? I mean, it seems like, just lately, things aren't breaking like they used to. That must be somewhat of a relief for you, isn't it? Less to keep fixing all the time?"

Jared twitched, then stared at me. He picked at his cheek, but seemed unaware he was doing it. "What do you mean by that? You trying to say something?"

I gave him a little shrug. "Not trying to say anything, Jared. Just noticing. Something changed."

Jared abruptly got to his feet. "You should leave. You don't have to stay all summer just because you took the job, right?"

I paused a beat. "I made a commitment, though. I never leave jobs early. Never have, no matter what I find myself in."

"Too bad, then." He looked back as he put his boots on. "Thanks for the coffee. It's better than that stuff down in the break room."

After he left, I looked at Papa on the shelf. "That whole conversation was disorienting," I told him. "Did that make any sense to you at all?"

He smiled, as always. I used to get so much from Papa's facial expressions. We had entire conversations without speaking, and laughed about it. Other times, I checked his face to see if I should take something seriously, or shake my head and let it go.

"What do you think?" I asked him. "Serious? Not?"

Jared was holding down a job, there was that. No one mentioned mental illness—not that they necessarily would. I sighed. "My money's on meth. He's using, big time." But he seemed to focus when he needed to, and the things he fixed seemed to work perfectly afterwards.

"And what's EOD?" I got up and went down to the pasture, where Max and Ben were trying to fix an automatic waterer. "Max, in the military, what does EOD mean?"

Both heads swung in my direction. Max set down his tool. "Bomb squad. *Why?*"

I didn't want to talk in front of Ben the Fed. "Nothing. Thanks." When I looked back, they were both staring at me.

I turned in and found Walt in the office. He looked up from his paperwork.

"Walt, have you noticed any changes in Jared lately?"

He hesitated. "Lost a lot of weight."

I sat backwards on one of his chairs, leaning on the backrest. "I'm concerned about him. He's showing signs of possible meth use." I tipped my head. "Probable."

Walt sat back, closed his eyes.

"I'm not saying I know for sure," I said. "I think it's enough of a concern, I wanted to mention it."

"Alright. Thank you, Abby."

I nodded and went back upstairs.

Ben looked at my framed pictures of Papa and myself. He focused on an old one—I was a child, holding my favorite stuffed animal. "That's a crazy looking lion."

I was pleased that he'd noticed. "That's Argyle."

He laughed out loud. "Its name was Argyle?"

"Yes. I thought it was a grand name." I smiled, remembering. "I used to march around the house with him, shouting, Argyle! Is an interesting lion! He's not! A boring old lion! And Papa would shout, Say it again!"

I glanced at Ben. Was that too much disclosure? But no, he was grinning broadly. "Anyway." I cleared my throat. "What do we need to do for dinner?"

Ben looked great with laugh lines. Eyes crinkled with humor, he moved to the counter and pulled groceries out of bags. "I went for easy." He lined up a box of pasta, a jar of sauce, tomatoes, and colorful peppers. "We can spice up the sauce a little bit with chopped vegetables. I wasn't sure if you had Worcestershire sauce, so I brought some."

"That sounds fantastic." I got out a pot and filled it with water.

Ben looked in the cupboard, found a frying pan, and started browning meatballs. I liked his comfort in the kitchen. I perched on the counter, swinging my legs.

"What have you got I can drain grease into?"

I hopped down and got a glass jar from the recycling bin. "Let me know what you want me to do."

He waved me away. "I've got it. This is me buying you dinner."

I scooched myself back up on the counter, and watched him cook. "Tell me about yourself."

Ben talked easily about growing up in a small town. We shared childhood stories, and I found myself talking about Papa. He, in turn, talked about ice fishing, snowshoeing, the mutt he'd raised as a pet.

He was a good cook. He'd made everything well. I found myself having so much fun, I decided not to ask him about college or careers. I hoped Ida wouldn't be too disappointed in me. I'd planned on grilling him, but I lost the inclination along the way. He finagled his way around it, and I let him.

Washing the dishes, we talked about music and dancing. We ended up pushing aside the furniture, putting in a CD. He remembered some dances slightly differently than I did. At one point, we pivoted into each other and laughed so hard, we lost the beat entirely. Ben threw up his hands and sat down. I stopped the music and sat across from him.

"This has been fun," I said. "We'll have to do it again. My treat next time."

He smiled and touched my arm. "Let's."

After he left, I moved the furniture back. I looked at Papa. "I am a failure at counter-intelligence," I told him. "I didn't even want to go there." I shook my head. "I wonder what he was planning to say if I asked him again about being a fed? Or what jobs he's had? He probably thought it was weird that I agreed to avoid the entire conversation."

I sat for a while, pondering that. "It was nice, though."

"Abby, you cannot, can NOT fall in love with the fed." Ida actually shook her finger at me.

I put my feet up on a chair and took a swallow of coffee, to stall. "I didn't say I was in love with him. I said I need to work on my interrogation skills."

She pointed her cup at me. "Looking is one thing. Look all you want. You need to be hardcore, Abby. Save the romance for after we figure out what's going on. And when he's willing to have an honest conversation with you. You've got an advantage here, him being all smitten with you. He might slip up and tell you something."

I put my feet down. "Smitten? He is not. What a thing to say!"

"Abby, if you can't see the way he looks at you, you definitely need to up your game. You're right. You are a terrible spy."

I set down my cup. "That was harsh."

"Did you find out anything at all?"

I thought back. "I found out the name of the dog he had when he was ten. Basically." I drank some coffee. This was going badly. I should get out some cookies.

"He likes to dance," I said, getting a plate down from the cupboard. "Maybe I should invite him to the next street dance, is there one coming up? I saw a sign somewhere. He's from around here. I could watch for people to recognize him, come up and start talking to him. That would be so awkward, there's no way he could keep up with it. At least I'd find out who he really is."

"Don't think you're going to distract me with cookies," Ida said, taking two of them and dunking one in her coffee. "I don't think an undercover fed will take time off to go to a dance. You need to get him off alone, someplace where you won't get so distracted. Get him off on the trails." She punctuated with her cookie. "Yes. Get him to help you clear the trails, that's the ticket, and give it another go. Focus on listening for misdirection. You can do this, Abby. I know you can."

I hesitated and bit off a large piece of cookie.

"I dare you," Ida said.

I chewed and swallowed. "You dare me?"

Ida folded her arms over her chest. "I double dog dare you."

I blew out a breath. "Okay. I'll do it."

Chapter Fourteen

I saw Ben in the barn later, and started over to grab a muck rake and reel him in. Jared came around the corner, saw me, and reversed course. He disappeared behind the hay shed. Huh. I couldn't see where he was going.

"What do you suppose that was about?" Ben startled me. I hadn't seen him come out of the barn.

"I have no idea. Maybe I somehow offended him when we were having coffee." By asking him why the sabotage stopped, for example. I hadn't meant to be accusatory, but maybe he thought I was. Maybe meth was making him paranoid.

I realized Ben was studying me, as if waiting. Had he asked me something else, and I missed it? His face wasn't giving anything away. "I'm going to grab a rake and go clear the trails," I said. "It's my favorite job, peaceful, in the woods. Want to join me?"

Ben's eyes sparkled with humor, although he kept a straight face. What was he up to? He almost seemed like he was waiting for me to ask him. That didn't make any sense.

"Sure, I'd love to. Let me grab my gloves."

We started with the closest trails, scooping manure and heaving it into the brush.

"I know they drag the trails with the Kubota when they have time," I said. "I suppose that might be something you do. But I figure I can do this, and free people up for things like fixing fences. And I find it relaxing." I tossed a rakeful and listened to the swish as it went through the bushes.

Ben still looked like he was privately amused about something. "I appreciate it. It's not hard to drag the trails, but it's just one more thing. I can't get to it all."

I needed to set an atmosphere somehow. Maybe start by sounding confessional, myself. "I like so many things about this job. But of course, I'm always thinking about the next placement. At some point I need to start looking on-line to see what's coming up. I'm finding myself reluctant to think about it, though. I'm going to miss flinging manure." I illustrated the point by forking up a huge piece and hefting it into a bush. It landed with a rustle and a thump. "I really love it out here."

Ben seemed alarmed. He looked down at his rake. "I forgot that part of being a temp worker. How soon will you leave?"

"It was a three-month gig. Just to get them over the summer season. Then they hire someone more long term."

Ben took a few steps and shoveled up a long line of smaller bits that some horse dropped while walking. He gathered the whole pile in his rake before tossing it. "Where do you think you'll end up? Nearby?"

"That's impossible to say. I have no idea where jobs will be opening up." I had successfully changed the mood. Now to wrangle him to my advantage. "Maybe someplace warm. How do you feel about working the ranch in a Minnesota winter?"

Ben walked further down the trail. "I've lived in Minnesota most of my life."

"But from what I understand about ice fishing, you're in a little shack with a heater. Not like fixing the heated water trough in minus twenty temps. It just sounds a little overwhelming to me. Or heading out into the wind chill every single morning to manage the herd. I kind of like coffee and warm slippers in January. Maybe you haven't thought that far ahead yet, to all the seasons of having an outdoor job in this climate."

We reached a fork in the trail. Ben stopped, waited for me to choose.

"Let's start left, and do the fence line." That would be the most remote. I turned that way and waited for Ben to answer me, or admit that he didn't plan to be here by January. He walked and scooped quietly. No matter. I plotted my next move while I waited.

"I guess I'll have to see how things go," he finally said.

I nodded. "So, you basically end up having temporary assignments, too? In effect, I mean."

Ben took a breath and started churning things around inside his head again. If only I could surprise him somehow, jolt him out of it. I found a particularly dried out, non-sticky piece of manure and tossed it at his legs.

He jumped like he was on fire, and let out a little yelp.

I laughed. "I'm sorry. For laughing, I mean. You—" I laughed harder, pointing at him because I couldn't talk. I took off a glove and wiped tears from my eyes. For a ranch hand, this guy really had a thing about his clothes.

Ben glared at me, hands on hips, rake at his side.

I looked at his eyes and erupted into another fit of laughter. "I just wanted to disrupt your inward focus, get you to talk to me." I leaned on a tree to hold myself up, glanced at him, and giggled.

"Has anyone ever told you that you're impossible?"

I smiled warmly. "Yes."

Ben shook his head, and stepped closer. His eyes were full of something he wanted to say, but I wasn't sure what it was. He took off one glove, cupped the side of my face with his hand, leaned in and kissed me. He gazed into my eyes and tenderly said, "You smell like a horse."

I laughed and kissed him back, and made it a good one. "You taste like a horse." I could never tell Ida about this. Never.

I walked away with my rake. I glanced back.

Ben looked a little disoriented. "Wait," he said.

I shook my head and scooped up a pile. "Tell me one honest thing about yourself, Ben. And not about when you were twelve. Tell me one thing about now." I sighed. Ida was right. I was a terrible spy. "I really shouldn't kiss you. Really. Who are you?"

Ben passed me on the trail. "If you really believe the things that you accuse me of, Abby, you shouldn't expect me to talk about it."

I took a minute to digest that. "You mean calling you a fed?"

Ben did a little "cannot confirm or deny" head waggle. "If you think that's what I am, you shouldn't expect me to blab things around. Unless you're calling me an extremely unprofessional fed."

He had a point. If he really was a fed. Otherwise, that was a masterful deflection.

"Well, you know who I am," I said. "You know I'm not some kind of a plant."

He waved a hand in the air. "No, I don't!" He started to raise his voice. "You were here before me, but for all I know, you're an itinerant hitman! Hitwoman! That doesn't even seem unlikely! I'd believe anything at this point!"

"Oh, please!" I raised my voice right back at him. "Why would I still be here?"

"To avoid suspicion!" Ben yelled. "If you leave right away, that would look a tiny bit suspicious, wouldn't it?"

"Well, you shouldn't be kissing me at all," I shouted. "Is that what you do? Go around undercover, kissing murderers? That's the stupidest thing I've ever heard! You'll probably get herpes!"

"What?" Ben ran his hand though his hair, making it stick up. "Are you nuts?"

"And what would constitute a guilty response, Ben?" Now I was waving my arms around. I felt my face getting hot.

Ben blew out a long breath. He squeezed the bridge of his nose. "Look. I'm sorry I called you a hitwoman. I was just trying to make a point."

I turned my back on him and walked down the trail. I needed a minute to regroup. This was not going at all how I envisioned it.

Ben followed me. "Abby. Let's start over, here. This whole thing went off the rails somehow."

I raked up a pile and looked at Ben sideways. "It was around the time you said you'd believe anything about me, at this point. What was that about?"

"I don't know if I want to kiss you, or tear my hair out!" He was raising his voice again. "I can't even describe you! Everyone else around here, I can pretty much sum up, but you—you defy description! Words fail! You're impossible!"

I squinted at him. "Who are you describing everyone to, exactly?"

He threw his rake. "Dammit!" He turned his back to me and leaned against a tree.

I rounded the next turn and heard him rustling in the brush, retrieving his rake. I wondered idly if he was in the poison oak.

He came up behind me. The controlled anger in his voice gave me a chill. "Abby, I was speaking hypothetically."

I was suddenly aware that I was on the most remote trail, alone with an angry man both larger and stronger than me. How old did I have to be, to stop doing stupid things on a dare? I looked around for escape routes.

He noticed, and stopped in his tracks. He took a deep breath. "Abby, I'm just frustrated. I would appreciate it if we could forget this conversation ever took place, and do a bit of a restart."

I kept my rake between us. "Sure. But you know, I've had enough raking for one day. I think I'll head in."

He nodded and stood back to let me pass.

I pointed down the trail with my rake. "You go ahead, I'll be right behind you." No way I was turning my back on him.

Ben looked sad, but turned and walked toward the barn. When we got there, he put away his rake and left without another word.

Ida walked up to me, looked around, leaned in. "How did it go? Did you get anything?"

I put my mouth by her ear. "He's talking to someone and giving them descriptions of everyone here."

"No! How did you get him to say that?"

"He got a little rattled and called me a hitman. Woman. Then he was trying to apologize, but he got upset again."

Ida stared at me. "He—" She shook her head. "Why was he rattled?"

"I don't want to talk about it." I put my rake away, and brushed my hands on my pants.

"Wait! Why would he call you a hitman? And why does he look so depressed? Because he slipped up and told you what he was doing?"

"I guess so. That's when he got angry. We need to keep this on the down-low. And I need coffee." I fled the barn.

Ida followed me up the stairs. "Pour me a cup too. We need to talk about tomorrow."

I didn't reply until we were sitting at the table, eyeing each other over our mugs. "What about tomorrow?"

"We need to cover for Walt and Max tomorrow. They're going down to the grass drags. I'm so glad, too. They both need a little time off. We've got lots of volunteers coming in to cover."

I tried to figure it out so I wouldn't have to ask. Finally, I set my cup down. "They're going where?"

"You got any cookies left?"

I got up to get her some.

"Grass drags. Drag races. With snowmobiles. But on grass, seeing as it's summer."

"Ida, sometimes I'm not sure if you're serious."

"Oh, it's a big thing, Abby. Both the guys really enjoy it. Sometimes people race across water, too, but not everyone does that. If you don't go fast enough, your snowmobile sinks, and I imagine it's done for, once it's at the bottom of the lake."

"Do they do it more than once a year? I like seeing things that you can't find in other places." I didn't say bizarre regional customs, but this would qualify.

"They do. I'm sure either of the guys would love to take you."

I nodded and tried to decide if I wanted any more cookies today. Probably not.

"You seem subdued, Abby. What happened out there, that you don't want to talk about?"

I stared at the cookie plate for a moment. "It didn't go the way either of us wanted. We both ended up unhappy. It seemed like a funny thing to do, especially after you double dog dared me, but Ida, we really don't know that he's a fed, or any kind of a cop. That's a whole narrative that we came up with. We don't know that he wouldn't do anything to hurt me out there. I'm not big or strong, I don't know karate, I don't carry a weapon. Maybe I should." I nodded thoughtfully. "Maybe I should look into weaponry. Why not? I just need to figure out the laws state-to-state about carrying and all that."

Ida looked alarmed. "It was that bad, that you want to go buy a gun? I'm so sorry, Abby. What did he do?"

"He didn't do anything." I shook my head. "I don't even know why I'm upset. All he did was yell, and there aren't enough numbers to count the people who have yelled at me in my life. Generally, I just think it's interesting."

I studied my coffee, looking for an answer in a chipped ceramic mug. "It wasn't the yelling. It was when he got angry. For a minute there, I didn't feel safe. I hate not feeling safe, Ida. I hate feeling helpless. I hate being aware of how small I am, seeing people as potential threats. There's probably not a guy on this ranch that couldn't kill me with his bare hands. Except maybe David. All I have is the ability to run, and that doesn't always work out."

I met Ida's shocked eyes, and felt bad for upsetting her. "I'm sorry. It's just one more thing we don't think about because we don't want to. We can go back to not talking about it."

Ida sat back in her chair. "Well, you're right, Abby. Look at me. I'm not young anymore. I'm fairly strong, but I damn sure can't run. I'm so sorry I pushed you into luring a man we don't know into a remote area, alone. That was a terrible thing to do. I just got a little carried away."

"But then I get angry," I said. "Why should I have to live like that? Why should women in general? I'm damn well not going to be afraid my entire life, flinching every time a man raises his voice or walks close to me or behind me. I should challenge Ben to a rematch. We didn't finish the trails. I should ask him to go do the fence line with me, and just be prepared to whack him across the head with my rake handle."

I nodded to Ida, meeting her eyes. "By God, I'm going to. He doesn't look right past me like he does you, but he'll underestimate me that much. I'll get one good swing in."

Ida stared at me.

I raised my mug to her in a toasting manner. "Another cup?"

We planned out the schedule for the next day, and Ida left.

I looked at Papa. "I don't even have to ask. I know exactly what you would think about me whacking men across the head with muck rakes."

I heard a knock at the door. "Hold that thought," I said.

It was Ben. He held his hands up in a "don't panic" gesture. "Abby, I just want to apologize. Can I just have two minutes?"

I stood back to let him in. "Really, it's not like you did anything that terrible. I'm not sure why that escalated so fast."

Ben stepped in, but stayed in the entryway. "Abby—your eyes. I looked at you, and you were afraid of me. I really can't bear that." He waved a hand in the air. "If you never want to talk to me again, I'll accept that, but I can't stand thinking I scared or intimidated you. That's the last thing I want."

I leaned back against the wall. "I guess seeing you angry triggered something. Must've hit a nerve for me."

Ben shrugged and waved his hands again. I wondered if he was capable of talking with his hands full. "I come from loud people, Abby. We raise our voices. We wave our hands around. We shout."

"Not very Midwestern," I said.

Ben smiled. "That repressed Midwesterner thing is really about the huge Scandinavian influence on the area. I'm Irish. The Irish aren't known for being emotionally subtle."

I looked him over. He was still in his work clothes. "Want to finish the trails?"

He opened his mouth to say something, but stopped. "Sure. Let's go."

We got some rakes and headed out to the fence line. Ben stayed ten feet away from me. I supposed he was trying to be nice.

"Ben, have you ever raced a snowmobile on grass? Or a lake?"

He grinned. "Never. I've put in countless hours on a sled, but only on snow." He held a gate open for me. "I've watched a few times, like Walt and Max are doing tomorrow. It's a whole fair-like atmosphere. Park on someone's field for ten bucks, eat mini-donuts."

That sounded like fun. "I really need to try that before the summer's over. You okay with both of them being gone tomorrow?"

Ben shrugged. "Sure. You and Ida are dealing with all the people, anyway. All I have to worry about is the physical property and the horses. What's gonna happen?"

Chapter Fifteen

Ida came up while I was starting breakfast, my hair still in a towel from my post-run shower.

"Grab a mug," I said. "Want some eggs?"

She peered at the line of chopped veggies on the counter. "Sure. If I'd known you hadn't eaten yet, I'd have brought something."

"You can help cook. Grab the little sausages out of the fridge, we'll throw them in, too."

Ida cut up the sausage links I'd browned a few days ago, and threw them in with the bowl of veg I was stirring. I dumped them all into the pan of half-cooked eggs and made a big scramble.

"Abby, this looks wonderful. Do you eat this every day?"

"I try to," I said, adding some diced avocado at the last minute. "I feel better when I do. Lately it's been too easy to grab something else. Do you like a lot of pepper?"

She nodded and put dishes on the table. "Let's plan our strategy for the day."

"I thought we did that yesterday." I scooped a pile of eggs onto each plate. "There's hot sauce in the fridge if you want."

"I mean our behind-the-scenes strategy," she said, searching the door of the refrigerator and pulling out a bottle. "With Walt and

Max both gone for the day, it's the perfect opportunity to snoop. Safely, of course."

"Ben and I worked it all out last night. It was fine. I don't think he was ever a threat to me. I just reacted when he actually got angry. We finished the trails, and got past it."

Ida sampled her eggs. "I'm glad to hear that. I had a terrible dream last night, that Walt and Max got back from the grass drags and found our bodies in the tack room, and Ben was gone."

I put down my fork. "Ida!"

"I know. I wasn't going to say anything."

I stared at her for a moment, then started in on my eggs while they were hot.

"And then I dreamed that Ben was chasing me with a shovel, screaming."

I rolled my hand in the air, in a 'let's move on' gesture. "What kind of snooping did you have in mind?"

"There will be lots of volunteers here, with Max gone. Doing all his chores. They really do enjoy it, you know. He should take time more often. Good for everyone." She paused to eat a few bites. "Abby, this really is very good. So, we should pull people in for coffee breaks. Set out some cookies in the break room, create a relaxed, chatty atmosphere. 'Cat's away' kind of thing."

I sat back in my chair. "So, maybe emphasizing this as a day without supervisors might create a whole different vibe, loosen people's lips?"

Ida nodded enthusiastically. "Exactly! And we'll be right there, shamelessly eavesdropping."

I pointed my fork at her. "Cookies are great, but in workplaces all over America, if you want to make it feel like a special day, you put out boxes of donuts. I can run into Deergrass and be back with donuts in under half an hour."

Ida beamed. "That's perfect, Abby. You do that, and I'll make a lot of coffee and do up the dishes, here."

I spread out the boxes on the break room tables.

"Oh, good." Ida opened the lids. "You went all out. Cake donuts, glazed, even sprinkles!"

"And donut holes," I said, popping one in my mouth. I took two more.

"We'll need napkins." Ida put out two piles. "I think we're ready."

Ben already fed the breakfast crew. A list of remaining chores was posted on the break room door, with extra tasks added. Car doors slammed as volunteers arrived. Within minutes, the break room was filled with happy chatter. Ida greeted each person cheerily and we started working the crowd.

Ben stuck his head in the door and scanned the room in his quick assess-and-catalog way. He took in the donuts and frowned disapprovingly. He knew exactly what we were doing. He threw me a withering glance. I ignored him.

Ida handed Ben a cup. "Have a donut!" she said brightly. "We've even got sprinkles!"

He took the coffee, but shook his head and left.

"Alright, folks!" Ida called the crowd to order. "We so appreciate you coming in! Here's the list of jobs we need to get done. Pick what you want, and stop by for re-energizing in between."

There was an immediate herding response as everyone crowded the list. The two high school sisters were giggling and dibsing horses.

Ida and I took turns tending the refreshments and doing quick chores in the vicinity of as many different people as possible. I noticed Ben doing the same. Jared stuck to mechanical repairs and upkeep, with David and Rodney. They clammed up every time I got within twenty feet. Ida went to get a rake, so I checked the coffee levels and started another pot. All in all, things were going quite well, when suddenly there was running and screaming.

Ida and I ran out of the barn. Ben sprinted out from behind a shed. Several volunteers were running across the pasture, toward the barn, shouting frantically.

One finally got close enough so we could understand him. "Fence down! Horses on the road!"

Ida sprang into action. "Get lead ropes! Get halters!"

Everyone ran for the tack room. Ben grabbed an armful of halters and handed them to me. He pulled Ida to the side. "I need you to take charge of this. You're the site leader. I'll hold down the fort here."

Ida instantly took command like a field general. She deployed people with halters. She had them running to the scene, but walking calmly toward the horses. She launched into implementation of an efficient strategy as though she had drilled for this particular catastrophe.

Meanwhile, I was rooted in one spot, my head on a swivel, watching Ida and wondering if someone should perhaps be watching Ben. What exactly did he want to do, while absolutely every other person ran the other way?

He saw me eyeing him, and leveled a very clear "Oh, come on!" glare in my direction. He impatiently jerked his head toward the pasture, telling me to just go, already.

I squinted at him, but turned to leave. Whatever he did, we would know it was him.

Volunteers stopped traffic. A few drivers used their trucks to block the road. A passerby pulled a length of rope out of her truck bed and draped it over a horse's neck, using it to guide the horse back into the pasture. Someone else took off his belt and did the same thing. A woman stood by the fence gap, waving a plastic bag at any horses who tried to escape again, startling them into retreat. Others guarded the gate to the next pasture, letting horses in as they were wrangled in that direction, keeping horses from getting back out. People from a neighboring farm came to help.

I couldn't see Rosie. I yelled into the crowd, "Rosie! Has anyone seen Rosie?"

Everyone scanned the pastures, the road, the ditches. No one had seen Rosie. Think. How far could she get before someone noticed? Down the road? To a faster road, with trucks and highway speeds? I couldn't breathe. I blinked madly to clear my eyes.

The seven-foot-tall stalks of corn in the neighbor's field rustled. The wall of green parted, and a volunteer waded out, dragging a reluctant horse behind him. Crunching and swishing, another volunteer parted the stalks a few yards down, lead rope in hand. A horse emerged with leaves hanging from its mouth.

I turned to a woman. "Can I stand in your truck bed?"

She agreed, and I climbed up. I scanned the tops of the corn. Mid-field, I saw movement. The plants were definitely swaying. I climbed down and worked my way in that direction, halter in hand. I pushed aside stalks. One smacked me in the face. "Rosie!" I called her name loudly. "Rosie!"

I reached the rustling, waving corn plants, and there she was. Standing with a mouth full of greenery, a defiant look in her eye.

"Rosie, you scared me!" How did this happen? How did I become so fond of a horse, of all things, that I was nearly frantic at the thought of losing her? "Don't you ever do this to me again!" She let me slide the halter over her head, but wrenched off another huge mouthful as I clipped on the rope. I pushed stalks aside as we worked our way out of the field, Rosie chewing steadily. A volunteer picked leaves out of my hair.

We finally got the last horses—the more skittish or stubborn ones—rounded up and moved into a secure pasture. Ida asked David to get a list of horses from the office and coordinate a head-count.

With wiped brows and handshakes all around, the passersby climbed into their pickups and pulled away. No one complained about their day being disrupted.

"Ida!" A volunteer shouted. "There's a cop pulling up by the barn!"

"Lord, help." Ida speed-walked toward the parking lot. I scurried along in her shadow.

The cop was just climbing out of his squad. I looked into the barn. Ben had a man in a headlock.

"Ida! Ida!" I hissed. "Look in the barn! Look in the barn!"

She looked. "Oh, Lord. What now?" She abruptly changed course.

The cop ran ahead of us. "Alright, let him go."

Ben let him go slowly, not backing away until the first cuff was snapped onto a wrist.

"I didn't do nothing," the man protested. "I just came to see if you needed any help!"

The cop looked at Ben. "What do you say, Murphy?"

Of course the cop knew him. Ben shook his head. "All the trouble was out on the road. He came in here thinking it was an empty barn, started digging around."

The man started swearing. The cop actually shushed him. The man actually shushed.

"Well, he's going in, anyway. Detective wants to talk to him. Property damage, gotta be a felony in there. Horses coulda been killed, people coulda been killed. Very least, a probation violation. Detective also wants to talk to him about homicide or accessory."

The man's eyes bulged. He still shushed.

The cop led him off by the arm. "I know you know your rights, Leroy, but I'm gonna tell you again anyway."

I turned to Ben. "What's the property damage? What did he do?"

Ben leveled a steely gaze at me. "Do you really think one of Max's fences just happened to break, all the wires at once, including the hot wire?"

I felt a little stupid. I hadn't gotten that far.

Ida watched the squad car pull out of the driveway, and pulled out her cell phone. "I really don't want to ruin the guys' day off, Lord knows they need it. But Walt will have a hundred fits if he hears about it from someone else, and doesn't know what they're talking about."

She typed a text message, narrating aloud. "First of all, everything is under control. You do not need to leave early. Send." She hesitated for a moment, framing her thoughts before typing again. Her phone rang. "Walt! I hope you're having a good time." Ida walked several feet and turned away.

My phone rang. It was Max. "What the hell's going on?"

I gave him a brief rundown, hoping he could hear me with all the revving of engines in the background. I assured him that everything was, in fact, under control. I promised to call him immediately if one single horse turned up missing, or injured in any way, or if anything else happened, or if anything seemed the least bit hinky. I was certain they were both walking toward the truck while talking to us.

Ida came back, shaking her head. "They'll be distracted, now. I hope they don't just leave. I told Walt there's really nothing for them to do here."

"I told Max the same thing. Let's talk to everyone, tell them what a great job they did, and see if anyone saw anything. Ida, just imagine if we hadn't been having a volunteer day today. If it was just us."

Ida shook her head. "I refuse to imagine that."

We gathered the troops, passed around the rest of the donuts, heaped praise on everyone. I studied facial expressions. Ben actually joined us, despite his scathing looks earlier. He was in full-on read-the-crowd mode, scanning, assessing, cataloging. I wished we could have an honest conversation about it and compare notes.

Most of the faces were highly animated, as people told the same story, over and over. It ended well, so it was a grand adventure.

Jared looked owly, sullen. No surprise there. Rodney seemed cross, but quiet. That was a bit of a surprise. He tended to be mouthy. Janice was silently drinking coffee, one donut in hand and another on a napkin. David looked solemn, but talked quite a bit, as usual. I focused on looking for a pattern, mentally categorizing people by their reactions, and eventually I saw it. With the exception of Jared, the people being quiet were on probation. The animated people were not.

That could mean something, or nothing, other than the understandable desire for people on probation to avoid trouble.

"Well, all right," Ida said. "You all did such a wonderful job. Now let's look at the chore list and see how much we got done, before all this happened."

Most of it was done, and several people asked to schedule another day. Ida promised a signup sheet, and a ride at the end of the day next time. The crowd dispersed. After a smattering of car doors, it was just the three of us.

Ben leaned back against the countertop, legs crossed, arms folded across his chest, watching Ida and me. This was just too much. I was not going to be scrutinized. I scrutinized him back. "What?"

Ben shook his head. "It would help if you trusted me."

Ida and I both broke out laughing. We simultaneously tried to stop, looked at each other, and laughed again. I put a hand over my mouth. "I'm sorry," I choked out. "But really."

Ida turned to clean up the donut boxes. "Ranch hand, my fanny."

I gave him a hands-up "what do you want from me?" gesture. "I actually do like you, Ben."

He stormed from the room.

"Alright," I said, when we were alone. "What's in the barn that someone wants?"

We did a walk through, tried to see with new eyes. Tried to notice something we likely looked right past, every day. Looked for places that something might be hidden. Neither of us was really surprised when we came up empty. We had just given up when Walt and Max pulled in.

We told the whole story again, Walt's face darkening, Max fiercely grim.

Ben left the damage for Walt and Max to see, as well as the cops. The fence was shorted out with metal rods leaning against it. "Short to ground," Ben called it. The wires were cut. Someone deliberately opened the fence, letting the horses out into the roadway. If the guy in the barn was guilty, he was lucky to be in the safe confines of the local jail.

I went on a taco run with some of the volunteers, and came back with a bag of tacos for Max. He was too busy rewiring the fence—and too angry—to stop and make himself lunch. He looked annoyed when he saw me coming, as though he didn't feel like being polite about it. Then he smelled them. He set down his tools and came into the break room.

I grabbed us each a soda, and sat down to keep him company. I watched him unwrap a taco, squeeze a packet of hot sauce over it, and take a bite. I probably shouldn't ask him how the fence repairs were going. Or how difficult it was, not being able to use that corral. Or even how the grass drags went.

He paused between bites. "Thank you for this, Maguire. I didn't even realize I was hungry."

I smiled at him. "It didn't feel right, enjoying all that tacos are, while you toiled in the hot sun."

His mouth twitched at the corners. "I appreciate your support." He unwrapped another taco. "Thing is—" Max broke off, glancing up at the doorway.

I looked over my shoulder. Luke leaned against the door frame, striking a pose. I could see Ida's point. He really did look like something out of a western wear catalog. He would've made a great model, if he could tolerate being told what to do.

"Hey there," he said. "Heard you had a little trouble yesterday."

Max exhaled through his nose, closed his eyes for just a moment, then started eating again.

"You don't miss much," I said. "How many people called in to report how it went down?"

Luke narrowed his eyes, frowned.

Max cut a glance between Luke and me, now keenly interested.

"What's that supposed to mean?" Luke twirled his keys on his finger.

"You tell me, Luke." I was feeling testy. "Just wondering why a probation officer knows every time a piece of wire gives way on a fence."

Luke just managed to stop himself before correcting me about what happened. I wondered if he knew about it before we did.

"Just trying to be friendly," he said. "Glad it all worked out for you."

"Thank you," I said sweetly. "It's nice that you're so concerned about the ranch."

We stared at each other for a few beats. I wasn't sure who was challenging who.

"You think you know a lot, Abby, but you know almost nothing. That was one of the first things I ever found out about you."

Max put down his taco.

"First day we met." Luke gave me his charming smile. "I didn't want to piss you off when there was a chance of going out with you, but you know, Abby, you're dead wrong about sex not being transactional."

I blinked. Max said nothing, but moved his feet, poised to stand.

"Thing is," Luke went on, "it's in women's best interest that sex is transactional. Basic economics. You control access to a desired commodity, you call the shots."

I waited a beat. "How do men and women tend to get along in your family?"

"They get along great! And if the guys start acting too much like guys, the women reel 'em in."

I could feel a headache coming on. "I have no interest in playing 'adorable bad boys' with you, Luke."

He shook his head. "You don't really understand how men and women interact because you were just raised by a man." There was a split-second glimmer in his eye—he knew he'd irritated me. "It's not all intellectual, Abby. In real life, men might act like we're in charge, but we're only in charge so far, because we want what women got. Women are never going to have as much power as men, if they refuse to use the power nature gave them. Isn't that right, Max?" He nodded, agreeing with himself, pushed off from the door frame and walked away.

I looked at Max. He remained expressionless as the sound of Luke's boots retreated out of the barn.

"What a dumbass," he said.

I blew out a breath in relief. "I was afraid you were going to agree with him."

He raised both eyebrows.

"I'm not putting you in the same category as him. Not even close. It's just, everywhere I go, I have to figure out cultures and subcultures. Underlying beliefs. You really never know what people think about so many things, that don't come up in conversation."

"Until someone makes a point of telling you, just to irritate you," Max said.

"Well, there's that." I frowned at the doorway. "It will surprise you sometimes, when you find out what people believe. Or even yourself, I guess. Sometimes we don't even know our own underlying assumptions. We believe a whole lot of things we don't think about."

Max snorted. "I believe it's pathetic for a man to say right out that he needs someone to make him act like an adult." He shook his head. "Some things are too important to act like it's a game. A woman is definitely one of those things." He looked up at the sound of approaching boots, and Ida leaned in.

"What are you two all serious about in here?"

I looked up at her. "Ida, did you ever get Johnny to do things by promising him sex?"

Ida threw her head back, laughing. "Oh, Lord." She looked at Max's grin, and laughed some more. "Honey, Johnny never had to earn sex a day in his life." She smiled broadly. Her eyes got a lively twinkle, just thinking about it.

Alrighty then.

I finished documentation, and closed the file cabinet, rising to leave. A thought occurred, and I sat back down. Walt had files on all the volunteers. Background checks, contact information. Probation details when applicable. I pulled open that drawer and took out the first file. It wasn't a ton of information, but it helped fill in the overall picture. Any corrections or warnings, notes of appreciation. I worked my way through, scanned, occasionally jotted down a note. Janice lived in a trailer court in Jack Pine, with a cousin. Probably the cousin's trailer. David had been around for six years. Mason. I winced. I didn't expect him to have a file. He must've started as a volunteer. I pulled it out, set it aside, and finished reading the rest of them.

I sat back and took a breath before opening Mason's file. His father was listed, with a rural address outside Deergrass. Mason lived in the same trailer court as Janice and three or four others. A girlfriend, Jamie, shared his address.

A plan formed in the back of my mind. I really should understand more about Mason. I made a photocopy of his file to read more carefully later, and returned the original to the cabinet.

I opened the bottom drawer, and found a catch-all stash of miscellaneous things. A sticky note on a sweatshirt, dated a few months ago, caught my eye: "Mason left in round pen."

Well. His girlfriend might be wanting that back.

Chapter Sixteen

I locked up the cabinet and grabbed the hoody and file.

Ida pulled in as I reached the parking lot. "You look like you're on a mission! What are you up to?"

I leaned on her window frame, and waved a sleeve at her. "This is Mason's. I'm taking it to his girlfriend. If it were me, I might want it back."

She grabbed the sleeve and pulled the whole thing in the window. "Not without me, you're not. Get in."

There was no point arguing. Ida would lend an air of credibility, anyway. We would pay our respects. I climbed in and she backed around in an arc, reversing course. "What were you planning to say?" Ida stopped to look before pulling out on the road.

I read the address aloud. "It's a trailer court."

Ida nodded. "I know where that is. Not the best area. Of course, Jack Pine is depressed in general, but that's a depressed area of Jack Pine."

Just as well I wasn't going alone. "I suppose I should've called first. She might not be home."

"Only take ten minutes to find out," Ida said. "So, what are you planning to say?"

I sat back in the seat. "Ok, so we found this sweatshirt. It says it's Mason's. We thought she might want it. You knew Mason for several years, liked him. He helped me when I first came, was nice about it." I paused. "I'm not going to say I found him. Let's not say that."

"Probably best. All right, I can work with that." She drove in silence until we reached a dismal looking trailer court on the edge of town. There was very little grass, mostly dirt and gravel. The cars were all beaters. Strewn bicycles and toys wore dust like a coat of paint. An old toilet next to someone's door was filled with petunias, though. A central playground was in good repair. The weeds under the swings were pulled. Someone was trying.

Jamie's address was in the middle of a long line of trailers, down an interior road. A brown, older model sedan with rusted wheel wells and hail damage was parked outside. I hoped Jamie could afford lot payments without Mason's small paychecks.

Ida led the way up the wooden steps, and knocked. A thin young woman in a loose shirt and jeans opened the door. She had dark hair pulled back with a ponytail holder, and dark circles under her eyes.

"You must be Jamie. I'm Ida, and this is Abby. We worked with Mason. We came to bring back a shirt he forgot at the ranch. We thought you might want it." Ida held up the hoody.

Jamie stood back to let us into the entryway, reached for the sweatshirt. "Thank you. I do want it. I gave it to him." Jamie focused on me. "You're Abby? You're the one who found him."

"I—yes, I was. I'm so sorry." I didn't know what to say.

"What was he like? When you found him."

I hesitated. "At first, I thought he was just passed out. Like sleeping, only he was on the ground, so I thought he must've gotten drunk and passed out." I hoped I could leave it at that.

Jamie swallowed hard. "Thank you."

"Jamie, I knew Mason for years," Ida said. "I liked him. We miss him."

I nodded. "He was nice. He helped me when I first came, and didn't know anything."

Jamie looked at me, one hand resting on her abdomen. "He was clean. Clean and straight. He was working real hard. Do you know what happened?"

I paused. "No. But I want to."

Ida's eyes widened.

I studied Jamie. She looked level-headed, determined. "I'm sure the police came by to talk with you?"

She nodded. "They just dragged him through the dirt. Talking about was he dealing, was he hanging out with people dealing. He wasn't." She glanced down, seemed to notice her hand on her belly, moved it to a hip. "He didn't want any trouble. He wasn't into anything. He even asked me to marry him. We're gonna have a kid. Mason was real happy."

Both Ida and I stood with our mouths open for a tick longer than was socially acceptable. Ida recovered first. "Jamie! We had no idea. I know that makes everything harder, but congratulations."

"We weren't gonna tell anyone yet," Jamie said. "That's why Mason didn't say anything. I didn't want him to, yet."

"That's even more reason," I blurted. "To find out."

Ida gave me a side-eye, but Jamie nodded. "Are you really gonna try?"

"Jamie, I'm just a therapist. I will do my best. Did Mason say anything? Has anyone come by? Anyone Mason seemed worried about?"

Jamie was eyeing Ida with her peripheral vision, her face turned to me. Ida wore her polite smile and didn't seem to notice.

"His boss came by," Jamie said. "He was real nice. He helped Mason's dad pay for the funeral. Otherwise, he was gonna have to sell his car, and I don't know what he'd do without his car. He already sold his boat and trailer to pay for something."

"Walt." I didn't know what else to say about that. "Anyone else?"

Jamie hesitated. "There was an old guy came around a few times. Mason really didn't like him. I don't know what he wanted, they stayed outside. Mason was real upset afterwards. One time, I looked out, Mason was yelling at the guy, pointing a finger at him, telling him to stay away, leave us alone."

"Did you tell the police that?"

"Yeah, but they just wanted to know about drugs. People they know are dealing. I just kept saying no, no, no, he hasn't been around them, not them either."

"Ok," I said. "He wasn't acting like he was worried about anything?"

She looked away, shook her head.

"Thank you," I said. "Let me give you my phone number. If you think of anything else, please let me know."

Jamie went into the next room, and came back with a pen and a scrap of paper.

I wrote my name and cell number. "Are you going to be okay?"

"Mason's dad is gonna help," Jamie said. "He wants to be involved, be a grandpa."

Ida leaned in. "That's wonderful. I'm so glad. Good for everyone."

Jamie nodded, and we turned to leave. I looked back. She met my eyes, but said nothing.

We were quiet until Ida pulled away from the curb.

"Abby! What was that? Did you lose your mind?"

I couldn't think of a single good response. "You sound like Max."

"I can't believe you did that." Ida's head pivoted between me and the road. "We didn't go there to say we'd solve Mason's murder, Abby! What are we supposed to do now?"

"I said I'd try. I didn't promise anything, except I'd try. We were going to do that anyway."

Ida pulled out of the trailer court. "Lord, help."

"Ida, you can't pretend we went there for any other reason than to snoop. And the only reason to snoop is to find out who killed Mason. So—what?" I turned in my seat, threw open my hands.

"I didn't think we were going to tell Mason's girlfriend that. That's not what we talked about, not at all."

We drove in silence. Ida stared at the road.

"This child will have enough strikes against them from day one," I said. "It matters."

Ida pulled into the parking lot. "Alright, Abby. Just try to be careful, will you? Don't just assume you can trust people."

I reached for the door handle. "You think she was talking about David? The old guy?"

"We need to find out if it was him. And what he was doing." Ida drummed her fingers on the steering wheel.

"I'll ask him about Mason," I said. "Say I keep thinking about him, after finding him like that. Which is true. David likes people to ask his opinion. Maybe he'll start talking and not know when to stop."

"That'll work." Ida swung down from the cab.

Max walked out from behind a shed and watched the two of us climbing out of Ida's truck. He frowned and turned toward the barn without a word.

"He's got some nerve," I said. "Assuming we're up to something, just because we're together."

"Hmph." Ida threw a glance at his back. "He can just keep wondering where we've been. I'm not going to say a word, see if he dares to ask."

I turned up the stairs to my apartment. I pulled out my laptop bag and tucked the photocopied file in the middle of temp agency paperwork. I leaned back against the stove and looked at Papa. "She wasn't going to talk in front of Ida. And I don't understand that one bit."

I went out running the next morning as the sun came up. I happily watched the horizon as rosy pink turned to coral. A golden orange glow spread across the sky, breaking over the dark tops of the pine trees. Sheer delight gave me extra energy. The horses and cows I jogged past were motionless in the fields, their breath forming puffs of mist. My nose and ears were cold. Cooler air settled with a dank chill in low spots where the road dipped, turning past wetlands. I shivered, running through it. Rising into a bright, open stretch, I felt the warmth of the sun. The day would heat quickly.

I heard a car behind me on the gravel road, and edged closer to the side. I was coming up on the neighbor's farm, only a few fields from home. The car slowed abruptly, then turned around behind me. I heard a loud pop, and something hit the road a few feet ahead of me. I pulled up short in surprise, then started running again. They must have kicked up a rock with their sudden turn.

I heard another pop, and something hit a tree to my right. I turned around, confused. A dark green sedan, the back bumper held on with a bungee cord, faced away from me. I couldn't see who was in it. Someone reached out a back window. Another pop, and the ground beside me exploded in a puff of flying dirt.

I jumped sideways. Fear and adrenaline surged through me. I ran away from the road. Another pop. The side of my arm burned. I sprinted full out, ran for the trees. The gate! The ranch, through the fields. I threw myself at the gate, launched over it, landed hard, scrambled up. I staggered a few steps—

"Hey! Get out of there!"

I rolled, hid behind the gate. I peered between the boards.

"What the hell you doing in there?" An older man in denim and a dirty ball cap strode toward me.

"I'm sorry!" I looked at him over the top of the gate. He did not have a gun. "I'm sorry! Someone—shooting at me!"

"The hell you say." The man reached the gate. "Get out of there!"

I opened the gate and walked out. My heart was pounding. "I'm sorry. I was running—" I waved a hand toward the road.

He looked me over, took in my shorts and running shoes. He nodded. "I've seen you running."

"Someone—shooting at me! I swear!" My breath came in short gasps. "I was going to cut— through the fields—to the ranch—by the trails. Off the road."

The man frowned. "Can't get through there. Electric fences."

"Oh, hell." I'd forgotten. I looked down at myself. "Not in shorts."

He squinted at me. "Your arm bleeding?" One of my sleeves was torn, bloodied. "Say, was that the truth? Someone shooting at you, out here?"

"Yes!" I poked at my arm, winced.

"I was just coming out to give those kids hell for shooting off fireworks. You come on in the house." He saw me hesitate. "You don't need to be afraid of me. Walt's been a real good neighbor for a lot of years. I don't know what the hell's going on over there, but we're not having shooting. Someone's going to get hurt, or someone's going to lose some stock."

I followed him up concrete steps, through a screen door and into a small kitchen. I could smell coffee and bacon. A sense of unreality hit me as my adrenaline leveled out. The man walked across the floor. "Sharon! I need the phone!"

A gray-haired woman in jeans and a worn sweatshirt came around the corner. "What in the world—"

"We need to call the police." He continued into the next room. I stayed by the door.

"Oh, my Lord. Are you hurt? You come on in here and sit down." The woman pulled a chair out from a Formica table. "Can I get you some coffee?"

"Yes. Please. I'm sorry to trouble you."

She took an orange mug from a cupboard, filled it with coffee and set it in front of me. "You just take it easy," she said, and followed her husband.

Minutes later, a silver extended-cab pickup pulled into the driveway. Walt. He trotted up to the door, and the woman let him in. They murmured to each other, shook their heads.

"Walt." I didn't know what to say.

He put a hand on my shoulder, looked at my arm. "Are you ok? You need a doctor?"

"I don't even know." I wore a t-shirt under my top layer. I took hold of my waistband and started to pull off my long-sleeved shirt, but quickly lowered my arm again when it throbbed. "I might have to cut this shirt off."

The woman leaned over me. "That sleeve's ruined anyway. You want me to cut it off for you?"

I paused, looked at Walt for cues. He was looking at my arm. "Ok," I said. "If you don't mind."

She opened a drawer, and pulled out a large pair of kitchen shears, turning towards me. The oversized blades glinted in the fluorescent light. I blew out air, glanced at Walt. He was still focused on my sleeve. I closed my eyes.

The woman moved my arm gently as she cut the sleeve from the shirt, and slid it down over my arm. "It's just barely grazed. Looks like an abrasion. The bleeding is already slowing down. You're gonna wanna clean that up, though."

Her husband came back into the room. He and Walt shook hands. Walt thanked him. They nodded at each other. I was starting to feel lightheaded.

We all trooped outside. I was trying to show them where it happened, when the police pulled up. "It happened so fast," I said. "One hit a tree. A couple hit the road." I was relieved when they found the tire marks from the U-turn. None of this seemed real. If it weren't for the hole in my sleeve, I would've doubted my own sanity.

"What do you think this was about?" one of the cops asked.

I was wondering the same thing, once the adrenaline wore off. "They can't have been trying to hurt me. I reacted far too slowly. Standing in the road, processing what was happening."

Another cop pointed at a tree trunk. I squinted in the sunlight. "They probably hit my arm by accident."

The cop studied my face. "Early in the morning for kids messing around. That kind of wildness is a middle of the night thing. Alcohol induced. Any reason someone wants to scare you?"

I glanced at Walt. He was watching me soberly. I shook my head. "I'm still pretty new here. I don't even know that many people."

The cop turned to Walt. "Lot going on at your place lately."

Walt's voice was tired. "Let me know if you need anything." He was silent driving the mile to the ranch. Coming to a stop in the gravel lot, he turned in his seat to face me.

"Abby, I'm so sorry. I'm sorry for what this has turned into. I'll understand if you cut it short. You don't have to stay. You'd probably be smart not to." He sighed heavily. "And I feel I need to make you aware of something. This is not public knowledge—the police are withholding it. I need you to not repeat it. Mason was shot before he was hit on the head. He was already dead when he was beaten."

I didn't say anything, absorbing that. Then I shook my head. "I'm not leaving early, Walt. We have clients. We've made a commitment to them. They're scraping up enough hope to come out here, to try. I'm not just dropping them. And I really believe that whoever did this, did not want to hurt me. They could have. I was stupid. I just stood there."

He sat for a long moment, then nodded. "Maybe you could stay off the road for a while. I know running is important to you. Max has a treadmill." His voice faded. Walt looked older than when I met him.

I nodded. "I'll figure it out."

Max ran out of the barn and pulled open my door. His eyes quickly scanned me, lingering on the graze on my arm, the sleeve in my hand. "Maguire. You're okay." It was a statement.

I nodded agreement. "I'm okay, Max."

"Come up to the house. I've got a good first-aid kit, I'll clean that up for you."

I climbed down from the cab. My arm hurt when I moved it. I turned to Walt. "Thank you for coming to get me." Walt tipped his head in response and started toward the barn.

I followed Max up to his kitchen and sat in the chair he pointed to.

He knelt on the faded linoleum beside me and examined my arm. "Okay. It's really not bad. Tell me what happened." He got a wet cloth and squeezed it over the wound, letting it run into his wastebasket.

I described everything in the detail I knew he'd want, including my stupidly slow response.

"You need to stop that," he said, dabbing antibiotic onto my arm with a cotton swab. "Stop insulting yourself, Maguire. You're not a trained combatant. You're a civilian. You're not supposed to expect getting shot at while you're out running."

"I'm not used to being so slow on the uptake," I said. "I'm normally extremely good in emergencies. I'm the one who tells everyone else what to do."

"No one excels at every single thing they've never had exposure to, been trained in, and practiced. You expect too much from yourself, and it's starting to seem like some kind of a disorder."

I looked down at the top of his head. "Excuse me?" He peered up at me, one eyebrow raised.

I had to laugh. "Max. Ow!" I frowned at him.

"Sorry." He wrapped a bandage around my arm. "Come back tomorrow. Dr. Max will have another look at it." He picked up my sleeve. "You want me to throw this for you?"

I nodded, and he tossed it in the garbage. I pulled the rest of the shirt over my head and added it to the trash. I looked around the room. He must have just moved in, kept the 1950's house as is, and personalized very little. Even the furniture looked original.

It was extremely clean and neat, give him that. And what was that on the wall? I moved closer. It was a very colorful, framed picture of a rooster doing a high-kick walk through the grass, a barn in the background. It was made entirely of seeds and beans. Different colors, different sizes, apparently glued on. It was...a seed picture. I stared at it. I was afraid to say anything.

"That's crop art," Max said.

I turned to study his face, look for cues. Did he love it? Was it just there? "Crop art?"

"It's a thing. Especially at the state fair. Kind of a fair tradition. Ida bought it for me one year, clearly thought it was hilarious, but she was playing it straight. So I acted delighted, called her bluff, hung it in pride of place. Neither one of us has ever flinched, so there it is." He smiled reluctantly, as though he wasn't in the mood, but couldn't help it. "I have come to like it, though. Makes me think of Ida."

I looked back at the seed rooster.

"Listen. Whatever the hell you're doing, Maguire, you need to stop. You might've been hit by accident, but someone's sure as hell sending you a message."

"All I'm doing is talking to people, Max, and listening. What I'm trained in. What I've practiced."

"Well, keep it for sessions, and stop trying to flush out bad guys. You're sure as hell not trained in that, and you're gonna get hurt if you refuse to listen."

"Thank you very much for the first aid, Max. I appreciate it." I glanced back at the rooster one more time.

He saw me eyeing his crop art, but refused to be distracted. "And the advice, Max," he said. "Thanks for that, too. I can't wait to follow it."

I smiled at him and returned to my apartment to change. I needed coffee. And ibuprofen. And a minute to think. I certainly wasn't going to tell Max that Ida and I visited Jamie. All the same, I should warn Ida.

Who would even know we were there? I closed the door and leaned back against it. "I hope Ida's not right," I told Papa. "She thought I was foolish to trust Jamie at all." I wanted to keep liking Jamie. Wanted to help her. It might be a very bad idea.

Chapter Seventeen

I woke up the next morning feeling groggy and cranky. My arm hurt. It hurt every time I rolled over on it in the night. Coffee helped with the grogginess, but not with the crankiness. I grouched my way down the stairs.

Ida beat me in, which was unusual. She was alone in the office. "Abby! Are you okay?" She assessed me, decided that I was. "Did you hear about Ben the Fed?"

"No! What about him?"

She nodded. "He's moving into the house with Max. Gonna be on-site from now on, in the basement bedroom."

We looked at each other. "As a ranch hand," I said.

She nodded again. "Uh-hunh."

I looked at the schedule. "There's nothing going on for a few hours. I'm going to go see if I can jog on Max's treadmill. Maybe I can spy on Ben at the same time."

I wandered up to the house. As soon as I reached the door, it opened. Max smiled out at me. "Morning. How's the arm?"

I scowled. "Sore, and I'm crabby. Walt said you had a treadmill. Would you mind if I take out my frustration on it?"

Max grinned. "Come on in. You don't look like you're dressed for jogging, though."

"I thought I'd ask before I bothered changing." I followed Max through the kitchen and down some ancient wooden stairs. The basement was partially finished, probably over a half century ago, and never updated. It felt dark despite the overhead lighting, with small glass block windows and cement floors.

I glanced into the bedroom as we walked by. The window looked like it was slightly enlarged to meet the legal requirement of an egress window. Dark wood paneling. Linoleum curled up around the edges. An oval braided rug, faded, worn. Ben stood by a full-size bed, unpacking a suitcase into a small dresser. He looked up as we passed, and stopped what he was doing to stare at us.

Max walked past a small bathroom and into a second bedroom. The treadmill was not expensive, but it looked functional. He also had a punching bag, a rowing machine, and a stationary bicycle. A weight bench and barbells were against one wall.

"Wow! You've got a whole set-up here." I squatted by the rowing machine and looked it over.

"The winters get kinda long," Max said. "Granted, I get a lot of exercise around here anyway, but sometimes it feels good to get a little cardio, burn off some steam."

I briefly wondered if Max, living alone, had intense midnight workouts in January, instead of strapping on a holster and wandering the property. None of the equipment looked dusty. Maybe the punching bag was his answer to nightmares and panic attacks. Maybe I should try it.

"Feel free to use whatever you want. You're welcome to it."
Max shook his head, frowning. "I still can't believe what happened
yesterday. Seriously. You come on over here, any time." Max looked
up at Ben, who stood in the doorway. There was an uncomfortable
silence. They were probably both considering how to spin Ben's
presence. Neither of them looked at me or spoke. I could try to
help them out, but I was feeling surly. I straightened up and went
to look at the treadmill instead. It had a basic display, and a simple
incline if I wanted to run uphill. I despised running uphill.

Ben turned and walked back into his bedroom.

Max looked relieved. "You can work out right now, if you want.
Don't knock, just run over and change, let yourself in when you get
back. If you ever want to come in and I'm not around, just make
yourself at home." He didn't say anything about announcing my
presence for Ben's sake. Apparently, he assumed Ben could close
the door if he wanted to walk around in his underwear.

I nodded. "Thanks, Max." Alrighty, then. We were all agreed.
We were going to pretend nothing was going on. "I'll be back in a
minute."

After our session the next morning, Max needed to run into
town, pick up a part. "Go ahead," I told him. "I'll clean up here. I
have lots of time." I planned to enjoy a leisurely pace.

Maverick and Rosie wandered in the indoor arena as I put things
away. I talked to them casually, scratched a neck, patted a rear.
Gradually I became aware that Maverick was standing purpose-
fully, rather than lounging. He watched me with one eye, one ear
cocked in the other direction. I moved a few feet to look around

him. Maverick moved with me. "What are you doing?" I walked up and ran my fingers through his mane. "What's going on with you, huh?" I looked around, didn't see anything, and picked up my rake. I moved the wheelbarrow. Maverick moved too, flanking me.

"Huh." I set the wheelbarrow down. I still didn't see anything. Rosie was watching Maverick. Her ears were swiveled away from me. "What are you guys up to?" I stood next to Maverick, looking over his back. There was someone in the shadows, leaning against the wall. "Hello," I called out. "I didn't see you there."

The figure straightened, walked toward the rail. It was Luke. "Hi there. I just got done talking with someone and saw you in here. Didn't want to interrupt you, looked like you were busy."

I gave a smile and wave, and he left. Huh.

I found Walt in the pasture, haltering a horse. "Have you ever heard of a horse standing between two people?"

Walt glanced at the horse standing between us, glanced back at me.

"No, I mean on purpose. Like in a protective manner."

Walt's face changed. "Yes. We had a family coming in for therapy, Maverick started standing in between the dad and the kid. Wouldn't move. Turned out the dad was abusive. Turned into a whole child protection thing, kid removed from the home. None of us had a clue, until the parents said they had no idea why Maverick would do that, and the kid called them out on it." He buckled the halter and clipped on a lead rope. "Maybe you'd better tell me what you're talking about."

"Maverick was standing between me and Luke. I hadn't seen him—I didn't even know Luke was there, but Maverick did. And Rosie noticed. She was watching the whole thing."

Walt leaned on the horse's back, regarded me seriously. "Luke that's a P.O. Luke that's out here multiple times a week, interacts with all kinds of people here. Abby, I'm not telling you how to run your life—"

I shook my head. "I already told him I'm not dating him. Maybe he's angry about that." I thought about Maverick standing there, on alert, while I puttered around. "It took me awhile to even notice Maverick. I guess I'm still learning how to listen."

Walt sighed. "I guess I'm still learning how to see. Maybe I need to open my eyes."

I woke with a start—sitting up, heart pounding. I swung my legs out of bed. I was dreaming—the sound of running footsteps in a hallway. I walked out to the living room and put on water for tea. I went to turn on the lamp by the door and saw a car in the parking lot. Max's girlfriend. I'd never met her, but I'd seen her drive in and out a few times. Max wouldn't be out doing rounds tonight.

I sat and looked out the window, into the darkness. The dream was still heavy. I couldn't shake it. Screaming. An attacker. Physical restraint. Calming, being released, and suddenly attacking again. You could never relax. It was never over. You could never turn your back. That was the nightmare that woke me in the early hours. Someone turned their back. Sometimes, I got there in time to help them. Other nights, I couldn't move. Couldn't save them.

Couldn't help. And tonight, when I finally reached the co-worker, it was Mason, lying on the floor.

I shook my head. The constant flooding of adrenaline was toxic, I knew that. Eventually I would have to find my next job. I thought about the years of split-second decisions. Putting out fires all over the building, all at once. Pencils and chair legs turned into weapons. Co-workers bleeding—or worse. I just didn't want to do it anymore.

The stars were clear over the pastures. The air coming in the window felt warm. I turned off the tea kettle, slid on my boots, grabbed my Maglite, and went down the stairs. I would do the night watch tonight. I had no idea where I would go from here, but I didn't have to know right now. Moving around would help.

I walked through the barn, through a few corrals. Everything seemed quiet. The moon was bright, so I turned off my flashlight and stood by a lean-to, looking out on the woods. Even the horses seemed quiet tonight, standing in clusters. I heard a door close and turned to look. Max's girlfriend walked from the house, got in her car, and drove away. No doors were slammed. No gravel flew from under her tires. I looked at the house. I hoped Max was ok.

Max seemed subdued the next morning, moving horses into the barn. I grabbed some buckets and distributed them. When the last horse was nose-in to its feed, Max came and stood by me. I waited. Max sighed. "Did you see her leave last night?"

"I did. You ok?"

He rolled his shoulders, stretched. "I think so. We finally called it. She needed us to be done."

"I'm sorry, Max."

We leaned back on the fence and watched the horses eating. One of them was making a huge mess, dropping food everywhere. "I better get him looked at," Max said. "Might need his teeth floated."

I'd heard that term for horse dentistry, so I just nodded. Neither of us moved.

Max sighed. "I got nothing bad to say about her. Nothing. I've been hard to have a relationship with for a long time. I can't be mad at her. She thinks maybe this guy at work will be a nice, steady partner. Start a family. Said the guy isn't a real deep thinker, but he's always predictable, always happy. She just wants to be happy."

We stood there together, let that settle in. "I hope it works out for her," I said. "I hope you're ok."

He nodded, pushed off from the fence and stretched. "I think I am, Maguire."

One of the horses picked up its now empty bucket with its teeth, and tossed it. I smiled. "I guess he's done, then. I'll take him out."

I wandered around in the afternoon, watching Ben lurk. Every time I turned around, he was in a different shadow, watching someone. I walked around to the machinery sheds, and found Max lurking. He was checking hinges, hasps, gate closures—and watching people. I started to feel self-conscious about walking around, watching people.

I moved back out to the main corral area. David and Jared were out by the fence, talking. I didn't often see Jared chatting with anyone. I thought about that, and jumped when someone spoke right behind me.

"What are you up to?" Ben sounded light, conversational.

I gave him a level gaze. "The same thing as you. Getting anywhere?"

He hesitated a beat. "I was thinking about cooking up some dinner again. Are you free tonight? I could make a quick run, pick up some ingredients?"

I was free. Did I want to deal with it? I could try to redeem my counterintelligence efforts. Maybe he would let something slip. "Why not? What time should I expect you? I'll put on clothes that don't stink."

Ben smiled happily, and we agreed on seven. He turned and wandered toward the machinery sheds. It might be fun to see Ben and Max lurk their way into each other, but I turned instead toward the barn.

I'd just showered and changed into clean clothes when Ben knocked at the door. He had a paper grocery bag in each arm, so I held the door for him to ease in sideways.

"Go ahead into the kitchen." I closed the door and locked it.

"Ok if I just dig around for pans?"

"You have full kitchen privileges. Knock yourself out."

Ben unloaded the grocery bags. There was a lot of produce. "I thought I'd whip up a stir fry."

"Wonderful!" I leaned back against the table and watched him. A direct approach had not worked with Ben. I would need to come up with a different angle. "How do you like living on-site?"

Ben looked up at me from the cutting board, where he was lining up vegetables. He held a cleaver that would probably take my arm off. "It's convenient. Saves on gas. I might be in Max's hair a little, but it works for me. How about you?"

I nodded. "This is ideal for a temp situation. Where were you living before this? Did you have to worry about getting out of a lease?"

"Nope. Wasn't a problem." He kept chopping. "Do you like mushrooms?"

"I do. So, you must've been in a month-to-month situation?"

"Great, some people don't like the texture." He scraped some chopped vegetables onto a plate to make room on the cutting board. "You must get a lot of month-to-month setups, being you move around so much."

He was enjoying this. Thrust and parry. Duck and roll.

"It must be somewhat uncomfortable for you," I said. "Starting a new job is considered a major life stressor under the best of circumstances. It's been pretty tense around here. I imagine people haven't been as warm and welcoming as you might hope for."

Ben smiled. "Yet, here I am, sharing dinner with you." He stopped chopping, set down his knife, and turned to lean back against the counter. "I hope you won't think this is too forward. I brought something for after dinner." He wiped his hands on a dishtowel, reached into one of the bags and handed me a CD.

I hadn't expected this. "What is it? Something new?"

"Not new at all. You didn't have any country music to dance to, so I thought you might like this." Ben ducked his head, looking almost—shy? "There's a song about moving the furniture to dance in a tiny living room. I thought you'd like that."

I did like it, which left me feeling off-balance. Ben watched me read the label. He looked a little nervous. I studied him. I wasn't prepared for nervous and sweet. He waited for me to respond.

"Let's try it right now!" I ripped off the plastic covering and popped out the CD. I loved the song immediately. We moved the furniture. We played the song repeatedly, dancing in several different styles. We tried other songs and other CDs. We laughed when the music and our steps were awkwardly mismatched. We grinned at each other when it all came together smoothly. Finally, I put a hand on his arm.

"Ben. It's been two hours. I'm starving."

Ben smiled. "Me too." He pulled me in and kissed me.

A tingle ran through the whole center of my body. My toes curled. I kissed him back, but stopped well short of the point of no return. I put a hand on his chest and took a step back. "We should have dinner." My voice sounded unsteady.

Ben took a deep breath, blew it out. "Dinner. Right." He turned and looked around as if he'd forgotten where he'd left the kitchen. He looked at me again, blinked hard a couple of times, and walked to the counter. Picking up the knife, he glanced at me, then shook his head as if clearing it. "Stir fry. On it."

I tried to regroup. I couldn't tell Ida that I'd failed again because he kissed me and I lost my mind. I watched as Ben finished chopping the vegetables and pulled chicken out of the refrigerator. He'd stuck it in there before we started dancing. I didn't even notice.

Ben studied me as he unwrapped the chicken. "Abby, I'm here because I like you. Not to talk about weird things going on at the ranch."

I blinked. "The weird atmosphere bothers me. Plus, I don't know if the police are getting anywhere with Mason's death. I can't help thinking about it. It's reasonable to wonder if you've noticed anything."

Ben cut up the chicken with that large, very sharp cleaver. He gave me a side glance with a little smile. "If I come up with something, will you kiss me again?"

I narrowed my eyes at him. His smile turned to a grin.

"Kisses aren't transactional," I said. "But you could try to impress me."

Ben laughed and turned back to his food prep. He turned the stove on under a pan I didn't see him dig out. He was quick. I'd only turned my back for a minute.

"It's not like you don't have an agenda, Ben."

He turned to look at me.

"It's not like you're really a ranch hand. It's not like you ever address that fact. I don't want to ruin the evening, but I also don't want to kiss someone who never reveals himself, beyond an obviously false persona."

Ben sighed and stirred the chicken. "I thought I'd be able to cleverly avoid the issue for a while longer."

"I'm surprised no one has told you this before, Ben Murphy." I shook my head solemnly. "You are not slick."

"I'm usually better," he said. "You've got me off my game a little." He put the chicken and vegetables together. "Now I don't even have rice or anything going here. I'm all out of whack."

I got some plates out of the cupboard. "This looks perfect by itself. And I'm hungry enough to eat it all, so you'd better get some on your own plate, quick."

I made a conscious effort not to wolf my food. It really was delicious. I told him so, but the mood was lost. Probably just as well. I really didn't want to kiss a stranger, even if I did like him. I resisted the impulse to rub his leg with my foot under the table. I needed to keep my resolve, at least until I knew who he really was. I sat back in my chair. "I don't suppose you have any idea how long you'll be working here. You must've lived locally, though, before moving in with Max?" Surely, he could tell me that.

Ben considered that for a moment. "I grew up in Deergrass. Been staying with a friend in Jack Pine for a while. We stay out of each other's way for the most part. I give him something towards his house payment. That was always going to be time-limited, we just haven't set the limit."

I nodded. "Thank you." It wasn't much, but it sounded honest.

"Tell me something about a previous job," Ben said. Telling benign stories carried us through the meal and the cleanup, which Ben refused to leave for me. I walked him to the door.

"Thank you for the CD," I said. "I really do love it."

Ben smiled, touched my face with the back of his hand, and walked to the house.

Chapter Eighteen

Considering his earlier efforts to avoid me, I was surprised when Jared approached me, calling out to get my attention. "Hey, Abby. I heard about how you ran over that bear. I got my jacks and jack stands in the truck. If you want me to look at your car, I got time. I mean, I won't charge you or anything, just to help you out."

"Jared, that's really generous!" I studied him. His eyes seemed clear, focused. His pupils looked normally dilated. His speech seemed lucid. "That would be amazing! Thank you!" I looked at the parking lot. "Where do you want it? Some place with a little more room?"

Jared turned and looked at the pickups and cars half filling the lot. "Yeah, why don't we move it back behind Max's house there? Then I can slide in and out easier."

"I'll get my keys!" I ran up the stairs. Jogging back to my car, I saw Max coming out of his house. "Jared's going to look at my car for me! Do you mind if I move it behind your house, so it's out of the lot?"

Max made a sweeping motion with his arm. "Have at it!" He continued toward the barn.

I maneuvered around the logs delineating the parking lot, and onto the level patch of thin grass.

"Just leave the keys in it." Jared backed his truck up close to my car. "Give me a couple hours. I'll let you know what I find."

I brought Rosie in for a quick ride. We were walking toward her post when Rodney came through the barn, frowning. Rosie flattened her ears against her head and pulled away. I blinked at her, caught off guard. Rodney glanced over, snorted, and kept walking. Rosie swung her hindquarters away from Rodney, pivoting on the lead rope. I stopped and waited until he walked out the back door.

Rosie's ears stayed pinned to her head for a moment. She watched Rodney leave, then seemed to relax. She let me walk her to her post and clip on her halter.

"What was that about?" I waited for a few minutes, making sure he didn't come back, before leaving her alone while I got her brush and tack. Horses sensed people's moods, I got that. Did Rosie just not like Rodney's crabbiness? Maybe she could tell I didn't like him! That was a terrible thought. I had to rein this in.

The moment passed. We had a good practice ride, and I returned Rosie to the pasture. I made a mental note to ask Walt about it, and went to check on my car.

Jared wiped his forehead with his sleeve. "Well, prob'ly not what you wanna hear...does your air conditioner work?"

I thought about it. "Yes! I have used it. It worked just fine."

"Well, you're lucky, then. Ok, so, the lower radiator support is pushed back. The bottom plastic covering was broke loose, but I pulled it back together and put some zip ties on there to hold it. I just took off another piece that was broke, but that's just to make it more aerodynamic and fuel efficient. You could replace that, but you're never going to get the money back in the gas it saves. I'd just leave it, if I were you."

"Ok! Thank you!" I hesitated. "There was some...hair and stuff before. Could you still see anything from the bear?"

He grinned. "Couple chunks."

I shuddered. "Jared, thank you again. I really appreciate it."

He nodded. "My pleasure." He put his jack stands in his truck and climbed into the cab. He drove almost to the main road, then stopped and got out. "Oh, Abby! Here's your keys." I jogged over to him and took my car keys, and waved as he drove away. I turned toward my car but glanced up as a pickup came rolling down the road. A fast-food bag flew out the passenger window and landed in the ditch.

"Hey!" I yelled as the truck drove away. "Hey! Get back here!" Another few pieces of trash flew out. Laughter, and a hand out the window, middle finger extended. The truck drove off in a spray of gravel. I opened my mouth to shout insults at them, but remembered I was supposed to be acting like a therapist. Representing the ranch. I kicked at the ground. Pigs. I walked to the barn for some gloves and a trash bag. I was so sick of cleaning up other people's messes! I should get a job where I could swear at people without worrying about maintaining an image. That would be a worthwhile career change. I should put that in the search engine for the temp agency and see what comes up. Meanwhile, I didn't want people bringing their kids to a place with garbage lying around. I stormed off to pick it up.

I woke in the darkness. I stared at the ceiling, gradually registering that I wasn't sleeping. Again. I rolled over to look at the clock. Two-thirty. I sighed and rolled back away, putting the glow of the clock behind me. I tried to breathe slowly. I willed myself to sleep, to relax, to not panic. I felt the familiar rise of anxiety. My pulse quickened. I struggled to breathe. I threw back the covers and bolted out of bed, wrapping my robe around me. I turned on a small lamp and sat listening to the growling and hissing of the electric kettle as my water heated. Footsteps sounded on the stairs. I started for the door, paused, grabbed my Maglite.

Max was rumpled—his clothing, his hair. His face looked tense, his eyes bloodshot and slightly swollen. He slowly blinked at me.

"Come in here," I said. "Come and sit down. I'm making tea."

"I saw your light." He glanced at the flashlight in my hand, but didn't say anything. "If you want to be alone, just say so. You don't have to always talk to me in the middle of the night."

I sighed. "I wasn't sleeping. You know." He did know. I could see that. "How long has it been since you slept a reasonable amount of time?"

He rubbed his face. "I haven't been that great at it for years, but now..." his voice faded away.

I took two mugs from the cupboard and dropped a lemon teabag in each. "I didn't think it was possible, but you look worse than I feel." I filled the cups and handed him one.

Max smiled slightly. "I feel even worse than I look. Thank you for this. And—I don't know. Thank you for all of this. I almost didn't come over here this time. I intrude too much. You listen to people's problems all day, then I come over here, a mess, dump on you in the middle of the night. Nobody sees me like this. Maybe I'm wrong to keep coming."

I shook my head slightly, tried a sip. It was too hot. "This is what we do, isn't it?" I blew on the tea, watched it ripple across the top. "We're all such a mess. We hold it together, and help people whose messiness comes out around the edges or blows out the center. Then we try to hold the mess for each other."

Max cupped his hands around his mug and shivered.

"You're too spent," I said. "We spend ourselves, and wonder why we're broke. Max, don't ever worry about being a mess around me."

Max's face was drawn. He looked strained. "I want to talk." He started with the smells. I hadn't expected that. He described assaulting odors. Stenches that revealed situations his eyes hadn't yet registered. Scents that transported him back. He talked for maybe fifteen minutes. Then it suddenly became overwhelming.

"This is bullshit!" Max smacked his hand on the table, a loud crack in the quiet night. "This is so damn stupid!" He launched out of the chair and stormed across the room, stopping to turn and glare at me. "I don't know what the hell I'm doing, listening to you!" He pointed a finger at me repeatedly, as if stabbing me with it. "You have no damn idea. You think there's some kind of touchy-feely bullshit going to make it all go away? The hell with you! You and your psychobabble crap! You think you can understand this?"

"No," I said quietly. "But I can hear you."

He radiated anger. We waited in silence. The tension level in the room gradually settled. Max leaned against the wall, sideways. He didn't want to look at me, but couldn't turn his back. Finally, he spoke. "I'm sorry." His voice sounded choked.

"Max, that was huge. You opened the door." I paused for a moment. "You know I'm not patronizing you. Opening the door is huge. Now you know at a gut level that you control it—you start, you stop. Next time you'll go into it knowing that. This is the beginning of not being all locked up anymore."

Max walked back to the table and sat down. "I'm sorry. I have no call to swear at you. I knew this was a bad idea."

"I've been cussed at by experts, Max. You barked at me. You didn't hurt me. And this wasn't unusual at all. Pretty often, when something powerfully emotional has been bottled up and you start to talk about it, it's like a boil being lanced, and a lot of ugly stuff comes pouring out."

Max pulled back a few inches in his chair. "That's the worst metaphor I've ever heard you use."

We sat, drank our lukewarm tea, looked at nothing together. Max drained his cup and set it down. "I'm just so tired. I feel like maybe I could sleep now."

"Maybe you should lay down on the couch," I said. "I'll give you a pillow and some blankets. Really. You walk out in that cold night air, you're going to wake yourself back up. Just crash here, and maybe we can both get a few hours."

He hesitated, then gave me an exhausted smile and a little nod. He stretched out on the couch, taking the pillow and blanket without comment.

I left my bedroom door ajar. The sound of his deep, even breathing calmed me. When I woke, the sun was bright in the windows.

Max left a pot of coffee, his blanket neatly folded on the couch. I threw on some clothes and poured myself a cup.

Max had the breakfast crew in the barn. He tried to smile. Uncomfortable, restlessly moving a rope around in his hands. "Thank you. Even if it was just a few hours, I haven't slept that hard in ages. Maguire—" His face compressed as if he were in physical pain.

I stepped in closer. "Listen. That all made total sense. The parts of the brain that process smell are also used to process emotion and memory. You see? Your brain is behaving in a reasonable way. Even if it's incredibly difficult."

He draped the rope over the fence, shrugged helplessly. Afraid to speak.

"No, that's good, Max. Your brain is trying to heal." I smiled, watching him struggle to balance embarrassment with a desire to be polite. "The actual brain isn't manly, macho, or a hundred percent self-reliant."

Max waved a hand in frustration, disgust. "Yeah, I know, I know. You break your leg, you get it fixed. I got that." He leaned over to spit on the ground.

"We're good, Max." I raised my mug in a toast, and walked into the office.

Walt blocked off the next day for a "staff mental health day," taking the horses to the state park to ride on the trails. Walt, Max, Ida, and I were off for the day. Ben stayed back. No one commented on him not really being staff.

"We'll trailer them in the morning," Ida said. "They all trailer really well, as long as you put them in the right order. Rosie does get a little cantankerous, so we plan for that." Points for not telling me, "The horse mimics the person."

I was excited to watch. I hadn't known 'trailer' was a verb, let alone how it worked. Max backed up to the barn, and one by one the horses were led in.

Quincy stepped right in without hesitation, and was secured in the first spot. Rebel took a few tries. Ida walked her in a circle and back to the trailer, where she put one hoof up and changed her mind, backing away. Ida didn't seem at all upset. After a few more approaches, Rebel stepped up with all four hooves and took her place by Quincy. Max brought Maverick out, and Maverick assumed his place as though he were in charge. He reasserted himself when Rosie stepped in, giving her a look.

"Wow," I said. "Did you see that?" Rosie did, that much was certain.

Max laughed. "That's why we put them in that order. Rosie's not gonna start anything with Maverick, and they both know it."

There was more carefree laughter than I'd seen since my first week on the job. It was nice to see Max and Ida excited. Even Walt was smiling. The energy level continued to grow as we led the horses back out of the trailer to saddle them.

There were tie lines, but we tied the horses to the outside of the trailer while we tacked them up. There were wheelbarrows and a designated manure dump. Max brought his own rake.

Max and Walt swung into their saddles from the ground. I took a breath, put a foot in the stirrup and copied them, heaving myself up and onto Rosie's back. I tried to look nonchalant.

Ida led Rebel over and climbed up on a picnic table bench to mount. No one cared in the least. "There are places here where we run them," Ida said. "They love it. We love it. It's a whole 'nother thing than the trails on the ranch."

"We'll let you know where we run." Walt turned in his saddle to make eye contact. "The horses know, and they'll start getting keyed up when we get close. We'll let you know for sure whether to let Rosie go or not."

Max also twisted around to face me, and grinned. "That's a fast horse you're on."

I narrowed my eyes at him. "There's no need for sarcasm."

Max laughed. "When I tell you to be ready, just be ready. Keep your balance, keep your hand firm on the reins, but let her have her head."

We walked through long stretches of pine woods, and prairies covered in tall grass, dotted with wildflowers. The sky was a deep, vivid blue. When we reached a creek, Ida circled Rebel a few times, coaxing her to walk on the wooden bridge. Ida laughed. "She doesn't like the sound of her hooves, echoing."

We came into an open meadow where the path widened, turning up a hill with clear sight lines. I could feel Rosie's energy building. She felt like she wanted to take off. Max turned in his saddle to look at me. "Are you ready?"

Rosie gathered herself under me, taking a deep breath. I relaxed the reins, and Rosie exploded. She flew into a gallop, flying past Rebel and Quincy, who were running full out. Ears pinned flat on her head, she pulled even with Maverick at the top of the hill. Walt let Maverick slow to a walk, then stop. He laughed as Rosie slowed slightly ahead of him, breathing hard.

I laughed too, from pure exhilaration. My heart was pounding, adrenaline coursing through my body. Walt turned and looked behind us. Max and Ida came trotting up from the rear and stopped.

"Oh, Lord," Ida said. "That was good!"

"I told you, you were on a fast horse," Max said.

"I thought you were being sarcastic! I thought she was the slowest horse on the ranch!"

Max grinned. "She's one of the fastest. She was slow because you were scared! She was taking care of you."

I looked down at Rosie, shook my head in disbelief. "She loves to run. I could tell. She moves slowly to take care of me?" I scratched Rosie's neck, astonished and grateful. "You've been keeping me safe, this whole time? I had no idea, Rosie."

Walt nodded. "Now you know her better. Now you know who you've been working with."

"Let's run again," I said. "I want to let her go."

We explored different trails, running at times. I was amazed at how the choppy, bouncy trot smoothed into a faster, flowing lope. Rosie clearly relished it. We gave the horses water and let them graze while we ate lunch, then took another ride before trailering the horses and heading for the ranch.

"This has been the most wonderful day," I said. "I think it's the first 'staff mental health day' that has ever made a real difference in my happiness."

"Me too." Ida was glowing.

Max and Walt seemed perfectly relaxed, the tension melted away. We turned the horses out, and carried the saddles back into the barn. Max grabbed a rake and a hose to clean out the trailer.

I trotted up the stairs. My door was unlocked. I been so excited earlier about watching horses being trailered. Did I forget to lock the door? I must have. I pushed the door open and peered in. I stood for a moment, listening. Nothing. Quiet.

I reached in and picked up my Maglite from the floor, gripping it tightly as I pushed open the bedroom door. Everything looked normal. I opened the closet, pushed aside the clothing. I knelt and looked under the bed. Should I have looked through the whole place first, before being on my hands and knees with my back turned? I was bad at this.

I held the flashlight in front of me like a club as I walked through the living room, and into the bathroom. Nothing looked out of place. I pulled the shower curtain aside. Nothing. I realized I'd been holding my breath. I stood for a minute, willing my heart rate to slow.

I went back to the kitchen and set down the flashlight. I felt a little lightheaded. I hadn't eaten much lunch, maybe a sandwich would help. I took the bread from the cupboard, and opened the refrigerator. There was a wrapper sitting in the middle of the top shelf.

An empty wrapper. From Max's cookies.

Chapter Nineteen

I stood, frozen. What?

Then my mind processed what I was seeing. A chill rippled over me. My heart started pounding. I couldn't breathe. Someone was here. The wrapper. Someone knew. My stomach tightened. Someone knew about the wrapper. And left one. For me.

I looked around wildly. There was no one here now.

I heard footsteps on the stairs. I didn't lock the door! I grabbed the Maglite, pressed myself back against the wall. The door opened.

"Hello! You up here?" It was Ida. I tried to answer her, but couldn't get words out. I walked to the doorway, shaking.

"Abby—" she stopped when she saw my face. "What is it?"

I pulled her in, closed the door and locked it. She followed me into the kitchen. "Ida. Someone was in here. The door was unlocked—I can't swear if I locked it this morning or not. Ida—" the words stuck in my throat.

She looked around. "What is it, Abby?"

I opened the refrigerator and pointed. Ida looked confused, then her eyes widened in comprehension. The blood drained from her face. "That was there?"

I nodded. "Ida. Someone knows."

Ida sank into a chair.

"Abby." She reached out for me, so I pulled up a chair and sat by her. "No one could know about that wrapper unless they were there. You're talking about a killer, Abby. You haven't told anyone?"

"No. You?"

She shook her head weakly, holding on to my arm. "What does this mean?"

I took a deep breath, blew it out slowly. "Everyone knows I found Mason. No one knows you took the wrapper, or even saw it. So, this isn't going to blow over onto you."

I thought some more. "The killer really can't know for sure that I saw it. He's guessing. There's no reason to think I even noticed it." I paused. "Unless he has access to police reports and knows it wasn't part of the crime scene."

I stopped again as that sank in. "This has to mean it was left in the tack room on purpose. What is that? Why would someone do that? I guess you talked about someone framing Max. It sounded unlikely."

Ida said nothing.

"They're assuming I at least saw it. There's no point leaving it in my fridge, if I wouldn't associate it with Mason being killed."

"Everyone knows you hate trash," Ida said. "If they expected you to find Mason, they could've left it for you in the first place."

My stomach clenched. I stopped breathing.

"Either Max or I was going to find him," I said. "That particular wrapper could've been a poke at Max, too."

That brought a few spots of red to her cheeks, a furrow to her brow. She would be angry for Max. We both needed to be angry.

"Alright." I stood. "I'm not cowering in here. I'm damn well not." I opened the fridge again and reached for the wrapper, then stopped. I really should call the police. But that would mean explaining the first wrapper, and where it was now. And how likely was it that someone would do this, and leave fingerprints? I grabbed a napkin and used it to pick up the wrapper, opened a drawer I rarely used and dropped it in.

Ida watched me. "What are we going to do?"

"We're going to think about this differently. This probably alters our suspect list."

"You should come home with me," Ida said. "You shouldn't stay here."

I hesitated. That sounded inviting. I blew out a breath. "I'm not giving them the satisfaction. This is my home. I'll just absolutely make sure I lock the doors. I may have gotten careless."

"Are you going to tell anyone about this?"

"Nope. If I don't react at all, whoever it is will get frustrated. Maybe they'll show their hand."

Ida shook her head. "I can't believe it's come to this. Please be careful, Abby."

I was cleaning up my lunch dishes when I heard a knock at the door. I looked up and hesitated—it was Luke. I waved him in, walking toward him, drying my hands.

He carried a duffle bag. "Hey, I'm just heading out for a run in the state park. You want to come? I heard you've been kind of stuck on the treadmill."

I blinked. "Wow. Word gets around."

"Just thought you might want to check out the trails in the park. There's some nice dirt trails, easy on the knees. Some woods, some prairie. You'd like it."

"The state park! I don't know why I never thought of that!" Did I really want to go running with Luke? How bad an idea was this?

He leaned over my garbage to spit out a wad of gum. He pulled a new piece out of his pocket, unwrapped it, stuck it in his mouth. I could smell it. Peppermint.

"I'm not real fast," I told him. "Seriously. You can probably walk as fast as I jog. Thanks, though."

He leaned against the counter, smiled. "I'm not doing speed training or anything. Just want to stretch my legs after a day of sitting in meetings. Come on, no judgement here. Really. We aren't feeling it, we can even walk up the hills."

I thought about heading out into a remote area, alone with Luke. He obviously knew everything going on around here. Maybe I could find out who he was talking to, getting reports from. What else were people telling him? He might know things no one wanted to tell me.

"Ok, you're on." I hung up my dish towel.

"Great! Do you mind if I change in your bathroom?"

"Feel free." I changed quickly and dug out a waist pack for my phone and keys. I added my ID and met Luke in the kitchen. I tried not to look at him in his shorts.

"Did you want to drive separately?" I asked. "You won't have to come all the way back out here."

"Nah, you can hop in with me. Then you don't have to pay." Luke wore a waist pack as well—a bulky one.

"Your pack looks heavy," I said. "What have you got in there, a water bottle?"

He hesitated, then unzipped it to reveal a handgun. He smiled with a shrug. "Just a habit, I guess. Never yet ran into a bear, but you never know."

I got a water bottle from the cupboard to buy myself a moment. He was running with a gun? That little revolver was not for bears, unless he just wanted to scare them off. "Did you want some water?"

He shook his head. "I threw a little cooler in the truck, with some cold drinks."

He planned this. What were we doing? I was hoping to grill him. What was he doing?

"Ok, just let me make a quick call. I was supposed to get back to someone, and never did." I dug out my phone and dialed Ida. I got her voice mail. "Hey, I know we talked about getting together this afternoon. Sorry I didn't call earlier. I just got a chance to go running out in the state park with Luke Morgan—he even packs heat for bear encounters! So, I'm going to do that. I've never run there—hoping I can learn something. Have a great rest of your day! Talk to you later!" I turned to smile brightly at Luke.

He studied me. "Who was that?"

"Oh, just Ida. We talked about looking over recipes or something. Ready to go?" I locked the door behind us.

"So," I said, as Luke pulled out of the driveway. "Were you just passing by today and decided to swing in?"

Luke grinned at me. "Well, I thought it might be nice to come by and see if you were interested. I know it's not a date, I got that, but it could still be fun."

"That was thoughtful. It kind of surprises me how often you're out at the ranch. Your folks aren't on intensive supervision, are they?"

"No." He shook his head. "Just makes it easy. I don't have to drive all over, finding people. Honestly, I'd rather not sit in the office all day. I probably see people more often than I'd need to, but it's better than losing track of them."

"Sounds like you don't lose track of much. Someone keeps you pretty well informed."

He gave me a side-eye. "Small community, Abby. People tend to talk."

I shifted my weight in the seat. "People talk a lot less since Mason was killed. I've really noticed that. People keeping to themselves, a lot more defensive."

Luke glanced at me. "Probably not surprising. You're still an outsider." He reached over and laid a hand on my leg. "I don't mean that bad. Just that you haven't been here that long." He patted my thigh, then put both hands on the wheel again. "So, how far are you thinking about going today?"

I paused a beat, cleared my throat. "I usually go anywhere from three to eight miles or so. But like I said, I'm slow, so if you want to do just a couple, that's fine too."

"There's a real nice trail in the back of the park. Quiet, hardly any traffic. Just under six miles. Want to try that?" Luke had a state park pass on his windshield, so we drove right past the office. He turned down a gravel road, past the main parking lots and trailheads. I didn't see any other cars.

"You must know this park well," I said. "Have you run here a lot?"

"All my life. I know all the places no one else goes." He slowed, pulled into a gap between two stands of trees, and parked on a grassy expanse hidden from the road. A chain link fence surrounded a small yard with equipment and piles of gravel. We climbed out of the truck, and Luke put his keys in his waist pack.

"You've never really seen a bear out here, have you? I've never heard of anybody running with a gun."

"I've seen them," he said. "Not up close. Thing is, out here, there's no one to rescue you."

I leaned against his truck to stretch out my hamstrings. Did I even have coverage out here, if someone tried to ping my cellphone to locate me? I pulled out my phone. Zero bars. Could they still do that? The phone company probably could. I put it back.

Luke was watching me. I smiled brightly. He led me into the woods, picking his way through pines and oak trees, until we came upon a trail.

"We can start running from here," he said. "The trailhead is back by the visitor center, but part of the trail washed out one spring, and they haven't repaired it." He pointed to the right, so we set off that way, jogging side by side. "When it gets narrow, you go on ahead of me. That way you can set the pace."

I loved the trail. Dirt and wood chips made a gentle surface, winding through the woods, opening into meadows. Squirrels rustled in the brush. We came to a break in the trees. I stopped to look at a ravine—I hadn't known it was there, behind the thick wall of pines. A creek ran through the bottom.

Luke stood beside me. I felt his hand on my neck, his thumb stroking my throat. I pulled back slightly. "Hey. Luke. Colleagues, remember?"

He smiled. "Yeah, that's right. You said that." He squeezed my shoulder, slid his hand onto my neck again. His fingertips reached halfway around my throat. I stepped away. His fingers brushed across my shoulder as I moved. "Ok, Abby," he said quietly.

"Let's just run."

Luke ran by my side for about a half mile, and the trail narrowed. He slowed and tucked in behind me. I could hear him breathing, hear his footsteps following me. "Your shoulders look tense," he said. "You'll get better form if you can shake it out."

We came to another clearing. I paused, pulling to the side. Luke massaged my shoulders. "You gotta loosen up. You run all tense, throw off your form, it impacts your whole body."

I exhaled. "You're right. Maybe I'm just having an off day. Maybe we should cut this short."

"You're doing fine. Just need to relax."

I rolled my shoulders. I should be making better use of this situation—not letting him keep me off balance. I started jogging again. A long, shaded stretch turned down into the ravine. "So, Luke," I said. "Why did you decide to become a probation officer?"

"I kind of fell into it. Majored in criminal justice, but didn't want to work in a prison, didn't want the shift work of being a cop."

The shade was cool. I felt goose bumps shivering up my arms. Worse, I realized I had to pee.

"How about you?" he asked. "You always want to be a therapist?"

"No. I guess I kind of fell into it, too."

"That's most people," Luke said. "No one really grows up wanting to be something and that's their career, anymore."

What was I going to do? On my own, I'd just pee in the bushes off the trail a ways.

"Now, it's more like life just happens," Luke said, "and you see where you end up."

Ignore it. Just keep going. "Do you like being a P.O.?"

"It's just a job. There's a whole lot more to life than just making sure felons behave. Hold up here a minute."

My bladder was getting more insistent. If I'd known I was going running, I'd have had less coffee.

Luke rearranged the pack on his waist. "It's rubbing wrong. Let me try to adjust something here." He probably wasn't used to running with a gun. I didn't want to think about that. "Ok," he said. "I'm good."

The trail was damp as the woods deepened. "People seem nervous about making you mad," I said. "Like they're afraid of getting violated."

"Nobody has to get violated."

I slowed to avoid stepping in a washout, and Luke bumped into me. His hand came up to my shoulder, then slid down to the small of my back. "Everyone knows what to do, to keep me happy. It's not that hard." Luke took hold of my arm. "Most of them are pretty motivated. Especially if someone's been to prison, you'd be surprised what they'll do to keep from going back. You seem tense again, Abby. You ok?"

I looked around at the bushes. "Luke, I'm sorry, but I have to pee. I didn't know I'd be running today."

He grinned. "No worries. Pick your side. I can just water the bushes on the other side."

I picked my way through the brush to a deep, thick circle of trees to hide behind. He would have to work at seeing me in here. I'd hear him coming. I paused, listening for footsteps. Then I quickly pulled my shorts to my knees, dropped to a squat, and finally relaxed my bladder.

Leaves crunched loudly behind me. Rustling—something big—exploding through the brush. I jumped, and pulled up my shorts, and spun to look, and tipped over sideways.

A deer. It crashed away, pushing off powerfully with its back legs, bounding through the bushes. The pounding of its hooves reverberated through the hard earth.

I exhaled, heart pounding. It was bedded down in the dense greenery. I startled it. I brushed myself off and finished peeing, not relaxing until my shorts were back where they belonged. The things men didn't have to worry about. "Are you decent?" I called through the bushes.

"All set!" Luke answered.

His eyes focused on my shorts as I walked out. I hoped I hadn't splashed on them when I jumped. This was ridiculous. I had to get out of here.

"That deer must've been right on top of you," Luke said. "That was pretty cool."

"I nearly had a heart attack." We settled back into a rhythm.

"You seem pretty interested in my caseload," Luke said. "Any reason?"

"I'm interested in a lot of things. Just how I'm wired. That's why I like temp jobs. I'm always curious about different walks of life."

Deeper into the ravine, the shadows. "So, you think my people are afraid of me?" Luke asked.

"Well, they must like you, or they wouldn't talk freely with you. It seems like you always know what's going on around the ranch. Sometimes more than I do."

He didn't say anything for several steps. "What do you think happened to Mason?" he asked. "Must've been kind of scary, finding him like that."

I hesitated. "It was awful."

"You think any of my people were mixed up in it, I hope you'd tell me. That's a little more than a violation. They'd have reason to be afraid of their P.O., wouldn't they?"

"I don't know what to think, Luke." That was certainly true. "Did you know Mason? Any idea what he could've been mixed up in?"

"People get mixed up in a lot of things, Abby. They don't always end up dead. I'd say he crossed a line. There's lines you don't cross.

Sometimes people don't know when to quit, leave well enough alone."

I couldn't think of a good response, so I ran in silence. Our shoes beat a dull cadence on the trail as we wound back up out of the ravine. I shortened my stride as the path steepened, but Luke stayed behind me. We broke out into bright sunshine, and I saw the equipment yard ahead. I hadn't realized we went in a circle.

Luke pulled up beside me as the path widened. "There we are. Nice run."

"It's beautiful out here," I said. "I wonder if it's really safer than the road."

Luke gave me a long look. We reached his truck, and I leaned against the tailgate, stretching my calves. Luke leaned beside me, his right arm straight against the truck. He reached around me, resting his left hand on the tailgate, trapping me in front of him. I twisted around to face him. I could smell his sweat, feel the heat from his body.

"Luke?"

"Do you feel safe, Abby?"

I blinked. "Could you please back up?" My stomach was tight.

He smiled, waited a few beats, then leaned in and kissed the side of my throat.

"Luke," I said. "There's lines you don't cross."

Luke grinned. He pushed off from the tailgate and walked toward the cab. "You're a cool one, Abby." He handed me a cold Diet Coke, and I drank it as we drove out of the park. We passed the main parking lot and I saw Ida's truck pulled to the side. She and Max were sitting in it—Ida pointed at us, and said something.

Luke didn't seem to notice them. Ida swung out of the lot and followed us.

Luke commented on a few passing vehicles. "I suppose you don't know much about trucks, what with driving a hatchback and all."

"You're right, I don't. Luke, I keep wondering what you meant, when you said it's surprising what people will do, to keep from going to jail?"

He gave me a sideways glance. "Pretty self-explanatory, isn't it?"

"Well, it's a curious thing to say. It shouldn't be surprising to remain law abiding, follow probation requirements. Is that surprising? Or did you mean something else?"

Luke paused, turned his head to look at me. "What would surprise you, Abby?"

How far should I go with this? I shrugged. "I don't know. I'd be very surprised if people did something illegal, thinking it would keep them out of jail."

He was silent for a few minutes, staring through the windshield, slowly drumming his fingers on the steering wheel.

I tried to look relaxed, feeling the tension emanating from Luke.

He glanced at me, back to the road. "You wanna be careful, talking like that, Abby. That's how rumors get started. Things take on a life of their own. You might want to watch yourself."

"Yeah, you're right. That was kind of a reckless thought."

He nodded.

"So, Luke, what is the most surprising thing you've ever seen someone do, to stay out of jail? Is it about acting out of character?"

Luke took a breath, blew out air through his nose. "Yeah, I prob-ably can't get specific. Confidentiality. No offense." He pulled up in the lot and I climbed out.

"You're fun to run with, Abby. Let's do it again."

I met his eyes. "If you could get the colleague thing, and keep your hands to yourself, it would be more fun."

He laughed. "See you around." He drove away, and Ida pulled in. She hadn't quite stopped when Max ejected himself through the passenger door.

Chapter Twenty

Max launched across the parking lot. "You—are you—" He strode up and glared at me, eyes shimmering with anger. "Do you—" He waved his hands in the air.

I started to feel guilty, seeing him so upset. "I'm sorry, Max. I was just trying to pick his brain."

Max's eyes bulged.

"You know," I said. "Interrogate him."

Ida joined us. She glanced at Max, then at me. "Abby, we were worried sick. Did he really have a gun? Did you see it?"

I nodded. "In his waist pack. He didn't seem like he was used to carrying it. After he showed it to me, he never pulled it out."

Max's mouth hung open. He closed it again, and shook his head as if he couldn't quite process what he was hearing.

"I was ok," I said. "The worst part was when I had to pee."

Ida gasped. "No! What did you do?"

"Well, I tried to ignore it as long as possible, but I couldn't take it anymore. I hid behind a bush."

Max spun on his heel and walked away. He stopped, hands on hips, and stared at the ground, breathing heavily.

"I'm sorry, Max. I really am." I looked at his back. "I didn't mean to worry you." I thought, somewhat randomly, about not having cell reception in the park. I wouldn't mention that. "He just stopped by unexpectedly, and wanted me to go for a run. There wasn't a whole lot of time to think."

Max blew out a long breath and put his hands to his temples.

I turned to Ida. "I just left you that message as a worst-case scenario kind of thing. So someone would know where I was."

Ida nodded. "That was smart." She glanced at Max. "He'll be ok," she whispered. "He was worried sick." She threw another quick look at Max, and leaned in. "Did you figure anything out?"

Max's back was still turned.

"I need to think about it. He's squirrelly, Ida. I think he's in this, waist deep. I have to process all the comments he made."

Ida straightened as Max turned and walked back to us. He gave me a long look, then shook his head again.

"Maguire, I swear to God. If you ever do this again." Without finishing, he turned and strode toward the house.

Ida nodded at me. "You think. I'll see you in the morning."

I walked into the barn the next day, to grab a rake. There was time to clear some trails. Walt saw me and came out of the office, carrying a halter and lead rope. His expression was dark, angry. I stopped in my tracks. Walt pointed toward the door with his head. "Come with me."

I followed him to the outdoor arena. He pointed with his head again. "Wait here."

"Okay." I smiled. Walt did not smile back. He walked out to the woods and came back with a big horse. Really big. I'd never worked with this horse—he intimidated me. In fact, I'd never seen anyone work with him.

Walt tipped his head toward the arena. "In there."

I swallowed, and obeyed. "What are we doing?"

Walt led the horse in, draped the loose end of the lead rope over the horse's neck and walked away. He stood outside the fence with his arms crossed over his chest, watching me with a steely gaze.

I glanced at the huge horse in the arena with me, and back at Walt. "What are we doing?" I repeated nervously.

"Walk him in a circle."

I eyed the horse. It snorted. I looked back at Walt. He still looked thunderous. I blew out air. "Ok." I walked up to the horse—it was even bigger up close. I reached for the lead rope draped over its shoulders. It turned and glared at me. I froze. I took a deep breath, and grabbed the lead rope. "Ok," I said. "Walk."

The horse leaned in with its massive head and shoved me, knocking me several steps sideways. I got my balance and looked at Walt in alarm. Walt didn't move.

"What are we doing?" I asked myself in a small voice. The horse was still glaring at me. I walked up to it again, moving my hand back up the rope. "Walk!"

The horse leaned in and smacked me with its thick neck, knocking me to the ground. I scrambled backwards away from it, and clambered to my feet. I looked at Walt. He was glaring at me. The horse was glaring at me. What was Walt doing? This was some kind of a test. I walked up to the horse again. The horse blew air from its nostrils. I hesitated, then grabbed the rope. "Walk."

The horse took a step, then another. I started to relax. The horse slammed its neck into me. I bounced on my butt and slid several inches in the sand. The horse stood, looking at me. I got up again, blinking back tears. I looked at Walt. He didn't move.

"I don't know what to do," I said.

"Walk him in a circle."

I walked up to the horse, and took the rope. I didn't even have my hands positioned properly before he swung his head and knocked me down again. I scrambled away and looked at Walt. "What are you going to let him do to me?"

Walt took a step forward and pointed at me. "What are YOU going to let him do to you?"

I hugged myself with my arms and looked at the horse, then back at Walt.

"You gonna let him do that?" Walt asked. "Who else are you letting do that? You need to figure this out, Abby, before you get yourself killed!"

Had Walt lost his mind? How could I figure this out? I walked up to the horse again. He planted his hooves. I took hold of the rope. "Walk!" The horse shoved me. I sprawled backwards, and pushed myself up from the dirt.

Walt climbed through the fence and stabbed his finger at me. "Tell me, who and what are you allowing to push you around? You re-enact your own life in this arena, Abby. How are you ignoring your own safety? How are you acting like it doesn't matter what happens to you?"

I bit my lip, rubbed my wrist where I'd landed on it.

Walt pointed at the horse. "Go ahead! Walk him in a circle!"

I didn't move.

Walt pointed at me again. "There's nothing wrong with your hearing! You hear and see better than most, until it's about you. What's it going to take? Go on! Walk him!"

I took a step back. "I don't want to do this."

Walt threw his hands in the air. "Good! It's about damn time!"

I was bewildered. "That was what you wanted?"

"Yes! I wanted you to damn well stand up and say no!" He put his hands on his hips and glared at me. "Now, horses establish dominance by who can move who around. You let it end there, letting him push you, you've established he has a right to." He stood, scowling, and watched me.

I looked at the horse, then back at Walt. How much did I care if a sixteen-hundred-pound horse I never intended to have anything to do with, thought it could push me around? I was absolutely not going to walk that stupid horse. I narrowed my eyes at the horse, then nodded.

"Alright," I said. "I get it." I walked over to Walt, put my hands on his chest and shoved him. He wasn't expecting it, and staggered several steps backwards. I turned and walked away, not letting Walt see my eyes widen in horror. What had I done? Did I just assault my supervisor? Great. Now I'd get fired. I climbed through the fence, and saw Max standing by a lean-to, watching. A surge of anger made my face hot. They were both in on it! Well, screw them. I turned and glared at Walt over the fence.

Walt was grinning widely. He laughed. "'Bout damn time."

I was done. I went up to my apartment and closed the door. I was pacing angrily when someone knocked. It was Max, glowering at me through the window. I opened the door, but stood in front of him. I narrowed my eyes, hands on my hips.

We glared at each other. He leaned in. "I can't protect you, if you won't cooperate!"

I held up a finger. "One: it is not your job to protect me." I added a finger. "Two: controlling me will not change or right anything that happened in the past."

Max's eyes bulged. "*Cont*—I'm not controlling you!"

"No, and that's driving you crazy, isn't it?"

He turned and stormed out, slamming the door behind him.

I locked it. I went to the kitchen to rant at Papa. "He is going right back to the top of the suspect list! If he thinks he can resolve his survivor's guilt by turning into Super Alpha Male and defending his turf at all costs, there's no telling what he might do! And I am damn well not his turf! Excuse my language."

I was apologizing to a photograph. "This is what it's come to!" I kicked a chair leg. "And I don't trust Walt either, if he thinks he can toy with people, the ends justify the means, even if someone gets hurt. I trust zero people here. Zero. None." I rubbed my temple. "And I have a killer headache coming on!" I winced at my own words.

"And my wrist hurts! And Ida's weird when it comes to Max, and I'm not even sure I want to know why. They could all be in on it—there is no doubt whatsoever that they would cover for each other. I've got to get out of here. I don't even know why I think I can never leave a job early. I just made that rule up. I can't even take a nice, relaxing job without people trying to kill me! What's wrong with me? Why do I always land in it?"

I kicked the garbage can. "And Ben! He's a liar from day one, whatever his deal is! An ex-fed could be a mercenary as easily as anything else! He's probably the killer himself, prowling around to find whatever it is, before anyone else does! Or maybe he's not an ex-fed. Maybe he's a fed wannabe who washed out of spy training and never got over it! And now I've rubbed his face in it by calling him a fed! He'll probably kill me in my sleep! Luke is a creepy freak, but he is not the only one! Far from it!"

I was suddenly exhausted. Drained. I didn't even want to be here. Maybe I should go get a motel room for the night. I grabbed my purse and opened the door. Max and Walt were standing in the parking lot, talking. I closed the door.

What could I do? My world was effectively shrunken. I couldn't go for a run outside, and I was not going to Max's treadmill. There was no one here I wanted to talk to. There was no one I wanted to call, either. How had it come to this? It wasn't as if I had no friends. I just wanted to go home, but no such place existed. I opened my laptop to get caught up on my billing. I was here to do a job. I could by God do that. I could do it well, and then I could get the hell away from here.

I woke in the night, but I didn't turn on the light. I didn't want to talk to Max. I sat in the dark, and wondered if he was wandering around down there, thinking about other night patrols in other places. Or thinking about the entertainment value of watching me get shoved around by an animal that weighed fourteen times as much as me. I went back to bed and pounded my pillow into shape. Max could stay in the dark.

I was relieved to see my morning schedule was with Ida. I pasted a smile on my face. My voice was friendly and encouraging. After our client drove away, Ida pulled me into the break room. "Sit down," she said. "You seem tired."

I sat, but didn't say anything.

She poured water into the coffee maker. "You're quiet today."

I rubbed my temple, where another headache was forming, and debated how to respond. Clearly there was a question there, but "Walt is a jackass" wouldn't satisfy it.

Ida watched me. "The horses, though, they didn't seem to respond like you were low energy, dragging. If anything, they seemed like maybe you were a little agitated inside."

I sighed. It came out as a growl. I shook my head. "No, Walt is right. Maybe I am being too passive. Why should I let people push me around? Why should I retreat into a shrunken, tiny world? Why should I always be in observation and reaction mode? I should be more aggressive." I nodded to myself. "I should go kick the damn hornet's nest open and see what comes out. If I can find it. If I even know it when I see it."

Ida studied me dubiously. "Walt told you that? What exactly did he say?"

I frowned, sat back in my chair. "He put me in with a monster horse that kept slamming into me, knocking me down. He wasn't happy until I refused to listen to him."

Ida arched her eyebrows, and took two mugs from the cupboard. "I bet that wasn't the message he had in mind."

I certainly wasn't going to tell her that Max was in on it too, standing there watching me get bashed around until I got scared. Max was Ida's golden boy. All hail Max.

I realized I sounded like Jared. What was wrong with me? I didn't like feeling scared and helpless. I wanted to lash out. What did I care, anyway? I was here for a couple of months. I never had to see these people again. Unexpected, hot tears welled up in my eyes. This was infuriating. I blinked angrily, and then everything got immeasurably worse.

Walt was leaning in the doorway. Listening. I closed my eyes and put my forehead on the table.

I heard the scraping of chair legs on the wood floor. I turned my head and squinted. Walt and Max were both sitting across from me. I closed my eyes again. This was turning into a nightmare. And here I was, being passive. What could I do? Pick up my chair and throw it at them? I might enjoy that, for thirty seconds. I sat up and opened my eyes. Walt had a kind look on his face, damn him. Max at least didn't look all compassionate. He looked annoyed.

"Maguire, you want to get out of your head and talk to us for a minute?"

Good. We could argue. I narrowed my eyes at him.

Walt interrupted. "Abby. You know I was not setting you on a course of self-destruction. That's the exact opposite of what I was trying to do."

I looked around at the three of them. "Is this an intervention?"

"You need one," Max said. "Walt was just trying to get you to stop putting yourself in danger."

I glared at him. "You were a lot of help. You do that with all your therapists? You realized it was Beat the Therapist Up with a Horse Day, and grabbed a good seat?"

Max glared back. "I've never seen him do that before. He cares about you, Abby. We both do. We don't want to see you get hurt because you put no value on your own safety! Now you're mad, you want to go down fighting. Maybe you don't have to go down. Did you ever think of that?"

I scowled. He should talk. Fighting is better than feeling, isn't it, Max? I didn't say it out loud, didn't want to throw that in Max's face. What was wrong with me, that I always pulled my punches?

Walt saw me do it. He met my eyes, acknowledging that I sheathed my sword. "We get out there with clients, we need to always remember this is painful," Walt said quietly. "It hurts, pulling that shrapnel out."

No one said anything. I stared at the table. Ida set cups in front of us, breaking the tension. She poured the coffee. I picked mine up and tasted it. It was terrible. This is what it's come to. I took it with me anyway, and went in the office to do my documentation. No one spoke to me for the rest of the morning. I wasn't sure if they were angry, or giving me space.

Ida and I had more sessions in the afternoon, but she acted like nothing happened. I saw her watching me a few times, but she didn't comment. Staying out of it, I supposed. I didn't blame her.

I managed not to think about it until I tried to sleep that night. Then I couldn't stop thinking. I knew perfectly well what Walt intended. Obviously, I got his point. And somehow, Walt seemed to get the deeper point. He could see me.

I looked at Papa and thought about climbing into his car that first time, just a scrap of a thing, all bony elbows and skinned knees and tangled hair. Navigating a whole new world. Trying to be good. Trying to be perfect. A scared little girl, trying to make the world safe. Never understanding that a child can't make the world safe.

I still couldn't make the world safe. I saw that now, saw myself. I picked up Papa's picture, dusted it. Held it and touched his face. I'd gotten into such a habit of trying to make the world safe, before I really knew for sure that he was my safe world.

And Max was at the door. I let him in, but without the usual smile. He sat at the table, and I set a mug in front of him. I heated water for tea. "You remember that old show, Grizzly Adams?" I asked.

Max blinked slowly. "Yes." He picked up his mug, examined it, turned it over in his hands. "Guy lived out in the woods with a bear?"

"Right." I nodded. "I've been thinking about what I'll do from here if I give up trying to make the world safe."

Max set his cup down. "You wanna go live with a bear?"

I shrugged. "Maybe."

"Sometimes," Max said, "I come up here at night, I feel like I'm still dreaming."

I leaned back against the sink, studied the floor. "You get mauled by a bear, you probably should've seen it coming. It's a bear. It's what they do."

Max didn't speak for a long moment. "Maguire," he finally said, "I'm sorry. We weren't trying to make you feel hurt or betrayed. We just want you to care if something bad happens to you."

I ripped open a couple of tea bags, threw them into our cups, and poured the steaming water over them. I sat down in front of Max. Neither of us spoke. I fingered the little paper tab stapled to the string of my tea bag. "Yeah. I get it."

He nodded. We listened to the old barn creaking in the wind.

"Maybe I always knew I couldn't make anything safe," I said. "Maybe that's what the dream is about. When a co-worker turns their back, and I can't get there. Can't move. Can't save them."

Max froze. I'd struck a nerve. There were ghosts reflected in his eyes.

"But here's the thing, Max." I tugged the string up and down in my cup, sending dark plumes of tea through the water. "I really was creating safety, for a minute. Being a safe place. For long enough to take a breath. Some of the kids, they actually thanked us for restraining them, for keeping them safe while they lost control. Losing control was so scary for them." I set down my mug. "This one girl, I can still see her pushing back her wispy blond hair, tucking it behind her ear. Got her alone, away from an audience, she told me, 'We don't treat you guys bad because we hate you. We do it because we know you won't hurt us.' Like they felt compelled to prove to themselves that there was such a thing as safety in the world, so they could keep trying to live."

Max sat back in his chair. He didn't say anything.

"And all those kids," I went on, "who witnessed the explosive behavior, listened to the physical restraints, all the screams, and needed to say out loud that they were scared. Or the ones whose homes were raided by police the night before—the twelve-year-olds, thirteen-year-olds, who sat at gunpoint while their homes were searched. At gunpoint, Max. Because the adults couldn't get it figured out. The kids who saw violence, even death, and just got packed off the next day, but couldn't sit still, couldn't focus, and people think they're just being bad again. They all came to me, Max. The office space changes from one job to the next, but the need to be seen and heard never changes. Never changes, Max. The need for a safe person."

I shook my head to clear it. "I still see their faces. Some of them gave words to such unspeakable things, the images from those words are still vivid, years later. But they were able to speak them. For a minute, they mattered."

Max reached across the table and put his hand over mine. He sat with me, quiet.

"I don't know what to do. I can't be that person anymore, Max." I felt tears welling up in my eyes. "I hope they find a new one. I hope they find someone. I hope they're safe."

Max stood, and pulled me with him to the couch. We sat, and he held me, my head on his shoulder. He never spoke. Neither of us knew what to say. I buried my face in his neck, and we sat through the darkness.

Chapter Twenty-One

I was cleaning the kitchen the next morning, putting away dishes, when Walt showed up. He knocked, and waited for me to open the door. He met my eyes, neither of us smiling. "You told me once that there was always coffee."

I stood back to let him in, then waved a hand toward a kitchen chair. I measured water into the carafe.

Walt set his hat on the table, settled his weight back in the chair, stretched out his legs and studied me. "I need for us to work through this, Abby."

I sat across from him, gave him a direct look. The coffee maker gurgled behind me—the soundtrack of my life. "Here's the deal, Walt. Yes, that was very effective. As an intervention, yep, totally cut to the chase. 'Where else in your life are you just doing things that you think are a bad idea, and probably not in your own best interest? Where else are you just waiting to see how far someone will go, instead of protecting yourself?' All right. I get it."

I leaned back in my chair, started to stretch my legs out, then realized I was mirroring him. I leaned forward again. Damned if I was going to be the client mirroring the therapist. "But there's a cost. There's a cost-benefit analysis here. Because now I can't trust you. I am completely out of my element in this place. You're the expert—and my direct supervisor. I'm supposed to be able to rely on you."

Walt nodded. "That is a high cost. I'll accept that. And I might regret it, if I hadn't believed your life could be at risk. I'm sorry you are hurt, Abby, but I will not apologize for trying to wake you up. A man died on this ranch. In my barn. A man I knew, an employee of mine, lost his life. By a deliberate action, and I don't know who took his life or why. If I lose you as an employee, as a co-worker, as a friend, but you keep your life, I'll accept the loss."

I stood up and took some mugs out of the cupboard, setting them by the coffee maker. I leaned back against the counter, crossed my arms. "So, what do you want? What are you looking for?"

"I will not have you using yourself as bait to catch a killer. I won't have it."

I thought about that. Looked at the coffee to see if it was done. Looked at Walt's hat on the table. "I wasn't using myself as bait. I was trying to figure things out."

Walt sighed. "Abby, I am completely overstepping now. I'm not speaking as your employer. If you want me to stay in that box, let me know, but I've grown fond of you. If it were Ida or Max, I'd speak up."

I poured a cup of coffee and set it in front of him. He nodded, picked it up, smelled it. He took a small sip and sighed. "As a friend, Abby, I note that your papa's passing was only a year ago. I wonder if you don't quite have your feet under you."

I sat down.

"I'm sorry you lost him. Do you think that's what you're tripping over?"

I reached for my empty coffee cup. Looked inside, as if it might be hiding an answer, or an escape. "I don't know. I used to be better. At everything."

"You know you don't need to grieve and be perfect, all at the same time? Way you talk about him, I bet your papa didn't expect you to be perfect."

I shook my head. "He never did." I turned my empty cup in my hands, thought about getting up to fill it, but didn't. "I never had to achieve anything, for his approval. He wanted me to enjoy life, more than he wanted me to prove anything to anyone."

Walt set down his coffee. "I wonder if perhaps losing your papa has made you feel a bit like you felt, before you had him." He tilted his head in a shrug. "Your nomad lifestyle probably felt somewhat different when your papa was your home."

We were silent. I could hear horses moving around outside, their nickers in the woods. I heard a gate clanking shut. Voices by the parking lot. I couldn't make out what they were saying. An airplane hummed overhead, grew louder, then faded.

"I was four years old," I said. "I remember very little from before I was with Papa. Except immediately before, which I remember vividly. No one could decide whose problem I was, but they all knew I wasn't their problem, they had enough problems." I thought about the relatives on the phone, in the kitchen, in the yard, reminding each other I wasn't their problem. I was so surprised and saddened to learn about this. I hadn't known I was a problem.

"Then Papa drove up, put me in his car, and we drove away, and then I was his. But not his problem." I tilted my head in acknowledgment. "You're right about that, though—Papa was my home. I never did the math to figure out how old he was when he became a single parent to somebody else's four-year-old girl, but he never once acted like I was a problem."

We sat quietly again, Walt with his coffee, me with my empty cup. I was thinking about Papa. I didn't know what he was thinking about.

He took a breath. "Abby, you may see yourself as just a temp worker that we'll forget about as quickly as you came, but you're not. It appears to me that you are treating yourself as though you are disposable. And I wonder if somewhere inside, you believe that being with your papa was the only thing that made you not be disposable."

He waited, but I had no response. Walt's phone buzzed in his pocket. He ignored it. "It's obvious from how you talk, that your papa made you feel valued. Just don't convince yourself that your only value was with him." He took a deep drink of his coffee, signaling that he was done talking.

We sat and looked at each other over the table. "I'm not sure where to go from here," I said.

"Can we work together effectively?"

"Absolutely."

Walt set down his cup, acknowledging the quickness of my answer with a grim smile. "You are nothing if not professional. I've no doubt you will continue to be professional, and fulfill your obligations. I rather hope we'll be friends." He stood, picked up his hat, and walked to the door.

"Walt."

He stopped, turned.

"There is always coffee for you. Any time."

He nodded, and left.

Ida came in as I was tacking up Rosie, and called across the barn. "Hey, Sunshine. What you up to?"

"I'm just going out for a thinking ride, Ida. Come with me."

She nodded. "Hold on while I go get Rebel."

We brushed and saddled Rebel together, and rode out quietly. The woods were cool, a slight breeze rippling the trees. Birds were singing, trilling, whistling— different songs overlapping, all around us. We rode into an open bit of field, where killdeers ran through the grass, and over the dirt. I decided we were far enough away from the barn. "We shouldn't assume the sabotage is connected to the murder."

Ida said nothing for seven or eight hoofbeats. She turned in her saddle to look at me. "Well, it has to be, doesn't it?"

"It could be separate. Or, maybe the resulting tension escalated something else."

"You think you know what's going on?"

Rosie stopped and reached down to nibble at her leg, scratching an itch. I loosened her reins, giving her freedom of movement. "Ida, the last time I knew what was going on, I was somewhere around Lake Michigan. But I can't come up with anyone that makes sense for the sabotage, other than Jared."

Ida stared at me, waiting for Rosie to walk on. "How does that make sense?"

"I can't find anyone else with ability and opportunity. Especially with Max prowling around continuously. It's either Max or Jared, and it's not Max."

"But, *Jared*?"

"At first, I thought it was so he could get paid to fix things, after he broke them. Then, I thought it was swings of disordered thinking, from drug use. But then I thought about how angry he is, how he feels like Walt and others here think he's stupid. Look down on him. Max is exalted, and he's excluded."

I held up a hand as she opened her mouth to protest. "All I'm saying is, he thinks it's true. Right or wrong, that's how he feels. And not only that, but he feels somehow vindicated. By what? 'Who's the smart guy now?' That's vindication. That's 'See, I did something.' So, what did he do? If he's been leading Walt and Max on a merry chase, watching them tear their hair out, now he's the smart one and they can't keep up."

Rosie started walking again, and Rebel joined her. Ida stared silently ahead. I waited for her to respond. "Abby," she said, "that makes me incredibly sad. That's not how we are, here. That's not *who* we are." She looked away. "It's not who we mean to be."

The horses' hooves were rhythmic in the quiet pasture, like heartbeats on the dry ground. Killdeers sounded shrill cries of alarm, announcing our approach. The sunshine was warm on my skin, my legs feeling the heat through my jeans.

Ida stopped Rebel just before the land bridge over the culvert. She set the reins down across Rebel's neck and turned to face me.

"I'm sorry to say, that does make sense. That's why there was no answer—we didn't want to see the only answer there was."

Rebel grazed, cropping the grass. I lowered Rosie's reins so she could do the same. They moved slowly, finding slightly longer patches here and there. I registered that I was not afraid, letting Rosie drift around unpredictably. I was getting my legs under me.

"But what about Mason?" Ida looked tired. "What about that wrapper, you getting shot at?"

I shook my head. "I can't conceive of a way that's all Jared. Maybe the murder, but not the psychological taunting. I mean, he was in the army, so I'm sure he knows how to shoot, but it just doesn't feel right. It's someone else."

"People around here often grow up knowing how to shoot," Ida said. "Whether they hunt or not. Boys and girls."

"So, motivation. Looking at ability is a non-starter. Or, with mental health, we often ask what changed? What happened that made things go sideways?"

"What made Jared start using, after all those years of being clean?" Ida shrugged. "If he is, in fact, using again. We may never know why."

"Every time I try to talk to him, he gets suspicious," I said. "I wonder if anyone else would know?"

Ida crossed her arms over her chest. She had absolutely no concern for her reins. I was still holding onto mine, however loosely.

"Abby, do you think we should say something to Walt and Max? About suspecting Jared?" She made up her mind while I thought about it. "I'm telling Walt. We can at least awaken him to the possibility. Maybe the sabotage is over, but if it's not, we need to be on top of this." She hesitated. "Say, just so you know…"

I watched her fuss a bit, search for words. "What?"

"Well, Max's ex? She already got married." She shook her head, tsked loudly. "He's well rid of her, you ask me. But in case he's upset."

I gaped at her. "It's been five minutes! Do you think he and Max overlapped, or did she just up and marry a co-worker?"

"I don't know. In the end, I don't suppose it matters. I just thought you should know."

We heard someone coming, and looked back. It was Ben, on Lucy.

"Here comes the fed," Ida said. I didn't have a chance to respond before he caught up to us.

"Hi there! What are you two so serious about, out here?"

"Oh, nothing," Ida told him. "Just giving the girls some fresh grass before we finish our ride." If he wanted to get anything out of Ida, he'd have to work harder than that. He could join us, but if he hoped to learn anything, he would be sorely disappointed.

The break room was crowded. A sizable trail ride was scheduled, with many hands to do the work. Arms crossed, Rodney leaned his back against the wall. "Somebody else go get Sally Mae. I hate that damn horse."

Max gave him a side glance. "That's a good horse."

Rodney scoffed. "Her and Rosie. They're both such damn mares."

I glared at him. "Don't call her that! I hate it when you use 'mare' as an insult."

"What you want me to say? You rather I call her a bitch?"

"I can't help but notice when a male horse is cranky, everyone thinks there must be something wrong. He's trying to communicate something! Or else it's an individual quirk. When a female horse is cranky it's because she's a mare! Even if the vast majority of the mares here are sweet and patient, everyone knows mares are cranky! Of course they are! They must be! They're mares!"

Rodney waved his hand in the air as if I were a gnat.

"Maybe you can't catch Sally Mae because you don't like her," I said. "Everybody knows that, do you think *she* doesn't?"

He stabbed a finger at me. "You don't know nothing about horses!"

This irritated me coming from his mouth, even if it was true. "Here's what I'd like to know. Why is Rosie terrified of you? What's that about, Rodney?"

The room went silent. Every head swung around to look at him.

Rodney turned and stomped out of the room. He glanced back at me from the doorway. "Bitch."

Max stood up. "I'll get Sally Mae." Seconds later, the sound of raised voices came in from the arena.

I stuck my head out. Max and Rodney were face to face, shouting, sticking their fingers in each other's faces. I sighed. I should not have started this.

"I'll call her what I want! It's the damn truth!" Rodney stormed out to the parking lot and climbed into his truck.

Max stalked over to grab a lead rope and halter.

I was too embarrassed now to look at anyone. I went to the tack room and lugged out saddles. Someone else brought out brushes. Ben swung into full ranch hand mode, carrying saddles, bringing in horses. Give him credit, he was all in. Everyone got busy. No one looked at me.

Walt and I finished a morning session, and moved into the break room. Ida dug in her purse, fussed. Walt stopped on his way to the refrigerator, and studied her. "You all right there, Ida?"

She tsked, shook her head, bent over her purse. She looked like one of her chickens pecking for a piece of corn. "Well, for heaven's sake, I can't find my keys! I always put them in the same place in my purse, for exactly this reason. Oh, Lord, help."

Walt raised his eyebrows, but said nothing, and opened the fridge.

"Oh, well here they are. Thank heavens. I must've stuck them in the wrong compartment, although why I'd do that, I have no idea. I must really be getting old." She left, with a smile and a wave.

Walt set a Diet Coke in front of me. He sat down across the table, leaned back, and put his feet up on the chair beside him. He popped open a can. "So, Abby, why's that mare thing bother you so much?"

I sighed. "I'm sorry if I made a problem for you there. I don't need to be bickering with volunteers."

"That was a real question, though." He shrugged. "I really was wondering why it gets under your skin."

I put my own feet up. "I hate it when people use female as an insult. Men mock other guys by calling them 'girls, ladies. Are you having a tea party?'" I did air quotes, with the appropriately sarcastic tone of voice. "It's just like every time a guy's asked me if I was on the rag because I called him out on anything. Or when men ask if it's that time of the month, any time a woman raises a complaint, or just isn't submissive and docile." I scowled. "And there's no equivalent for being so arrogantly dismissive to a man. No one would ever tell a guy who was angry about something, he must have jock itch."

Walt smiled. "Folks often forget we're talking mares versus geldings. Castrated males. Add in a couple stallions, suddenly mares aren't the problem. You're going to keep hearing it, though. That's a common theme in a lot of the horse world, mares being thought of as difficult."

"In a lot of the *world*." I took an angry swig.

He put his feet on the ground. "Let's go finish that arena. Might's well clear up the crap we can, before our meeting."

Staff meetings were not as much fun as they used to be. The ride at the park had helped, but tension settled over the ranch like a fog that clouded the windshield each time it was wiped away. Max sat with his feet poised under him, ready to spring from his chair if his constantly moving eyes landed on a threat. Walt was settled back, quietly watchful. I had an image of a couple of junkyard dogs—a younger, leaner one running with lightning speed toward an intruder, the older, stockier one sauntering along behind, ready to rip someone's throat out. I shook my head to clear it. That was awful. What was wrong with me?

All the same, maybe I should add a profound lack of situational awareness or a blinding degree of pride to the composite picture of who we were looking for. Who would take these guys on, threaten them on their own turf? We should be thinking about that. I made a mental note to bring this up to Ida, and realized everyone was looking at me. I blinked. "I'm sorry. What was that?"

Max shook his head. "Honestly, Maguire."

Walt smiled kindly. "Max has been telling Ida and me, when we have time here and there, about the things you've been teaching him about trauma, PTSD, how it affects people."

Ida nodded. "Like when people have a huge reaction to something that doesn't seem like that big of a deal, they might be reacting to something prior, we may not know about."

"Well, that's exactly right," I said. "While other people have numbed their emotions, so they can keep going. They might under-react to situations that really are dangerous or significant."

Max snorted.

I raised my eyebrows at him. "Excuse me?"

He shook his head, raised a hand in a "don't mind me, just carry on" gesture. "Not like we know anybody who does that."

I narrowed my eyes at him.

Walt interrupted. "It's good for us all to keep learning. Abby, I appreciate you bringing your experience to what we do here. As we go on, I'd like you to help us all with these things. Now, let's take a look at the next week or so."

Max gave me a side-eye, one eyebrow raised snidely. I squinted at him, but we both turned to Walt. Class was called to order.

Chapter Twenty-Two

The volunteers were using every loud tool they could find. The skid loader growled away. Someone had a chainsaw. The Kubota dragged the pasture to gather dried manure.

I put on my gun range headset and went down to the barn to grab a rake and help clean out stalls. David looked at me and said something. I pulled the headset away from one ear. "Sorry, what?"

He smiled. "You shoot? I hadn't heard that."

"No," I said. "I got them when I worked in a nursing home. I'd wear them when Jeopardy was on."

David grinned. "Well, listen. Several of us shoot together. Friend of a friend has a range set up on his property. You're welcome to come out tonight, if you'd like."

"I don't have anything to shoot."

"I have several firearms, if you'd like to try your hand at it." David held up his hands. "No pressure, really. Purely for enjoyment. Group bonding, as it were. Just let me know before I leave, I'll give you directions."

I found Max in the office, and sat down next to him. "Is this a bad idea? David invited me to come out with a bunch of people, shooting. Like team-building. Tonight. What do you think?"

Max sat up from his paperwork and studied me. "I think we've made a hell of a lot of progress, if you're asking my opinion instead of going off half-cocked." He raised one eyebrow. "Do you want to go?"

I shrugged. "I like doing new things. David seems nice. Might be fun?"

Max nodded. "Well, you're not going by yourself. I'll go with you. Guy that owns the place is a good friend of mine, actually. Consider me your shooting buddy. We breathe the same air, all night long. Alright?"

I smiled. "Perfect. I'll tell David."

Max and I rode together in his truck. Max pulled into the long, gravel driveway without hesitation. The home of an old service friend, he explained.

The range was a brightly painted, eight-by-ten wooden backstop. Behind it were stacks of tires two layers deep, filled with dirt, and beyond them a low-lying marshy area. In front of it, a small shelf sat under the empty frame of an old metal swing set. The ground was nicely covered with wood chips.

About a dozen people were gathered, comparing weapons. Everyone had ear protecting headsets. A handful of children wore little colored headsets and small plastic safety glasses. I wondered if whoever shot at me when I was running might be here. I'd never know it. Or the person who shot Mason before clubbing him in the head, although I wasn't supposed to know about that. I wondered if Max knew about it. Maybe this wasn't a good idea. I took a step closer to Max.

"Turner!" Our host hustled out and wrapped Max in a muscly hug. "Damn! Good to see you! Didn't know you were coming out." He eyed me with speculation.

"Vig, this is Maguire," Max said. He didn't specify our relationship. Vig clearly wanted to know.

Vig put his left hand on my shoulder. "Glad to have you, Maguire." His right hand was in a cast—the kind of cast I'd seen on boys with boxer's fracture, from punching walls. I wondered what Vig hit, and why he hadn't used proper alignment to avoid injury. Whether he'd been messing around, or angry. Whether alcohol was involved.

"Thank you for having me." I smiled warmly.

Vig hugged Max again, slapped his back, and wandered away.

Max brought two different sized handguns and what seemed like an awful lot of ammo. "It goes fast," he said. "You'd be surprised." He showed me how the cartridges slotted into the magazine, and how the magazine snapped into the butt of the pistol.

I didn't think the first gun looked that big. "That's nice. It probably recoils less? I don't want to look stupid."

"This is a compact 9mm," Max said. "It's actually going to have more of a kick than this full size one. The larger weapon absorbs more of the energy, so you feel less of it. You can try them both out."

I recognized several faces from the ranch. Rodney pulled up after us, with Janice in the passenger seat. David walked over and talked through the window. Rodney backed out and drove away. Max shook his head.

"What was that?" I asked.

"They're felons," Max said. "Can't be around firearms. And both on probation. David shouldn't have to enforce that. That's ridiculous, showing up and putting him in that position. Vig doesn't likely know, but he'd be pissed if he found out. He runs a clean place."

"Max, Janice made a big deal out of getting off probation. She's got five years hanging over her. Why would she risk a violation for something like this?"

"Good question. And I just heard Rodney telling someone he had one week left before he's off paper—so close he could taste it. So go figure."

Everyone seemed genuinely glad to see us. Max was relaxed, even happy. Camaraderie looked good on him.

David went first, aiming at paper targets duct taped to the backstop. No one said anything about Vig not shooting, with his hand in a cast. People went in turns, some taping up targets, others placing cans on the little shelf. They bent down in the grass, picking up empty cartridges that came flying out to the side. I got into a rhythm of wearing my hearing protection when someone was shooting, and pulling it off one ear for conversations.

A few people brought full soda bottles, which were hung from the frame to dangle or swing. Everyone cheered when people hit their targets, and laughed when carbonated bottles exploded. I found myself laughing and cheering with them. A bottle of water became a fountain, with multiple streams flowing from the sides. One person put a small, round watermelon on the shelf. It blew apart in a spray of juice and rind that covered the backstop and the ground.

The children seemed completely familiar with their boundaries. They waited obediently for their turns to shoot rubber band guns—a few older kids had BB guns. The parents helped their children with proper stance, safety, and etiquette. How to hold their toy guns and aim at the targets, how to respect weapons and other people.

I stood in the hot sun, on the dusty ground, holding a cold soda and an ear of fire-roasted sweet corn. I felt a familiar sense of amazed gratitude that I always experienced when being welcomed into another culture—especially the more intimate aspects of a culture. "This is our home, our food. This is how we teach our children."

Max got into a friendly competition with Vig's wife —both had vastly better marksmanship than anyone else. When he beat her by an edge, they did high-fives and hugged each other. I hadn't been sure what to expect—maybe a bunch of armed whackos—but this was the most deliberately careful, reasonable group of people I could imagine, and possibly the nicest. Certainly, the most welcoming.

"Ok, Maguire," Max said. "You're up."

"Oh boy."

"Don't worry," Vig said. "You're among friends. No one's judging here."

They all settled back to watch. I heard soda cans cracking open. Someone brought out a bag of chips.

Max showed me how to hold a handgun, starting with the compact. "Here's the safety." He showed me how the lever flipped. "This is the slide—you pull it back and let it go forward again, that puts a round in the chamber. Hold your index finger straight until you're ready to pull the trigger—don't put your finger on the trigger before you're ready to shoot. Now, you can use your other hand to steady it, like this. You are gonna get some recoil here, so don't be surprised by the kick. Just relax, aim where you want to hit, and squeeze." He pointed it at the ground while someone put up a target. When the range was clear, he handed the gun to me, turning to walk away.

"Stay here," I said.

He laughed and stood near me. "Alright. Give it a try."

I exhaled, and tried to stand right. They all had such a relaxed confidence, when it was their turn. I tried to look relaxed and confident. I pointed at the target, blew out air, and squeezed. Nothing happened. I looked at Max. He raised an eyebrow.

"Ok," I said. "I got this." I aimed at the target, and squeezed. Nothing happened. I looked at Max. He was grinning.

"You're stuck in your head, being a perfectionist again, aren't you?" He stepped in. "Ok. Maguire. Two things. First, you need to get out of your head. Second—" he took the gun from my hands. "You need to flip off the safety." He grinned and handed it back to me. A murmur of laughter ran through the group.

Ok. I used my thumb to flip the safety lever, and tried to stand right. Tried not to obsess about standing right. How do I get out of my head? Breathe out. Squeeze. The gun jumped in my hand. Holy crap! The inside of my palm was tender from the butt of the gun scraping it. Could I hold it tightly enough? These people had some serious hand muscles.

I looked at the target. "Did I hit it?" I bet I didn't. I bet it went high. Holy moley. I probably took out a bird.

Max laughed, and waved downward with his hand. "Finger straight, point at the ground. I'll go look." He walked over to the target. "Let's try it again."

I waited until he was behind me, then tried it again.

Max went to check. "You got the edge of it!" Everyone cheered.

I was thrilled. "I did it! Let me try the other one!"

Max put away his compact handgun and took out the full-sized one. He walked me through it again—the safety was different, I noted. The slide was difficult. Max watched me awkwardly pulling on it, but made no remarks. I would really have to start doing hand exercises. I'd had no idea.

I liked this gun much better. I not only hit the target, but got fairly close to the center. I tried a few more times, getting a little better each time, then let someone else take over. I beamed at Max. "That was great! I love doing new things!"

He laughed and mussed my hair. "Good job, Maguire."

We stayed and watched for a little longer, then drove back to the ranch.

"That was way more fun than I expected," I said. "I'm so glad we came. And I'm so glad you came with me. I would've felt stupider with someone else teaching me. But everyone seemed so warm and welcoming. Why did you insist on coming?"

Max paused. "I didn't know who would show up. Until we figure out what's going on, I'm not assuming anything."

We pondered that in silence while he drove.

The next day was sunny and hot. It was shaded but stifling in the barn, away from the breeze. I went up to my apartment for a cold drink. It was convenient, living right on site. I should do an inventory of my groceries, while I was at it. I'd been going through a lot of Diet Coke and coffee, with all my attempts at interrogation.

I leaned into the refrigerator. My veg was getting wilty. That never happened. Too many trips to Taco Tio and Burgers 'n Bait, with anyone who asked. I sighed. I would get my car out of Max's backyard, go to the store, and get more produce—and eat it this time.

I dug in the crisper under the sagging lettuce. There was a paper bag under the kale. What would that be? I had no memory of this. I hoped it wasn't moldy. Did Ben or Ida leave something? I unrolled the bag and looked in.

I stood, blinked. Tried to process what I was seeing. I reached in and pulled out a stack of bills—twenties, fifties, hundreds. Over a thousand dollars. A few thousand.

What?

Chapter Twenty-Three

Who had been in my apartment? Just about everyone. Who was alone? Ben. Ida. Luke. Max, for sure. Jared had never been out of my sight. Nor Walt. Janice? I didn't remember. Did I go into my bedroom for egg money? The kale was getting mushy, so it may have been that long. I was so careful about locking my door—but not always during the day, if I was just in the barn or corral.

I leaned back against the counter to think. If someone hid money to come back and retrieve it later—which seemed farfetched—they would expect it to be under the kale. Not exactly a vote of confidence, that they didn't think I would find it there. Kind of rude, now that I thought about it.

If someone reported me for having illicit cash, which they would claim to have seen, they would expect the money to be under the kale.

Whatever was going on, I wasn't leaving it under the kale. The toilet tank or a coffee can would be too obvious. I thought back to previous jobs—to crafty teenagers with drugs—and pulled up a chair. I climbed on it, lifted out a ceiling tile, and pushed the bag in so it was partly on the framework between tiles. I replaced the tile, climbed down, and studied the ceiling. There was no sign of a tile being moved or weight being up there.

I should tell Ben the Fed to put a hidden camera by my door. Or maybe he already had! He'd better not have. That was assuming the money wasn't his. I already knew he was capable of hidden agendas.

Ben was in the barn, raking the sand. I took him by the arm and pulled him over to an empty stall. "Listen. I need to know right now if you're any kind of a cop or not."

He blinked. "I'm not a cop."

I released his arm and turned to walk away.

"Wait. What's happened?"

I shook my head. "If you're just a ranch hand, it doesn't matter."

"Abby, wait." He pulled me back. "You absolutely cannot tell anyone this. I'm a private investigator. I often work with law enforcement. Please, tell me what's happened."

I narrowed my eyes at him. "So that's why your microphone in my purse didn't have to be admissible as evidence. Does Walt know this?"

"Yes."

"I assume Max knows, too."

"Yes."

"So, when you say don't tell anyone, you mean Ida?"

He exhaled loudly. "I'd prefer you didn't even talk with Max and Walt about it. You never know who's listening. Will you tell me what's going on?"

I looked him straight in the eyes. "Did you leave something under my kale?"

Ben looked at me like I'd lost my mind. "Did I what?"

I studied his face. "Did you leave something in my crisper?"

He stared at me blankly. "Was I supposed to?"

Another thought occurred to me. "Who hired you?"

"What? Does that remotely matter?"

"Yes," I said. "It matters."

"Mason's father hired me. Now tell me what's going on."

"Listen." I told him about finding the money, and about relocating it. I didn't tell him where I put it.

"You need to report this. Abby, this is not a laughing matter." He pulled out his phone. "I'm calling this in." Ben patted the air with his hands, as if holding something down. "In terms of anyone else, though, this conversation never happened. Okay?" He walked away, touching a few buttons on his phone. A saved contact, not an entire phone number.

I walked out of the barn and leaned against the fence to watch the horses wandering in the corral, grooming each other, drinking at the trough. Their lives went on, and so did ours. Mason's father probably worried about him—he was one of the guys who wore a rough life on his face. Yet he was apparently clean, sober. He worked at the ranch. He was starting a family. He looked like he was making it. Whether he walked in on something or was actively involved in it, Mason had to matter. His father mattered. Hiring Ben would be what Mason's dad sold his boat and trailer to pay for. The very thought seemed overwhelmingly sad.

I went back upstairs, grabbed my grooming gloves, and pulled them on as I walked out to the corral. I found Rosie and brushed her with my hands. Every few minutes, I lightly slapped my gloves together to clear off the hair. I watched Ben walk out of the barn and up the stairs to my door. He knocked, waited, knocked again. He looked around. Would he try the doorknob? I stroked Rosie's haunches as I watched.

Ben pulled out his phone, and seconds later, mine rang. He heard it, and located me. He waved me over. "I left a message. Will you be home this evening? The detective will probably want to talk to you right away."

I nodded. "I'll stay home. Just let me know."

Of course, that meant no grocery shopping. Should I eat anything out of the fridge? Would they dust my aging produce for fingerprints? It might be embarrassing to admit I had no idea what was going on in my kitchen. Maybe I should look up my credit card statement so I'd know when I last bought groceries. That bag wasn't there when I bought the kale. I went up to Max's door and knocked loudly. Max appeared in minutes.

"Can I borrow a sandwich?"

He grinned. "Come on in." He stood back to hold the door open.

I looked closely at his face. "My kale went bad."

Max laughed. "It started out bad. I sure as hell don't have any kale you can borrow. There's ham and turkey in the fridge—dig around and find whatever you want."

"Thanks!" I opened the refrigerator door, then turned and looked into Max's eyes. "I guess I've fallen off the pace a little. I haven't looked in the crisper for a long time. The kale got soggy and brown, and I wasn't even in there."

"No judgement here, Maguire. You know how I am with vegetables. Cooked with a roast is about all I'm up for." He opened cupboard doors and pulled down a loaf of bread and two plates. "I haven't eaten yet either. I'll join you."

We sat at his table with sandwiches and root beer. "Thanks for this," I said. "We can eat at my place next time. I'll go grocery shopping tomorrow."

Max chewed and swallowed. "Least I can do, Maguire. You do a lot for me."

I felt momentarily guilty for trying to provoke a response from him. No, I had to shake that off. I drank my root beer and looked around the room, taking in the worn furnishings, the faded linoleum, Ida's brightly colored crop art. Did anything reflect Max? He'd lived here for years.

He must have seen me. Max glumly surveyed his home. "I guess when we've put money into this place, it's been the plumbing, HVAC. Windows. Insulation, making it weather tight."

"That's smart." I nodded, studying him. Max didn't seem happy, but I wasn't sure why. He frowned at his half-eaten sandwich.

"What, Max?"

"Well, you know, my ex…"

I knew as much as I needed to. Idiot.

"She said no woman in her right mind would ever want to live here."

"Oh, for God's sake. What a stupid woman."

He raised both eyebrows.

"The house isn't the point. You are the point."

Max blinked, and seemed to stop breathing.

"I mean, I never met her. I suppose I should be polite, pretend I don't know she's an idiot. Max, she dumped you for a guy who she, herself, described as dim and predictable. Married him in a minute. What, because her biological clock was ticking? Seriously? And you're getting down about her judgement of your house? I wouldn't value her judgement of a housefly." I took a savage bite of my sandwich, shook my head in disgust while I chewed.

Max stared at me for a moment. A slow smile spread across his face. By the time I finished eating, he was beaming at me. That was more like it.

I returned to my apartment, but felt slightly uneasy. No. I couldn't let this happen. I was not going to become avoidant of my own kitchen, my own refrigerator. I defiantly walked over and took out a soda I didn't really want. I was proving a point. I cracked it open, raised a toast to Papa. "Here's mud in your eye."

That confused me as a child, when we toasted each other with grape juice. Papa said it came from horse racing—that the winning horse kicked mud into the eyes of all the horses and jockeys behind it. Then he took me to the horse races. Purely for purposes of illustration. At least, the first time. I smiled happily, and raised my glass again. "Here's mud in your eye, Papa. Remember when I asked if you could win with mud in your eye?" I took a swallow. "You said, Abs, you need to not give up when you're behind, and can't see." I took another drink. "Like right now."

I sat down at the table and opened my laptop. "You would be interested in so many things about this job," I told Papa. "Not so much the kale situation." No, he would not be amused in the least. "I'm not quite sure what my next move is, though." I started clearing emails and jumped when a knock came at the door. It was Ben and the plainclothes cop. I let them in.

The cop looked tired. I wondered if he always looked tired. He seemed to. He pulled out a notebook and pen. "You want to run through this for me?" He asked a long stream of questions. I felt stupid for not having better answers. He kept asking, as if I would know more the third or fourth time. He seemed annoyed when I didn't.

Finally, I sighed at him. "I bet you don't have any idea when you bought specific food, or when you last ate what. If you even have fresh food in your refrigerator. You always look exhausted. I bet you eat from the vending machine at the station. I bet you have beer in your fridge."

He stared at me. I glanced at Ben. He was staring at me. I cleared my throat. "Anyway."

The cop put away his pen. "So, where is this money?"

I got up, pulled my chair to the middle of the room, and momentarily forgot which ceiling tile I moved. I glanced at the two men, watching me. I exhaled. I picked a likely ceiling tile, lifted it, and peered underneath. I got down, moved the chair, and tried a different one.

"Hold on." I got down, got my Maglite, and climbed back up on the chair. I lifted a tile, stood on tiptoes to shine the light up into the ceiling, stuck my head up to look around. "Got it." I moved the chair once more and retrieved the bag. I handed it to the cop, who opened it, counted the money, and wrote me a receipt.

"It's not evidence of anything at this point. It's basically found money. You'll probably get it back." He paused. "Any thoughts as to what the point is? It seems like a strange move—a big cost, and what's the payout?"

"Oh, it was a very good move, assuming someone is flush with cash," I said. "I guarantee this will keep me off balance. Waiting for someone to come back for it. Wondering, on edge. It will hover in the back of my mind. I'll be suspicious of people, look at people differently. Especially anyone I trusted enough to leave them alone in the room."

My eyes cut to Ben. I quickly looked away, but he noticed. He narrowed his eyes.

"And I don't know who to suspect," I said. "Whoever it is, they're smart, and good at leading a double life, pretending to be a different person." I glanced at Ben again.

Ben scowled. The cop's eyes flicked from me, to Ben, and back again. I frowned, shook my head. I'd said enough.

"Don't mention this to anyone," the cop said. "The only crime at this point is potentially breaking and entering, if you weren't just in the other room. But there's enough going on around here that we need to see it as part of a whole. We'll keep this quiet, see if anything develops. In the meantime, keep your door locked. Whatever makes someone leave nearly three grand in someone's kitchen, it's not good."

"Can I throw away the kale?"

"You can do whatever you want," he said. "I needed to know about this, but I don't have a budget for chasing things that aren't crimes. Much as I'd like to dust for prints—there's a number of people around here already in the system. But it's not going to happen." He nodded. He and Ben left together.

Ida showed up the next day with a large plastic container. "I brought you something new. These are called mud pies. They have a date filling."

My eyes widened. "Pour yourself some coffee." I tasted one and swooned. Real butter.

Ida smiled. "It's an old recipe. I knew you'd like them. Now sit down, and tell me where we're at."

I took another bite, savoring it before answering. "We talked about Jared, but I keep thinking about Rodney, since he and Janice showed up for shooting. Max said the guy who owned the place wouldn't know they were felons. Obviously, David would."

Ida took a cookie. "All right. Go on."

"If Rodney had one week left on probation, why act like it didn't matter?"

"Maybe Rodney and Jared are both using." Ida dunked her cookie in her coffee, and bit off the soggy part. "Just because Rodney is behaving strangely, doesn't mean Jared is innocent." She paused with her cookie suspended over her cup.

I sat back in my chair, tried to think before speaking. I hadn't mentioned the money to Ida. I was keeping a secret with Ben the Fed, from Ida. I got up and walked to the cupboard, bringing back some napkins. We didn't really need them. I just wanted to move. "Drugs could cause delusional thinking. But maybe more sporadic. Maybe not a fixed idea that he has nothing to worry about."

Ida made a rolling gesture with the cookie in her hand. "I can tell you're thinking something, Abby. Come on. Spit it out."

"What if he had a personal guarantee from his P.O.?"

Ida sat up straight. "What are you saying?"

"Luke said I had no idea what people would do, to stay out of prison. What else could that mean?"

Ida took a breath. "Do you think Rodney killed Mason?"

"It would help if we knew why, but I could see it. He's not afraid to argue with Max, which puts him in a very small minority." I realized I was waving my cookie around. I set it down. "Let's say Luke was making people do things for him. It would involve a lot of moving parts. I could easily see Luke getting in over his head. Maybe this is an attempt to contain something."

I took a bite of cookie, and another thought occurred to me. I held up a hand while I chewed and swallowed. "Wait, though. If Jared was the saboteur, upsetting the equilibrium, why wasn't he the one killed? Luke said Mason probably got killed for crossing a line, not knowing when to quit. What line did Mason cross, that Jared didn't?" I waved my finger for emphasis. "Luke told me something there, whether he meant to or not."

And the money. Three grand was a lot of money around here. People were always trying to figure out how to buy hay for the year, with a short growing season and a long winter. Luke wasn't a rancher, but he lived in this economy. How much money were we talking about, if he would throw nearly three thousand away?

Ida stood and put her cup in the sink. "If someone was trying to contain things, and it wasn't Luke, who else could it be? Who else organizes things, oversees things? And don't say Walt."

"Okay, that's a good question. Who organizes things?" I squinted at her, thinking. "What about David? He organizes group activities that feel incredibly unifying."

I gasped. "Ida! What if he didn't send Rodney and Janice away from shooting because they're felons, on probation—what if he sent them away because Max showed up with me? What could've happened if Max hadn't come? David invited me by myself!"

I dropped my cookie. "That could explain why Rodney thought he could go in the first place! Maybe he went before. Max assumed that David told Rodney he could *never* come—maybe he told him, don't come tonight."

Ida leaned back against the counter, arms crossed over her chest. "Okay, David. He's here quite often. He's smart. Efficient. He was some kind of banking executive before he retired. Pillar of Society kind of thing. I don't remember what his wife did. They have a son who's getting into politics, local level. I didn't vote for him, but don't repeat that. Word is he has high aspirations. Or David does, for him. Eye on the senate, or some such. Hmph. Best to have a goal, I guess."

I stood and picked up my mug. "A bank executive. Huh. Well, let's not forget about the old man arguing with Mason, pressuring him. It wouldn't have to be David, but I bet it is. Plus, David keeps the horses straight by imagining dead animals slung over their backs."

"That doesn't really count," Ida said. "Everyone calls Molly the Llama Killer. I don't even remember who started that."

She turned toward the door. "I'll keep bringing cookies. We need to think about who to pull in here and schmooze. We should get David up here. Get him talking. He likes to talk."

"You're right." I added my cup to the sink. I'd wash them later. "Let's dig into David. That's good, Ida. And, hey, if you're going to the store before you bake cookies, I want to come. I need more coffee. And my kale went bad. I need to replace all my veg."

She didn't react to my kale going bad. Had I really thought she would?

Chapter Twenty-Four

The next morning, I heard commotion below. I stuck my head out the door. The parking lot was full. People milled around excitedly. A couple of volunteers walked around, passing something out. I trotted down the stairs to see what was going on.

"Abby!" One of the volunteers thrust a paper at me. "Are you in?"

I peered at the form. It was a numbered list of objects in the corral and pasture. The big tree. The log by the giant anthill. That rock right by the creek, but it can't go in. "What are we doing?" I had no idea.

"Disc golf!" The volunteer handed out pages to people walking by. "These are the holes. You hit whatever it says, in the right order. And count how many throws it takes—you get points for doing it in less throws."

"This sounds like fun!" It really did. "But I don't have a disc!"

"You can use one of mine." Ida came up behind me.

Max was with her. "And don't forget, any contact with a horse, at any velocity, is an automatic loss of twenty points. Even if the horse walks into it."

"Do the horses get hit a lot?" I didn't want to hurt anyone. My aim was not stellar.

"Almost never," Max said. "Most of them just leave. They go to the woods, watch us from there. But sometimes one will get curious, pick up a disc in their mouth."

"Oh, we get lots of hollering about that," Ida said. "But rules are rules. Twenty points." She handed me a disc. "Here, you can use this one. You can be on a team with someone if you want. I'd team up with you, but Max and I already signed up together."

David appeared. "You can sign up with me, Abby. I'll be your partner."

Team up with David? Game on. "I'd love to," I said.

"Ben suggested I ask you," David said. "He's too busy, but he thought you might appreciate someone who's done it before. As a guide, so to speak."

Huh. "I could use a guide," I told him. "I've never played a whole game of disc golf anywhere. If you still want to, you can direct me to the right rocks and anthills."

David smiled broadly. "I'd be happy to instruct you on technique as well. I have some experience in the matter."

We joined a line and waited. The starting team was having trouble hitting the first hole, which was described as the broad side of a barn. "That was supposed to be an encouraging beginning." David frowned. "Start with success, and all that."

At least they were having fun. Every time a gust of wind took a disc in the wrong direction, the laughter grew louder. Finally, they stood five feet from the barn and blocked the wind for each other. They entered their scores and moved on.

"Where have you played before?" I asked. "Here, or with your family?"

"Well, both," David said. "I played often with my son when he was growing up. Of course, he's far too busy now. Public servant. Making a career for himself. You'll know his name someday, Abby. Washington's not a far reach."

I gave him an encouraging smile. "What do you do with yourself, now that you're retired and your son is grown? Aside from coming here, I mean. You seem quite generous with your time."

Max and Ida hit the target with one throw each.

"They're the reigning champions." David shook his head. "They win every year. I do try to be involved in the community. I serve on several boards. I enjoy mentoring people who are at a crossroads in their lives. Ripe for input, one might say."

"David and Abby!" The moderator shouted.

"Go ahead," I said. "Demonstrate. I'm here to learn."

David took a careful stance, snapped his wrist, and threw his disc at the barn. He struck a triumphant pose, and people cheered. He really was a fan favorite. I tried to imitate him, and flung my disc. I threw it hard, so when the wind gusted up, it still hit the barn. Several feet farther down, but I just climbed over a fence to retrieve it.

"Excellent!" David busily wrote on our scoresheet.

The first team was now struggling with the next hole, going over Poop Mountain without touching it. One of them climbed up the back slope, with a determined look on his face. Max tossed a muck rake over the electric fence, and the man used it to knock his disc over the steep edge. The audience cheered as he worked his way back down.

"It appears we have plenty of time for chatting." David tucked the pen into his shirt pocket. "I hope you're settling in here, Abby. How's your dating life?"

I winced. "Quiet," I said brightly. "How's your marriage?"

David blinked, startled. "Oh—forgive me. I don't know why people always ask single women about their personal lives. We shouldn't."

He also didn't answer me. I mentally chastised myself—I would never improve as a spy if I kept getting ruffled. "Oh, look," I said. "We're up. What's the best throw for getting loft?"

David visibly inflated, and showed me how to throw a disc over a tall obstacle. His landed nicely on the other side of Poop Mountain. "You see? Angle and release."

My disc flew over the heap, but sailed over the electric fence and landed in a tree. "Totally meets the requirements." I grabbed the muck rake and opened the gate.

"Release," David said. "Angle and release."

I banged the rake against the branch until my disc came down. A woman from the team ahead of us picked debris out of my hair.

David cleared his throat. "I was really more wondering whether you're able to get away from the ranch at all. It must be different, living at work, out in the country. How often do you go into town during the evenings?"

"It really varies." Why did I feel defensive about this? It wasn't exactly a secret.

"I just notice your car never moves. Hope you're not feeling stuck."

I scanned the rest of the sheet while David talked, and realized the last hole was to go through the gap between Max's house and Abby's car, without hitting the car. Oh.

"No one with a truck ever wants to squeeze into my hatchback," I said. That wasn't my fault. "I guess other people drive me around a lot."

We heard shouting. Our heads both snapped in that direction. Quincy galloped past with a disc in his mouth. "Maybe it's Max's," I said. "Does he have to throw it from where he gets it back?"

Max walked after Quincy, followed by a woman wringing her hands. "Quincy, get back here!" Max called.

Quincy stopped, turned to look at Max, then trotted away. He threw a glance at Max over his shoulder and tossed his head haughtily.

The crowd erupted into laughter. "He just flipped you off, Max," a man shouted.

Max grinned. "He did. Quincy! Come here! Quin-ceee!"

Quincy picked up speed and disappeared into the woods.

"Here, Donna," another woman said. "You can use my extra disc. Just take the penalty shot and the twenty points, and move on."

The woman took the disc gratefully, and the game resumed. We made good progress through the course. David only needed a second shot on one hole. I made a respectable showing. Then I missed an obstacle and my disc shot into the woods. It smacked into Rodney, who was bent over, rummaging through the weeds.

"Oh! I'm so sorry!" I ran towards the brush.

"You don't lose points for hitting people," he said. "You just take a penalty shot for not standing in the poison ivy to throw it." He handed me a disc and threw another one toward the pond.

"Hey!"

He kept walking.

"Rodney! Come back here! This has chew marks! Give me back Ida's disc!" I ran past him and picked up the disc he threw, leaving the bitten up one in its place.

Rodney smirked. "My mistake."

David shook his head solemnly. "I remember when his disc got chewed up. It was that pony."

I scowled. I could picture it. Then another thought occurred to me. "How often are you out here at night?"

David shot me a startled glance. "At night? What do you mean?"

"Abby and David!" The moderator shouted. "You're up! Big tree! Move it or lose it!"

"It sounded like you come by in the evening," I said. "Seeing that my car is still there."

David threw his disc halfway to the tree. He pointed toward the bushes. "If you throw from where Rodney found your disc, you won't lose a penalty stroke." He hit the tree with his third throw.

I peered into the brush. It didn't look like poison ivy to me. I waded back in, and sent my disc sailing toward the big tree. I stepped on something. Pushing the weeds aside with my foot, I bent over, and picked up a billfold. It was most likely Rodney's, but I wasn't giving it to him without looking for ID. Not after he tried to make off with Ida's disc.

I opened it, and found Rodney's driver's license, and several hundred-dollar bills. I jogged past David. "Rodney! Did you drop your wallet? This was in the brush."

Rodney grunted, and opened the billfold to make sure his money was still there.

Honestly. I went back to my disc. It took me six throws to hit the tree. David marked the score without comment. He looked everywhere except at me.

"David," I said. What the heck, it couldn't get much more awkward. "Did you know Mason very well?"

He stopped breathing for a moment. "We worked here together for a few years. Why?"

"I'm just having trouble not thinking about him. I wondered if you knew much about him."

"Oh, forgive me. I forgot that you found him. That must've been awful. Of course you're upset."

I nodded. "What was he like? Did you know him well?"

The pause was so long, I thought he wasn't going to answer. Probably waiting to be rescued by the moderator. "Well, you know," he said, "Walt hired him on as paid staff after having him as a volunteer. Not many people can say that. That was quite a compliment from Walt." He looked at the sheet. "Our next hole is by your car. Let's see how many people are hitting it." He walked away.

The game nearly came to a standstill. Everyone but Max and Ida hit my car. Some repeatedly, as they took extra throws. David sent it sailing straight through the gap on his turn. He walked over to stand by Max. He was no longer coaching me.

There was no way I was going to get the release right. I moved this way and that, aiming, estimating. Angle and release. Finally, I faced the gap straight on. I held the disc vertically between flat hands, down between my knees. I heaved it through in what we used to call a granny shot, although I'd never tell Ida that. It was probably ageist.

After a shocked silence, the crowd broke out in cheers. Several people imitated me, improving their overall scores. Decreasing impacts with my quarter panel.

"We're going to call that move 'The Maguire'!"

I didn't see who said it, so I grinned at everyone. We all turned in our scoresheets. After a break for tabulations, it was announced that Ida and Max won again. Everyone applauded. David walked away without a word.

I did two sessions that afternoon with Max, and a third with Ida. It was now a comfortable routine—client, cleanup, paperwork, repeat. I liked the activity level, the variety. The utter unpredictability of the most well-planned session. Weaving it all together to stay on course with an overall treatment plan. There was a lot of potential here.

Ida followed me up to my apartment. She sat down and put her feet up on a chair. "David looked unhappy toward the end of the game, Abby. How did it go? Did you interrogate him?"

"Well, I tried." I scooched up to sit on the counter. "At first, it seemed like he was interrogating me. He wanted to know if I leave in the evenings."

Ida frowned. "Why on earth would he want to know that? Does he want you out of here?"

"No idea. I asked him if he comes here at night. He got a little upset." I started swinging my legs, thinking back. "And then Rodney tried to swipe your disc!"

"I saw that." Ida furrowed her brow. "Leaving me that chewed up one. Some nerve."

"When he swapped out discs, he dropped his wallet in the bushes. I looked to make sure it was his, and Ida, there was a lot of money. Several hundred dollars. In hundreds."

Ida said nothing for a moment. Then she shook her head. "That can't be good. If Rodney has any paid employment, it's part time, and low wage. He spends half his time here, working off community service hours. He's up to his eyeballs in something."

"I asked David if he knew Mason very well, and he didn't like that one bit. Hemmed and hawed, never answered. He seemed shaken that I asked at all."

"So, he probably was the old man at Jamie's house," Ida said. "Seems like a guilty reaction, to me. Very suspicious."

"I wonder why he wants to know how often I leave at night," I said. "That's kind of creepy."

"I think this will be helpful, Abby. We know they're both up to something. We can't eliminate them at all." She looked at the clock. "Why don't you come over for dinner? We can make something. It will be fun, and if David's truck is here when we get back, we'll catch him red-handed."

Ida dropped me back around ten. David's truck was nowhere to be seen. Ida waited, headlights shining on me, until I was inside with the door locked behind me.

Max came up sometime in the dead of night. I wasn't even sure what time it was. I was on the couch, wrapped up in a blanket, thinking about David, and Rodney, and Luke. The more I thought about it, the guiltier they all seemed—but there was no way David and Luke would share being criminal alpha male. It was one, or the other. Or someone else. I had no idea. I was tired.

Max was tired. When I returned to the couch, he sat down next to me.

"Oh," I said. "Do you want some tea? It won't take a minute."

He shook his head. "I just—" He turned red-rimmed eyes toward me. "Maguire, I know it didn't go so well last time, but I'd like to try again. If you're willing. I want to try to talk."

I nodded, sat back, and waited.

"I—" He shook his head. "I don't know where to start."

"Just start talking," I said. "It will work itself out."

He talked for a few hours, staring at the air in the middle of the room. From time to time, he paused. We sat in silence until he spoke again. There was nothing I needed to say, nothing he needed to hear. When he was finally spent, the sun was breaking over the trees. The horizon was orange and gold.

"I'm sorry," he said. "It's going to be a long day. I'm sorry I kept you up."

"You know I'm not sorry." I studied him through bleary eyes.

"It's been a lotta years. I want to be done with this." Max didn't look at me while he spoke. "You got me thinking I could have my life back, or a life, anyway. You got me thinking things could be different."

I nodded. "Let me pull some jeans on. We can do the breakfast crew together. We'll do the long day together. This was good, Max. I think it will help."

He nodded. "I do too." His voice cracked. He swallowed. He waited while I made a few cups of coffee and changed into barn clothes. We were quiet as we walked out to the woods to bring in the herd.

Max, Ida, and I perched on a picnic table after our last sessions for the day. I wanted some sunlight before heading back in to finish documentation. I smiled gratefully and waved at Janice and David, who were scooping out the arena, giving us a little extra time. I laid back on the hard, rough table. The wood was hot beneath me. I dangled my feet over the side, baking in the afternoon sun. Ida teased Max. He laughed affectionately. A loud bang came from the barn. A horse came galloping out and skidded to a stop just before crashing into the gate, head pivoting wildly, half of a lead rope swinging from its halter.

Max was on his feet and moving before I could register what was happening. Voices, shouting. I jumped up. Rodney came flying out of the barn, backwards.

Chapter Twenty-Five

Rodney landed and slid on the gravel. I froze. Walt came striding out. His tan face was flushed five shades darker. He picked Rodney up by his belt and shirt, and hurled him through the air. Rodney landed on his back, rolled over and scrambled to his truck. He looked back at Walt, stabbed a finger in the air. "This is assault! I'm going to press charges!"

Walt stood, hands on hips, and watched as Rodney started his engine.

"You think you're such a big man!" Rodney screamed out the window. "You know nothing! You're so damn great! Right under your own damn nose! How big a man are you? You don't see nothing!"

Ida and I stared. Walt watched until Rodney drove off the property, then turned and strode back into the barn. We followed wordlessly.

Max stood near Sally Mae, talking to her. She skittered back and forth, eyes huge and panicky. Walt bent over and picked something up from the ground, and handed it to Ida. Her mouth dropped open. Ida turned to look at Sally Mae, then flushed dark red, and went in the office.

Walt went to Sally Mae, examined her. He spoke soothingly, stroking her neck. Walt's presence seemed to calm the horse. Her eyes were still wide, but she stood, breathing heavily. Walt stood with her. Max took a few steps away, looking at the ground, breathing heavily himself. I walked to the office. Ida was sitting with her head in her hands.

"What was that?" I asked.

She lifted her head. "It's a stun gun. And she was wet."

I stared at her. "Why would someone shock a restrained horse in a barn?"

Ida didn't answer. She didn't need to. Rodney hated Sally Mae. I felt sick, thinking about it. The difference in her demeanor with Rodney, and with Walt, was beyond clear. She tried to tell us. She knew where she was safe. She knew when she was not.

Max walked in, but didn't sit. He leaned back against the wall, scowling, arms tightly folded to his chest.

"Max, what is going on here?" Ida braced herself on the table. "How would anyone dare to bring a stun gun onto this property? And use it on a horse, with Walt right in the office?"

Before Max could answer, Walt came in. He stood in the middle of the floor. Ida turned to him. "Walt? Do you think he'll really try to press assault charges?"

"Let him. Chief of police keeps horses. I like my chances." Walt shook his head. "I will call his probation officer. That's illegal for him to own." Walt left a message for Luke to call him, disconnected, and slipped his phone into his pocket. "I'm not going to be any good here, now. I feel I should stay to watch over things, but I need to pick up Clara from school."

Max gave him a hard look. A chill ran down my back. "You go ahead, Walt," he said. "Your family needs you. I'll be here."

Walt nodded and walked out without another word. We heard his truck start, and tires on gravel. Max stared at the floor for a minute and left. I opened the file cabinet, pulling out folders. "I can't do much, but I can do the documentation so those guys don't have to worry about it."

"Give me some of those," Ida said. "I'll do the ones I was in on. Then we're going to talk about this, see what else we can do. We're damn sure not helpless. There's got to be something. Abby—"

I looked up.

"If Rodney did kill Mason—what if he comes back, to hurt Walt? He wouldn't go after Walt's family, would he?"

I thought about that. "I don't think so. If he wants to prove he's a big man, bigger than Walt, he wouldn't prove it by going after a woman or a child. He'd come after Walt." I hoped that was true. Who knew what Rodney was capable of? Why should he be rational? "If he does come after Walt, I hope he does it here. I know it would be bad for the ranch, but Max is here, and Max carries. Ben, too, for that matter. Walt doesn't carry, does he?"

"No." Ida shook her head. "He used to hunt, but he's never carried. This just doesn't bear thinking about. None of it." We turned back to the paperwork.

"Abby." Ida was still distracted. I met her eyes. She hesitated. "I know you have your two rules. I just want to know how you feel about this. Not saying anything one way or another."

I waited.

"The part about everyone keeping their dignity, that there's always another way to handle things. Do you think Walt crossed the line, that he was wrong in his reaction?"

"Rodney's lucky Walt didn't hurt him," I said. "Lotta guys would've beat him up. And Ida, it's not just Sally Mae. Now I know why Rosie was afraid of Rodney. Those were the two horses he talked about hating, but who knows how many he was torturing?"

Ida closed her eyes, shook her head silently. We finished the paperwork, and went to bring the horses in for dinner.

I woke with a start. My heart was pounding. I looked at the clock. Two-thirty. Again. I closed my eyes, but felt panic building. A bad one. I swung out of bed and walked out to the kitchen, tried to slow my ragged breathing. I thought about Max, wondered if he was awake. I went to turn on the lamp by the door, but saw lights on the road. A vehicle, idling. The headlights were off, but the running lights showed what looked like a pickup at the end of the drive. I froze—but no, everyone knew that Walt wasn't here at this hour. It wouldn't be someone coming after him. Probably nothing. Probably kids, out messing around.

I grabbed my Maglite, slipped on my boots, and stepped out the door. It was hard to see. The yard lights were off, and it was a dark night. Two people were out of the truck, passing in front of the running lights as they walked around. They climbed into the bed of the truck and heaved a bag into the ditch. It landed with a thud.

More garbage! Suddenly furious, I ran down the stairs and toward the road, shouting. "Hey! Stop! You can't dump that there!"

Both people jumped into the cab. The truck pulled away, then slowed to a stop.

"Hey!" I was almost to the road. "You put that back in your truck! You can't dump your garbage here! We have horses here! And children! Get back here and pick this up!"

The driver hesitated, then pulled away.

"Hey!" Hot rage flooded through me. I bent over, picked up a broken spark plug from the side of the road, and hurled it at the pickup as hard as I could. I heard a sharp impact as the back window of the cab shattered. Rage turned to shocked fear.

The pickup spun its wheels, throwing gravel as it sped away. I ran to the shadows and stood with my hand over my mouth. I couldn't believe I did that. What if they came back?

Max came running out of the house, gun in hand.

"Max! It's me!" I called.

He slowed, jogged over to me. "What the hell is going on?" He put a hand on my shoulder, felt me shaking. He pulled me in. "Hey. Hey. Hey, Maguire. You're okay. It's okay. I've got you."

I leaned on him, grabbed a handful of shirt. "I'm sorry. I'm really sorry. I woke up...they woke me. These people. Out here. Dumping garbage. I was just so angry. I just didn't think. I came tearing out here, yelling at them."

Max pulled back enough to look down at me. "Are you nuts? Especially after today. Do you know what could have happened?"

I nodded shakily.

"What did happen?" he asked.

"I picked up a piece of trash and threw it at them. It broke the truck window, Max. I thought they were going to come back here..." my voice trailed off.

Max exhaled loudly, hugged me again. "Maguire. You threw something at a guy's truck, all alone out in the middle of the night? Do you ever think?"

I shook my head into his chest, took a deep breath, and pulled back. I turned to look at the ditch. "They dumped a huge bag of trash. As if garbage pickup out here wasn't ungodly expensive. Now Walt has to pay for that! Where is that money supposed to come from? Programming? Hay? I heard it thud when it hit the ground. I'm just so tired of selfish jerks making problems for everyone else to clean up—" I stopped myself.

I turned on my Maglite and shone it into the ditch. It *was* a huge bag of trash. Except it wasn't a bag. It looked like a blanket wrapped around something. I stepped closer, shining my light over the dark heap.

Max grabbed my arm and pulled me back. "Stay here. Give me that light." He pulled out the gun shoved in his waistband and took the Maglite from me. He walked up to the blanket, hooked a toe under one edge and pulled it back. My legs went limp. I hit the ground. Max came running.

I tried to move to my hands and knees to get up, but a wave of dizziness swept over me.

"Sit down," Max ordered. "Stay here." He hesitated for a second to make sure I was listening, and turned back to the ditch. There was a man in the blanket. I saw a person. "I have to check for vitals," Max said over his shoulder. "Stay there."

I couldn't breathe. I couldn't believe I was reacting like this. I never in my life fell apart in a crisis. Never. I tried to focus on the cold ground under me, the sounds of Max moving in the grass, the cold air around me. Focus. Breathe.

Max came back and took my arm, pulling me to my feet. "Let's go inside and call the police from there."

"I'm sorry," I said.

"Maguire." He put an arm around me, holding me up. "Stop apologizing. Everyone has a limit. Just walk now."

"Max, is he—"

Max tightened his grip on me. "He's dead. Gunshot." Max hesitated, then started walking.

I stopped cold. "It's not—Max—it's not—"

He shook his head. "It's Rodney."

Max went down to wake Ben. I huddled on the couch. Max offered me a blanket, but I couldn't bring myself to wrap it around me. He brought out a flannel shirt and draped it over my shoulders.

They both went outside. When they came back in, they brought the police.

I couldn't say if I knew the truck. A lot of people have pickups. I didn't know what color it was. It was dark.

One of the cops wanted to know why I happened to throw a spark plug at them.

"It was lying there on the road," I said. "I wasn't exactly stopping to think. I thought they were dumping garbage, so I threw garbage at them. I know it was stupid."

"It might be helpful," the cop said. "A cracked window at least narrows things down. Broken ceramic from spark plugs is actually amazing at shattering glass. It's a thing."

We covered the whole day, over and over, from the afternoon with Rodney and Walt, to the truck, the body. "David was here, he shoots," I said. "Not that I think he did it, I'm just saying. And he drives a pickup. Janice was here. They were cleaning the pasture. She doesn't drive. Walt called Luke Morgan and told him about it, since Rodney wasn't supposed to have a stun gun."

Walt arrived, looking haggard. We covered it all again. Walt's daughter could confirm he'd been home all night.

The cops wanted the stun gun. One of them went with Max to the barn office to get it. Emergency vehicles lit up the yard. Crime scene tape was posted around the ditch. The detective asked us to call if we thought of anything to add.

I had no idea what to add. Nothing made any sense. "If he was killed for shocking a restrained animal, I don't know who would do that. The way gossip travels around here, it could be anyone in three counties." I rubbed my face. Half-formed ideas seemed to flit around the edges of my mind, but I couldn't take hold of them. "How often is it clever?"

The detective looked at me. "Excuse me?"

"When people kill each other. How often is it clever? Tricky? Elegant?"

"Never," he said. "It's almost never even interesting. People die for really, very few reasons."

"It seems so complicated and convoluted," I said. "Maybe when it all settles out, it will be simple. We just don't see it yet."

Ben walked out with the detective. They talked by the detective's car for quite a while. The rest of us sat numbly in Max's living room, in silence. Max got up and put an arm around Walt's shoulder. "We're gonna get through this. We will."

Walt looked at him. "We'll have to close. We can't have clients here."

We all sat with that.

"Let's start with a week," Max said. "The police may come up with something. We can always extend it if we need to."

Walt nodded slightly. "I'll be back early. I'll call Ida. We can start phoning people."

Max saw him to his truck, then came back.

I didn't get up. "Can I stay here?" There was no way I was going back to that apartment by myself.

Max sat at the end of the couch by my feet. I curled up on my side, thinking about the very few reasons people die. Barring psychosis, I could boil it down to two: someone is a threat, or in the way. How did Mason and Rodney intersect, with that lens?

Nothing tricky or elegant with either murder. They were simply dead.

Max and I stayed on the couch until the sun came up.

Chapter Twenty-Six

Ida and I sat in the office, cancelling sessions, calling volunteers. We were vague. They would hear soon enough, if they didn't already know. After we spoke with or left messages for everyone, we stepped outside to breathe. Max was leaning against the far picnic table, smoking a cigarette. We walked over and sat on the bench near him, but no one knew what to say.

I heard a vehicle drive in, and looked up to see an unfamiliar car. It pulled to a stop, and Luke climbed out of the driver's seat.

I looked at Max. "Where's his truck?"

Max pointed his cigarette at me. "Maguire, keep your mouth shut."

Luke walked over. "You got some kind of problem here? Looks like the place is deserted. I've got some meetings this morning. What's with the tape by the road, there?"

"Nothing to do with us," Ida told him. "We had to close for a bit, anyway. Just to help the police, keep people out of their way."

"Where's your truck?" I asked.

Max glared at me.

"Alternator gave out," Luke said. "Got a rental 'til it's fixed. You not going to have people in here all day, then?"

"Sorry, no," Ida said. "It'll be a few days. If we'd known you were meeting folks here this morning, we'd have let you know."

"Hey, no problem. I'll catch up with them at the office." He nodded, got back in the car, and drove away.

"Maguire, are you out of your damn mind? That was not funny." Max glowered at me, bent down, and stubbed out his cigarette in the dirt. "If that was him last night, you do not want him thinking you know it."

"Don't you think it would've looked weird if I didn't notice he was driving a car?"

Max shook his cigarette butt at me. "You could work on sounding curious instead of confrontational."

"Alternator, my ass," I said. "We gotta call the cops and tell them to find out where Luke's pickup is. Probably at the auto glass shop."

"I will call them," Max said. "You stay here and talk to Ida about the benefits of staying alive." He stalked off toward the barn.

Ida put a hand on my arm. "Abby. This has been left right on Walt's doorstep. I'm not going to let this lie."

I thought about Walt. I was furious with him about the giant horse, but still. I nodded.

Walt was leaning on the fence, looking out over the pasture. I took a spot next to him. He glanced at me out of the corner of his eye, sighed heavily. "I feel paralyzed, Abby. How do we come back from this? How do I just start up again? Two men have lost their lives. I can't act like none of this happened. I don't know how to move forward."

We stood in silence. Leaves rustled in the trees. Horses grazed in the growing heat of the sun. I could hear soft whinnies as two horses called to each other from different parts of the woods, crackling and rustling as they moved through the brush. I shifted my weight as the fence pressed into my forearm. I studied Walt. "When you're stuck, pay attention to what you're looking at."

He turned his body toward me. He stared at me, said nothing.

"Look where you want to go," I said.

He closed his eyes for a long moment, then put his hand on my shoulder. "Alright. I hear you."

I tried to order my thoughts as I chopped vegetables for dinner. There was absolutely nothing I felt completely sure of. I scraped the vegetables into a pan and checked Papa's face. What would he tell me, if he could? Would he tell me to leave? It was one of my favorite pictures. I caught him in an unguarded moment, in his later years. I was an adult. He was looking at me with comfortable affection, a fleeting expression startled away by my camera. He shook his head, smiling. I didn't regret capturing that look, even if I spoiled the moment. Now, I cherished it.

"Would you tell me to stay out of it, like Walt and Max? You always encouraged me to think, to satisfy my curiosity. To learn everything I could about things that captured my interest, regardless of other people's opinions." I tried to think back on different situations and what Papa said about them. It seemed critically important to decide what he would say now, but I just couldn't tease it out. I stirred the vegetables, pulling some of the thinner ones to the edge of the pan to cook more slowly.

When I wrote that seventh-grade research paper about spontaneous human combustion, everyone else was writing about pop stars and pro athletes. He never cared what the teachers thought. He told me to carry on being Abby. Would this be different? Would he tell me to stand down and protect myself? Or to follow the threads, to see where they lead?

"I guess Rodney is out of the equation, now. Although I never thought he was any kind of a mastermind. More of a henchman. But whose henchman? I've seen him talking with David. I need to get Janice to talk to me. She might know something without realizing it. Maybe she made an offhand comment to someone, gossiped to the wrong person. She works with David all the time. Maybe she talked with him, not knowing he could be the murderer, and she can tell me something he said. I'll have to pay for more disgusting eggs, to get her up here." I realized that while I stared at Papa, my vegetables were burning. I pulled them from the heat and turned off the gas.

I left the burned vegetables on the stove. The mess was too hot to clean up now. I changed into running clothes, and went to knock on Max's door.

I checked the clock. One-thirty, early for me. I sat up and swung my legs over the edge of the mattress, rubbed my face. Had I been dreaming? Something about the smell of mint. Why was I awake? I heard a noise—the barn always made noises, especially in the wind. This one sounded like it was right in the apartment. Probably the old wood shifting with a temperature change. I got up and walked toward the bedroom door.

I heard a crinkling noise as I stepped on something—it crackled under my bare foot. I stooped down to pick it up—and froze. It was a wrapper. A cookie wrapper. On my bedroom floor.

Someone was here. The killer. In my room. Stood over me.

A board creaked in the hallway. I backed up, pressed against the wall. I fought down panic. What could I do? I looked around. What was heavy? What could I grab? I tried to be silent, invisible. I heard my doorknob turn.

The door opened partway. I tried not to breathe. My empty bed was visible from the doorway. The door stayed half open. Silence.

I slowly stooped down and picked up a cowboy boot. I held it with the heel pointed out, and waited.

The door closed. I heard creaking in the hallway. The outer door opened and closed. I waited. Listened.

I tiptoed over and pressed my ear to the door. I heard nothing. I slowly turned the knob, eased the door open. Peered around the corner. No one. I crept out to the hallway and picked up my Maglite. Put my face to the window. It was dark. I couldn't see anyone. I locked the door, grabbed my phone, ran to the bathroom, and locked the door behind me. I called Max. He answered after four rings. I couldn't speak.

"Maguire?"

I struggled for breath.

"Maguire? Are you ok?"

"Someone's out there." My voice was shaky. "They were in my bedroom. While I was sleeping."

"Are you safe?"

"I'm locked in my bathroom."

"Stay there. I'm on my way."

"Max, be careful," I said. "Someone's out there!"

"Stay where you are." He hung up.

Max opened the door with the spare key. I didn't unlock the bathroom door until I heard his voice. Ben came from my bedroom, shaking his head, holding his gun in front of him.

Max holstered his and pulled me into a hug. I was shaking.

"There was a car out on the road," Max said. "Pulling away as we came out. Whoever it was, walked in." He pulled back to look at me. "Are you ok?"

I nodded. "There was someone in my bedroom. While I was sleeping." I rested my head on Max's shirt, clenched the side seams in my hands. "They were out in the hall when I woke up. Then they come back. They must've seen my bed empty. I heard them leave."

"Did you see them?" Ben looked at me, standing there wrapped up in Max, breathing on his t-shirt.

"No," I said. "I heard them and saw my doorknob turn. The door opened and closed. I didn't see who it was. Did you see anything?"

"I didn't even see the car," Ben said. "There was no one there when I got up the stairs."

I pulled away from Max. My pulse was still racing from adrenaline. I started pacing.

Ben stuck his gun in his waistband. "Who had keys?"

"Any number of people living up here, over the years." Max frowned, crossed his arms over his chest. "Always turned the keys back in. Never had any idea someone might've copied them."

Ben took out his phone. "I'm calling this in." He stepped away.

I stopped pacing, hugged myself. "Someone stood over me while I was sleeping, Max."

Max's dark eyes looked black, thunderous.

"A squad's going to come by and take a report," Ben said, moments later. "What do you want to do for the rest of the night?"

"I'm not staying here! My door was locked. I know it was."

Max put a hand on my back. "Come up to the house. We'll leave every light on outside. Light the place up like daylight. No one's coming back then. Tomorrow, we change the locks."

We waited in my apartment until the squad car arrived. I began to feel a little foolish, going through it all again, but I knew someone was there. I wasn't so sure the police believed me. Even if I told them about the wrapper, they still probably wouldn't.

After they left, I followed the men back into the house. Ben paused at the top of the stairs, watching me from the corner of his eye.

Max got me some blankets and a pillow. When I settled down on the couch, Ben went down to the basement.

Max sat at my feet for a moment. "You gonna be ok?"

I huddled up in the blankets. "Yes. Thank you."

"You need anything, Maguire, you even just feel nervous, come get me. I've bothered you enough in the middle of the night. You don't want to be alone, just let me know."

I tried to smile at him. "Thank you, Max."

He went in his room and left the door ajar.

Walt took the news like a physical blow, reeling back a step. He took hold of my shoulder. "Abby. My God. If anything happened to you—"

"Whoever it was wanted to scare me, not hurt me, Walt." Someone was toying with me. I still felt residual fear in my gut, but anger was growing, displacing it.

Walt gripped my shoulder. "Abby, whatever you're doing—asking around, talking to people—you've got to stop. You've got to. I can't have you hurt." He studied me intently, to see if I was listening. "Please, make it obvious that you're not poking around. Don't be stubborn about this." He was called away before I had to answer.

Ida leaned in close, eyes wide with shock. "Abby, are you alright? Truly?"

I pulled her to the corner, away from the doorway. She turned her ear to hear my whisper. "Ida, they left a wrapper on the floor of my bedroom. I stepped on it. The killer stood right over me."

Ida paled. She put a hand to the wall, steadied herself. She opened her mouth, closed it wordlessly.

Our faces jerked toward the door as footsteps neared. Ben walked by the office, but didn't come in.

"Did you tell anyone?" Ida whispered.

"No! Who would I tell? What would I say?"

We were quiet for a couple of beats.

"You want to come live with me?" Ida asked.

I was momentarily tempted, but shook my head. "They're changing the locks. It should be ok." I wasn't sure I believed it.

"Ida—it's like I have a stalker. I've never even thought about stalkers, Ida."

"You going to listen to Walt? Stop asking around?"

I paused. "I didn't even feel like I was getting anywhere, Ida. I don't get it." I waited while another person walked past, then shook my head. "Whoever it is, they definitely have the upper hand. They've got me walking around scared. I'm—" I broke off as a thought occurred to me. "Ida. I'm being lunged. Someone's got me running in circles, going this way and that. They're lunging me! Damned if I will be lunged."

Ida glanced at my hands, and I realized my fists were clenched.

"What was it Max said? The clients that try to lunge us, we just don't respond like they expect. Then if they keep coming, maybe they get a different result. Well, whoever's jerking me around is going to get a different response, Ida."

Ida cocked her head, squinted at me. "What are you planning on doing?"

"I gotta figure it out. When I was trying to lunge that horse, it totally messed me up by going a different direction. Especially coming towards me. I'm not going to cower in fear. I'm taking it to him. I'm coming straight at him." I walked away, then turned back. "Don't say anything."

Ida gave her head a tiny shake, almost imperceptible. "I'm still in."

Leaving the barn, I stopped short. Someone was standing at the top of the stairs, at my door. I peered around the corner. It was David. I watched as he knocked, looked around, and tried the doorknob.

"Hey, Abby!"

I jumped. Ben appeared from behind. I glanced up again. David was looking down at me.

Ben stopped, reassessing the situation.

David walked down the stairs. "Abby! There you are!"

I made myself smile. "I was just in the office. What's up?"

David glanced at Ben, then back at me. He hesitated. "Just came to issue an invitation for shooting again, make sure you know you're welcome."

"That's nice, David. Thank you."

David nodded and walked away.

"When is shooting?" Ben asked.

"I have no idea. He didn't say."

David retreated across the parking lot.

"I gotta go," I told Ben. We could talk later. I went upstairs and forced myself to walk in, to sit at my table. It was daylight. The locksmith was coming. People milled around busily downstairs. Nothing would happen.

I sat for a long time. Not even trying to think, or understand. I gave up on sustained mental focus. I let my thoughts drift and settle around me like cottonwood seeds floating, lifting, eventually coming to ground. Finally, I stood up and looked at Papa. His picture looked back at me. I reached out and picked up the frame, and turned it around to face backwards. "You're not going to want to hear this," I told him.

Chapter Twenty-Seven

I opened my computer case and took out the file I photocopied from Walt's office. I called the number on the contact form, and Mason's father answered. I introduced myself.

"Jamie talked about you," he said. There was a slight hesitation. "Is there—something I can do for you?"

"I understand that Jamie needs to keep out of this," I said. "And I totally understand if you do too, I promise. Totally. I just wondered if you would like to be seen meeting me for coffee. Here. At the ranch. In my apartment."

There was a longer pause. "I guess you mean at a time when a fair number of people will be watching."

"That's right. I'd walk you out afterwards. Back to your car. Shake hands, nod at each other, promise to call, with the hand-up-to-the-ear phone gesture."

Silence. I was just about to speak, when he did. "What exactly is it you're aiming to do here?"

"Fire a shot over the bow," I said. "Get their attention. At the very least, cause a disruption, shake something loose."

Another long pause. I was getting used to it now, and just waited. "Well," he said slowly, "I don't know as how that's a very good idea." He didn't sound like he was done, so I waited some more.

"I tell you what," he said. "I'm gonna wait until tomorrow, and then I'm gonna take you up on it. Reason being, I got an appointment later today, I'm making up a will. I gotta make sure, anything happens to me, everything I got goes to Jamie. Soon's I get that straightened out, why, I'll come out. I'll meet with you. We'll make it look like we solved everything here, and world peace on top of it. Then we'll see what happens. You just hold on, then, and I'll give you a call."

We disconnected. I blew out a long, slow breath. I reached over and turned Papa's picture back around. I glanced quickly at his face, but looked away. "I know," I said. "I don't want to talk about it."

I buried the file in my bag. I needed to be busy. I grabbed my laundry hamper and soap. It gave me a focus, loading the washer in the barn, setting up my drying racks upstairs. I wandered around downstairs while things dried, not wanting to sit up there, thinking about my doorknob turning in the middle of the night. Thinking about someone standing over me. And that wrapper, where I would be sure to step on it. What was that? Who did that?

I stayed as busy as I could for the rest of the day, helping with sessions. Bringing in horses. Putting away obstacles. I swept the barn. Eventually, it was night, and there was nothing else to do.

I stayed in bed for about two and a half minutes. This was not going to work. I got up and folded laundry, piling t-shirts and jeans in stacks on the chair. I closed the drying racks and put them away.

I pulled out a paperback I'd read three times, and settled onto the couch. At least it wouldn't take a great deal of concentration.

A few hours later, Max showed up. I locked the door behind him. He looked me over. "How are you? Obviously not sleeping."

"Not even close."

He took off his flannel shirt and draped it over the arm of the couch, set his holster on the floor. We sat next to each other. I pulled my feet up under me.

"How are you tonight?" I studied his face.

Max hesitated. "It's been so crazy. I don't want to add to that."

I reached out a foot and poked his leg with it. "At least we're sitting together through the night. What do you need, Max?"

He swallowed hard, took a breath. "I'd like to try talking again. Go a little farther, if I can. I shied away from a lot of stuff last time. There's so much I don't know if I can say out loud." He met my eyes. "Maguire, you've gotta say if it's not a good night. I'm trusting you to be honest. I don't want to pile it on."

I nodded. "I appreciate that. I'm ok, Max. Actually, it helps just having you here." I sat back and watched him expectantly.

He hesitated for so long, I felt like I needed to help him. "Just start anywhere, Max."

He started in the middle somewhere. It took me awhile to figure out a context for the raw emotions, a setting for the snapshots of vivid experience. He started in the middle of catastrophe, and it struck me that it probably happened like this. Out of nowhere. Bewildering, needing reaction and response without time to process. That much I could relate to.

He talked, and then stopped, staring blankly. He talked again. He cycled between words and tense silence for hours, not coming up for air. At one point, I thought he was going into a full-blown PTSD dissociative state, and would forget where he was, who I was—but he slid to the floor, sat on the ground with his back against the couch, and croaked out my name. "Maguire."

I slid to the floor as well, scooting over to lean against the chair, giving him a little space.

Max's shirt was wet. He was trembling. "We were trying to do the right thing. That's all we tried to do. Stand up and do the right thing. Again and again."

I nodded. "I know, Max." I paused. Studied him. Stretched out my legs. "I know you did. We did, too. I'm not equating my work with your service, Max. I'm not. We weren't protecting the nation, we weren't getting killed. We did protect people. And we got hurt. And some of us got hurt bad. And we kept standing up and taking care of people while we were hurt."

Max rubbed his hand over his face, through his hair. "We tried to take care of each other. We did." His voice cracked, and tears trickled down his face. "I really tried."

I nodded again. "I know you did, Max."

Max's shoulders trembled. "I really tried." He pulled his knees into his chest, hugging his legs. Holding himself together. "But it wasn't enough. It didn't matter. It was all for nothing."

"You've got to let yourself shake, Max. Let your body get rid of it. You gotta let go. You can't worry about looking strong in front of me. Let your body shake."

He glanced at me, eyes wide, but then he listened. He relaxed his body and started shaking, shook hard. Then he was lying on the floor, spent, soaked in sweat.

I pulled a folded t-shirt off the chair and tossed it to him.

He pushed himself to sitting, wiped his face with my shirt. He picked up the conversation as though it hadn't stopped. "But you damn sure can't cry, so you laugh. You laugh at the damnedest things."

"You do." I smiled. "Things really do seem funny, though, in a crazy kind of way."

Max looked down at himself and pulled the front of his t-shirt away from his skin. He frowned, lifted it over his head and dropped it in a wet heap on the floor. He reached for his flannel shirt and put it on. "One more thing you can never talk about. No one will ever understand the things that were funny."

"I think you have to be very familiar with darkness, before you can laugh there." I tossed him another t-shirt.

Max dried his neck with the new shirt. "You make it seem funny, and you talk about that, and you don't talk about the people who get destroyed. You don't talk about how it could be you, next."

He shook his head, draped the shirt over his knee, and leaned back against the couch. "You going back?"

"No." I'd settled that. "You?"

"No. I'm here now." Max started to go on, then smiled ruefully. "I was going to say, no one's shooting at me now, but—" he gestured at me with the shirt.

I giggled, then shut it down and covered my mouth. "I'm sorry." Too much stress and exhaustion. I'd finally gone over the edge.

Max grinned and scolded me. "It's not funny, Maguire." He shook the t-shirt at me. "It's really not."

I started laughing and couldn't stop. I pulled down another shirt and buried my face in it. I snuck a look at Max. He was trying to scowl at me, but his shoulders were shaking. We both gave up and laughed until tears streamed down our faces. I pulled a handful of shirts from the chair and threw them at him. He giggled and wiped his face with them. I laughed at him for giggling.

"Look at us," I said.

Max looked at my strewn laundry, at the two of us on the floor, faces streaked with tears that wouldn't stop. He laughed harder and tipped over, holding his stomach. I couldn't see through the tears. It was hard to breathe. Finally, we lay quietly on the floor, breathing heavily. My abs were aching.

"It must be three in the morning," Max said.

I bunched up a pile of shirts and put my head on them. "Let's just sleep here."

He pulled down my sofa throws and tossed me one, and made his own shirt pillow.

I smiled again, at the sight of us.

"Maguire." His head was down, eyes closed.

"Yeah?"

"What was that shaking thing?"

"Your body releases trauma by shaking. People don't let themselves, because we're embarrassed, so our bodies hold it. Store it. Some people think that's why animals don't get PTSD like people do. They shake after something bad happens, then move on."

"Huh."

I closed my eyes.

"Maguire?"

"Yeah?" I felt like we were at a slumber party, and resisted the urge to start giggling again.

"Thank you."

I smiled in the dark. "You're welcome, Max."

There was quiet. I heard the noises of the night outside my window. The vibrating croaking of frogs. The howl of coyotes—one, then others joining in.

"Max?"

"Mm hmm?"

"It wasn't for nothing."

Max didn't respond. A long moment. Then he scooched himself closer on the floor, reached out a hand, rested his knuckles against my arm. Just a touch. Just the warmth of human contact. We stayed there, amid the tossed, heaped laundry, feeling each other's presence.

The next time I opened my eyes, Max was breathing deeply, evenly on the floor beside me. I closed them again and didn't wake up until sun lit the room.

I sat up and looked around. I giggled again, but it hurt to laugh.

Max stirred, opened his eyes. He saw me grinning at him, and arched one eyebrow. He looked at the room. "Oh." He sat up and leaned against the couch. "No one would ever believe we weren't drinking."

I clambered to my feet, groaning. "I'm going to be stiff for days. We're too old to sleep on the floor."

"I hope you're making coffee," Max said.

"As soon as I can get there." I stretched and my body made cracking noises.

Max smiled tiredly and made his way to the bathroom.

Ida was down in the office. I texted her. "When you get done, will you come up? Just you."

She appeared ten minutes later. "I said you needed help with some female thing or other. Max said to tell you, 'Girl stuff, my ass. Stay out of it and let the police deal with it'."

"Duly noted," I said. "Get some coffee. I want to run through this."

I waited until she was at the table, then spread my hands in the air. "It's the game playing, Ida. Toying with me. Shooting past me is straight up intimidation, but food wrappers? Trying to terrify me? Granted, it worked. But listen. That has to narrow the field. Most of the guys here would just throw a brick through my window."

She took a sip. "Go on."

"Let's simplify. That cop said that people die for really, very few reasons. Let's not complicate this." I rubbed my foot against the table leg, thinking. "Let's talk David, or Luke. Either of them could influence or control other people. David's got more prestige. People really like him. He thinks he's a mentor for the next generation. Luke has more power."

Ida set her cup down. "What power? I've always thought of him as kind of a joke."

"Yeah, well, he's not your P.O. I've been thinking of Luke as childish. Self-absorbed. Talks like everyone's playing games with each other. What if he is playing some kind of game here? What if, besides being a gorgeous, charming emotional toddler, he's also a sociopath?"

That set Ida back in her chair. I stabbed a forefinger at the tabletop to mark a point. "Luke's hanging around way more than he needs to. David volunteers all the time, says his wife wants him out from underfoot. He wants to know when I'm gone at night. Plus, he was at my door when he didn't know I could see him, and tried the doorknob. I almost wish I hadn't locked it. I could've caught him in the act. Whatever he was doing."

"What?" Ida said. "When was this? He tried to go in?"

"I can't prove he would've gone in, but he definitely tried the knob. He made up a lame story when he saw me." I poked the table again. "Luke's people are afraid. Like it doesn't matter if they keep the terms of their probation—if they make Luke mad, he'll violate them. After Mason was killed, people really clammed up. Luke has enormous power over people's lives. Mason wasn't on probation, though."

"He used to be," Ida said. "And he was one of Luke's. But he was off paper. Not under Luke's thumb anymore."

"Imagine being on Luke's caseload," I said. "Talk about not having a voice. You're a convicted felon, on probation, can't buy a job. I know, they made choices that got them there. But say you're trying to turn it around. Now imagine your P.O. is dirty. Of all people to never be able to complain about! Who's going to believe them?"

"What do you think he's making them do?" Ida asked. "Kill people? Really?"

"Not everybody would kill someone. But some people would."
I paused. "Do you think drugs? Mason was back in the tack room,
at night. People keep trying to get into the barn."

I realized I was drumming my fingers on the table, and stopped.
I put my hand on my lap. "Doing it here would give Luke deniability, instead of running it through his office. David probably
couldn't do it from his house, unless his wife is in on it. One
problem with being retired and running a drug ring."

Ida nodded slowly. "There's a tremendous amount of drug use
around here. A lot of meth. If there's meth distribution out of the
ranch, Walt will be devastated, Abby."

"He's already devastated," I said quietly. "Ok, Jared started to
unravel. Using. Paranoia, grandeur. Breaking things just to out-
smart Max, feeling powerful. But while he reveled in it, he put the
place on high-alert."

"Jared used to be on probation with Luke, too. That's how he
got started here."

"Huh." I nodded.

"How could there be drugs in the tack room and we wouldn't
know?" Ida asked. "How could we not see something?"

"It wouldn't have to be in one spot, all the time. Just long
enough to make a handoff. There are endless places to temporarily
hide something. Plus, Jared's tool area is always locked. Jared is
angry. Either Luke or David could manipulate that anger, recruit
someone who feels like an outsider. But Jared is in push-back
mode. Not so convenient anymore, him having the keys. Gives him
power, some protection from reprisal." I shifted my weight back.
We were still missing something.

We sat quietly for a few minutes, while we both juggled our thoughts.

"Ok, try this," I said. "What if Rodney didn't get killed for shocking a horse? What if he got killed for shouting that Walt didn't know what was going on in his own place, under his own nose? Rodney was getting too hard to control, and he was about to be cut loose. Like Jared is. But Jared doesn't talk."

"David was there. He witnessed the whole thing."

"You're right. Walt called Luke and told him about the stun gun, but probably not about Rodney running his mouth." I pushed the plate of cookies away. "The way gossip travels around here, Luke could've found out about that part. But not that many people were there. David was there."

Ida looked old. Tired. Sad. "You're right. I don't know between David or Luke, but it is less complicated. One person in charge, tying it all together. But what do we do?"

I made an I-have-no-idea gesture. "Would anyone believe this? And what would they do about it? How many people do you suppose local law enforcement has, to put on this? Luke's in corrections. David's a respected community member."

Ida rubbed her temples. "Alright. It's a start. I've got to get back downstairs. Let's both think about this."

Chapter Twenty-Eight

It was a good afternoon. Meaning that several volunteers were in, Luke was meeting with people one after the other, and David was adjusting a gate. I straightened my kitchen, made a fresh pot of coffee, and set out a plate of cookies. I walked down to the barn and stood outside, waiting.

Mason's dad pulled up two minutes early. I met him as he climbed out of his car. He turned back to hit the key fob, locking the doors. I held out a hand. "Abby Maguire. Thank you for coming."

He shook my hand and looked me in the eye. "Stan Hobbs. I hope you don't regret this."

"So do I." I led him up the stairs, resisting the urge to look around to see who was watching. I locked the door behind us. This would be a better idea if one of us carried.

I waved him toward the table. "Please, sit. Would you like coffee?"

"Yes, please. Just black." Stan sat, but looked uncomfortable. "Did you know Mason?"

I brought him a steaming mug. "Yes, but not well. He was kind to me." I pushed the cookie plate slightly closer to him.

"Please don't be offended, but I have no appetite." Stan sampled his coffee, but didn't seem to taste it. "Jamie said—from talking to you, she—well, it sounded like you didn't think Mason suffered?"

Suddenly I had no appetite either. Neither of us was going to be able to force a smile, away from watching eyes. "I believe that's true, Stan. Honestly, it looked to me like he never saw it coming. Like it was that fast."

Stan looked away, swallowed hard. "I appreciate knowing that," he said. He turned his gaze back to me. "I'm not sure I understand why you're doing this. This here."

I hesitated, thought about Ida telling me not to trust people. "I guess it's complicated. I've gotten really angry."

He nodded absently, drank some coffee. He was turned inward, eyes unfocused. He shifted his weight in the chair. "This was a good job for Mason. Best thing that ever happened to him— that, and Jamie. Got his self-respect back, self-confidence. He'd had some trouble, sure, but he was proud of what he was doing here." He paused, then went on. "Mason did better here than he'd ever done. Only the one problem, couple years ago. Got into it with some fellows out in the parking lot. Think he got written up over that, but that was the only time. Other than that, he got all good reviews. All good."

I'd ask Ida about that. I'd never heard anything about it.

Stan sucked on his teeth, deep in thought. "I always thought there was something funny there, but Mason wouldn't say a word. I was terribly worried, then. Thought he was going to backslide again. It had that same feel, you know? Like when he was getting in trouble, but wouldn't admit it. Kids never are as smart as they think they are." He shook his head sadly. "Can't always do anything about it, though." He shrugged one bony shoulder. "Somehow Mason kept himself out of it. And that was the last time I ever felt that way. After that, he just seemed like he was solid."

Stan looked at the window. The sky was slightly overcast. A couple of Canadian geese flew by, honking loudly. Their calls gradually faded as they disappeared from view. I wasn't sure if Stan heard them, or the continuous ticking of the second hand on his watch.

"He was just starting off with Jamie then, and was he starry-eyed. That boy was whipped, from day one. I credit her for a lot of his success. She encouraged him, built him up. She's going to let me know my grandchild, now. I believe she will, too. I don't believe she'll falter on that." Stan blinked and straightened, as though something startled him. "Oh, I'm going on. I didn't mean to ramble." He looked at his watch. "How long do you suppose we need to stay here?"

"Probably not long." There was no need to drag this out. It was excruciating. For both of us. What was I thinking, asking him to come to the very building where Mason was killed? I felt ashamed for having gotten so caught up in strategy. "We probably already look like we've said whatever we need to say."

He put his feet flat on the floor one at a time, as though it were an effort. He set down his cup, still half full, and rose. "Please let me know. And please watch yourself. You seem like a real nice young woman. Please watch yourself."

I followed him out, and walked him to his car. We put on a little show, to convince anyone watching that we were partners, if not friends. I watched him drive away, and slowly walked back.

David stood in the corral, staring at me. He held the gate for a young volunteer to come through, and closed it after her. I made myself smile and wave. He did not smile back. His eyes followed me to the stairs.

Behind him, a small group of people walked in from the trails, rakes in hand. One of them appeared to point at Stan's car, and said something to the person next to him, who shrugged. The others were lost in conversation, laughing.

I realized I was holding my breath. Had he pointed at Stan's car? I wasn't sure. He could have been looking at anything.

I glanced back as I started up the steps. Luke stood just inside the barn with his briefcase, Janice behind him. Luke waved and walked over, while Janice edged her way towards David.

"Hey, Abby," Luke said. "What are you up to?"

"Not much, now. How about you?"

"Just finished here, last meeting. Want to grab a quick lunch?" He smiled—the charming flirt smile. "Just as colleagues. Friendly trip for tacos. I'll drive, make it easy. Heck, I'll buy, too." He pointed toward his car with his head. "Been awhile. Come on, hop in."

Like hell.

"Oh, I just ate." I waved. "Thanks, though." I locked the door behind me. I leaned against the wall and closed my eyes for a moment, then went to clear up the dishes.

There was a knock at the door. I hesitated, then opened it. Walt looked angrier than the day he beat me up with a horse. I stood back to let him in.

"Just what in the hell do you think you're doing?" He stayed in the entryway, making no pretense that this was a social visit.

I decided to meet his directness. "I will not be lunged, Walt."

His eyes narrowed slightly, but continued boring a hole through my head. "You what?"

"I. Will. Not. Be. Lunged." I met his gaze without flinching. I was at least as angry as he was.

"What the hell are you talking about? The shooting on the road? The intruder up here? You think taunting a killer will answer to that?"

"It's the same person, Walt." I made my voice quiet, but hard. Meeting with Stan had affected me. I became more furious with every word. I would apologize for nothing.

I told Walt everything. The wrappers. Ida protecting Max by taking the first one, me protecting Ida by keeping it quiet. The one in the refrigerator. The one on my floor. Right next to my bed. The money the police told me not to tell anyone about. Walt let me talk without interruption, his face growing darker as I went.

He waited to make sure I was done, then spoke in a voice as hard and quiet as mine. "I ought to fire you on the spot."

I had no good response for that. I said nothing.

"This was a reckless thing to do, Abby."

"And now I've done it. Help me, Walt."

He wasn't glaring at me—his anger wasn't hot. It was cold, deep, perfectly controlled. "What exactly would you have me do?"

"See who else recognized Stan. You are beyond a doubt the most observant person I've ever known, Walt. Help me see a reaction. Maybe nobody has any idea who he is, but if someone does, and has reason to fear his presence, there should be a tell."

He looked at me for a long, silent moment. "Did you for one minute think about what you're going to do, if you manage to provoke a response?" As usual, Walt put his finger right on the crux of the matter.

"That's a fluid concept," I said.

"That's what I thought." He turned and walked out.

I watched him go down the stairs. He stopped, looked around. His gaze lingered on each person in range of sight. He would miss nothing, forget nothing. I hoped he wouldn't really fire me. I hoped I hadn't destroyed our friendship. I was surprised by the depth of my feelings about that. But I didn't have time right now. I went down myself, locking the door behind me.

David came out of the woods, leading a horse. I walked right up to him. "David! Hi! I meant to ask you—"

He brought the horse to a halt, and tilted his head at me.

I made myself smile. "You invited me to shooting, but didn't say when it was. Any time soon?"

His face lost all expression. He seemed to be searching his memory. "Oh. Well..."

He didn't even remember the conversation. For crying out loud. I got a sudden image of my second-grade teacher smacking her pointer stick on Tommy Jarski's desk. "Tell the truth, and you won't have to remember what you said!" I was tempted to tell David that.

He recovered. "Forgive me, my mind was elsewhere. I'll let you know. Say, who was that gentleman you were speaking with earlier?"

I gave him a bigger smile. "Nothing to do with the ranch. Just a personal matter."

He missed a beat. At the same moment, the horse glanced at him. Aha. Gotcha.

David began to be unhappy with the conversation. His posture stiffened. He drew back slightly. "He seemed to resemble an acquaintance. Perhaps I was mistaken." He walked away with the horse. David got a bit pompous when he was unhappy. I looked around. Luke was gone. Ben was doing something by the barn. I waded into the middle of the group of volunteers with rakes.

"Hi, guys."

They all looked up. One of them tossed a pile into the wheelbarrow, missing me by inches. They all laughed. I put a grin on my face, waved and moved on. No guilty consciences here.

Janice was scrubbing feed buckets. She saw me coming, grabbed a few clean ones and carried them away. I pretended I hadn't noticed, and called out a greeting. Janice paused, throwing me a tiny head jerk over her shoulder, but accelerated and fled for the feed room. This wasn't enormously informative. Janice stood with both Luke and David within minutes of Stan leaving.

I saw Ben out of the corner of my eye, stopping to examine the sliding door. He appeared to be so unaware of my presence that he must be working at it. He stooped, and I saw his holster under his shirt.

Max and Ida were just finishing a session. I didn't even want to think about facing Max, after he talked with Walt. Enough visibility. I went back upstairs, to do my own chores and wait.

Halfway through cleaning the bathroom, I heard my phone buzz. It was Ida. "I'm outside your door. Didn't want to frighten you by knocking." I let her in and locked the door behind her. She looked subdued. Worse, actually. She looked like a walking mug shot. Pale. Slightly disheveled. Dazed.

"Ida, I'm so sorry I didn't warn you. I didn't plan to tell Walt everything. I shouldn't have implicated you without giving you a heads up. It all happened so fast."

She sat down. "I'm not angry with you, Abby. I just don't know how it's come to this. When did you decide to parade Mason's father around?"

I swallowed. "A couple days ago. I wanted you to have plausible deniability."

"Well, I had that. You know Walt was watching my face when he told us. I'm actually glad I looked surprised. The look on his face, he might've strangled me with his bare hands." She paused. "I think Max might have popped an artery. He should probably take it easy for a little while. Just in case."

I didn't want to think about Max right now. He would certainly share his opinion, when he became functional enough to make it up my stairs.

Ida tilted her head. "Walt didn't mention the rest of it in front of Max. At least there's that. I suppose he was showing me respect by not giving me a dressing-down in front of someone. He said he needed to talk to me alone, so Max left, closed the door."

That was interesting. "So, Walt held back the whole story. The wrappers, all of it."

Ida processed that slowly. "Well, the wrappers. That was it, wasn't it? Am I forgetting something?"

He hadn't told Ida about the money. "No, I'm just a little off kilter." That was the truth. I hoped I could keep it straight, in this big, happy work family, who knew about what.

"Ben the Fed is hanging around in front of the barn, pretending to work."

"I saw that," I said. "Good. He can stand around packing heat all day long. If he wants to swoop in and take the credit, that's fine by me."

"Did you say anything to him?"

"What? No! I'm not spilling anything to him until he antes something up himself."

She nodded. "He must know who Mason's father is, then. Otherwise, how would he know to start shadowing you?"

I hadn't thought of that. Ben must have been surprised when the man who hired him showed up. He probably had a moment. I wondered what Ben thought of our charade. "Are we okay, Ida?"

She rested a hand on my arm. "Of course, we are. I'm just not sure where to go from here. I can't decide if I hope the killer shows himself, or not. This could be terrible, Abby."

We both jumped when someone knocked on the door. We looked at each other, and froze.

Chapter Twenty-Nine

I slowly walked to the door. Another knock. I heard a cupboard door close, and glanced back. Ida was poised with a frying pan raised over her head.

"That's not a bad idea." I opened the door.

David's eyes cut between me and Ida, who lowered the pan and was trying to look nonchalant. "I'm sorry," he said. "I'm interrupting." He turned and left.

"Pack a bag," Ida said, as I locked the door.

"Then the whole thing will be for nothing. Stan put himself in danger, coming out here. I can't bail on him."

"Tell Ben the Fed to sleep up here. He can give us the all-clear when it's over."

I hesitated. "I wonder if Max will loan me a gun. No, he'd just yell at me."

"He would. He's going to yell at me, too. He'll work himself into a state wondering what Walt wanted me for. You know, Abby, I do get tired of being yelled at by men."

She had a point.

"What would Johnny have said?" I asked.

Ida pondered that for a moment. "Well, he would've been upset, thinking I was in danger. But he always had an element of, you get 'em, Ida! You give them what for!" She smiled warmly, absently slapping the frying pan against her hand.

"I don't want you in danger, Ida. I'm the one who started this. You should probably head home."

"I talked you into the whole thing in the first place." Ida poked the pan at me, punctuating her words. "Let's not forget that. Do you have any popcorn?"

I blinked.

Ida bobbed her head. "That's it. We'll have a sleepover." She looked around the room. "Say, where's the TV? I never noticed it was gone."

"I put it in the closet. Ida—"

"Well, let's haul it out. What did you do with the rabbit ears? They work if you put a little tinfoil on them."

The sky darkened. We were huddled under a blanket on the couch when the next knock on the door came. I set down the popcorn.

"Good thing I put my truck behind the shed," Ida whispered. She pushed off the blanket and reached for the pan beside her. "They think you're alone. We should have made a more detailed plan, though."

I gripped my Maglite. "Are you ready?"

She took a deep breath. "Ready!"

Ida crept behind me as I tiptoed toward the door. I stopped, and she walked into me.

"Sorry. But I don't need to be sneaky. That will make it look like something's up."

Ida made a little gasp. "You're right! I'll sneak, you play it cool."

We moved to the door. I made sure Ida was in place behind it, and threw the lock.

Arms folded over his chest, Max had the air of a man being extraordinarily patient. He glanced from my face to the flashlight in my hand, and back. He closed his eyes and turned his face away for a moment. "May I come in?"

I opened the door wider. Max stepped in, noted Ida behind the door, and moved to see what she was hiding behind her back. I locked the door, even though Max was standing there, fully armed. He raised an eyebrow.

"Distractions make for moments of vulnerability," I said.

"Damn straight." Ida raised her chin defiantly.

Max looked at Ida's frying pan and took a deep breath. He closed his eyes again, blowing out slowly.

Ida leaned in, but frowned and pulled back again. I could tell she was struggling not to warn Max about his arteries.

Max raised a hand and rubbed his temples, eyes still closed. "I saw your truck."

"We were right in the middle of Kojak," Ida said. "Can we help you with something?"

Max opened his mouth, closed it, turned, and left. I locked the door behind him.

"At least he didn't scold us," Ida said.

There was a commercial on, so I went to get a glass of water. We settled back in with the volume low, so we could hear someone coming.

Around midnight, I gave Ida an extra toothbrush and a pillow. I locked the windows. There were ladders in the barn.

I was staring at the ceiling when Ida came in. "Abby! Abby!" she hissed.

I sat up.

"There's someone downstairs!"

I listened. "Are you sure? The barn makes a lot of noise at night. You'd be surprised. And Lego is in the medical stall. She might be banging against the wall."

"I know horse banging! Just listen!" She sat on the end of my bed.

We both leaned an ear toward the floor. She was right. I heard scraping, like a chair being moved. I tried to locate the noise and orient myself.

"I think that's the office," I whispered. "It's under us. That's not the tack room." We stared at each other.

Ida set her pan on the bed beside her. "What should we do?"

"I'm not going down there. There could be ten of them, for all we know. We should call Max." I reached for my phone. There was shouting, a crash. The lights went on, glowing out through the open sliding door. "I think he knows."

We peered out the window. "I can't see anything at all," Ida complained. "Do you think we can go down there?"

All the exterior lights went on.

"We're concerned," I said. "We have our phones ready, to call the cops."

We paused at the door to the barn, peering around the corner, then crept in toward the office. Ben had David in a half-nelson. Max appeared from somewhere in the back. He put zip ties around David's wrists while Ben held them.

Ben looked up and saw us. He did his scanning assessment, registered the frying pan and flashlight, and looked away. He said something to Max.

Max pulled up a chair and sat David into it, while Ben pulled out his phone. Calling his cop friend, no doubt.

"What would David be doing in the office?" Ida hesitated, then strode over.

Everything looked to be under control, so I followed her and stuck my head in the door. The filing cabinet was open, a keychain dangling from the lock. I gasped, and rounded on David. "You can't have keys for the files! This is too much!" I shook my Maglite at him. "You cannot have access to client files! You cannot! I don't know who you think you are! Client files are absolutely confidential! There is no excuse for this!" I took a breath.

Ben interrupted. "He wasn't in the client files." He picked up a file folder from the desk, and turned to David. "Why did you want Mason's employee file?"

David ignored him.

"David was in here when the cabinet was open, not long ago," Max said. "I thought Ida forgot to lock it after our session."

Ida gaped at him. "You what?"

Max pulled up a chair and sat in front of David. "What did you take that time?"

David stared resolutely at the wall over Max's shoulder.

Ben set the file down, and Ida picked it up. She paged through it, scanning. "There is absolutely nothing noteworthy in here."

I grabbed Ida's arm and pulled her out of the office. Ben narrowed his eyes at me.

"Ida," I whispered. "Mason's dad said he got written up a few years ago for getting in a fight in the parking lot. He said it felt like trouble. Something bad. Is that in his file?"

"I remember that."

The men were all watching us.

"That was earlier," Ida said. "He hadn't been hired on, yet. That would be in his volunteer file." She walked back into the office, closed the drawer, and opened another one. She flipped through the files, frowned, looked through them again. "Well, it's missing. The whole file's gone."

"What's gone?" Max moved to her side.

"Mason's volunteer file. It's not here."

Max flipped through the files. "What are you looking for?"

"You remember, Max. A few years back. There was that brawl in the parking lot. Walt was so angry, went storming in and broke the whole thing up himself, said if there were any clients on the property, he would've had them all arrested. Some of them did get probation violations. Mason got a written warning, and a suspension. He came back, though. I was happy about that. I knew he had promise."

Max glanced at David, tense in his chair. "I do remember that. Some people came here to pick a fight with Mason, that was in his favor." Max walked back to the file cabinet, flipped through it again, then looked through the other drawers. "It's not here."

"I don't know what that would have to do with David," Ida said. "I don't know that he was even here that day."

We heard a car door, and a cop walked in. He looked at the zip ties and the frying pan. Turned to Ben and Max. "What've we got here?"

Ben filled him in.

The cop looked at Max. "He had no legal right to the keys?"

"None."

The cop looked at the key ring, and nodded. "So, you think this could be the second time, here? He took one file, thought about it, came back for the other one?"

"That's what we figure," Ben said.

The cop loomed over David. "You got anything to say?"

"You clearly don't know who I am." David glared at him. "These men have committed assault and unlawful restraint. I expect immediate action—rest assured I will be discussing this with the mayor. This will impact your career. You decide how."

"Alright. Well, you're under arrest for breaking and entering." The cop looked at Max. "Any idea why he'd want that file bad enough to get himself a criminal record, man of his age and social standing?"

"No idea," Max said.

"How about the other homicide? You check to see if his files are missing?"

Max opened the cabinet again and quickly located Rodney's volunteer file. He paged through it. "If anything's missing, I don't know what it would be. There's only the one file, he wasn't an employee."

"Alright." The cop pulled out his cuffs. "Well, the detective's going to want to talk to you tomorrow, I can pretty much guarantee it. If you could come up with a date for that fight, it would help. You got something to cut these zip ties off?"

Max brought snippers from the tool area.

"Doesn't look like he's going to be too forthcoming," the cop said. "Going through processing, night in a cell might help. Previously upstanding citizens tend to struggle with all that." He put a hand under David's arm. "Sir, I need you to stand up."

Ben glanced at Max. "Anything you can think of, could've been in that file besides a written warning for fighting? I'm not following this."

Max shook his head, shrugged.

Ida absently slapped the pan against her open palm again, while she thought.

David eyed the pan.

"Well, his body language changed when we started talking about the fight," Ida said.

Every head swung towards David, who stiffened under scrutiny.

Ida frowned. "The warning would be pretty much factual. Not likely anything we don't already remember. I tell you what, though. Walt does let people have their say when they get written up. He always gives people a chance to write their own version of things, and attaches it in their file. I wonder if Mason did that? I wonder what he said?"

"Hard to imagine Walt missing it, if David was implicated," Ben said. "Say he did. David's worried there will be eyes on Mason's files again, digging up something that was supposed to be long forgotten. Unless he's stupid enough to have kept it, we may never know."

The cop watched David closely. "Homicide, pretty good chance for a search warrant. Judges around here really don't like people getting killed. Give us a little leeway. Wonder what his wife will think about the whole house being turned over?"

He paused to let that sink in. Then everyone seemed to decide at once that David wasn't going to be provoked, and turned away.

The coin finally dropped. "Oh," I said.

The cop paused with one hand on David's arm.

I cleared my throat, hesitated. "I actually have a copy of that file."

Even David stared at me.

Ida spoke first. "Abby, what in the world do you mean? Which file?"

"Mason's volunteer file."

The cop was the only one whose mouth wasn't hanging open.

"I was just glancing through all the volunteer files one day." I was getting flustered. "Just for background information. I hadn't expected Mason to have one, since he was an employee. It kind of threw me. But I wanted the contact information for his family, and I ended up photocopying the whole file, to read later. I figured I'd just shred it afterwards. I haven't. Read it, I mean. Only the contact page." I hurried up the stairs, retrieved the file from my computer bag, and gave it to the cop.

He flipped through the pages, stopped, and read silently for several minutes. He looked up, frowning at David. "Oh, dear." He shook his head solemnly.

Ben and Max crowded the folder. The cop laid it flat on the table. Ida and I stuck our heads in.

"Well, now. Just the word of a guy who's no longer here to testify—" the cop cut a glance at David. "But I bet an enterprising reporter could find corroboration, word gets out." He addressed David directly. "I'd say your son has a potential problem with his budding political career. Isn't this the candidate promising to clean up meth in the county?" He looked back at the file. "Distribution, assault, what else we got?"

David squirmed uncomfortably in the handcuffs. "Are we done here?"

I turned on the photocopier, waited while it warmed up, and ran off some pages for the cop. When he drove away with David, we went back upstairs.

"I don't know how I'm going to sleep now," Ida said. "Do you think David's the killer? Trying to keep a lid on things?"

"Probably. Trying to protect his son. Maybe he even took over the kid's drug empire. This could just make things worse."

"What?" Ida checked to make sure the door was locked. "What do you mean? Why would it be worse?"

"He's only charged with breaking and entering. He'll bail out pretty quick, and he'll be mad."

Ida peered out the window, at the parking lot. "Not tonight, you don't think?"

"No. It must be two in the morning."

"Well, he'll be banned from the ranch," Ida said. "That will help. He'll have way less opportunity to kill us."

"I hope he will. He's stealthy. Who knows how long he's been walking around, with how many keys?"

We propped a chair under the doorknob, and went to bed.

Chapter Thirty

I walked around in the woods, looking for Teddy. My cellphone rang. I draped the lead rope over my shoulders and pulled out my phone. Unknown number. I answered professionally, in case it was someone I wanted to talk to.

The voice was hesitant. "Hi, um. This is Jamie? Mason's fiancée."

I snapped to attention. "Jamie! Yes! How are you?"

"Hi, um, listen." Words poured out. "When you came out here, I didn't really talk about everything. I just don't want any trouble with the ranch. I really don't know what the deal is, I just know it's something to do with the ranch, so I didn't want to talk in front of that other lady, you know?" She took a breath. "But, you're like, new here. So, I thought maybe. Especially if you're really trying to help."

I paused a moment to process that. "Well, you're right, Jamie. I'm new, and I'm also a temp worker. I'm not even really a ranch employee. What did you want to talk about?"

There was silence at the other end of the line. I thought I might have lost the connection, and looked at my phone screen. Then I heard her voice again.

"So, it wasn't true that Mason didn't have trouble with anyone, besides that old guy I told you about. Someone from the ranch did come out a few times? It was worse than the old guy, Mason wasn't just irritated. It was like he was scared of something. They both yelled at each other. I couldn't really understand, they were outside, but Mason said, 'I don't know, alright? I don't know!' Then another time, he like shouted, 'I can't help you!'"

Silence. Jamie composed herself, then went on. "He wouldn't talk to me about it, but he'd be real uptight afterwards." Her voice quavered, her hand likely trembling, holding the phone. "He'd go to work, and come home stressed out. I could tell there was something really wrong going on, but he wanted that job to work out so bad. He just kept telling me don't worry, it's not good for the baby, it'll be okay." Her voice broke. "I mean, it's sure not okay, is it? I don't know if this will change anything or not, but I wanted to tell you."

I leaned back against a tree. "Did you say anything to the police, Jamie?"

"No. Like I said, they weren't listening to me anyway. And I don't want any trouble following me back here. I have to protect our baby, okay? I can't have ranch people coming here, thinking I know anything."

"I won't get you in trouble, Jamie." Okay, think. "Was it a man who came by?"

"Yes. Mason never said his name."

"Can you describe him at all? What did he look like, or what was he wearing?" Here we go. Good looking? She would definitely remember seeing Luke, and he saw Mason at the ranch all the time.

Or another old guy? It could still be David. I braced myself. Which way would she go?

"Older than us," she said. "But not real old. Kind of brownish-blondish hair. A beard. Some kind of tat on his arm, like a military kind of thing. One time he wore a flannel, with the sleeves rolled up. And he was carrying. A side holster."

I dropped my phone in the brush. Little spots danced in front of my eyes. I knelt in the dirt and groped for my phone in the bushes. I finally pulled it out. "Jamie? Are you still there? I'm sorry, I dropped my phone for a minute."

"I'm here. Don't forget, I don't want any trouble."

"Yeah. I know." I sat on the ground, my back against a tree. I couldn't breathe. "Okay. Thank you for telling me this."

"You promise, if you figure anything out, you'll tell me? I just don't want to wonder, for the rest of my life."

I closed my eyes, leaned my head back against the bark. "Yes. I don't know if I will, but if I do get any answers, I'll get in touch. And if you think of anything else, please call me again."

She agreed, and we disconnected. I sat there in the dirt, lightheaded. Okay. This didn't necessarily mean anything.

But there was no way it was good. In fact, it sounded so bad, it was just as well she hadn't told the police. Or was it?

When I opened my eyes, three horses were standing in front of me, looking at me curiously.

"I don't know what to do," I told them. I sat with my head in my hands. A cold knot was forming in my stomach. Was it even possible? What if it was Max all along?

No one would believe me, for one thing. I was supposed to be getting Teddy. I pushed myself up against the tree, and started walking. He wasn't in the woods. I'd try the pasture. I barely registered the horses I passed.

All right, Abby. Get a grip, here. So Max got into it verbally with Mason. Big deal. He does that. Needing anger management classes didn't make someone a killer. Or a stalker. Why the big reaction? Maybe I was just overwrought. Max was right—everyone has a limit.

Or was my subconscious trying to tell me something that I didn't want to hear? I had to approach this logically. The benefit of an outside viewpoint is supposed to be independent thinking—for example, not getting pulled into a person's golden aura, that others choose not to see through.

No matter who it was, they were enlisting others. Well, Max had friends. He'd lived here for years. All it would take would be one or two wingnuts in the crowd. Somebody knew exactly what was going on, and was pretending not to. It could just as easily be Max.

Could Max possibly be my stalker? He was so upset when I went running with Luke. More than co-worker upset. He'd been incoherent.

It niggled at me that Ben hadn't seen anything the night the intruder was in my bedroom. Not even taillights from the car Max reported. If there really was a car, why didn't Max see it earlier? I didn't wake him. Ben stashed his gun in his waistband. Max was fully dressed, wearing his holster. He had a key. After changing the locks, he still had a key.

Could Max be scaring me, so he could run in and comfort me? And why did I instinctively call Max, anyway? How might he react if I called Ben instead? Maybe his survivor's guilt was compelling him to create danger and rescue me, again and again.

The message behind the wrappers could be simple. "You know me."

"You know me. Look at me. See me."

It was possible.

Max could have killed Mason. He could have had a hand in killing Rodney. If so, he pretended to find both bodies with me. He wasn't emotional, not one bit. He snapped into efficiency. I thought of it as combat mode.

I got to the pasture and looked around. I saw Teddy and angled off in his direction. He was happy to stick his head into his halter. I snapped on his lead rope and turned toward the barn.

I assumed that Ben moved in with Max to better watch the ranch. Maybe he was watching Max. Trying to get proof. If he was, and slept in the same house, I hadn't given him enough credit.

Max lunged that horse so gracefully. He was so smart, so attentive, so aware of tiny changes in behavior, stance, movement. Was Max lunging me?

I thought about late nights with Max, talking, crying, laughing. Sleeping on the floor. Rumpled, worn Max showing up at my door. Holding me in the darkness, when I ran out of words. Max always understood. Max always came running. I barely made it to the nearest bush before throwing up.

Wiping my face on my sleeve, I tottered over and leaned on Teddy, who hadn't moved when I dropped his lead rope. He looked at me curiously.

Max wouldn't have to be acting, though. If he was doing these things, he could be dissociating. Checking out. Walking around in an altered state, his mind defensively making him unaware, protecting him from more pain. It was possible. Trauma could trigger dissociative states. He could be doing things in a state of extreme stress, and not even know it. Not remember.

And Ida, acting like Max is her cherished son. Was she zealously over-protective of Max because she knew at some level that he was broken?

And—no. I didn't want to think about it. I steadied myself with a hand on Teddy's side.

Could I have triggered this whole thing by offering to help Max process his trauma in the first place? Was he too fragile? He was reluctant. I more or less talked him into it.

"I was just trying to help," I told Teddy, burying my face in his back. "What have I done?"

I hadn't known his girlfriend would dump him and get married immediately. Did that push him over the edge? Maybe I should've told him then to stop digging up the deep trauma. Ended relationships are huge stressors. Could Max see the ranch falling apart and think he had nothing left? How much mental resilience could one person be expected to have?

Here I was, telling Ida we look at what changed. What happened, to make things go sideways. Max had a whole list of things.

I dropped Teddy off in the barn, clipped to his post, and left. It wasn't my session. They would be fine without my help. I hurried upstairs and locked my door behind me.

Alright, breathe. My head was spinning. What was wrong with me? I couldn't even think straight. Breathe. My phone buzzed. It was Ida, texting. "Are you ok?"

I paused. "Sorry, I got a phone call," I texted back.

My phone rang. "I thought it would be easier to talk," Ida said. "Walt and Max are going into town to meet with the police. Are you free to cover?"

"Be right down." Good. This would buy me some time. I helped with Ida's sessions. She helped with mine. When Max and Walt did return, they went into the office and closed the door.

"Let's go out to dinner," Ida said, when we were done. "We've certainly earned it. What a day. It went well, though. We did a fine job. We deserve a little something."

We got tacos and took them to Ida's place. We made an evening of it. We baked cookies. Ida threw me a few curious glances. "You seem a little off, Abby. Are you okay?"

I nodded. "It's just a lot. It adds up." She couldn't argue with that.

It was late when she dropped me back at the ranch. I thought about changing clothes and going to bed, but I wouldn't sleep. That much was obvious. I could sit and read a paperback, but I didn't want to leave a light on. I didn't want Max to come up. I was in no way prepared to deal with that. I slipped into my boots and went outside for a walk. I could go see what Rosie was up to. Go scratch Teddy.

The air was cool, with a slight breeze. Thousands of bright stars filled the sky. I was so amazed by those stars when I first came, first walked the trails at night. Such a beautiful place. I thought about Max and his memories linked to smells. Years from now, what would I associate with the smell of manure? Friendship, laughter, Rosie? Or death and a sense of overwhelming dread?

I heard Max's door open and close. I stepped into a lean-to, pressed myself into a back corner. The sound of his footsteps carried in the quiet of night. It sounded like he was right next to me. And then, he was.

I held my breath as he walked in front of the lean-to, stopped, and looked up at my apartment. He stood for several long minutes, staring at my window. I focused on the ground, afraid Max would feel my eyes on his back. Finally he moved again, walking away from me.

I felt lightheaded. I shoved aside a dried manure pile with my foot and sat in the dirt, leaning back into the corner. I closed my eyes, just breathing, giving Max time to get a little farther away.

"Maguire? Maguire!"

I jumped. I was still in the lean-to. In the dirt.

"Maguire, are you okay?" Max leaned over me. The sun was bright. The first few horses in the breakfast crew stood behind him, lead ropes dangling. They watched with interest.

I looked around, disoriented. "Oh."

"Are you hurt?"

"Um, no," I pushed against the wall to heave myself up. "I fell asleep."

"Dammit, Maguire, you scared the hell out of me! I thought—what the hell are you—" He stopped, but clearly with great effort. He took a deep breath and blew it out slowly. "Why are you sleeping out here?"

I blinked. I could hardly tell him I was hiding from him. "Oh, well, I just sat down, I didn't really mean to sleep there. My gosh, I slept for hours! That's amazing!" I sidestepped past him, climbed over the fence, and scampered up the stairs. I looked back from my door. Max was staring at me with his mouth open.

I couldn't remember if my door was locked or not. I pulled out my key, went through unlocking-the-door motions. I made my way to the bathroom and looked in the mirror. Ouch.

I dropped my clothes to the floor and eased slowly into the shower. I was going to be stiff for days, after sleeping on the ground, leaning up against a cold metal wall. I tried to focus my thoughts as the hot water ran over my sore muscles. I wasn't even sure what day it was. It was early enough that I could look at the office calendar, check the schedule, but Max would be down there. I had to be able to work with him, to somehow act like nothing was wrong. I rested my head against the tile wall. Think.

I'd have to compartmentalize. Snap into professional mode. How did things get so personal with Max, anyway? I would pretend he was a client. The rigid boundaries that came with that would get me through. That's it. Professional smile, easygoing professional demeanor. Switching off my personal life during sessions was second nature. I would think of it as one long session. Think and respond in therapist mode. I could do this.

I toweled off and slipped into my robe. I was halfway across the living room when I heard a knock at the door and froze.

Calm. Professional demeanor. In a bathrobe. Think.

My phone buzzed. It was Ida. I opened the door and peered out. She was alone, so I let her in.

Ida gave me a long, searching look. "Abby, are you alright?"

I cleared my throat. "Sure. Why?"

She raised her eyebrows. "Well, Max said you were sleeping out in the lean-to with a clump of manure as a pillow, looking like you were dead, and when he woke you up, you ran away from him."

"That's a little dramatic." I paused. "Actually, I pushed the manure aside before I even sat down."

Ida crossed her arms and leaned back against the door. "What's going on?"

"I don't know what I can tell you, Ida." That was the truth. "Sometimes I go out at night, see the stars, walk with the horses. I don't sleep well. I sat down and the next thing I knew, Max was shouting."

Ida shook her head, eyeing me doubtfully. She decided not to push.

"Um, what day is it today?"

Ida's eyes widened. "Did you hit your head?"

"No! I'm just tired. Not quite in gear yet. Do we have a session?"

Ida looked at the ceiling and sighed. "You and I have two sessions this morning, and we all have a staff meeting this afternoon."

"Great! I'll just get changed and get my hair dried. I'll be right there."

Ida gave me a look, and left.

The morning went fine. Max kept his distance. He gave me odd looks from across the barn, but looked away if I glanced at him. Was he afraid I would bolt if he spoke to me? Or was he afraid I knew the truth about him? If he was my stalker, how would he react if he thought I knew? None of my studies ever had even a single chapter on stalkers, let alone murderous ones. What do they do if their secret delusions collide with reality? I had no idea.

Ida gave me odd looks too, but reined it in when the clients came. We cleaned up after the second session. I attempted a smile, and told Ida I needed some fresh air. I needed more than that, but fresh air would help.

Ida nodded. "Good idea. I'm going to run a few quick errands before the meeting."

I watched her truck recede into the distance. Teddy came up and presented his neck. I scratched him with both hands, occasionally shaking loose hair off my fingers. The breeze blew the hair back to me. It stuck to my clothes and face. I was spitting hair out of my mouth when I heard footsteps.

"Need some help there?" Luke walked up and wiped hair off my face with his fingertips. He stroked my lip with his thumb.

I recoiled. "I'm good. I got it."

"Just trying to be nice."

"Yeah, I'm good." I stepped back, wiped my face with my hand, and spread another layer of horse hair over my mouth and cheeks. I tried wiping it off with my sleeve, but made it worse.

Luke grinned at me. He looked around the parking lot. "I'm meeting someone here. If you need help when I'm done, let me know." He walked into the barn, stepping carefully around dirt clods in his leather slip-ons. Must be court day. He was wearing slacks and loafers.

I turned back to Teddy, who was giving me a side-eye. "Sorry, sweetheart. I bet I felt nervous for a minute there. Don't worry. The mountain lion's gone."

Chapter Thirty-One

The fresh air did help. I sat on a picnic table bench in the warm sun. Most of the horses were out in the woods, but a few wandered around in the corral or visited the water trough. A bird circled overhead—I guessed some kind of hawk. The smaller birds vanished.

Before I knew it, Ida pulled back into the parking lot. I'd completely lost track of time. I hadn't mentally prepared myself for the staff meeting.

Ida gave me a little wave as she climbed down from the cab. "We've got about a half hour. I see Walt's out by the round pen. I'm going to go see if he needs anything."

I should at least look presentable. I ran upstairs, gave my boots a quick scuff on the rug, and slid into my bedroom to change into a shirt that wasn't covered in horsehair. I popped back out into my hallway and ran into Luke.

I took a step back. "Luke. I didn't hear you *knock*." I looked at the door pointedly.

Luke gave me a grim smile. "This has been fun, Abby, but I don't want to play anymore."

"I knew it."

"Knew what?"

I shook my head. "What did you think we were playing?"

"Why did I just get a call that Jared Wills and half my caseload got pulled in for questioning—on a tip?"

I blinked. "What?"

"A tip? Who you been talking to, Abby?"

"What?" I didn't have to pretend to be confused. Did Ida say something and not tell me? Surely not.

He paused. I could see him recalculating. "You expect me to believe it's not you? You never stop talking, Abby. You been asking all kinds of questions about my caseload. Talking to everybody. You think I don't hear? Now they all get pulled in? I don't believe in coincidence. Who you been talking to?"

Suddenly I could see it in his eyes—hostility, a cold anger. What Rosie and Maverick tried to show me. It took a second to register. That was enough time for him to grab my arm. His grip was painfully tight.

Instead of trying to pull away, I took a step in. I grabbed my own wrist with my free hand and yanked my arm out through the weak point between his fingers and thumb. I registered his surprise as the momentum carried me several steps away from him. I took another few steps, turned, and quickly straightened. "I don't know what you're talking about. You need to leave. Now." I tried to move, but he blocked my way.

"Luke. Assaulting me is a 'crime against a person.' You will lose your job. Your career. Think about this. You've made your point. Just walk away."

"You talk too much, Abby." He lunged, grabbed a handful of my hair, and jerked me backwards. Regaining my balance, I put both of my hands over his and pulled his fist into my head. Again, I felt his momentary confusion. He'd probably never attacked someone who had years of training on how to not hurt an attacker. Was that what I wanted? I'd never in my life tried to hurt another person. I'd never been attacked outside of work. Think. With the hair pull, there would be coworkers coming to help, to peel back the fingers one by one, while I immobilized the hand, kept as much hair as possible in my head. No one was coming.

His hand tightened in my hair. He pushed me into the wall, knocking down a picture. It crashed to the floor. The glass shattered. Luke leaned in. He smelled like sweat and peppermint gum. The flirtatious twinkle in his eyes was gone, replaced by hardness, darkness. "I should have stopped when you broke my window."

A chill ran down my back.

"All alone, out in the dark. I should have dealt with you then. You're alone now, Abby."

I argued with myself. Can't harm—not a client—hurts. Hard to think. I had to get out of this. No one coming. I struggled for something to say, something to divert him.

"Did you kill Mason?" I blurted. Damn. That was not it.

"No. I didn't kill Mason." Luke frowned, as though disappointed. "I don't have to kill anybody. People don't want to go to prison, I told you that. I warned you not to cross the line, Abby. You play your part, or you step back and keep your mouth shut." He exhaled sharply through his nose, shook his head. "Mason wouldn't just keep quiet and look away. Easiest thing in the world to do. Rodney couldn't keep his mouth shut. And you never, never stop talking. You won't play nice, and you won't shut up."

"But—Rodney—your window. That was you."

Luke tightened his grip on my hair again, lifted me slightly off my feet. The pain made my eyes water. Luke saw the tears and smiled, a spark returning to his eyes. "You don't know! All those questions, all that endless talking." He laughed. "You'll never see it coming. You think this is all on me? You don't even know what to look out for."

I made an inarticulate grunt. Tried to think.

He smiled again. He was happy, if he had the upper hand. "Watch your blind spot, Abby. Where do you think you're safe? Out on the road? In the park? In the barn?" He stroked under my chin with a finger. "In your bed at night? Where are you safe, Abby?" He lowered me to my feet, took a step back. "You have absolutely no idea the mess you have made, that I'm expected to clean up. So, one more time. Who you been talking to?"

I turned sideways, raised an elbow into his chest, gaining a few inches. I'd only talked to Ida. I would never tell him that. I tried to take a deep breath. Think.

Luke shoved my face into the wall, gouging my head on the empty nail. I tried not to cry out, but it hurt. A lot. Blood ran down my face, into my eyes. Face wounds bleed a lot. Don't panic. Think.

"I'm done playing, Abby. I'll do you myself, right now. I'm in this too deep to screw around with you." He slammed my face into the wall again.

Sparkles of light filled my vision. Pain. Blood. Something finally clicked. Predator. Get out of your head. I felt a surge of adrenaline, fear, rage. Damned if I would be prey. Flip off the safety. I jammed a knuckle into his eye as hard as I could. He jerked. His hand in my hair loosened. I drove my boot heel into his foot. He yelled, and his grip loosened again, and I tore myself away, and some of my hair ripped out. He was off balance. I shoved him into the wall and turned, but he grabbed my belt and pulled me back, and fell over, and I came down sideways on top of him. I struggled off of him, and got to my knees, and drove an elbow into his eye. His hands went to his face. I crawled away and scrambled to my feet. I couldn't see. Blood. My face. Breathe.

I tried to run, but he grabbed my ankle, and I twisted as I fell, and slammed into the floor. I kicked back at him. My heel hit his nose with a crunch. He grunted and let go. I struggled to my feet again, tried to wipe blood from my eyes. He was facing away, but still blocking me in. He growled and started to get up. I kicked him in the back, kicked him again. I could hear myself yelling something. I kicked him again and again. He made a gurgling noise and curled, his arms wrapped around his torso. I kicked him once more, stepped over him and stumbled toward the door.

I wasn't grabbed, pulled back. I got to the door and staggered down the stairs. Tried to wipe the blood from my eyes. It kept coming. Ben and Max, running. Shouting—I couldn't make it out. Had to keep going. Ben reached for me. I pulled away. Max shoved him, yelled. I ran a few more steps, but started shaking. Ben stopped, stared at me, turned and ran up the stairs.

Max stood near me. Said something—I couldn't understand. Couldn't stop shaking. Max took off his flannel and wrapped it around me. He took off his t-shirt and wadded it up, pressing it to my forehead. I swayed, and he stepped closer. I leaned into him. I started understanding his voice. "I've got you. Let it come. Let yourself shake, Maguire. You're safe now. I've got you."

Max led me over to a picnic table, and we sat. I was still leaning on him when the cops came. They ran up to my apartment. Some of them came back down. They stared at me. I was having trouble tracking what was going on.

I focused on my ragged, shaky breathing. He wasn't a killer, or a stalker. He was still Max. Wasn't he? He had to be.

More cops came, and an ambulance. The EMTs talked to the police, and they all turned to stare at me. The EMTs took out a gurney and maneuvered it up the stairs, angling it through the door. Max gave me a squeeze. "Don't you worry, Maguire. I hope you did hurt him."

I couldn't think. Who expected Luke to clean up? Luke was the stalker. Who was the killer? Breathe. Just breathe.

A second ambulance arrived, and Walt was there, talking with the police and the new EMTs. They were all looking at me. Max gave me another squeeze. The EMTs walked towards us.

"Looks like this bus is for you," Max said.

I stopped shaking. I could barely sit up. "I don't think I can walk." My voice sounded strange.

"I got you." Max sat with me as the EMT looked at my head. As soon as Max moved his shirt, the blood ran down my face again.

"She's gotta go in," the EMT told Max.

"Hold this," Max said. He put my hand to the shirt on my head and picked me up. He carried me to the back of the ambulance and supported me from behind as I climbed in.

Ida took me to her house. We sat at her kitchen table. She looked at my stitches. I listened to her bird clock chirping in the next room.

"You stay here as long as you want," she said. "You can move in, if you want to."

I felt numb. "I didn't even know what was going on. Did you say something that got a bunch of people pulled in for questioning?"

"Of course not," Ida said. "We just had a theory. We were going to figure out together what to do about it. Guess we didn't have to."

"Huh." My head hurt. I spent so long talking with the police at the hospital, going over things again and again. Now I struggled to string words together.

"Apparently, Luke's people are claiming ignorance," Ida said. "That's what one of the cops told Walt. I guess Jared confessed to all the sabotage. Said he was just jerking Max around, he's not getting pulled into any homicide. Wants to make a deal."

Ida shook her head, tsked. "Sounds like someone was running drugs out of the barn, we got that part. Jared's not going to spill it all, until he gets some assurances. I don't know. Most likely, Rodney was coerced into killing Mason, then Luke killed Rodney to keep him quiet."

"I don't think so." I stared at the table. "I don't think so, Ida."

"They'll sort it out." She looked at me. "You want something to eat?"

"Huh." I tried to put my head on my arms, but it hurt. I picked it up again.

Ida got up and walked to the freezer. She brought me a carton of ice cream and a spoon.

I started eating. "What do you think made this all blow up all of a sudden?"

"I have no idea," she said. "Walt and I were out by the round pen when Max and Ben came running out of the house, shouting."

I took another bite. "That makes no sense."

"No, it doesn't. We'll find out eventually. Walt is shutting things down for the rest of the week. He's pretty shook up."

I thought about asking about Luke, but I didn't want to know.

"Don't worry," Ida said. "Those black eyes will fade in no time."

I took a bite of ice cream.

"Sometimes you can't even tell someone's nose got broken."

I sighed. I couldn't think of anything to say, so I dug out a chocolate-covered peanut with my spoon and stuck it in my mouth.

Someone knocked at the door. I froze.

"It's alright," Ida said. She got up and soundlessly moved across the linoleum.

She should take a gun. Did she own a gun?

Ida came back. "Do you want to see Ben the Fed? If you don't, just say so. I'll run him off."

I paused for a beat. If he was here to kill us, he wouldn't wait for permission to come in. "Yes. I mean, yes, I'll see him. But don't leave!"

She nodded and let him in. Ben got halfway across the floor, stopped, and looked at me in horror.

"You're going to want to work on that," I said. "Not exactly encouraging."

Ida shook her head and leaned back against her sink. She casually reached over and pulled a steel meat tenderizing mallet out of a utensil holder.

Ben sat down facing me. "I'm so sorry." His eyes teared up. He blinked to hide it. "I'm so sorry this happened to you."

I didn't know what to say.

He noticed the carton of ice cream, the spoon. His mouth twitched a little. "I won't stay long. I just had to see for myself that you were ok. Are you ok?"

I made an I-have-no-idea gesture with my spoon. "I don't know, Ben. I feel like I got hit by a train. I'm staying here tonight. Then I'll see."

Ben pulled his chair close to mine, touched my cheek. "You let me know what you need, Abby. You want me around, you want space, whatever you need."

"I need to know," I said. "Who's gonna be in my blind spot? Will they just lie low, with all this police attention? Will they come after me?"

Ben shook his head. "It was Luke, Abby. He can't hurt you anymore."

"No, it wasn't, Ben. I mean, yes, it was, but not just him. He said he was playing a part. He was expected to clean up the mess. Who would expect that, Ben? I don't know who to watch out for. Just like he said. I can't see it coming, if I don't know."

Ben gave me a kind look. "He was messing with you, Abby. It was him. That was just emotional manipulation. Terrorizing you. You're safe now."

I shook my head, but it hurt, so I stopped. "There's someone in my blind spot, Ben."

He looked so patient and understanding, I wanted to kick him. He was going to be dismissive until I ended up in a shallow grave somewhere. Or dead in the tack room.

"It's alright now, Abby."

I tried to shake my head again. A wave of dizziness swept over me. "I need to lie down."

He stood, put the ice cream back in the freezer, and helped me to my feet. Ida led us into the guest room. She pointed with the meat mallet.

Ben didn't seem to notice. "You want me to sleep on the couch and help with concussion protocol, I'm glad to."

"I got it," she said. "But thank you."

"Abby, you want me to sleep on your couch for a while, if it makes you feel better, say the word. Whatever you need."

I closed my eyes and spun into darkness.

I stood in the doorway of the barn apartment, took a breath, steeled myself. I was not going to be controlled by this. I would

SIMPLY DEAD 331

not allow my world to shrink. I had a right to live in this world—as much right as anyone.

Max stood behind me, waiting for me to enter, or decide not to. "Maguire, you don't have to go in. You don't have to stay here one single night. Ben's moved out of the basement bedroom. You want to move in, we can do that right now."

I leaned against the wall, hugged myself. I was getting a headache. I didn't want to take painkillers. I had to stay sharp.

"I'll move your stuff," Max said. "You can just turn around and walk right back out."

I swallowed. "I'm not giving up my home, Max, even a temporary home. I'm not letting fear—or Luke—take that much ground."

Max nodded. "I get that." He stood, weight comfortably balanced on both feet, settled in for as long as he needed to wait.

The glass was swept up. The wall was repainted, after the blood was washed off. The paint smell was still strong. The nail was removed, the hole filled.

I was stalling.

"What do you need, Maguire? Just let me know. Anytime, anything."

I looked around, making sure the place was empty. "There's someone in my blind spot, Max. I don't want to be stuck, but I don't know what to do."

Max regarded me silently. Then he nodded. "I'm here now, Maguire. Why don't you make us some coffee? That will normalize things a little. Then we'll talk about this."

I blew out a breath. That was a good idea. I started going through the familiar routine, measuring coffee grounds, pouring in water. We sat at the table. The coffeemaker gurgled, and I panicked. I leapt to my feet. Adrenaline flooded me. I couldn't breathe.

"Maguire?" Max was on his feet, next to me. "What is it?"

I blew out a few breaths. "I'm sorry. The noise. That—" I gestured vaguely at the coffeemaker. I leaned on the table, tried to slow my panting, gasping. "He was going to kill me. I really had to kick him."

"Yes." Max's voice was firm. "There is no doubt about that, Maguire. None."

"I might need someone to be here when I'm making coffee. For a while. So I can—" I pointed at the coffeemaker again—"associate that—"

Max very slightly raised one questioning eyebrow.

I glanced at the coffeemaker. "It sounds like...when I kicked him."

Max registered the gurgling, and comprehension filled his eyes. He shook his head. "You are not losing your enjoyment of making coffee, Maguire. None of us are losing that. That's a big deal, you and your coffee. You just look at me." He reached out and took my hand. "I totally get it. Just look at me." He smiled, and his eyes showed affection. "You're going to be okay, Maguire." He gave my hand a squeeze. "You got it? You got my 'watching you make coffee for me' smile?" He lightly touched my hair with his other hand.

I focused on Max, his smile, his hand—and let the coffee gurgle. That is what gurgling means. It means Max. Ida. Walt. As many times as my brain needs to know that. I felt lightheaded. I had to be desensitized to my own coffeemaker. The things you don't see coming. "You're going to get tired of running up here to sit and smile at me so I can make coffee."

Max actually grinned. "Or not. Now talk to me. What is it that makes this feel unfinished to you?"

I repeated for Max what I'd tried to tell Ben. "He was boasting, Max." I shivered. "He was so triumphant. He would've gloated about being the killer, if he was." I met Max's eyes—looked for patronizing kindness, dismissiveness. I saw neither. I recognized the deeply serious man I spoke with in the darkness of night and felt a flood of relief. He was listening.

Max waited to make sure I was done. "You don't think it was just him being unhinged?"

"No." I almost referred to the run in the park, but stopped myself. I didn't want to bring that up to Max. "He said he doesn't have to kill anyone. People don't want to go to prison. Like holding that over people's heads is his role. I thought he was in charge, but he talked like he was a player." I hugged myself, tried to think. "At first, he seemed disappointed in me for not getting it, but then he really got energized by being so much smarter than me. Max, I don't know if whoever killed Mason and Rodney is five states away by now, or if they're out there wondering exactly what Luke said to me, what I might know." I sat back in my chair. "No, they won't go anywhere. Whoever it is will quietly wait, hoping it all sticks to Luke."

Max stood up and got two mugs from the cupboard. He poured coffee in both, set one in front of me, and sat down with the other.

"All right. Luke's probationers, that's a fixed number of people. He can't play jailer for anyone else. I'm going to call that cop and get him to listen to me. Get him to listen to—well, you need to talk to Ben yourself. Anyway. The door was unlocked when Luke came in, right? You just came up for a minute?"

I blinked, trying to process that. What did Max stop himself from saying? "The door wasn't even closed. I just ran in. Is there something I need to know, here?"

Max shook his head. He looked disgusted. "So, the new lock isn't compromised. We're closed for the week anyway, so there'll be fewer people in and out of here. The minute you want to come stay at the house, you let me know." He paused to assess me. "We'll get through this. Okay? I'll be up here several times a day to make coffee. I'll come up at three AM for some tea, so we can take back the night as well. I'll set my alarm."

I nodded. I was processing a little slowly. What did the cop need to listen to? Ben didn't take my concerns seriously, but maybe he knew something. I needed to hear it.

Chapter Thirty-Two

I heard a knock at the door. I peered through the window—it was Ben. I unlocked the door and let him in, then locked it behind him. He walked down the hall and stopped. He wasn't smiling.

"Oh, no," I said. "What is it now?"

"No, no, nothing else has happened." He looked at the window. The linoleum. "Abby…"

I stared at him. "What? What's going on, Ben? Talk to me. What do you know?"

He finally looked at me. He took a breath. "I know how angry you were when you found that bug I put in your purse."

I narrowed my eyes at him.

He seemed to be searching for words. I didn't want to help him with this, but I was getting impatient. I made a get-on-with-it gesture with my hand.

Ben took another breath, and I knew. "You left another one. You hid one in here somewhere. You didn't. Tell me you didn't."

I saw confirmation in his eyes. I felt like I'd been kicked in the stomach. I turned away.

"Abby—"

I held up a hand to silence him. He stopped talking. "When?" I asked, not looking at him.

"The first time I was up here."

I felt my last bit of strength drain away. "When I was getting the Bigfoot FTA shirt. I was laughing at you, but you've really been laughing at me this entire time." Tears of exhaustion and humiliation filled my eyes. I was furious that he saw them.

"Abby—"

"Take it. Get it out of here. Take it and get out."

There were two of them. If I dusted more thoroughly, I might have found them. I bit my lip. This entire time, I'd had no idea. I was wrong about absolutely everything. I liked him, and he knew it. "Go."

"Abby, please talk to me. We need to talk this out."

I glared at him. He looked away from whatever he saw in my eyes.

"There is absolutely nothing to talk about. You knew what I thought. You got me. You got me good, Ben. You were smarter than me. Well done. You're good at what you do. Now get out."

He opened his mouth to say something. I felt panic building inside. I had to get him to leave. "GET OUT." I sounded hysterical. I couldn't help it.

He turned and walked away. Ben was halfway out the door when another thought occurred to me.

"OH."

He froze, turned back.

"You never know who's listening, Ben? Was that supposed to be funny?"

He looked blank.

"When you said not to talk to Walt or Max about you being a private investigator, because you never—" I picked up my boot and hit him with it— "know"—I hit him again—"who's listening?" I threw the boot at him. "Was that just one more way you've been laughing at me, mocking me this entire time?"

"Abby, I swear—"

I pushed him out, slammed the door and locked it. I heard his voice through the door. "Please call me, Abby."

I walked back to the kitchen. I looked at Papa and felt the weight of the time he'd been gone. "I've made such a mess of things," I told him. "I can't see anything. I can't get anything right."

My face hurt when I dabbed it with a tissue. I couldn't even cry right. I felt like breaking things, but I'd only have to clean it up.

Several minutes later there was a knock at the door. I ignored it. My phone buzzed. I looked at the message. "It's Ida. I'll go away if you want."

I walked over and opened the door. "Who sent you?"

"Walt and Max wanted me to make sure you're ok. They said Ben came down crawling on his belly like a dog that got kicked."

"He's not a dog. He's a rat." I stepped back, holding the door open.

Ida stepped in, then stopped. "You didn't think for one minute I would come up here because that man told me to?"

"He's a good liar. He could tell you anything."

I sat down on the couch and pulled my feet up under me. "Ida, he's been spying on me this whole time. He had listening devices hidden in here. He's been eavesdropping on everything. I'm such an idiot. I thought we liked each other. I can't believe he's been listening to every conversation. How many times did Max and I bare our souls to each other in the middle of the night? Walt has been up here talking about being depressed, being afraid. Would they have done that if Ben the Rat was sitting in the room? That's stealing! It's taking something that has not been given to you. He had no right."

I narrowed my eyes at her. "On the other hand, they both knew he was a private investigator, so maybe that's on them. But, Ida—" I took a deep breath. "I talk to my papa. I talk out loud to his picture." I could feel tears running from my eyes, but didn't have the energy to stop them. "No one is supposed to hear that." I wiped my mouth on my sleeve. My mouth didn't hurt. "How could I be so stupid? This is why I don't date. I should have known he just wanted something."

Ida shook her head. "He's the one who's stupid, not you. I don't know much, but I know that." She pulled her boots off and settled back in the chair. "Don't let that man knock the wind out of you, Abby. I don't blame you for being angry—I'd be mad too. Damn straight, I would. Just don't get down on yourself on account of him."

I wiped the bottom of my face again and got up to get some sodas from the refrigerator. I handed her a can, then froze. "Ida! He heard us talking about him being a ripe tomato!"

She burst out laughing. "Well, that won't hurt his ego any."

"No! I didn't want him to hear that!"

She shook her head. "Does it matter if he knows you find him attractive? I guarantee he's known for a while you think he's aggravating. And that was before all this."

I conceded the point. "Aggravating doesn't half cover it." Having a girlfriend in my corner made me feel better, at least temporarily.

"I wonder if he was surprised how often we talk about him," Ida said.

"What? We do not."

"Well, we do. We call him a fed, or a rat, or whatever, but here we are talking about him."

Realizing she was right irritated me. I took a drink of soda so I wouldn't have to respond. I had another thought mid-swallow. Coughing hurt, and it made my eyes water.

Ida leaned forward in her seat, eyes wide. She wordlessly handed me a tissue.

"Ida, he heard us talking about finding that wrapper. We both talked about concealing evidence from the cops." We sat with that, neither of us knowing what to say. I dabbed at my eyes.

Ida sighed heavily. "Well, I guess we reported it, didn't we? We just didn't know it."

"I hardly think that's going to count."

"Abby, we'll deal with it when it comes. We can't pretend we didn't think about what we were doing, so we'll just see how it shakes out. Did he say who was listening?"

"He said just him."

"Ok, then," Ida said. "We'll see if Ben the Rat turns us in or not. Hopefully he's too entranced by you to do it."

"He's not entranced by me, Ida. He was using me."

She shook her head, but with little energy behind it. "You don't know much."

"Ida, I thought there was no way it could be both David and Luke, but maybe that was wrong. Luke did talk about being reeled in and told what to do, if he wanted something the other person had. Maybe that includes money. If David took over his son's drug connections, maybe Luke found out, and David had to let him in on it. Even if he wasn't in charge, it could be lucrative."

Ida settled her weight back in the cushions. "Well, Ben wrapped up his case and left. Sounds like the cops are done, too. They all seem to believe it was just Luke. I can't decide if it's the right thing to do, to keep talking about this, or if I should encourage you to let it go."

"Maybe David thinks he's safe now," I said. "Maybe he won't come after me. He knows it's all been laid on Luke. He's smart. Anyone does accuse him, he could talk his way out of it. Unless he wants revenge for his son's political career. Other than that, he's better off taking his breaking and entering, and leaving it at that. Don't you think? Isn't he? He'll probably get probation himself! But he'll wait too, won't he, to see how it shakes out?"

Ida gave me a long look. "We'll see, Abby. Eventually, we will."

Max and I took an afternoon break in the barn. He used one foot to push back the chair his boots were propped on. "Might's well go get the dinner crew." He angled out of the break room, grabbed a few halters and started for the woods.

"I'll be right behind you." I wiped our crumbs from the table, straightened, neatened. Picked up abandoned, half-empty water bottles.

I heard footsteps and smelled cigarette smoke. "That was fast. Just wanted to grab a quick one? I'm coming." I turned, and saw Janice holding a paper grocery bag.

"I brought you some more eggs," she said. "Been a hard week around here, thought maybe you didn't get to the store."

I made myself smile. They would be disgusting. I'd give them to Ida, tell her to use them in cookies. "That was nice of you."

Janice reached in the bag, pulled out a gun and pointed it at me. She set the eggs on the floor.

"Oh, for crying out loud," I said. "Talk about assumptions you don't even know you're making. Here I am, talking about other people's underlying beliefs."

"What?" She squinted at me.

"You've been right in front of me this entire time. Men aren't the only ones who underestimate women."

Janice shook her head. "Luke Morgan was right. You never do stop talking. And I have no idea what you're talking about."

I slowly took a few steps back. "Granted, I've worked with way more aggressive males than females. But females can be hell on wheels. You know what I mean?"

Janice kept pointing her gun at me. "Maybe. I've known women like that."

"Yeah." I nodded, agreeing with her. Think. Keep her talking. I had no idea where I was going, but she seemed to be coming with me. "People always say boys will fight and get over it, but girls get mean."

Janice nodded back. "That's for damn sure true."

I moved a little farther away. "Boys try to explain how there's rules. Fighting. You just don't do certain things. Girls don't usually grow up with physical fighting, so they don't grow up with the same rules. A girl, she decides to use violence, she'll just take the person out. Have you noticed that?"

"I do know women like that," Janice said. "I had an aunt like that."

I'll just bet you did. I tried to think of what to say next.

"Kind of like what you did to Morgan," Janice said.

A wave of nausea swept over me.

Janice laughed. "Oh, you weren't even thinking about that, were you? No one would've expected that. Maybe talk people to death, that I'd believe."

I swallowed hard. Don't think about Luke. Focus.

"No worries," Janice said. "You did a lot of people a favor there. Everyone's talking about it. Lot of people real happy."

"Okay," I said. "So, what are we doing here?"

Janice aimed the gun at my chest. I was sure she wouldn't mess up and leave the safety on. "I wasn't sure what you knew, what Morgan told you. I ain't gonna live watching my back. Figured I better come and find out."

I sidled closer to my cell phone on the table. "All I know is, you have a gun. That's no big thing. Everyone around here has a gun. And everyone knows Luke is guilty, so you're all good."

Janice moved in front of me, blocking my way. "How do I know you're not gonna tell my new P.O. I have a gun?"

"Janice, I don't care if you have a gun. Just leave it at home after this. Bring the eggs in, that's why you came here."

"Head for the door. We're leaving."

I pulled a chair between us.

Janice snorted. "Move. Morgan ain't exactly an expert witness anymore, and I'm out. The cops let me go. I take care of you, I'm staying out."

I felt stirrings of a deep, burning anger. This is what it comes down to? Killing people, so she can continue to do whatever she damn well pleases, without consequence? Mason was loved. People were devastated. Rodney was not disposable. She had no right. None. Who did she think she was? Damned if she would dispose of me.

I made my voice calm. "So, what? Your profits too big to walk away from? Luke found out, so you had to cut him in? You'd have each other over a barrel, wouldn't you? Especially after killing Mason and Rodney. Both of you under each other's thumbs. Boy, I bet you're glad that's over!"

She frowned. "See, you just contradicted yourself. You said you didn't know." She took a step sideways, aiming around the chair. "Morgan got some kinda weird thing about you. Got careless. Maybe I'll go pay him a visit, take him some flowers or something. Tell him you had an accident, see what he says."

Fury surged inside me. My stomach tightened. I rested my hands on the back of the chair, thought about flipping off my own safety. I knew where it was, now.

What of Janice's right to dignity? I shook my head. Doesn't mean the gloves can't come off. I had no desire to humiliate or shame her. Just take her out.

"Luke did get a couple things right," I said. "I do talk a lot. And I guess I am a pain in the ass when I get irritated, but that was Max, who said that."

Janice rolled her eyes. I swung the chair in an arc, hit her, knocked her down. The gun went off so loudly it felt like a physical impact. It blew a hole in the wall. My ears started ringing.

Janice shoved the chair off and looked around for me. She struggled to get up. I came up behind her and kicked her in the head. She caught herself with both hands on the floor. I kicked her gun hand out from under her and jumped on her arm. I heard a crack and she cursed, but didn't let go of the gun.

I dropped on her back with my knees, and she grunted. I grabbed an arm and pulled it behind her back. I leaned on her head, shoved her face into the floor. She mule-kicked back at me. I grappled around, then got ahold of her leg and pulled her foot up under me. I leaned all my weight into her. We rocked and slid around. The force of her struggling lifted us off the floor, and I pushed her down, again and again. My grip loosened, and I pushed a foot against the floor for leverage as I tried to hold on.

I heard boots pounding, and Max burst through the door. He came into Janice's field of vision and aimed his gun at her head. I heard him shout over the ringing in my ears. "Drop your weapon right now!"

His tone sent a shiver through me. I'd never heard that voice from Max. He was in full-on command and control mode. Engage and neutralize. If he'd been talking to me, I would've wet myself.

"I can't move my hand!" Janice twisted her head to glower at him. "She broke my damn wrist!"

Max moved in and used his boot to push Janice's gun away. He picked it up and shoved it into the back of his waistband. "Alright, Maguire, I've got her."

I rolled off Janice's back and leaned against the wall, exhausted. I was going to be seriously bruised from her kicking me. If she'd hit my face, I would've been done.

Max pulled her arm behind her in a much more effective position than I managed. He took his phone out and called the cops. I stayed on the floor.

Max looked over at me. "Are you okay?"

I nodded.

Janice held still while we waited. Max seemed to accomplish this effortlessly. I was thinking vaguely that I should learn how to do that, when the police came in. Max set both guns on the floor. He waited as a cop picked them up, then stood next to me.

We told them as much as we could, each from our own viewpoint. Janice told them to piss off. They looked at the bullet hole in the wall, and wanted to hear it all again. Janice was led away, with assurances that her wrist would be seen to. Then the detective arrived.

Great. I sighed heavily and leaned against Max's leg. Then I reached up and Max helped me heave myself off the floor.

The detective sat at the table, making notes. I worked on holding myself upright. Max stood, arms crossed over his chest.

I explained that I smelled cigarette smoke and thought it was Max.

Max recoiled as if I'd slapped him. He closed his eyes, turned his face away.

The detective rubbed his forehead. "Alright. I don't quite understand how you got the jump on her, when she was holding you at gunpoint. How did you get from there, to her on the floor and you on top of her?"

"I had a split second," I said. "That was when I hit her with a chair."

The detective's pen hovered over his notebook. "You had a split second--?"

I sighed. "When she rolled her eyes at me."

The detective's mouth twitched. He looked at his notebook, cleared his throat. Max glared at him.

The detective took a breath and exhaled. "Why did she roll her eyes at you?"

I squinted. "What difference does it make?"

"I'm just trying to get the full picture." He waited.

I sighed again. "I agreed with her that I talk a lot."

One of the uniformed cops coughed. Max glared at him.

The detective wrote a few more notes and slid his notebook into his pocket. "Alright. I'll let you know if there's anything else." The remaining cops followed him out.

"I let you down again." Max's voice quavered. "I can't get anything right anymore."

"That's not true, Max. You came running in when I was about to lose my grip on her. I don't know what I would've done."

He wouldn't meet my eyes. "I let her get by me. You got hurt again. She got close because of me smoking. I'm sorry, Maguire." He looked miserable. "When I heard that gunshot..."

"Max. Please don't." I couldn't come up with words. I reached a hand toward him.

He shook his head and walked away.

One of the chairs was still on the floor. I sat and looked at it for a long time.

There were cops walking around in the barn, talking about trajectory, looking for the bullet. The horses from the dinner crew crowded the gate, looking over the fence, probably hungry by now. I wasn't sure where Max was. I went up to my apartment, laid down and pulled the edge of the bedspread up over me.

I must have fallen asleep in my exhaustion. I hadn't seen it get dark. I got up and turned on the light, and heated some water, waiting for Max.

Max didn't come. I didn't believe for one minute that he was sleeping. I pulled my tea bag up and down in the steaming water. I drank slowly, hoping Max would show up, wanting a cup.

He didn't.

I put the mug in the sink and turned off the light. No point looking like I was begging. He didn't have to come up if he didn't want to.

I took a picture of Papa from the shelf and set it on the table. I looked at his face and thought about how alone I was. "I don't know how it came to this," I told him.

For the first time, it felt stupid talking to him, knowing that he would never answer. I put the picture back on the shelf. Not wanting to talk to Papa was like watching the clouds roll over the final star in the night sky.

We used to watch the clouds at night. Papa said the moon was playing peek-a-boo with me, ducking behind the clouds and popping out again. I laughed, calling to the moon, and Papa laughed at the sight of me.

No more laughter, now. No more playful moon. Just me, alone in the dark.

Feeling sorry for myself would get me nowhere. I got up, grabbed my Maglite, slid into my boots, and went out to walk with the horses. Surely, there were no villains left. It had to be over, now.

Chapter Thirty-Three

I was morose the next morning. My entire body ached. I made an instant coffee so I wouldn't hear it brewing, and went downstairs. Max saw me coming and veered off to check the fence line.

I sat on the steps and leaned against the barn. I could add Max's name to the list of people I felt stupid for having cared about.

Ida walked up, looked me over. Frowned. "Abby, you need to get out of here."

I was so shocked, I didn't breathe for a couple of beats.

"No, no," she said. "I mean you need a break. A change of scene. Come on, put some clean clothes on. I'm taking you into town. We'll go get a roll or something. You simply have to get away from this ranch, Abby. Go on, now."

I couldn't think of a reply, so I obeyed. I even brushed my hair. I'd been avoiding that since having some ripped out.

Ida chatted with a forced cheeriness while she drove, but I had no energy to chat back. I leaned against the door. She studied me soberly. "Abby, we're going to get through this. We will."

I sighed. "I'm sorry, Ida."

Ida clucked, tsked. Shook her head. "You don't owe it to anyone to paste on a smile. I mean we're really going to get through this.

You just keep walking. We'll move through it together." She angled her truck into a parking place and bustled into the café. I followed in her wake.

The aroma of freshly baked donuts and breads pulled me in the door. I felt hungry for the first time in days. Most of the tables were filled with people chatting, drinking coffee, eating pastries. They fell quiet as we entered. Some people gazed at us openly. Others pretended not to look. I turned to tell Ida we should leave. Then I saw Jamie and Stan at a little table for two. They stared at me, mouths open. I guess I really did look that bad. I walked up to them.

Stan rose, took my hand in both of his. "I'm so sorry." He shook his head slowly. "I'm so sorry."

I looked between Stan and Jamie. "I want you to know something." The entire café was silent, every ear trained on us. Good. Let them hear. Let it be the juicy gossip of the month. I wanted everyone to know.

"It wasn't for nothing," I said. "Because I found out why. Luke Morgan told me why."

Stan and Jamie both drew ragged breaths. Jamie's lip quivered. Stan gripped my hand more tightly.

"Mason refused," I said. "He was determined to stay clean, straight. Law abiding. Take care of his family. That made him a threat. Luke Morgan told me straight up. Mason was killed to keep him quiet. Because he refused to be a part of it."

Jamie buried her face in her hands. Stan trembled. A single tear tracked down his face. He nodded, tried to speak, couldn't. He nodded again.

I squeezed his hand, released it, and turned to Ida. "I gotta go."

Ida put a hand on the small of my back, and guided me out the door and to her truck. She drove for a few blocks and pulled over to the side. "Well, that should be all over the tri-county area by nightfall."

"I hope so," I said. "That family doesn't need to be under a shadow of community shame."

Ida nodded. "That was good, Abby." She sat for a moment, then drove to her house. "We'll take our break here, in my kitchen. It will be a change, anyway. I've got a few bars in the freezer. We'll just have a little visit here."

That sounded perfect. I followed her in.

I made it down for a session with Ida, but I still ached. Max turned and walked the other way when he saw me. I was probably just as obvious when I was doing it to Ben.

Ida did all the heavy lifting. I mostly stood there, smiled, made a few observations. When the clients drove away, I walked out and leaned on the fence. At least the horses were still reliable. No matter what happened, they went back to being horses. I stood in the sun for a long time, not even thinking. Then I heard footsteps, and turned.

"Maguire. Are you okay?" Max. Ida must have scolded him.

"No," I said.

Max pulled me in for a hug. "I'm sorry."

"Good thing I'm a trained observer," I said into his shirt. "I misread absolutely everyone."

Max took a deep breath, exhaled.

I pulled back. "I've been thinking about taking Walt up on his offer, to leave this job early."

Max frowned, shook his head, absently reached for his shirt pocket. "A whole hell of a lot went on here, Maguire, on my watch. It's not right, you feeling humiliated. I'm truly sorry for my part in that. I'm just wallowing in my own failure." He patted his shirt again.

"Max. Did you quit smoking?"

His left eye was twitching. "Yes." He scowled at the fence, as if it were at fault. "I nearly got you killed. I'm never going to smell like smoke again." He ripped a handful of leaves off a tree branch. "I might be a little testy for a couple days."

I rested my head on his shoulder. "You'll have to come up and help me with the coffee thing, if you're eliminating nicotine."

"Look at us. What a mess."

I nodded. Paused. "Max, why were you arguing with Mason at his place?"

Max stopped breathing.

I looked up at him. "I'm not criticizing you. Obviously, I'm in no position. Just wondering."

He didn't even ask. "Mason was off," he said. "Knew something about something. I thought it was about the sabotage, since I didn't have the first clue all the rest of it was even going on. So, yeah. Nailed that one, didn't I?"

I couldn't think of a good response.

"Maguire, I'm just glad it's all over."

I came down the next morning determined to normalize my life. I would focus on clients, sessions. Learning as much as I could. Practicing new skills. I would walk on the trails, until my head could take the impact of running again. No more time and energy spent on terrible things. And who needed Ben? Certainly not me. I had come to this job alone, with high hopes for a good experience. I didn't need the complications or the drama.

I looked around at the fresh, new morning. My car was still sitting behind Max's house. There was a prime example of needed change. I was embarrassed about it sitting for so long while I cadged rides with other people. Even after it became a golf course obstacle. I went right back upstairs and dug my keys out of my purse. I met Max walking out of the barn. "I'm finally going to get my car out of your back yard."

Max laughed. "Hasn't bothered me any. Gets clippings all over it when I mow, but the rain takes care of that."

Halfway across the parking lot, I stopped so suddenly that Max walked into me.

"Whoa! You alright?"

I blinked, frozen in place.

"Maguire? What?"

"I haven't moved my car since Jared worked on it." I swallowed hard. "You don't think—"

Max's eyes flicked between my car and me. "Give me your keys."

"No! If I can't start it, you can't start it!"

"Maguire!"

"Wait! I know! I have remote start!" I started pushing buttons on the key fob.

"No!" Max shouted. "Don't—"

My car exploded into flames. The hood bent up, straining against the latch. Black and white smoke poured out, thick, heavy.

I stood, paralyzed, speechless. Max sprinted into his house. He ran out with a fire extinguisher. He sprayed back and forth over the fire. The flames kept growing. He grabbed me around the waist with one arm, lifting me off my feet, and ran toward the barn. I heard loud popping noises. He set me down, and Walt appeared.

Max set down the fire extinguisher, shook his head. Walt was on the phone. I stood where Max set me, hands over my mouth. An eternity passed before I heard sirens. I watched the fire spread from the engine compartment to the cab. We all jumped when the tires exploded, sending debris flying.

Max wiped his forehead with the back of his hand. "I should get a hose and spray the house."

"You stay right where you are," Walt said. "There's insurance on the house."

Max looked at me. "What kind of insurance you got on the car?"

"Just liability. It's old." I watched as flames shot three feet high.

Walt gave me a squeeze. "We'll take care of you. It'll be alright."

We stood and watched as the sirens got closer. The wind blew the smoke into the pasture. The horses galloped away, stopping at the edge of the trees to look back. They stood, herded together, and watched as fire trucks pulled into the drive.

The detective had dark circles under his eyes. Exhaustion did nothing for his disposition. "I thought I was done here." Looking around the table at Max, Ben, and me, he took out a pen and focused on me. "Why did you start the car at all? After you thought about Jared Wills, why did you even start it remotely? Did you not think to call us before blowing up your own car? Yes, we have a small department, but law enforcement agencies talk to each other, did you know that? Someone would've come out here and checked it over! Do you think at all?"

He was right, of course. I knew that. But why did Ben get to witness this? He hadn't even been there. I sighed. "Why does he get a seat at the table?" I asked, tilting my head at Ben.

The cop's eyes flicked to Ben and back to me. "He persuaded me not to charge you with reckless endangerment."

I gasped, sputtered. "Charge—me? Charge me? For what? For starting my car? Charge *me?*"

He smiled grimly. "Kidding. Cop humor."

I squinted at him, and at Ben, who was trying not to smile.

"He's a material witness," said the detective. Without explaining that, he launched into questioning. He paused only once, stopping to stare at me when I described assessing Jared's speech and pupil dilation before handing him my car keys in the first place.

"And it didn't seem strange to you that he drove out to the road before giving you back your keys?"

"He acted like he'd forgotten," I said. "People do that."

We covered the whole thing only twice, which was something of a record for me. The detective closed his notebook and stood. "I'll let you know when the car can be towed away," he said to Max. He glanced at me, gave Ben a longer look, and left. What was that?

Max gave my shoulder a squeeze and walked the detective out. I looked at Ben. "What was that all about?"

Ben smiled. "Tom and I grew up together. Since before kinder-garten. College roommates."

"So that's who you've been talking to."

He gave me a head tilt, but said nothing. He was probably afraid to say anything.

I sat with that for a moment. "So what was that look he gave you on the way out?"

Ben paused and studied me. "He knows I like you."

I wasn't sure I wanted to know how that conversation went.

"He thinks I don't know what I'm getting into," he added.

My mouth dropped open. "Getting—who says you're getting into anything? That's a bit presumptuous, isn't it?"

Ben smiled, looked away. I was waiting for him to tell me I was cute when I was mad. Then I was going to clock him.

Ben shook his head. "I'm not assuming anything. I do owe you dinner. Do you want to eat in, rather than going to a restaurant? I know you're still recovering."

"As if you'd tell me where you live." I was irritated with his refusal to argue.

"I could bring supplies to your place. Then you won't need to worry about how to walk out on me, since you don't have a car."

Maybe this was how he did argue. He was pretty good at it. I got up and left.

I wandered into the office the next day. Max and Walt sat with their feet on the desk. They both looked up at me.

"Abby, come on in." Walt waved toward an empty chair. "Max and I were just talking about you. We were saying, you've come a long way since that first day when you cried because I asked you to brush Rosie's legs."

"I did not cry!" I gave a side eye to Max, who was grinning. "Rosie and I made a deal. I'd do the best I could, and she wouldn't trample me. We both kept our end of the bargain."

Walt put his feet down. "Abby, I know you took a pay cut to come here. Your time's not up yet, but we need to plan ahead, and I'm sure you do, too. It hasn't been the experience you were looking for, but we've done a lot of good, despite everything. We've helped a lot of people. And you've been an important part of that."

"We don't want you to go," Max interjected.

Walt looked at him. "I was getting there." He turned back to me. "You know we're hiring for a full year now. We've got some promising candidates, but if you're interested in adding a year-long gig, we'd rather have you. You're good for us. You don't just fit in, you make us better."

I sat back, blinked. I hadn't seen that coming. I'd never extended a temp job before. Just finished and moved on. "Have you talked to the agency about it?"

"No," Walt said. "I didn't want to get ahead of myself. If you're interested, I'll call them today. Of course, I would just hire you myself. I understand, though, you might not want to disrupt your employment."

What did I want? I had no idea what I wanted. "Give me a day to think about it," I said.

Chapter Thirty-Four

I was working hard on the pep talk. Okay, so I felt like I'd been trampled. I would double down on nutrition, rest, refusing to look in mirrors. It would be fine.

I got out a clean dishcloth and dusted my pictures. I held the last one for a moment, touched Papa's face. I couldn't help smiling at him.

Walt had asked me to come by. I stuck my head into the office, but pulled it right back out. Ben was sitting across the desk from Walt. I was too tired for Ben today.

Ben's posture was different. His presence. He might be a private investigator now, but Ben no longer just looked like a fed. He was exuding agent-in-charge. Walt sat straight in his chair, feet squarely on the ground. He did not seem impressed. I turned to leave.

"Abby," Walt said. "It's okay, come on in." They both smiled at me. I smiled at Walt.

I turned to Ben. "Did your cop friend say anything about that money?"

Ben glanced at Walt. "Ah, Luke Morgan never explained that. They ask, he laughs."

"Can I get that money back? I really need a new car."

"I'll talk to Tom. Try to speed that up. See what I can do. For the record, Abby, I didn't know about the wrapper in your bedroom. You absolutely should've told me, if you knew the intruder was directly connected to Mason's death."

"I guess I didn't talk about that one in range of your illegal surveillance equipment."

Walt's face was starting to darken.

Ben's eyes cut to Walt, and back to me. "I just stopped by to update Walt. Morgan's still in ICU. Kidney damage, from being kicked—well, anyway. They reconstructed his nose. When he does get out, can't imagine he'll get bail. He's charged with both accomplice and accessory to two counts of first-degree murder, the assault on you, probably attempted murder. Janice rolled over on both homicides, but she's claiming duress from Morgan. He-said-she-said."

I thought about that. "What about David?"

"David had nothing to do with anything," Ben said. "I almost feel sorry for the guy. Just trying to keep his son's history from coming out. Stupid, trying to engineer an impressive life for his messed-up kid."

Sorry for him? David and his son lost a lot, but really. I wondered what his wife thought of the both of them. And there was something wrong there. "I don't think so, Ben. I don't think that's all David did. And he's out on bail, on a minor charge."

Ben smiled kindly.

I narrowed my eyes.

Ben paused, studied my face, then continued. "They're trying to get Jared to cop to the car bomb, but there was a long enough gap after he worked on the car, his attorney's calling it circumstantial. Not sure what the thought process was there. Maybe he places the explosive thinking you could get out before the fire spreads to the cab. Figures it'll scare you off. That could affect the level of charges. If they do come up with enough evidence to charge him." He shrugged. "Lotta people sneaking around the ranch. Car sat there for a long time."

"What about the drugs?"

Ben blinked. "What about them?"

"The barn was, what, a transit station? So the cops wouldn't keep a log of people coming and going somewhere?"

Ben shrugged. "Like I told you, Abby, I'm not a cop. I'm not fully read into everything. It'll be dealt with, I assure you." He glanced at Walt again. "Anyway, we'll see how the bulk of the testimony goes. People start caving, they'll fall like dominoes. I should go." He left quickly.

I scowled at his back, thought about David and Jared, off in huddled conversation. And David pointedly asking why I hadn't driven my car in so long. And Jared, he told me I should leave this job early. "Too bad then," he'd said, when I told him I was staying. What was that?

Jared could end up skating. Most of the property damage, it could be argued, he subsequently fixed. He'd make a deal, go back on probation.

Ida said we'd find out, eventually. Ida understood the long game. But she wasn't the only one. I nodded to myself. I'd bet anything that David played a long game.

Walt thunked his pen into the mug on his desk. "Things you told me the other day, Ben Murphy never would've said a damn word. Look like a damn fool, not knowing what's going on in my own place." He straightened the papers on his desk and pushed back his chair. "Now, do you have time to take a little drive with me?"

I blinked. "Yes. I've got nothing all day."

Walt stood and stretched. "I want you to meet a friend of mine."

I climbed into Walt's pickup, and he drove to a used car lot. "Owner's a friend. He's going to help you out. Get you a real good deal, you don't need to haggle. Set up payments you can work with."

I felt tears welling up. I blinked them back. I was too exhausted, too emotional. "Walt."

He put a hand on my shoulder. "I told you we'd take care of you. It's going to be alright. You just come and look around at what he's got, here."

The owner, a balding, middle-aged man with a paunch, got up immediately when he saw Walt, and hurried over. He shook Walt's hand, with both of his. He turned to me and shook my hand. His eyes lingered on my stitches. He blinked hard and looked away. "Uh, Walt told me your situation. You just come on out here and take a look."

Walt wandered off to get a cup of coffee in the lounge, telling me to take my time.

"I'll give you a few minutes to look around," the owner said. "And don't worry about the price on the window. I'll do better than that for you. I believe you had a five-door? Is that what you'd like again?"

I felt disoriented. "I'm not sure. But thank you."

I wandered up and down the rows. There was a gray hatch-back—five-door, I guess, in car lingo—that I could probably afford. It looked like it should last a few more years. I should talk to him about that one, when he came back. I stopped to run my hand over the side of a bright red pickup truck. "Hi, there," I said to the truck. "Aren't you pretty?" I looked at the price. "Never mind."

I walked over to the hatchback. I gazed at the truck. I tore myself away. I was peering in the window of the hatchback when the owner walked up. He looked at the hatchback, read the window sticker. "I saw you looking at that half-ton, you like that?"

I smiled. "It's gorgeous, but my bank account likes this one."

He walked over and read the window sticker on the truck. "Let's take this for a test drive, see how she feels."

I started to refuse, but changed my mind. When would I get a chance to drive a beautiful red pickup? It really was lovely. I might as well enjoy myself. Then I could look at the gray hatchback.

I shouldn't have done it. It was glorious. I adored it. I pulled back into the parking lot, ran my fingers lovingly over the dash and sighed. "Okay," I said. "Back to earth."

The owner smiled widely from the passenger seat. "Well, I told you not to worry too much about the sticker price. I'll let you have this truck for the listed price of that five-door."

I stared at him. Blinked. Shook my head a little.

He grinned. "What do you think?" He was serious.

I gaped at him. "Why?"

He put his hand on my shoulder. "Walt Bravo saved my daughter. She was terribly depressed, as a teenager. Suicidal. Nothing helped. We tried everything. Last ditch, desperate, heard about some horse thing. Brought her out to Walt, turned her whole life around. I've got two beautiful grandchildren now. My daughter's doing so well." He smiled. "She named her little boy Walter."

I had to grin at that.

"I cannot tell you what it means, for someone to save your child's life. There was nothing I could do to help her, but he did. Now there's nothing I wouldn't do for Walt Bravo, and that's a fact. He's never asked me for anything—and he didn't ask me to do this, but I'm determined to. He just asked me to work with you, but it's a very small matter to take a loss on one vehicle. It's irrelevant. Let's go get the paperwork started."

I drove my glorious, bright red pickup truck back to the ranch. I climbed down from the cab, patted the tailgate lovingly, and followed Walt into the barn.

He grinned at me. "I'm real glad that worked out, Abby. That truck suits you."

I nodded. "I want to stay, Walt. Sign me up for a year."

Walt held up a hand, stopping me. "You know I want you, Abby, but I don't want you to feel obligated because of the truck. That's a whole separate issue. Your employment has nothing to do with it."

"I really love the truck." I looked back at the parking lot. "It's gorgeous. And red. But I want to stay because of the daughter. The girl who grew up. You've got something amazing going on here, Walt. I want in."

Walt smiled. "Let's do the paperwork."

Walt smelled his coffee and smiled happily, stretching his legs under the table. He settled his weight into the chair, took a sip, and sighed.

Max leaned his chair back on two legs. "I make a motion that we have all staff meetings up here from now on."

"I second that," Walt said. "Motion passed."

"You forgot to vote." Ida put a plate of cookies in the middle of the table. Max immediately lowered his chair to four legs and reached for the plate.

Ida smiled warmly at him, then turned to me. "I'm so glad you're staying. It's going to be a wonderful year. Things will settle down now and get back to normal. You're going to love it, Abby. Just wait, you'll see. A couple months in, you won't know what hit you."